THE BAD BRIDESMAID

RACHAEL JOHNS

*To Ali Watts, Publisher Extraordinaire – it's been a joy to work with
you on Bridget's and Fred's stories and
I can't wait to create many more books together.*

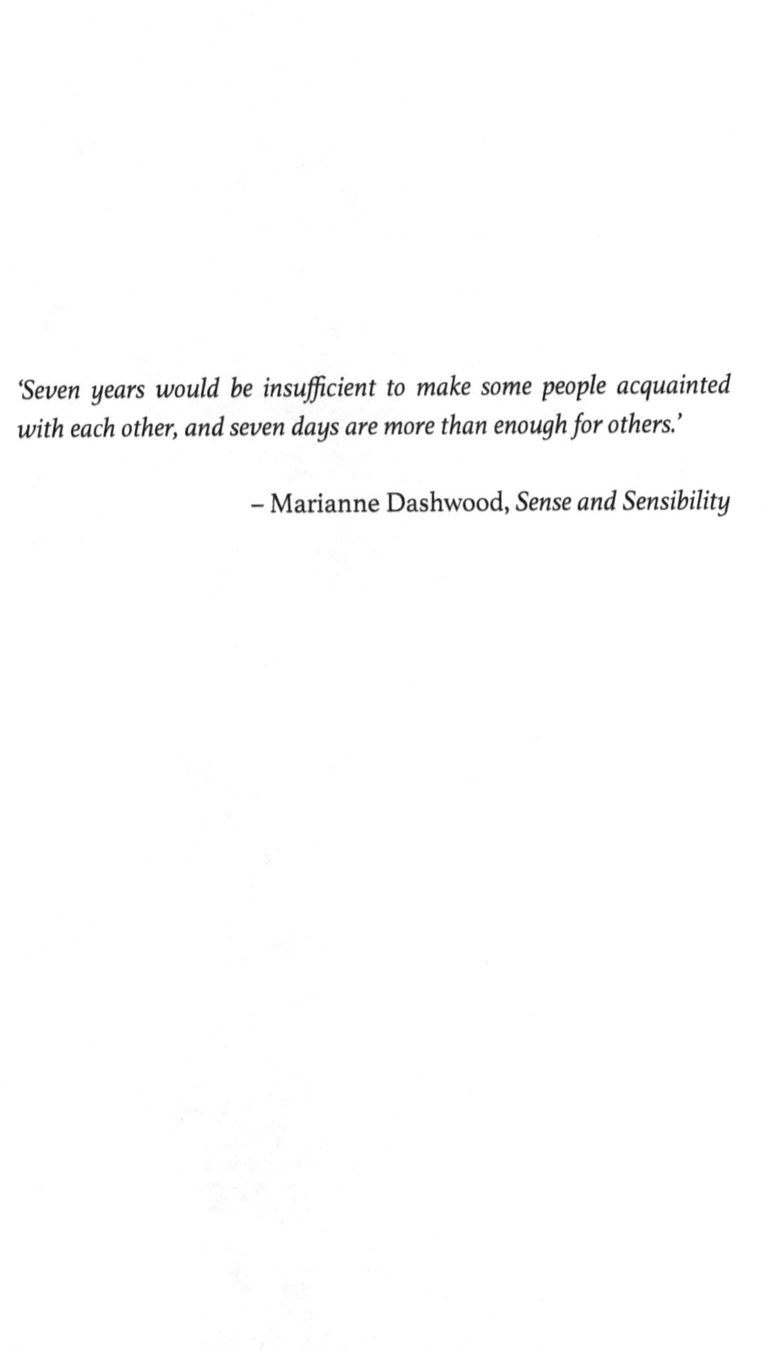

'Seven years would be insufficient to make some people acquainted with each other, and seven days are more than enough for others.'

– Marianne Dashwood, *Sense and Sensibility*

21 RULES FOR NOT CATCHING FEELINGS

1. No bullshit/Be honest.
2. Set boundaries before you meet.
3. Chemistry over connection.
4. Always meet first in a public place.
5. Never go back to your date's house.
6. Under no circumstances allow them to stay the night.
7. Expect nothing. Give nothing.
8. No jealousy or possessive thoughts.
9. Always pay for yourself.
10. No PDAs.
11. No selfies.
12. Keep seeing other people.
13. Limit your time together.
14. No text and in-depth conversation. No daily chats.
15. No labels.
16. Always put yourself first.
17. Never see the same person more than once a week.
18. Friends with benefits is not a thing.
19. No gifts. No favours.

20. Fit dates around *your* life, not theirs.
21. If anyone shows any signs of attachment, end it immediately.

1

RED FLAGS

'Let me get this straight.' My date leans his elbows on the table between us and looks at me like I'm deranged. 'You're writing a book about how *not* to catch feelings?'

Popping the olive from my vodka martini into my mouth, I nod. 'That's right.'

His dark-blue eyes bulge as he shakes his head and speaks slowly, 'And you're out on a *date* with *me*?'

'That's right,' I repeat equally slowly, wondering about this guy's IQ. Sometimes it's hard to tell from a Tinder profile.

Damon obviously only gave mine a cursory glance or he'd have known that I'm not on the prowl for a relationship. He probably got distracted by my photo. I'm not trying to blow my own trumpet, but I'm what people call 'striking'. I'm tall and thin, and ever since I was a little girl, people have been telling me I have a face that turns heads. Some say it's my almost jet-black eyes, others say my perfect cheekbones, occasionally someone even mentions my smile. I can't completely blame him; I saw his pic and thought he was hot as well. He's got a bit of a Jacob Elordi vibe going on; strong, square jawline and brown, floppy hair, longer than mine – not hard – that he keeps having to push out of his eyes every time he goes to take a sip of his beer.

I'm more interested in what's between his legs than between his ears anyway. If we get to that stage of the evening, I might just have to gag him or ask him not to speak while we're doing it.

Some people might think that just because I've slept with a lot of people, I'll sleep with *anyone*. But I've got standards. I might not be looking for Mr Right, but that doesn't mean I'll put up with any old Mr Right Now. I need to find them interesting in some way and respect them, which means going on a lot of dates to sort the wheat from the chaff. I guess dating is my hobby, along with writing, although I hope to one day make the latter my full-time job. I rarely indulge in one-night stands. Most of my hook-ups last for at least a few weeks, sometimes months, until I get itchy feet or the guy in question starts trying to blur our boundaries and I have to let him go. Not that I've got anything *against* one-night stands. My best friend and fellow librarian, Bee, who is obsessed with romance novels, reckons I'm ticking off some invisible list of book boyfriends.

Damon leans back and clamps his hands behind his head. 'What if you fall in love with me?'

Oh my God. Yet another guy with tickets on himself. I can almost see the cogs in his tiny brain churning as he mentally accepts this challenge. I should have guessed he was not my type when he made a joke about cancer when asking why I'd shaved my hair before we'd even ordered our drinks. *Red Flag #1.*

'I won't,' I promise, taking another sip of my drink. So far, it's the best thing about this evening.

Damon's not the first guy I've gone out with who thinks they can convert me, as if marriage is a religion and I just need to 'see the light'. Even if they don't want long-term commitment themselves, they see my stance as a personal affront. Most of the time I nip such interactions in the bud, but occasionally, if they're super cocky, I like to play their game. And – spoiler – I *never* lose.

One time I went out with this civil engineer called Lachlan, who decided after hearing my story that he could convince me to fall in love with him, even though he had no intention of having any such feelings himself. At first I pretended that I was falling for his love-bombing, but then suddenly ghosted him and he went crazy, trying to find out why I'd stopped wanting to be with him. He sent me flowers at work and at home, begging me to take him back. Poor guy – I do hope he learnt his lesson.

I'm pondering where Damon might fit on the scale from Billionaire Playboy to Virgin Boy Next Door when he asks, 'What exactly is the point of this book? Are you some man-hating feminist, Fred?'

I laugh. 'No, I *love* men, which is why I don't want to tie myself down to just one.'

'You know what I think your problem is?' he begins.

Oh, this should be good. *Red Flag #2 – a man who thinks he knows me better than I know myself.*

Two minutes later, he's still delivering his monologue when my phone vibrates on the chipped wooden table. Judging by the length of time it does this, someone is phoning rather than doing the respectable thing of sending a Snap or WhatsApp. The only call action my phone gets is from people wanting donations to charity or scammers warning me I haven't paid my tolls. More fool them, since we don't have tolls in Western Australia.

The only reason anyone else I know would call is if it's an emergency.

If I was enjoying this date, I still might let it go to voicemail, but Damon's theory about me is nowhere near interesting enough to quell my curiosity. I flip my phone over to read the screen.

Mum!

What could she possibly want at this time on a Thursday night? She, Waylen and I get together every couple of months for dinner. Sometimes I'll meet her outside of that if there's a show we both want to see, and we have a once-a-month agreement for a spoken update. Aside from that, we communicate by text message and the occasional meme about divorce and being better off single. Although her divorces were no laughing matter, I take the memes as proof that she's grown.

Have four weeks already gone by since our last phone call? I don't think so. Besides, it's not Sunday. Our calls are *always* on Sundays.

As if she realises I'm not going to answer, the vibrating stops, but before I can make a mental note to send her a message tomorrow, it starts up again. What the hell does she want? Has someone died?

'Do you need to get that?' Damon asks, lifting his pint to his mouth again. We've barely been here ten minutes and it's almost empty.

I shake my head. 'It's my mum. I'll call her tomorrow.'

He frowns. 'Sounds like she really wants to talk to you. You don't think you should answer? Maybe something's happened to her.'

'If she's calling me, she's obviously okay,' I say, not about to be told what to do by this bozo.

Before Damon can reply, my phone rings *again*. I glance at the screen. *Waylen.*

Okay, that *is* weird – my brother doesn't call me. We live together, so we have plenty of opportunities to speak to each other and will simply text if we need milk or toilet paper or other supplies.

I pick up my phone and stand. 'I think I'm going to have to take it.'

Damon nods. 'Shall I order you another drink?'

I'm too distracted to reply as I step outside and answer the call. 'Waylen? What's going on?' My heart plummets as I think of my deliciously fat Ragdoll cat, Aunty, short for Agony Aunt, because every single woman – even those of us single by choice – needs a cat to unload their problems on. 'Is Aunty okay?'

'Aunty's fine,' he says. 'She's sitting next to me and Benji on the couch right now, licking her butt.'

Phew. I love that cat more than I love *The Hunger Games*, op-shopping and seventies punk rock and that's saying something. 'Then what's going on?'

'Mum's about to call you, and I thought I'd better give you a heads-up.'

'She's already tried. Don't tell me she's got a new boyfriend.'

'Worse.' He pauses, then delivers the blow. 'She's getting married.'

'What?' I screech, earning myself a glare from two passers-by. I was joking about the boyfriend. 'Did you know she was dating someone?'

'Nope.' Waylen sighs loudly. 'I promise, tonight was the first I'd heard about all this.'

Here we go again, I think as I start pacing up and down South Terrace, the breeze from the ocean cool on my near-naked scalp. 'Is she trying to give Elizabeth Taylor a run for her money? Break some kind of world record?'

'She says it's different this time.'

I scoff – as if we hadn't heard that the last two times. After I supported her through the end of her fifth marriage, she promised me that she was taking a vow of chastity. Considering she's not the kind of person who can sleep with someone without catching feelings, I told her that was a very good idea, and she'd been going well.

Or so I'd thought.

'I told her you wouldn't be happy,' Waylen says.

Happy? I'm incensed! And terrified. 'Don't tell me you are?'

He sighs again and I can't tell if he's frustrated with me or our mother. 'She's fifty-seven years old; she can make her own mistakes.'

'Well, at least you agree this is a mistake,' I reply sarcastically. 'Why's this guy supposedly different?'

'His name's Paul – Paul Lewis – and she's known him for over forty years.'

What?! This renders me speechless for a few seconds. 'Do *we* know him?' I rack my mind for male family friends who might be a possibility but come up blank. We don't really have any family friends.

'No. She says he's an old school friend, and they met each other again a few weeks ago at their fortieth reunion. Remember she went to Brisbane for it?'

Usually, I'm good with a lot of information coming at me quickly – I'm a librarian after all – but I'm struggling with this. 'Hang on, did you say they only re-met a few weeks ago, and they're *engaged*?' That was fast even for her.

'Yep. And they're having a quick engagement as well. The wedding's in three and a half weeks, but that's not the only thing I wanted to warn you about.' He pauses again. 'She wants *you* to be her maid of honour.'

I freeze in the middle of the path, unsure whether I'm going to faint or vomit. Maybe both. How can she think I'd be excited by this news, never mind agree to be in her effing bridal party? In the end, I laugh psychotically. 'Like that's going to happen!'

My delusional mother calls again as I'm heading back into the Sail and Anchor. I reject the call, then send a message telling her I'm busy and I'll call her tomorrow. It's probably better for both of us if I take the night to calm down.

'I'm going home, Damon,' I say as I return to our table and notice a fresh vodka martini beside another half-drunk pint of beer.

He gives me a patronising smirk. 'Was that one of *those* phone calls?'

'What phone calls?'

'You know, one where you pre-organised a friend to call so you could bail on a bad date.'

It was clear he'd pulled this move numerous times – *Red Flag #3* – but I don't need to use such tactics. 'No bullshit' is Rule #1 for dating without catching feelings. If I don't like someone or I'm not feeling the spark on a date, I just say it to their face. No point wasting either of our time. Plenty more fish in the sea and all that.

Three strikes and Damon's out, or at least he would be if I wasn't already mentally out the door.

'If that were the case,' I say, pulling a twenty-dollar note from my back pocket, 'don't you think I'd have answered the first call?'

'True.' He nods and holds up his phone. 'Can we get a selfie?'

'Why?' I ask, as I slap the note on the table to pay for the cocktail I can't drink.

Damon gives me the sleaziest wink I've ever seen. 'In case you get famous with your book. Then I can say—'

'Definitely not,' I interrupt before he can finish. *No, thanks. Not now. Not ever.* I've already wasted enough time in this idiot's company, and anyway, Rule #11 is simple: No selfies. Selfies signify a level of commitment that I'm never going to give. The only photos I take are with myself, Aunty or occasionally my colleagues after we've had a few too many drinks at Darling Darling, which is exactly where I summon them right now.

Fifteen minutes later, after messages from my so-called friends refusing to meet me at our favourite hole-in-the-wall pirate bar at such short notice, on a work night, at what they deem 'late', I park my beloved bright orange Mini next to Waylen's sleek silver Ferrari 458 in our garage, climb out and slam the door.

Only people in committed relationships would think 9 p.m. is late – most of my dates are merely getting started at this time. Bee says she and her boyfriend, Sully, are already in bed and she isn't giving up a night of red-hot monkey sex when he's rostered to work all weekend unless I'm in hospital or she has to bail me out of jail. Persephone texted that her seven-month-old baby, Sullivan, named after Bee's boyfriend (long story), was in a fussy mood, and Xavier and Rory are apparently out for dinner with lesbian friends they're considering having a baby with.

I also slam the door that leads from the garage to the kitchen as I storm inside. The short drive from downtown Fremantle to the house I share with my older brother in East Fremantle has done nothing to calm me. Schmaltzy music is coming from the TV in the lounge room, but I grab a glass and my faithful cask of Aldi white wine from the fridge before I head in there to rage about our mother.

'How was your date?' Benji asks, grinning from the couch where he's practically sitting on Way's lap. Possibly because, despite it being a rather large couch, Aunty is taking up almost half of it, spread-eagled on her back, paws outstretched like a starfish. Her fluffy tail twitching ever so slightly is the only indication she's actually alive.

I ignore Benji and glare at my brother. 'Please tell me this is some kind of sick joke.'

"Fraid not,' Way says, his fingers gently caressing the back of Benji's neck, just beneath his thick, dark curls. It's still weird seeing my workaholic brother looking so relaxed, watching poor-excuse-for-free-to-air TV with a man on his lap rather than his MacBook. Until he met Benji a few months ago, Waylen was in an obsessive, monogamous relationship with his job.

Flopping down into a matching leather armchair, I pour wine almost to the brim of the glass and take a large gulp.

'How can you stomach that cheap stuff?' Benji asks, grimacing. 'It's even worse than what we serve in economy.'

Did I mention he's a flight attendant? Benji and my brother met when Way was flying to Melbourne for work, and although they are as different as Ted Lasso and Roy Kent, they've been seeing each other ever since.

'It does the trick,' I say as the wine slides down my throat. 'There's a nice bottle of red I brought over if you want me to fetch you a glass,' he offers.

In reply, I take a second gulp, then ask Way to tell me everything he knows.

He shrugs, reaching for the remote to mute the TV. If I wasn't so distressed, I'd give him hell for watching *Dancing with the Stars* or whatever this crap is.

'I told you pretty much everything already,' he says. 'You really should talk to Mum about this.'

I narrow my eyes, daring him not to push me. I'll call her when I'm good and ready.

He sighs. 'She and him were friends in high school, but lost touch after they finished. When they ran into each other again at the reunion, Mum says it was like no time had passed at all. After one drink they ditched their old school mates and went to have dinner alone. Paul lives in England now, like Toby Morpeth' – Way has even less of a relationship with his father than I do with mine, thus always calls him by his full name – 'and he was only in Australia a week, to catch up with his daughter and attend the reunion, but he and Mum spent that whole week together and have been talking ever since.'

I roll my eyes, thinking this story sounds like the kind of

romance novel Bee adores. 'Are we sure he's not got some fancy wife back in the mother country?'

It wouldn't be the first time Mum – Tracy's her name, by the way – has fallen for a married man. (Remind me, some time, to tell you about Husband #4.)

Benji sniffs, pressing a hand against his chest, as Waylen shakes his head. 'He's widowed. His wife died six months ago and—'

Almost choking on my wine, I spit, 'Six months! And he's already planning to shack up with someone else?'

This does not bode well. He's clearly one of those deadbeat men who can't manage five minutes without a woman taking care of him. He probably went to the reunion for the sole purpose of finding some desperate woman he already knew so he could speed up the process a little.

'Don't yell at *me*.' Waylen looks like he's stifling a smirk. 'I'm just the carrier pigeon.'

'And a very sexy pigeon you are at that,' Benji says, beaming like the lovesick puppy he is. Before I can pretend to vomit, he adds, 'I think it's kind of romantic.'

As my nostrils flare and my grip tightens on my glass, I see Waylen place a hand on his boyfriend's knee, but Benji does not heed the subtle warning.

'I think it's lovely that all Tracy's bad experiences haven't soured her on love. Maybe she and Paul were always destined to be together and that's why it never worked with anyone else.'

And maybe unicorns are real and there are pots of gold waiting to turn us all into billionaires at the end of rainbows.

'Have you unofficially moved in?' I ask Benji. He certainly seems to be here more nights than not. Don't get me wrong, I like him. He's easygoing, a fabulous cook, has a great sense of humour and clearly adores my brother, and I like the way Waylen has loosened up a bit since they met. But right now, he's getting on my nerves. 'No offence, but this hasn't got anything to do with you. You don't know Mum like we do, and you won't be the one having to pick up the pieces when her latest marriage falls apart.'

'Hey, don't take this out on Benji,' Waylen says. 'I know you're upset about this, but working yourself up into a state isn't going to change anything. You know what Mum's like. When she thinks she's in love, there's no stopping her.'

'That's a very defeatist attitude, Way.' I go to take another gulp of wine and realise I need to refill my glass. 'I know you divorce lawyers aren't in the business of stopping marriages from going ahead, but we're not talking about one of your clients here, we're talking about our mother! Maybe we should stage an intervention.'

Way throws back his head and laughs like this is the funniest thing I've ever said. 'What? And miss out on a week off work in an island paradise? Come on, relax. It'll be fun!'

I'm so distressed that I totally miss the phrase 'island paradise'. 'Oh my God. Don't tell me you're actually considering going?'

He nods. 'I emailed the office just before you arrived, letting them know I was having the time off.'

'Time off!' I can't remember Way ever having a holiday outside of the mandated public ones, and even then he usually works from home.

'Sounds like Paul's loaded,' Benji chimes in as Aunty lifts her head from slumber and gives me a look of utter disdain. She's not big on shouting. 'I'm invited too. One week in Norfolk Island, all expenses paid in a fancy resort. Bring on the cocktails.'

Normally, I'd be all about the cocktails and a free holiday, but I just can't bring myself to get excited about something I know will end in disaster. I can't understand why Way is being so nonchalant about it. 'Where the hell is Norfolk Island?' I ask.

'It's in the Pacific Ocean. Only a short flight from Brisbane, Sydney and Auckland. *And*,' Way adds, anticipating my next question, 'they've chosen to have the wedding there because apparently they've both always wanted to go.'

Benji all but swoons – 'So romantic' – as he reaches out to stroke Aunty's fur. She rubs her head against his palm like a total hussy and I resist the urge to snatch her away from him. He's already taken my brother, I'm not letting him take my cat!

'Didn't you say you were struggling to find the time to write?' Way asks.

I blink. 'What's my writing got to do with any of this?'

'I was just thinking that you could use the week leading up to the wedding as a kind of writing retreat. I'm sure in between all the stuff Mum's got planned there'll be time to work on your book.'

This gives me pause. Five months ago, I'd matched on Tinder with a photographer from the *West Australian* and although there'd been zero physical spark between us and we'd quickly realised we wanted totally different things in life, he'd been fascinated when I told him the rules I have for dating to avoid messy entanglements and emotions. 'I reckon that would make an awesome article,' he'd said. 'If you write it, I'll pitch it to the features editor for you.'

Not long before that, I'd finished writing my first novel after years of dreaming about winning the Booker or Pulitzer Prize. I'd thought I'd penned a witty, original masterpiece until Bee had risked our friendship to tell me it was an enormous pile of confusing and slightly disturbing sad-girl poop. Although I'd put on a brave face, telling her I appreciated her honesty and would of course continue pursuing my dream of writing – you can't expect to be an expert at something first try – her critique had knocked me, and I hadn't been able to put fingers to keyboard since.

'Would I be paid?' I'd asked the photographer, whose name I can no longer remember.

He'd nodded. 'If it's good.'

I agreed to give the article a shot, hoping that writing about a topic I was an expert in would get my creative juices flowing again. Not telling my friends or family what I'd done, I penned the article, titled '21 Rules for Not Catching Feelings'. It practically flowed from my fingertips, and no one could have been more surprised than me when the *West* shared it to their socials, and it went viral.

Within a matter of days, I'd been contacted by not one but three different publishers asking me if I'd be interested in writing a book on the topic. Hell yeah! It was a no-brainer. This might not be the debut book I'd dreamed of, but I was all about championing modern women and helping them realise that achieving a satisfying sex life doesn't have to mean giving in to traditional notions of love and the shackles that go with it. Besides, everyone knows that in the book world it's more about who you know rather than what you've written, and doing this could get me the contacts I need to really kickstart my writing career. With the assistance of my creative writing teacher, I scored myself an agent and he negotiated what they call in the industry 'a nice deal'. The money wasn't enough to quit my job – not that I wanted to, I love working in the library – but it paid off the loan I had for the Mini and that was worth celebrating.

A week of almost uninterrupted writing time *could* be good, although if I'm honest, time to write isn't the only problem I'm having with the book. Writing eight hundred words about my rules for casual dating was one thing, but writing sixty to seventy *thousand* is something else entirely. And I can't completely make it up like I did with my novel because people will be taking direction from my book, implementing the rules in their lives, relying on me to help them. This kind of pressure is something I never expected to feel.

'Anyway, we're off to bed,' Waylen says, swinging Benji's legs off his lap and standing before I can reply. 'Think about it. But either way, call Mum tomorrow morning, please. And be *kind*.

We might not understand her but that doesn't mean we can't support her.'

Be kind? Support her? What the hell has happened to my cynical older brother? Next thing he'll be encouraging his clients to talk it out, try all they can to stay together. He'll go broke. He won't be able to pay his mortgage and we'll both end up homeless. I blame Benji – he must be a God in bed, because no way would Waylen have been so blasé, even *happy*, about our mother's upcoming nuptials before their meet-cute.

I poke out my tongue at them as they head down the hallway hand in hand, then scoop up Aunty and carry her and the wine into my bedroom.

At least I know she won't try and talk me out of my mood.

2

CONGRATULATIONS AND COMMISERATIONS

My mood has only marginally improved the next morning when I walk into the Fremantle Library staffroom, sipping on the green juice I start every day with. Not because I'm a health nut or anything – I leave that to Waylen – but because my brother makes one for me when he makes his own and it actually tastes a lot better than it looks.

'So . . . what was the emergency?' Bee asks, her caramel ponytail swaying a little as she wriggles her fingers in a wave. Her other hand is holding her daily caffeine fix.

Xavier, library manager and possibly the sweetest man on the planet, and Persephone, back from maternity leave a couple of days a week, are already here as well, both nursing reusable cups holding their morning coffee orders from the Grouchy Sailor. After the Fabio debacle – in which my best friend almost fell for a sly 'Italian' barista – my colleagues road-tested numerous other local cafés but eventually went back to their old fave. I don't drink coffee, but apparently it truly does boast the best in town, and thankfully Fabio is long gone anyway.

'My mother is getting married again,' I announce.

'No way!' Bee says as Xavier's and Persephone's eyes widen.

They exchange guilty looks for ignoring my SOS calls to meet me last night. If all my cranky energy wasn't currently being hogged by Mum, I'd be holding grudges against the lot of them. What happened to sisters before misters?

'Oh my goodness!' Ursula, who has only just returned to work after extended sick leave, enters at that moment. Her complexion is so much healthier and she looks way less scary than when we first met her. Even her dress sense has improved; now, instead of black, buttoned-up outfits that look like they were made for 1950s school-teachers, she's experimenting with colour and the occasional pair of trousers. She rushes over to Bee. 'Did I just hear you're getting married? Did Sully propose?'

Bee laughs as she grabs the last coffee and hands it to Ursula. 'Not yet.'

Her eyes twinkle and I can feel in my bones that such an announcement won't be far off. Sully knows he's onto a good thing, and Bee has 'Marry me' written all over her.

'We're talking about my mum,' I say, still aggrieved. 'Oh.' Ursula blinks. 'Congratulations.'

'I think you mean commiserations.' She frowns. 'You don't like her fiancé?'

I huff. 'I've no idea. I've never even met him.' But what does it matter if I like him; it isn't like it's worth getting to know someone who will be in my mother's life for a few years at most. My throat tightens at the thought of what might happen *after* that. Last time she got divorced, it almost killed us both.'

Ursula opens her mouth to say something else, but Bee gets in first.

'I'm sorry, Fred. If you'd told us that's why you wanted to meet last night, I'd have put on clothes and come and met you. I assumed it was something to do with your date.'

The others nod grimly.

'Nick could have dealt with Sullivan if I'd known how serious this was.'

'Or you could have come to our place,' Bee adds.

Pre-Sully, I would turn up at Bee's cute little duplex, the front garden littered with gnomes, at all hours of the day or night, but ever since he moved in a mere couple of months after they got together, I've not felt quite so comfortable about doing so. It's not that I don't like Sully – he's perfect for Bee and always tries to make me feel welcome – but, just like Waylen and Benji, Bee and Sully already act like an old married couple, and nobody likes to be the third wheel.

'It's fine.' I shrug. 'It's not like talking to you lot is going to change anything.'

'I'm sorry to be dense,' Ursula says, 'but am I missing something?'

'Fred's mum's been married four times already,' Persephone explains, moving to the sink to rinse out her cup. 'And she promised Fred she'd find another hobby.'

I shake my head. 'Actually, it's five times, and—'

'Your mother's been married *five* times?!' Ursula exclaims. She'd once have given out a written warning if anyone spoke at that volume.

Downing the rest of my juice, I nod. The last one had ended even worse than the others and that was saying something. Except for Husband #3, whom she'd married when I was thirteen, my mother had a knack for choosing terrible men. Just like some people shouldn't be allowed to own pets, my mother shouldn't be allowed to date, never mind get married. Someone should pass a law that forbids frequent-flyer divorcees from tying the knot ever again. It should be like my red-flag rule – three strikes and you're out.

'Who's the groom?' Bee asks, her arms twitching at her sides as if she wants to give me a hug but knows better. Affection makes me uncomfortable, but out of all my colleagues, she's the only one who knows how bad this could be. She was the one who supported *me* through the end of Mum's last marriage.

I tell them everything I know. 'But you haven't heard the worst of it; she wants me to be her bridesmaid, or rather her *maid* of honour.'

'Excuse me?' It's clear by the expression on Bee's face that she doesn't know whether to laugh or cry.

Xavier laughs. 'You'd make a very bad bridesmaid.'

'The worst,' Persephone adds, a twinkle in her dark eyes. Maybe I can ask her to put a spell on Mum, or even this Paul guy. Surely if there are love spells, there are anti-love spells. Not that I believe in the gobshite about her being a witch, but desperate times and all.

'Why does she want you to be her bridesmaid when she knows full well you hate love-romance-marriage-and-all-that-mushy stuff?' Bee's quoting me directly. I've never been backwards in coming forward about my feelings on such matters.

'Because she's insane!' I cry. 'Certifiably bonkers. I should have her committed.' It wouldn't be the first time. 'Or maybe she simply doesn't have any friends willing to stand alongside her while she makes a fool of herself yet again.'

'Is Waylen going?' Xavier asks.

'Yep – he says only an idiot would turn down an all-expenses paid island holiday.' Not that he needs a free holiday; people like our mother keep my brother in business, designer suits, and fast cars.

Not that I'm complaining; no way I'd be able to afford the rent if not for the hefty sibling discount.

'He's your brother, right?' This from Ursula. 'Is he in the bridal party too?'

'Nope. I'm the only one she's asking to don a fancy dress and sign a stupid piece of paper that will mean nothing when they divorce a few months later.'

'What do you mean island holiday? Is it a destination wedding?' Persephone asks, glancing at the time on the kitchen microwave.

We're due to open the library in three minutes. Today is Rhyme Time, the most intense day of the week around here. Even if I hadn't woken up with a headache thanks to Mum, I'd be popping pain-killers as soon as the shrieking started. While Xavier and sometimes the others entertain the little *darlings* and their parents, the latter mostly spending the half hour on their phones ignoring Xavier and their children, I usually hide in the office doing whatever mundane, quiet task I can find until it's over.

'Yep, the wedding's on Norfolk Island,' I tell them.

'That's where Colleen McCullough lived,' Bee exclaims, grinning. 'You've got to do her house tour for me. I've heard it's totally extravagant, with outrageous gold wallpaper, hundreds of ferns hanging from the ceiling and furniture and sculptures from exotic countries all over the world. But you're not allowed to take photos there, so you'll have to describe it for me. You can take a photo of her grave in the cemetery though.'

'I haven't agreed to go yet.'

'I think you should,' Bee says.

When I glare at her, she adds, 'And not just because of Colleen. Hear me out.' Her tone is wary, as if she's talking to a child who might erupt in a tantrum any moment – fair enough. 'I know things haven't always been great between you and your mum, and this must be really hard and triggering, but a lot has changed since her last divorce. She's worked on herself, had therapy, and has been really trying hard to reconnect with you and Waylen. You even said a couple of weeks ago that you were proud of her and even starting to like her.'

'Hmm.' I cross my arms over my chest. I do recall saying those exact words after Mum and I had a pleasant night watching a play together at the local theatre, just before she went to Brisbane for the reunion. But Bee's supposed to be on *my* side. 'That was before this latest development. And what if another break-up sends her backwards?'

'What if it doesn't?' she counters. 'What if this ends up being forever and you not being there ruins what should be the happiest day of her life?'

'You sound just like Waylen,' I say, sulking. Lust and romance have ruined all their sensibilities.

She smiles. 'Well, he's a very smart man, but even if this doesn't last, isn't your relationship with your mum more important than that? Don't let another husband come between you.'

I sigh as Xavier clears his throat. 'Whatever you decide to do,' he says, 'we need to park this discussion because it's time to open. Come on, kids, cups in the sink, and let's go.'

While the hurricane that is Rhyme Time rages in the children's section of the library, I take a bunch of new adult fiction releases and a giant roll of clear sticky plastic and get stuck into covering books. This is one of the most hated tasks in the library – up there with cleaning vomit or picking up dirty tissues hidden in the shelves – and usually given to the most junior staff or work experience kids, but I find it strangely therapeutic.

And rarely am I in need of therapy more than I am today. I can't get Mum's news out of my head and think about calling my stepdad Jeff (Husband #3) because I'm sure he'll understand where I'm coming from. If anyone appreciates that Mum isn't cut out for married life, it's him, but I don't want to interrupt him at work. I should call *her*, but until I hear it directly from her mouth, I'm hoping that maybe last night was just a nightmare. I like this thought and I cling to it as I smooth my fingers over books, trying to work out the air bubbles.

When my stomach rumbles, I realise I've worked through morning tea and it's two minutes to midday, my allocated lunch hour. I head towards the staffroom to grab my bag and am almost immediately intercepted by my mother.

'Darling,' she exclaims, throwing her arms around me.

I pull out of her embrace fast. 'What are you doing here?'

She's almost as tall and almost as thin as me, but that's where our similarities end. My hair has been all the colours of the rainbow at one time or another, but I'm naturally dark brown, whereas her hair is the colour of honey. Mine is currently super short, but hers falls in thick waves to her shoulders, and her face is rounded while I've been told mine is heart-shaped like my father's. *How ironic.*

'Since you seem to be too busy at night to answer my phone calls, I thought—'

'I was going to call you tonight.'

She waves my comment away. 'I thought I'd come and meet you for lunch. You've got to eat, right?'

'How did you know what time my lunch break was?'

She grins – 'I called and asked' – and I scowl as I glance around the library trying to work out which of my colleagues betrayed me. Everyone is refusing to meet my gaze.

'Right then.' I nod. 'Let's go. But you're paying.' At least now I won't have to call her back after work, and I also get a free lunch for my troubles.

Mum smiles sweetly. 'Of course, darling.'

'Take your time. We can hold the fort here,' Ursula calls, waving goodbye as Mum and I head towards the escalator.

I think I liked Ursula better when she had a life-threatening, personality-altering tumour. Back when she was the boss and barely let us have a *tea*-break, never mind an extended lunch.

We end up on the rooftop bar at the National Hotel, one of my favourite places to relax with a post-work drink due to the view it affords over Fremantle and out to the Indian Ocean. The sunset is magic from here. The other good thing about this location is that if my mother annoys me too much or I can't convince her not to go ahead with this ridiculous wedding, I can just push her over the edge and save her the inevitable grief and heartbreak.

That might sound cruel but if you'd seen her a few years ago after Husband #5 dumped her, you'd realise I have her best interests at heart.

It's late January and the temperature is in the early thirties, but we sit under a sun umbrella and the breeze coming from the sea makes it almost pleasant. As Mum peruses the menu – I already know exactly what I'm getting – I notice her nails are uncharacteristically dirty.

She looks up and catches me staring, then chuckles. 'I've been getting into pottery. I mentioned to Paul that I'd always wanted to try it, and so he sent me a potter's wheel and gifted me a weekend beginner's course. Turns out I have the knack. I'll make you a mug.'

All I hear in those few sentences is the word 'Paul' and I try not to visibly shudder. 'Have you decided what you're having yet?'

Mum nods, puts the menu down and stands. 'I'm going to have the fried chicken burger and chips.'

I blink, surprised because I'd been expecting her to choose one of the salads – sans the dressing. For as long as I can remember, she's been watching her weight. I don't think I ever recall her eating chips in my life and 'fried' was practically a swearword in our house.

'What do you want?' she asks as I stare at her.

'The steak sandwich, please, and a vodka and soda,' I say, recovering.

'Should you be ordering an alcoholic drink? It's only just gone noon and you have to go back to work later.'

I raise an eyebrow; while I normally wouldn't drink at lunch, her shocking announcement has driven me to it. If I'm going to be civil, I need something to take the edge off. 'If you want to talk about what people should or should not be doing, why don't we start with people who have five failed marriages behind them getting married again.'

A middle-aged couple – the only other people currently on the roof – look our way, so I lower my voice as I add, 'To someone they barely know. Now *that* seems like a terrible thing to do!'

Whoops. So much for being civil.

'I *know* Paul,' Mum says, her expression soft but her voice firm. 'We've known each other since we were thirteen years old.'

Before I can scoff, 'With a forty-year break in between', she gets up and marches over to the corner bar to place our order, returning with my vodka and a lemon, lime and bitters for herself.

'How are things with you, darling?' She smiles, clearly attempting to reset the conversation. 'How's the book coming along?'

'It's fine,' I lie.

When I got the contract, she insisted on taking me and Way out to dinner – usually she's more than happy for Way to pay – during which she cried as she told me how proud she was of me. I couldn't recall her ever being so effusive about anything I'd done. She'd gone on about admiring my independence and wishing she was more like me. In a way, after that, I was kind of writing it for women like her as well as women like me; maybe

I'd help other women avoid making diabolical marriage choices.

I pick up my drink. 'But let's talk about the real reason you're here.'

Her fingers reach for a gold heart on a chain hanging around her neck that I've never seen before, and I guess must be a gift from her lover. 'I know this must seem very sudden to you, and I know I promised you that I was done with men, and I absolutely meant it when I said it. But then I met Paul again and the connection was magic. I'm sorry, but I can no longer keep that promise. Paul is the love of my life.'

Fingers tight around my glass, I say, 'If he means so much to you, why is this the first Waylen or I have ever heard of him?'

Mum picks up her drink and takes a sip, no doubt wishing she'd also bought an alcoholic beverage. 'It was an old friendship that never came up in conversation, but just because I never told you about him doesn't mean I didn't think about him. He was never far from my thoughts. I often wondered what had happened to him and—'

She stops speaking abruptly and turns away to look across the rooftop to the ocean.

'And what?' I ask, flapping a menu at her, trying to get her attention again.

'Sorry.' She shakes her head and smiles again. 'And nothing.

I was just thinking about how wonderful Paul is.'

My spidey senses tell me there *was* an 'and', but she doesn't give me the chance to press.

'I've never felt this physically attracted to anyone before.' She blushes, her grin so wide I fear her lips might snap. 'We barely left my hotel room the whole time we were in Brisbane and since he's been back in England, we've gotten very creative on FaceTime. Did you know—'

'Too much information,' I say, holding up my hand. I'm no

prude, but hearing about this Paul guy's prowess in the bedroom is not something I need if I'm going to meet him in a few weeks. Although that is still a very big *if*. 'And just because a guy is good in bed doesn't mean you have to marry him!'

'I promise this isn't about sex, darling. Paul ticks *all* the boxes for me. He's kind, he's intelligent, he's funny, he's interested in me as a person and wants to know my thoughts and opinions. He's like the missing part of me. Now that I've found him again, it's so easy to see why it didn't work out with any of my other husbands.' I can't help rolling my eyes. You might think I'm cold and heartless, but I have heard a version of this story more than once. I swear she called Colin (Husband #4) – or was it Bernie (Husband #5) – her missing half.

'Really? I thought it didn't work out with Waylen's dad because he ran off with someone else. And Colin because he was living a double life, and Bernie because—'

'Okay. Okay!' she snaps. 'I get it. Please, can't you just be happy for me for once?'

I notice the couple are no longer quietly enjoying their lunch but are now leaning towards us, blatantly eavesdropping, and I can't blame them. My mum's life is like a soap opera, one I've been acting in against my will all my life. The last few seasons might have been dull but this curveball has me back on the edge of my seat. She doesn't realise what she's asking of me. And if I'm honest, I'm also a little put out. Things have been getting better between us over the last year or so, and I foolishly thought that finally my brother and I were enough for her. That she was content with our little family of three.

'I would be happy for you, if I could be,' I say. 'But I'm worried. I don't know if *I* can survive another one of your heartbreaks, never mind you if you can.'

Her gaze softens as she reaches across the table to take my hand. Somehow, I manage not to flinch. 'I'm sorry for everything

I've put you and Waylen through, darling. I know I scared you, but I'm better now and I'm not going to go back to that dark place – ever. I know it's asking a lot for you to be my maid of honour, but I need you to trust that I know what I'm doing this time. I wouldn't ask if it wasn't important to me. I know how much you hate weddings, but it won't be the perfect day I want it to be if I don't have my babies there.'

'I don't hate weddings.' Honestly, I'm not that much of a Grinch. Some of the best nights of my life have been at weddings – everyone is happy, dressed up, drinking, dancing, all of which are my favourite things. 'It's marriage I'm opposed to, and I think *some* people should admit defeat.'

A waiter chooses that moment to appear, giving us both a few seconds to think before we speak again. 'Steak sandwich?' he asks, looking between us.

I tap my chest. 'That's mine, thanks.'

Grinning, he places it in front of me like it's a Michelin star meal rather than standard pub grub and turns his smile on my mother. 'Then the chicken burger must be for your sister. Enjoy, ladies.'

Mum positively glows while I roll my eyes. Is he flirting with her? She's got that kind of ethereal quality that men can't resist. No wonder she collects husbands like kids collect Pokémon cards, or whatever they're into these days.

I pluck a fry from my plate and take a bite. Like me, Mum can be very stubborn, and I realise that perhaps I've taken the wrong tack. Telling her not to marry her long-lost high school classmate will only make her want to do it more, but if I can get her to delay the wedding, it'll give me longer to come up with a plan.

'I'm glad you're happy, Mum,' I say, the words feeling like sickly sweet fairy floss on my tongue – I'm much more of a savoury gal. 'But . . . what's the rush? This all seems very quick.'

Even for you. 'Is it because he lives overseas? Is he planning on moving here? Or is it going to be a long-distance marriage?'

She shakes her head. 'I'm too old for nonsense like that. And Paul has a very successful business in England.'

'You're only fifty-seven. Pretty sure you're not on death's door just yet.'

'You never know when life can be cut short. We want to be together for as long as we have left. '

'So *you're* planning on living there?' I can't believe she wouldn't think twice about moving so far away from Way and I, especially after all we've been through the last few years.

Smiling, Mum reaches across the table to pat my hand. 'It might seem a long way, but you don't need to worry – we'll still see plenty of each other. Paul's promised me that not only will he fly me back here as often as I want, but he'll fly you across whenever you want too. First class.'

I'll admit the first-class flights to London tickle my fancy – how rolling is this guy? – but that is *not* what I'm worrying about here!

Feeling like I'm fighting a losing battle, I try another tack. 'You know, you don't need to rush into marriage. You could always get a working visa while you spend some proper time together again.' Not only are divorces stressful, but they're also expensive, even with Waylen's family discount; just ask my mum's non-existent savings account.

'At my age? With my non-qualifications?' Mum works at Fiona Stanley Hospital in their staff canteen; all her working life has been in shops or cafés. 'Sometimes you can be so naive, darling. Anyway, I want to marry him.'

Of course she does.

'We're only waiting as long as we are because we need to get the paperwork sorted. And of course, there's the dresses. Wait 'til you see what I'm thinking for your maid of honour gown.'

As she whips out her phone, presumably to show me a photo, I lift my sandwich and sink my teeth in. It tastes like I'm munching on cardboard. Usually the steak sandwiches here are to die for, so I'm pretty sure my emotions are the problem.

'What do you think?' Smiling so widely her facial muscles must ache, she angles the screen towards me.

I can't believe what I'm seeing. The pale pink dress looks like something a Disney princess would wear. Or Barbie – I swear I had a doll with that identical dress as a kid. 'Is that supposed to be your dress or mine?'

She laughs. 'Mine, of course. I'm not wearing white, because well . . .' She shrugs again. 'I may not be a virgin, but I still want to look and feel like a bride.' Swiping across to another photo, she adds, 'This is what I'm thinking for you.'

'Hell no,' I exclaim as my eyes are assaulted by a high-necked, floor-length gown that, if not for the satiny gold fabric, would look like a potato sack.

Reading my mind, Mum says, 'I don't want your youthful beauty to show me up on my big day.'

'Trust me, you don't want me to look like that either. I'll ruin the photos.' I change the subject. 'How's your burger?'

'Good.' She lifts it to her mouth for another bite. Silence lingers a few moments as we both eat, then she puts down her food and looks me right in the eye. 'I know it's a big ask, especially at short notice, but will you do it, please? Will you be my maid of honour?'

I'm not prepared to commit just yet. 'Does Paul have kids? Will they also be coming to the wedding?'

She nods. 'He's got two daughters and a son. Scarlett and Juliet are in their early thirties and Leo is about the same age as you. The oldest lives in Noosa and has three kids; the other two are in England, but he says they're all very excited to meet me, you and Waylen. That's why we're inviting all of you to join us in the week leading up to the big day. Spending time together on the island will really give you all a chance to get to know each other and become family.'

Her ideas of family differ vastly to mine. Just because they sign a legal document, doesn't mean we're family. Aside from Waylen and Mum, it's my friends – the people I've *chosen* to have in my life – who are my family.

I zone out as she talks more about their pre-wedding plans – it's like we'll be the next Brady Bunch. But my sibling card is full; I've got Waylen, not to mention two little half-sisters who have my previously-non-fatherly father wrapped around their cute little fingers.

I finish my sandwich and half my drink, then interrupt Mum mid-sentence, telling her I need to get back to work.

She looks up at me desperately. 'Please, Fred, will you do this for me?'

Sighing, I remember what Waylen said about a writing retreat and all the cocktails I can put on Paul's tab while we're on the island. 'Okay, I'll think about it.' As Mum's face splits into another wide grin, I add, 'But I'm not wearing that dress. I want a short red one instead.'

She springs from her seat and steps around the table to embrace me. *Ugh.* When will she learn I'm not a hugger? 'Thank you, darling. You're the absolute best. Are you free to go dress shopping on the weekend? I'm flying to London on Monday to be with Paul until we both fly to Norfolk for the wedding, and it would be so much easier to get this sorted before I go.'

'I can be,' I say.

'Excellent, and . . .' A slightly pained expression crosses her face as she stares at me. 'Maybe we can find you a nice wig to wear as well.'

Rubbing my hand over my soft fuzz of hair, I tell her not to push her luck.

3

NEWLYWEDS AND NEARLYDEADS

*A*s the crow flies, Norfolk Island is only 4951 kilometres from Perth, but it takes two flights and a ridiculous stopover for us to get there. We flew Perth to Brisbane on the midnight horror, landing just after 5 a.m. Queensland time, and our next flight isn't until 11.35. Even more ridiculous is the fact that we have to transfer to the international airport for the flight to Norfolk.

I mean, what the *actual*?

If Norfolk Island is part of Australia, which supposedly it is, why do we have to go through the rigmarole of customs as if we're flying to a different continent?

After collecting our luggage at the baggage carousel in Brisbane, Benji convinces us to put our stuff in storage lockers at the station and catch the train into the city for breakfast. While Waylen and I both look and feel like death, Benji has somehow managed to emerge from the overnight flight bouncier and looking even fresher than normal. Guess he's used to travelling all hours for his job. He says breakfast in Brissy will be better than anything we can find at the airport. Waylen counters that the free food in the Qantas Lounge isn't bad, but then Benji reminds him that I won't be able to come in with them because Way only gets one guest.

I'm about to say that Waylen would always pick me over him, but the way my brother looks at Benji with huge googly eyes makes me realise this is not the case. Are my days of being my brother's number one over? First Bee, then Way, and now Mum. It's a sobering thought that I might not be anyone's priority any more. Ignoring the tightness in my chest, I tell myself at least I'll always be Aunty's most loved.

After a fairly average breakfast at a fairly expensive café on Southbank, we decide to head to the airport and wait the rest of our time there. Waylen and Benji are stoked that our 'international' flight affords them duty free shopping, but I don't have enough money to get excited, so I wait at the café next to the news and book store. Of course I do a drive-by of the new releases, but I'm so tired that even the smell of books and their shiny covers don't give me the buzz they usually do. It's times like these I wish I drank coffee, but I make do with a bottle of Diet Coke.

I park myself at a corner table and FaceTime Bee to see how Aunty survived the night. My beloved feline is staying with her and Sully, and their adorable dog, John Brown, while I'm away, and I should just catch Bee before she heads off to work. At the library, we all work one weekend in three and this Saturday, Bee's one of the lucky ones.

'Hey, girlfriend,' she says when she answers. I can tell she's propped her phone up against her bathroom mirror as she's brushing her hair into a ponytail. 'How's Norfolk?'

'I'm not there yet,' I groan.

She grimaces. 'Oh, that's right. Sorry. How was the first flight?'

'It was a flight. More to the point, how's my girl? Is she missing me?'

'Um . . .' Bee picks up the phone and takes me into her bedroom where Sully is still asleep in bed, Aunty curled up on one side of him and John Brown on the other. 'I'm sure she is but she's still living her best life.'

I laugh. 'Where did *you* sleep last night?'

'Morning, Fred,' comes Sully's deep voice from under the sheets.

'Hey, Sully.'

Bee takes me and the phone into the kitchen as she makes toast. We're discussing the TV series I binged on the plane when possibly the most gorgeous guy I've ever seen walks into the café and joins the queue to order. He's about the same height as me but has deliciously broad shoulders and perfectly proportioned narrow hips, showcased by faded jeans, hanging low. They look so well-worn that even from this distance I can tell they'd be soft to touch. There's some kind of instrument case hooked over his shoulder; too small to be a guitar, but not the right shape for a trumpet. Is it a violin? He looks too cool to be a violinist. He's wearing a short-sleeved shirt in a modern art print, his dirty-blond hair is pulled back into a man bun – have I mentioned I'm a big fan of the man bun? – and his scruffy facial hair is on point. I immediately think about how it would feel between my legs.

'Fred, are you still there?' Bee asks through a mouthful of Vegemite toast.

'Sorry.' I look back at the screen, suddenly warm. 'My hot guy radar went off.'

Her eyes sparkle – 'Where? Show me!' – so I swivel the phone so she can see, uncaring if Hot Muso Guy catches us perving. Ask anyone and they'll tell you I have no shame. 'Ooh, he's a work of art. And is that a book tucked under his arm?'

'Oh my God, it is.'

'Smash,' we say in unison. There's nothing hotter than a guy who reads, unless the book is *12 Rules for Life*.

My libido perks up even more when he moves slightly and I see the cover of none other than my favourite book of all time. 'It's *The Hunger Games*.'

Bee presses her hand to her chest. 'That's gotta be an omen. Imagine if he's going to Norfolk.'

I don't believe in omens, and I hadn't even got as far as the island in my thinking. I was too busy wondering if I could lure him somewhere private pre-boarding, but if by pure luck he is on my flight, maybe I could tick Mile High Club off my bucket list. I'm contemplating how I'm going to engineer this meeting when a hugely pregnant woman in a chic travel tracksuit, shiny cinnamon-coloured hair falling in perfect curls around her shoulders, shuffles up beside Hot Muso/Book Guy.

What? I can't believe it. I take great pride in my Single Radar, and I could have sworn this guy was giving off those vibes.

'Oh bummer,' Bee says as the pregnant woman grumbles loudly to him.

'I thought I was going to burst.' The woman sighs and rests her hands, which I notice are French manicured, on her enormous bump. 'Did you order my hot chocolate?' When Hot Muso/Book Guy nods, she adds. 'Skinny milk?'

He nods again.

She beams sickeningly. 'What did I do to deserve you?'

'Never mind,' Bee says as I turn the phone back around so she's looking at me. 'I'm sure there'll be plenty of hot single guys in paradise.'

But I shake my head – that's not on my agenda for the next seven days. It's all about the writing. If I can get a good chunk of my book finished, it might take the edge off Mum marrying Husband #6.

Not too long after, I disconnect from Bee, and Way and Benji return laden with duty-free bags. They've bought grog, designer T-shirts, expensive aftershave and Lord knows what else. They each grab another coffee and then we head to the gate, where Hot Muso/Book Guy and his very pregnant partner are also waiting for the Norfolk flight. Maybe they're on their honeymoon after a shotgun wedding. According to Benji, who has been annoying us with facts about Norfolk Island since I agreed to go, it is a place for newlyweds and nearly-deads.

My gaze drifts to the couple's hands as I take a seat in one of the uncomfortable plastic rows. Yep, she's got a shiny, square-cut diamond ring, snug against a white-gold band. Very flashy, and definitely very expensive. He's not wearing a wedding ring, but I know from experience there are lots of reasons why men don't – most of them sinister.

'Attention, passengers flying on QF183 to Norfolk Island, your aircraft is now ready for boarding . . .' Some guy is halfway through his spiel when a dark-haired child, who looks to be about ten, rushes past me, almost giving me a black eye with a book she's waving about.

'Watch it,' I hiss, but she doesn't hear me.

She's too busy launching herself at Mr and Mrs Hot Muso/ Book Guy. The three of them share a big hug and seconds later two adults follow with a smaller girl and a baby. The woman is all smiles and looks a little like she's just come from Woodstock, wearing a long boho-style dress, her white-blonde hair hanging almost to her butt and piercings in her nose and all the way up her ears. The baby and the little girl have the same hair colour; the baby's is not much longer than mine and the girl's is not quite as long as her mother's. Lots more hugging follows, and the baby, held by a short guy with light brown dreadlocks and wearing colourful harem pants, almost gets squished in all the action.

Hot Muso/Book Guy scoops up the girl, who looks about five, and swings her around. She shrieks in glee. 'How's my princess?' he asks, drawing her to his chest in a big hug.

'Not a princess. I'm a pussy cat!' She adds an impressively realistic meow as she points to the cat ears on her blonde head.

'Sorry, Pussy Cat,' he says, winking at the adults, before swinging her around again. It's then I notice she's also wearing a tail.

When he puts her down, she drops to all fours and starts meowing loudly around her parents' feet. I wait for one of them to tell her off for disturbing the peace, but they're all talking a million miles an hour and no one in their little posse gives her a second glance. They're clearly heading to Norfolk for some wholesome family holiday. Not that I'd know anything about that. The only childhood holiday I remember going on was Mum and Jeff's honeymoon to the Whitsundays.

They couldn't get anyone to look after us for two whole weeks so had brought us along as well. Until then, I'd only been away for sleepovers at friends' places or my grandma's house and school camps, which were nothing like this vacation. When we got off the plane, I thought I'd landed on another planet – the blue skies and crystal-clear water were almost more than my eight-year-old heart could handle. Mum was so happy, and she even came snorkelling with us. We saw whales and went up in a helicopter, and although I'd never been one for sport before, I loved the bushwalks we took with Jeff pointing out all the colourful birds that called the island home.

Every day we had ice cream, and every night we were allowed to stay up late and watch a movie. Usually I'd fall asleep before it ended, and in the morning I'd find myself back in my bed, never remembering Jeff carrying me there.

I smile fondly at the recollection, thinking how different life might have been if Mum and Jeff hadn't broken up.

As soon as we board the plane, I praise the inventor of noise-cancelling headphones as I slap mine over my ears to drown out the family, who are seated nearby. The baby's grizzling now and the other kids are squabbling about who is sitting where, but I zonk out against the window, waking up mid-flight to see the back of my brother's head fused to Benji's in an X-rated smooch.

I shove my elbow into him. 'Knock it off. There are kids on this plane.'

The nap having revived me slightly, I pull my laptop out of my bag, try to ignore the lovebirds and do some work, but I've barely typed three sentences before it's announced that all laptops and large devices must be stowed away for landing. Sure enough, approximately ten minutes later, we start the descent and I look out the window to see the tiny island coming into view. In my head, an island in the Pacific Ocean would be all sun and stretches of pale-yellow sand contrasting with clear, aqua-blue oceans, but instead the skies hang low over the ocean in resigned slates and misty greys. The land mass sits upright from the sea like a cake, its rocky edges burnished, topped by a luscious green icing of thick pasture, the famous Norfolk pines popping up like candles, standing sentinel over the convicts who'd once called this so-called paradise their prison. Pure white foam gathers around its base, deep blue water crashing onto rocks. It's undeniably beautiful, just not what I was expecting.

As we touch down, I grab my phone out of the seat pocket. Expecting it to vibrate with a tonne of notifications when I switch off flight mode – it might have been a short commute, but I've been messaging a couple of very eager guys and expect a barrage of replies – I'm confused when nothing happens.

'My phone can't find a network,' I say. When Waylen doesn't reply, I elbow him. 'What is it?' he snaps, glowering at me. 'My phone isn't working.'

He nods as if I've told him the sky is blue. 'Yeah, neither Telstra nor Optus work on the island.'

'What!' My shriek earns me dirty looks from surrounding

passengers. 'Are you kidding me? What kind of backwards place doesn't have a mobile tower?' If I had any doubts that coming here was a mistake, now I'm certain. 'Please tell me they have wi-fi.'

'In some cafés, and the hotel should have it. Didn't you do any research about this place?'

'Why would I?' I pout.

Way shakes his head. 'And you call yourself a librarian.'

In my defence, the research aspect isn't what I love about being a librarian. These days the only real research I do takes place on Instagram or LinkedIn in the form of stalking guys I've met on dating apps. It's the books that drew me into my career, but surprisingly, it's the community aspect I find most rewarding. Sure, I still love reading more than almost anything else, but running workshops for women trying to get back on their feet after domestic abuse, movie nights for the local homeless, a safe space after school for teens who don't have a great home life and the conversations I have with the lonely patrons are why I do it.

'You can buy a sim card from the Visitor's Centre.' Benji's helpful information interrupts my reverie.

'Halle-bloody-lujah. That'll be our first stop once we've got our car.'

Mum and Paul were supposed to meet us at the airport, but she texted before our flight to say the wedding planner, who is also the celebrant, had to move their meeting to the afternoon and now they can't make it. Way has hired a car anyway, and I'll be in a better mood to meet Paul once I have a phone card.

Although it looked winterish as we came in to land, the temperature as we descend onto the tarmac says otherwise. The pilot mentioned it was only twenty-four degrees, but it feels at least ten hotter. Sweat is already pooling in the centre of my back, and I wonder how people with more hair cope with this humidity.

We follow the line of other passengers towards the tiniest airport I've ever seen. With a white roof, blue awnings, a hedge fence out the front and Norfolk Pines towering behind it, it almost looks like someone's house. Stepping inside is like travelling back in time into last century. The only thing that looks less than fifty years old is a shiny sign promoting Norfolk's history, culture and World Heritage Kingston settlement. Everything else, from the dull, grey striped carpet to the cream wood-panelled walls screams 1972. And yes, even though Norfolk is part of Australia, we have to go through bloody customs. There's even a sniffer dog winding between our feet as we – all cramped into the tiny area surrounding the solitary baggage carousel – wait for our things.

The carousel groans to life and as well as the expected suitcases, everything from trampolines, Ikea flatpacks and boxes of tinned food comes out. Most of the people around us are chatting like they're old friends at a school reunion and I wonder how many of us waiting here are actually tourists. Maybe Hot Muso/Book Guy and his family are islanders. He does have a bit of the laidback vibe you'd expect to go with such a lifestyle, not that I can say the same about his wife. She looks like she's stepped off the pages of *Vogue Pregnancy*, if there is such a thing.

As if he can feel me watching them, he looks over and our eyes meet. He winks and hits me with a *very* friendly smile. The kind of smile men in bars give me before asking if they can buy me a drink.

Jerk. What business does he have flirting with me while his heavily pregnant wife is standing right beside him? He's clearly in a committed relationship – about to become a dad – and while I might not want such a thing, that doesn't mean I don't respect the choices of others. I would never knowingly sleep with a guy in a monogamous relationship.

Resisting the urge to give him the finger, I turn my back on him just as my bright red suitcase emerges. Way steps forward to grab it for me, and his and Benji's bags follow soon after. Because my phone is all but defunct, I'm unable to check my dating apps, message Bee or scroll meaninglessly through Insta, so while we're in the queue for immigration, I find myself wondering how the government can afford to hire customs officers for only one flight a day.

'Right, where's the car hire company?' I ask, looking around as we exit customs, but there's no sign of any such thing.

'The email said there'll be someone to meet us outside.'

Sure enough, when we venture into the muggy afternoon, there's a woman who looks to be in her mid-thirties, with salon-dyed red hair, holding a sign with Waylen's name on it. 'Welcome to Norfolk,' she says after Way introduces himself. 'I'm Petrice. It's lovely to meet you all.'

We follow Petrice to a little white hatchback at the far side of the car park. She opens the driver's door and hands the key to Way with a map of the island. 'Now, you're staying at the South Pacific Resort, so just turn right as you head out the car park and then turn here.' She points to something on the map, and I hope Way's listening because it's not like we can use Google Maps. 'Then just keep going and the resort is on your right just after the main stretch of shops.'

'Thanks,' he says, as Benji opens the boot.

'Just park her here again and leave the keys on the driver's seat before you fly out.'

We all baulk at this. I mean, what is this place? It's like we've been zapped back in time to somewhere mobile phones don't exist, and people are still trustworthy.

'It's perfectly safe. Not much point stealing a car here.

There's nowhere to go.' She chuckles, then adds, 'Enjoy your holiday. No doubt we'll cross paths again.'

And with that, she's striding off back towards the building and we're left trying to wrangle our luggage into a car almost as tiny as my Mini. None of us has packed light. Not to mention all the duty-free bags Way and Benji have accumulated. Only my suitcase, Benji's and one of the bags fit in the boot, and even this takes much manipulation. The rest they pile in around me in the back seat.

'Does the map show where the Visitor's Centre is?' I ask as Way starts the car. My heart is feeling panicky with the knowledge I don't have access to civilisation.

Benji holds it out in front of him. 'There it is. It's on the main street too, so should be easy to find.'

'Excellent.' I flop back into the seat. 'Let's go.'

We arrive a few minutes later to discover the visitor centre closed at noon. I want to cry until I read the sentences below, informing me that on the weekends, phone cards are also available at P&R Groceries. Praise the Lord. I rush back to the car.

'Find P&R Groceries on the map,' I bark at Benji. He's not bad with the paper map and directs Waylen to head back the way we came.

Inside and out, the grocery store is a relic from the past, just like the airport, and I can't help turning my nose up at the fruit next to the counter as I approach it. The bananas are small, more brown than yellow and the apples make me shudder. I wouldn't touch any of them, even if they were the last food on the planet. 'Hi,' I say to the bloke behind the counter. He reminds me of Shane Jacobson, all smiles and in dire need of a good shave. 'Can I buy a phone card, please?'

'Sorry, luv, just sold the last one.'

'What?!'

He shrugs, grinning at me like this isn't a total travesty, when another woman enters the store and the two of them start speaking in what I can only guess is some kind of local slang.

'This place is the worst,' I tell the boys as I climb back into the car. Did I mention it's now bucketing with rain? So much for an island paradise. 'They've run out. I can't get a card until Monday. Our resort better have wi-fi or blood will be spilled.'

Way and Benji have the good sense not to comment as we head back down the road towards the resort. I glower out the window at the row of shops on either side, most of them named after people and quite a few of them empty and boarded up. Duncan's Jewellers, Max's Duty Free, Pete's Place, Craig's Knitwear, Ross's, and Benjamin's – no indication of what the latter two sell. Although most of my clothes come from op shops and I have a passion for vintage fashion, it's safe to say none of these shops – even the ones that are still in business – are likely to stock anything I'd be interested in or be seen dead wearing.

'I thought this place was supposed to be paradise,' I grumble as Way slows the car to turn into our resort.

Benji smiles over his shoulder at me. 'I think it's quaint. Cute.' I'm going to start calling him Pollyanna. The last few weeks, his eternal positivity has been grating on my nerves. And now, on this godforsaken island that is so stuck in the dark ages my phone has been rendered useless, it's all I can do not to lean forward and punch him in the head. It's amazing what being disconnected can do to a person.

A minivan pulls up just in front of us at the entrance to the South Pacific Resort Hotel – a brown building with a vomit-green roof – and Hot Muso/Book Jerk and his family pile out. Not islanders then, and just my luck they're staying at the same place as us. With those noisy, unruly kids, I'll never get a moment's peace. If I hadn't just missed the only flight back to the mainland today, I'd be on it.

Service is slow, and while the blue-uniformed man behind the desk checks the family into their rooms, I glumly take in my surroundings. You guessed it: it's unlikely the resort has had a reno since the 1980s. The floor is tiled in speckly, grey marble, and wood-panelling in browns and beige not only lines the walls but also a square-shaped pond in the foyer with a weird mushroom fountain in the middle and koi swimming in it. There are half a dozen old black-leather sofas in one corner, a TV hanging on the wall and some amps set up nearby as if they host gigs here. I shudder to think what kind of music it would be.

I wander over to look out the window onto the pool. Although not as clear blue as the photo Benji showed me at Perth Airport, it has sun loungers along one side that will make a nice spot to write. That's if it ever stops raining.

'Fred,' Way calls to me and I glance back to discover the family has vanished and it's our turn to check in.

We're given room keys, another map and, most importantly, the wi-fi password and then we head towards our rooms, passing an old-school games room with pool and ping pong tables, both of which have seen better days. The only thing that vaguely excites me so far is the book exchange housed in floor-to-ceiling wooden shelves. If I wasn't so tired, I'd take a look now – you can find gems in these places – but all I want to do is go to my room, order room service, connect to wi-fi, bury myself in the bed to sulk and then sleep for a year.

But my plans for the evening evaporate when Way reminds me we're meeting Mum, Paul and his kids for drinks in the bar before our first official family dinner in just over an hour.

Pray for me!

4

A PLEASANT TURN OF EVENTS

 ay, Benji and Mum are already at the bar when I arrive. She's wearing a floral pink maxi-dress and although it's not to my taste, she looks radiant. I'm guessing the man who is about six-three with salt and pepper hair and stylish black spectacles with his arm around her is Paul. He looks like a nice enough person, but all I can see is a few years, maybe even months, into the future, when he's cast Mum aside and I'm trying to help her put the pieces of her life back together. Only this time, she'll be in London, and I'll probably have to fly all the way over there to rescue her, by which time I doubt Paul will be magnanimous enough to pay for me to travel first class. Taking a deep breath, I linger a few moments at the entrance, gathering strength to go in. Thankfully, despite the patchy hotel wi-fi, I've managed to check my socials and bombard Bee with text messages outlining the hell I've landed in. She sent me half a dozen photos of Aunty playing with John Brown, which eased my crankiness a little.

As if sensing my presence, Mum glances over to where I'm standing and her eyes light up as she sees me. 'Darling,' she exclaims, rushing over, Paul following closely behind her. She throws her arms around me. 'I'm so glad you're here. Paul, this is my sweet, darling girl, Wi—'

'*Fred*,' I say; she knows I despise my legal name but insists on using it. 'And you must be Paul?'

He smiles warmly at me as he leans forward to kiss my cheek. 'Trace has told me so much about you. It's a joy to finally meet you and Waylen.'

His voice is deep and each word carefully enunciated, but even though he's been living in England for years, his Queensland twang is impossible to miss.

'Um. You too,' I manage, simply because my brother gave me a half an hour lecture about being on my best behaviour.

'Let me introduce you to my family.' Paul puts his hand on the small of my back and I try not to flinch as he leads me further into the room, right over to Hot Muso/Book Jerk and his family.

No way.

I'd been so focused on Mum and Paul that I'd failed to notice the others were even here, despite the middle kid rolling around on one of the tables, clearly pretending to be a cat, with the baby in the pram next to her watching and clapping her hands. And they were *Paul's family*? Maybe there's only so much stress one person can handle.

The oldest, seemingly oblivious to her little sister's antics, looks to be reading directly from a book to Hot Muso/Book Jerk.

'Kids?' Paul calls. 'Come over and meet your new sister and aunty.'

Aunty? The word gives me a visceral reaction. As if sensing I need it, Benji presses a glass of bubbles into my hand. Perhaps he isn't so annoying after all.

After a little more cajoling, Paul gathers everyone into a circle like we're on school camp and I wonder for a moment if he's going to start singing 'Kumbaya'.

'Let's go youngest to oldest, shall we?' He scoops the baby out of the pram. 'This is Miller, the apple of my eye.'

I'm not sure if Miller is a boy or a girl – they're wearing lime-green overalls and sucking on a purple dummy.

'I thought I was the apple of your eye, Grandpa,' the oldest says, pouting over the top of her book.

He reaches out to ruffle her already-scruffy hair. 'You're all the apples of my eye.'

The middle one frowns up at him from the floor where she's still on all fours. 'I can't see any apples in your eyes!'

Everyone laughs as he smiles down at her. 'And this is Kayla, our little pussy cat.'

She purrs loudly in response and swishes her fake tail.

'I'm Tallulah-Jane,' the oldest girl says, not waiting for Paul to introduce her. She looks at me with great suspicion. 'What's your phobia?'

'Excuse me?'

She sighs, rolls her eyes and speaks to me like I'm thick. 'What. Are. You. Scared. Of?'

'Tallulah-Jane is fascinated by phobias at the moment,' Paul explains, smiling proudly at her. 'Last month it was quantum physics. She's very smart. Always has her head in a book.'

'Oh. Right. Well . . . um . . .' I'm scared I can't finish *my* book, does that count? But no way am I going to admit that to a bunch of strangers. 'I guess I'm scared of needles.'

Mum chuckles. 'That's true, you used to scream blue murder when I took you for your vaccinations.'

'Trypanophobia,' Tallulah-Jane announces. I decide to refer to her as TJ.

'Sounds like some kind of dinosaur,' I say, which doesn't seem to impress her.

Paul chuckles, then clears his throat. 'Anyway, these three gorgeous girls belong to my oldest daughter, Scarlett.'

Scarlett steps forward and yanks me into a tight hug. 'It's so lovely to meet you. Isn't this so exciting? I just love weddings.'

I can't help bristling. It was bad enough when Mum wrapped her arms around me, never mind a stranger. And is she for *real* ? Either way, her sickly sweetness is bound to get on my nerves.

'I'm so sorry to hear about your mother,' I say as I disentangle myself.

Waylen glares at me. I shrug. *Just being polite.*

'Thank you. That means *so* much.' Scarlett yanks me to her chest again, which smells like milk. When she pulls back, I spy two wet patches on her dress. 'Whoops,' she says, giggling when she catches me looking, 'I think someone needs a feed.'

Paul hands Miller along the circle like we're playing Pass the Parcel and I'm so shocked when she lands in my arms, I almost drop her. I'm not sure I've ever held a baby before. She looks up at me with wide eyes and then starts to scream. I thrust her at Scarlett and let out a sigh of relief as she whips out a breast.

While Miller suckles loudly, the introductions continue.

Next up is River, who announces that he is Scarlett's 'soulmate' – I cannot help rolling my eyes at that – and then Paul's other daughter, Juliet, who, despite being hugely pregnant, is wearing a navy jumpsuit that screams designer. It's clear she's one of those people who always looks impeccable – she probably styles her hair and does her make-up before bed.

Thankfully she doesn't hug me, but merely offers a quick air kiss as Paul adds, 'Sadly, Juliet's partner, Henry, can't be with us.'

'He couldn't get that much time off away from work – he's an ENT surgeon – at such short notice,' she explains in a posh, lilting accent, but all I can think is . . .

If Juliet's partner isn't here, then Hot Muso/Book Jerk can't be him. He must be her brother!

'And last but never least is my boy, Leo.'

There's no mention of a partner, so perhaps he is single. Well, this *is* a pleasant turn of events. Maybe this week won't be as dire as I imagined.

And then I remember he's about to become my stepbrother. Obviously, his relationship status no longer matters because I draw the line at sleeping with relatives.

Leo gives me a cool nod – 'Hey' – and then takes a long slow sip from the beer in his hand. The flirtatious smile he'd hit me with in the arrivals hall is nowhere in sight.

Paul claps his hands. 'Right, now that we're all friends—'

'Don't you mean "family",' Mum interrupts with a soppy smile.

He pulls her into his side and his own grin grows even wider. 'Of course. Now we're all *family*, let's head into the restaurant and get even better acquainted.'

I can hardly wait.

The restaurant is called Cook's Landing and looks out over the accommodation part of the resort, where frangipanis line the paths and the ocean is only just visible in the distance. I find myself sitting between TJ and Juliet. As if this 'holiday' isn't punishment enough, TJ doesn't stop talking about phobias the whole time – she appears to have memorised that whole bloody book – and Juliet whinges about not being able to eat any of the food.

'Being pregnant sucks,' she tells me at one stage, almost as if it's my fault she's in this state. 'And I've still got thirteen freaking weeks to go. Kill me now.'

'Thirteen weeks?' I stare in horror at her stomach. 'Are you having twins?'

'No.' She sighs dramatically. 'I'm enormous, aren't I?'

I take another gulp of wine and glance across the table to Leo. No wonder my hot guy radar went off at the airport. He's undeniably gorgeous in a natural kind of way. He's now wearing darker jeans and a short-sleeved shirt, this one with seagulls on it, which shows off nicely sculpted biceps and forearm tattoos. Although I have a small tat myself, I'm hit and miss when it comes to guys and ink. I'm not a big fan of all-over body art and some men try way too hard, but the inscriptions on Leo's forearms, which I can't quite read, pique my interest and definitely enhance his appeal. His hair is damp as if he's just had a shower and that sparks all kinds of X-rated images in my head.

Wait 'til I text Bee and tell her that Hot Muso/Book Guy from the airport is Mum's fiancé's son.

I shriek as I feel something warm and slimy against my leg and look under the table to see Kayla beaming up at me.

'Did you just lick me?' I ask, horrified.

'Kayla, remember what we told you about personal space and boundaries?' Scarlett says sweetly, peering under the table. Then she looks back to me. 'Sorry, she's going through a cat phase.'

As if to emphasise this, Kayla rubs her head against my foot, and I somehow resist the urge to shake her off and point out that it's dogs that lick, not most cats.

'Do you have trichophobia?' TJ asks, hugging her book to her chest like it's the Bible or something.

Trying to ignore her little sister now wrapped around my legs, I say, 'I don't even know what that is.'

'Fear of hair.'

I blink – 'Oh, right' – then realise why she's asked this. 'No, I shaved my head to donate money in memory of someone I know who had cancer. I'm not scared of hair.'

'Who?' TJ asks, as Kayla appears from under the table.

I tell them about Lola, a young girl who used to be a member at Fremantle Library.

Paul dabs a napkin to his eye and blinks. 'Poor girl, but what a wonderful thing you did. And I think the short hair really suits you.'

'What hair?' Mum snorts. 'Please don't encourage her.'

Everyone except me and Leo laugh, but I find myself wondering how Paul's wife died. I know very little about the man my mother is going to marry. She'd tried to talk to me about him when we were dress shopping, but I'd paid little attention, not wanting to waste time getting to know someone who will only be in my life briefly. Been there, done that. Still, I promised Way I'd be polite, so I try to continue the conversation.

'What is it you do for a crust?' I ask him. 'I'm a landscape gardener.'

I couldn't be more surprised if he told me he was a milkman. How the heck does a mere gardener afford to pay for flights and accommodation for all of us to come here? Granted, it's not Hawaii or the Bahamas – more's the pity – but still . . . Some of them came all the way from the UK!

'Are you a TV gardener or do you landscape for celebrities or something?'

Paul chuckles. 'No, no. Nothing like that, and just run of the mill people. Now, who needs another drink?'

Run of the mill people? Something feels off here and I decide then and there I'm going to get to the bottom of it.

After dinner is ordered, Paul makes a concerted effort to get to know me, Way and even Benji. He might not have had need for a divorce lawyer himself, but he's clearly impressed by the dedication Way has had to get him where he is today. Paul asks Benji about his family and they all get excited when he tells them he's Vietnamese. Getting to know each other is then sidelined for a few minutes while the Lewises reminisce about a family holiday they took there just before Scarlett and River's commitment ceremony. Well, Paul, Scarlett and Juliet reminisce; Leo is stony-faced and quiet. In fact, the only people he talks to are his nieces. I get the impression that he'd rather be anywhere but here. His body language is tense, and there's this dark smouldering aura around him that doesn't match his dirty-blond hair. Not that I believe in auras, but you get my drift. Could it be I'm not the only one opposed to this wedding?

My heart lifts at this thought but before I can contemplate it further, Scarlett – the baby still glued to her chest – smiles at me. 'And what do you do, Fred?'

'She's a librarian,' Mum answers for me.

TJ tells me she reads ten books a week, and Juliet is hoping she'll have time to read again once the baby is born. Turns out she's the CEO of a high-end marketing company that caters mostly for boutique hotels, and she can thankfully continue to work while here.

'I'm crazy busy,' she tells me. 'It's a miracle Henry and I managed to get pregnant – half the time we're like ships passing in the night.'

'It'll be good for you to slow down and relax a bit when the baby arrives,' Paul says, as our kingfish and arancini are delivered to the table.

Scarlett laughs. 'Juliet doesn't know the meaning of the word. Are you even taking maternity leave?'

'Yes. Three whole months,' is her reply.

'Fred isn't just a librarian,' Benji announces with a wide grin. 'She's also a writer and just signed a contract for a book.'

The word 'oh' echoes around the table, all eyes focusing on me.

This has piqued everyone's interest.

'What's it about?' Juliet asks, piercing an arancini ball with her fork as if it is her mortal enemy.

'It's called *21 Rules for Not Catching Feelings*,' I say. 'And it's a guide for people who want to date casually.'

Scarlett pries Miller from her chest and passes her to River, so she can get stuck into her dinner. 'When you say date casually . . . you mean sex with no strings?'

Mum coughs. 'I'm not sure we should be discussing such things with little ears around.'

Everyone ignores her. Only TJ is listening anyway. Kayla is lapping up water from her plate, and Miller is now sucking on River's beard as if it's a teething toy.

'What are some of the rules?' he asks.

'Number one is No Bull— *BS*.' Remembering the little ears, I manage to correct myself just in time. 'You've got to be honest about what you want from dating and demand the same in return from whoever you're seeing. Number two is about setting guide-lines and being clear about boundaries before meeting in person. Number three is all about choosing chemistry over connection. And . . .' I say, reaching for my glass, 'if you want to know the rest, you'll have to buy the book.'

River chuckles. 'Surely family get free copies.'

We are not family. The only family I know I'll always have is Way, so he and Bee will be the only ones getting gifted signed copies. I bite back my reply and force a smile instead.

'And this book is based on your lived experiences? Your belief system?' Scarlett asks.

Mum reaches for her wineglass and downs the rest of its contents.

'Yep.' I nod, smiling unashamedly.

'What about kids?' Juliet rubs her hand over her bump. 'You don't want them?'

I shrug. 'I don't have a maternal bone in my body, but even if I did, you don't need to be in a relationship for that either these days.'

Mum half-weeps, half-smiles as she pats TJ, who is sitting next to her, on the head. 'Thank God Paul has given me grandchildren. Lord knows I've given up any hope with these two.'

Benji and Way blush, but Scarlett takes the pressure off them. 'Well, I think it's wonderful,' she says, exchanging a loved-up look with her partner. 'River and I have an open relationship. It takes all kinds to make the world go round.'

'Really?' I ask. Scarlett and River are getting more interesting by the second.

I see Leo roll his eyes as he takes another sip of his beer but can't tell whether the gesture is because of me or his sister.

'Aren't these arancini balls lovely?' Mum says, glancing around the table, desperate for someone to talk about something more sanitary. We all murmur politely in agreement, but the food *is* surprisingly good, considering the retro decor. While we eat, we learn that Scarlett and River have a small holding just outside of Noosa, where they unschool their kids and live almost off the grid. They can't completely go electricity free because of Instagram, where they apparently have a massive following of people who aspire to a lifestyle like theirs. From this they make a good income.

'Pretty much everything we and the girls wear is gifted,' she explains, gesturing to her long dress. 'This is from a really cool little boutique in Byron Bay.'

Bee is going to cackle when I tell her about this. We have a love–hate relationship with influencers – we love taking the piss out of them and hate the fact some of them earn more money than we can ever hope to, pimping themselves out.

'What's unschooling?' Benji asks.

Ten minutes later, I wish he hadn't. I now know more about what sounds to me like homeschooling for lazy parents than I ever wanted – or needed – to know. Although I have the good sense not to let my feelings show, Leo doesn't hold back, speaking to the adults for the first time since we entered the restaurant about how much of a joke their approach to education is.

Turns out, he's a teacher, so he has a horse in the race, but all I can focus on is his lovely accent. He sounds like Ed Sheeran, each word warm and confident, and I could listen to him all day. Why weren't there any teachers like him when I was at school?

'Do you teach music?' I ask when he takes a pause for breath. I'm curious to know more about him. I would *not* have picked him for a teacher. He's got too much of an edge.

'No. I teach English,' he says, all but glowering at me.

Not deterred, I add, 'So what was the instrument you were carrying at the airport?'

'It's a ukulele,' TJ states.

Ukulele. It takes great effort not to laugh – could there be a less cool instrument?

'Uncle Leo is in a *band*,' TJ adds. 'Do you know what being scared of music is called?'

I ignore her and look at him. 'How lovely. Will you be playing at the wedding?'

He merely shakes his head and turns his attention back to his dinner, indicating the get-to-know-Leo-better part of the evening is over.

Mum jumps on the lull in conversation to hand out our itineraries for the week ahead. It's pages long. Are they trying to pack as much sightseeing into seven days as they can? As well as daily group outings and dinners, there's a spa day planned for us along with Paul's daughters and two of Mum's best friends, who will be arriving later in the week.

I stare at the schedule in despair – where am I supposed to fit in my writing?

5

UNCHARTED TERRITORY

Despite the fact Norfolk Island is four hours ahead of Perth at this time of year, I wake at the crack of dawn to sun coming in the window. I'd forgotten to close the curtains when I fell into bed last night. I'm grabbing my phone off the bedside table when a rooster cockadoodles far too close to my window.

I groan, wishing I had a gun. So, *that's* what woke me.

After a quick scroll of my socials and an email and dating app check, I attempt to go back to sleep, but when this proves futile, I throw back the covers and climb out of bed. As Mum and Paul have jam-packed the week – and surprisingly, there isn't a cemetery visit on there – I decide now would be as good a time as any to check out Colleen McCullough's grave for Bee. The only problem being that the cemetery is a few kilometres away and I didn't bring suitable walking shoes.

Dammit. Then I remember the hire car and decide if the rooster has woken me up, it's probably woken the lovebirds as well.

'What the hell time do you call this?' Way demands as he opens the door to their room, which is right next to mine.

'The early bird catches the worm,' I say. 'I've already showered and done my morning meditation.'

He rolls his eyes. We both know I don't have the patience to meditate. 'What are you doing here?'

I hold out my hand. 'Can't sleep, so I thought I'd take a drive. Can I borrow the car?'

He closes the door in my face, then returns with the key. 'Drive safely. If you crash, you're paying the excess.'

I laugh because we both know that's not true. 'See you at breakfast, brother dearest.'

I follow the A3 map right out of the resort to find the town deserted. A few hundred metres up the road, I bump over a cow grate and then almost immediately have to swerve around two fat black-and-white cows. Another three are grazing on the lush green grass nearby, all of whom look up and give me the evil eye. Roosters and cattle! How many encounters with livestock will I have before the day is out?

This is more like Old McDonald's farm than paradise, I think, continuing until I get to a fork in the road and turn right. A compact little red ute that looks more like a toy than a real vehicle comes from the other direction and the driver lifts his finger in a wave. On the corner is another 'quaint' building that looks a bit like a saloon from the Wild West and announces itself as the Bounty Museum. Further on, the road becomes quite windy and steep; there are more cows out for a morning stroll, and houses sporadically peppered along the route. Down the bottom of the hill, I come to another turn-off but, following the map, I keep going along what is aptly called Country Road and soon spy what must be the Kingston historic townsite as advertised on the airport wall.

The buildings remind me of Port Arthur, which I'd visited while holidaying in Tasmania a couple of years ago, and I find myself taking the road towards the sea, rather than straight ahead towards the cemetery. It isn't like I haven't got hours to kill.

I admire the large waves chopping against the shore and am surprised to see a few early morning surfers. Further along where the Norfolk pines grow thicker on the non-sea side of the road, there looks to be some kind of camping ground and then I stumble upon the most perfect bay I've ever seen. Aqua-blue water ripples upon the palest yellow sand, the view literally stealing the breath from my lungs. So *this* is where they're hiding paradise.

I can't help myself. Colleen McCullough's grave forgotten, I park the car, hurry down towards the sand, then yank off my cut-off denim shorts, pull my Ramones T-shirt over my head and wade into the sea in my underwear.

Oh my God. The water is so clear I can see the patterns on the sand beneath my feet and colourful fish swimming by. There are a couple of other swimmers further out, an elderly woman walking a golden retriever along the beach and a bright yellow pontoon, which I swim towards. Once there, I climb up on top of it and relax onto my back, relishing the gentle rays of early-morning sun on my face. Now *this* I could get used to.

'Fancy meeting you here.'

'Holy shit.' I jolt upright and can't believe my eyes when I open them to find Leo Lewis pushing himself up onto the platoon beside me like Poseidon emerging from the depths. He's shirtless and water drips tantalisingly over his bare skin, his arm muscles rippling. I'd like to tell you he's not as good-looking as I remember from yesterday, but if anything, he's better.

Instantly, my nipples peak.

'You shouldn't creep up on people like that,' I scold, snapping my arms across my chest. I'm not usually self-conscious around hot guys, but then Leo isn't any ordinary hot guy. Come Friday, he'll be related to me. We're strangers and yet practically family. This is uncharted territory for me.

'Didn't mean to scare you,' he says, smoothing a hand over his wet hair, which hangs just beneath his shoulders now it's not tied back. He nods towards me, taking in my matching red silky bra and knickers. 'Nice swimming togs by the way.'

Thankfully, while I buy almost all my clothes from op shops, I spend big bucks when it comes to underwear, so at least he hasn't caught me in a saggy pair of Bonds cottontails.

'You're not flirting with me, are you?' I say, half horrified, half delighted. The other swimmers are mere specks in the distance – we could get up to some really saucy stuff up here before anyone noticed.

He laughs as if this is the funniest thing he's ever heard. 'Would be pretty weird if I was, don't you think?'

'I'll say.' Despite our situation, I can't help being a tad disappointed. 'Anyway, I wasn't planning on going swimming.'

'Oh?'

'I was on my way to the cemetery, but the water looked so nice, I couldn't resist.'

'Don't blame you. I was only planning a jog, but I couldn't resist a dip either. Don't tell me you're obsessed with cemeteries as well?'

I loosen my arms a little, there's so much to unpack there. One – his adorable accent. Out here in the middle of the water, it's even more alluring than last night. Two – he ran all the way from the resort? No wonder he looks so fit. He can probably do more than ten proper push-ups as well. Three – 'You're obsessed with *cemeteries*?'

He shrugs and almost smiles. 'Well, obsessed might not be quite the right term, but I do find them fascinating. I love reading all the headstones and thinking about the lives of the people who lie beneath the earth.'

I raise an eyebrow. 'Okay, you're officially weird.'

He half laughs. 'Why were *you* going to the cemetery, then?'

'There's an author my friend likes buried there. She's weird like you and asked me to take a photo.'

'Colleen McCullough?'

'You know her?'

He nods. 'I haven't read anything she's written but my mum had all her books.'

At the mention of his mum, the almost playful vibe between us falls flat. 'I'm really sorry that you lost her,' I say. 'Do you mind me asking how she died?'

'Melanoma.' He doesn't meet my gaze, looking up at the sky, which is getting brighter by the second. 'She had a spot on her back – she blames the girls' trips she took in her early twenties with her friends where they used to bake on the beaches in Ibiza. Anyway, it was in a place where she didn't see it and neither did any of us. By the time she started getting secondary symptoms, it was too late.'

'I'm so sorry. That's horrible.' The words don't seem nearly enough. 'Were you close?'

'Yeah.' He doesn't elaborate but I can tell so much by the way he says that one word. Leo is a man still hurting. And who can blame him – she's only been gone six months. 'You must have been close to the person you shaved your head for?' he adds.

I rub my lips together. 'I didn't actually know her that well at all. Lola was a patron at our library, but Bee – she's my best friend and we also work together – got to know her really well in the months before she died, and when Bee and her boyfriend, Sully, decided to do the World's Greatest Shave in her honour, half of us at the library did it as well.'

He nods as if he approves. 'What's Bee stand for?'

'Bridget. As in *Bridget Jones*.'

'No way.' His eyes widen and he chuckles. 'Like the book?'

I almost fall off the platoon. 'Don't you mean the movie?'

'I haven't seen the movie, but I read the book when I was home one summer and bored. Found it on Mum's shelves.'

'You've heard of Colleen McCullough, you know *Bridget Jones* was a book, and you were reading *The Hunger Games* at the airport. Who *are* you?'

He raises an eyebrow. 'You noticed what I was reading?'

Whoops. 'You were flashing it about under your arm. It's my favourite book, so I remembered. Anyway, I better go to the cemetery.'

'Do you mind if I join you?'

'Nope.' I shrug nonchalantly, but secretly I'm stoked – this might be the perfect opportunity to grill him on his feelings about our parents' rapidly approaching wedding. 'You can help me find Colleen's grave.'

'Sure,' he says and then dives smoothly into the water.

If he hadn't so firmly put me in my place when I'd asked if he was flirting, I'd think he was showing off and wanted me to admire his beautiful form. I resist the urge to do so as I plunge in after him and swim towards the shore where I quickly recover my clothes. Leo has the good manners to look away as I pull my shorts and T-shirt over my wet body, cursing myself for not bringing a towel, and then we head to the hatchback and drive to the cemetery.

I don't think our mission will be too difficult – if Colleen's such a literary icon and local celebrity, surely her resting place will be easy to spot and quite possibly outrageously decorated like her house – but I'm completely wrong. It's like searching for a needle in the proverbial haystack. A pretty haystack at that. The cemetery rests on a green hill that slopes towards yet another gorgeous beach, the varied stones popping out of the ground, making it look like a miniature city. We quickly get to know the prominent Norfolk families – Fletcher-Christians,

McCoys, Buffetts and Nobbs to name a few – but there's only so much of a good thing one can take. I begin to wonder if it's a fallacy that dear Colleen is buried here. Maybe it's a joke the islanders have played on tourists.

'So, what's Leo short for?' I ask as we walk down what must be the tenth row of gravestones.

He's right, they are fascinating. The best one is a stone on top of a miniature grand piano, and the saddest are those of babies or people whose lives were cut short in their prime. Two girls in their late teens rest side by side and as their death dates are the same, I assume they must have been friends. The double tragedy must really have rocked this small community.

'Guess,' he says, shoving his hands in his pockets as we continue our treasure hunt.

'Leon?'

He shakes his head.

'Leonard?'

'Nope.'

I sigh, wracking my brain for something else. 'I know. Leonardo!'

He laughs. 'Wrong again.'

I pause and scrutinise his expression to see if he's lying. 'How can I be wrong? There *is* nothing else!' It's then my eye catches on the name on a grave just off to the right – that of Charles Leopold Evans. 'Oh my God. *Leopold* ?'

He nods and I can't help laughing. 'No freaking way.' Someone as cool and sexy as him cannot have such an unsexy name. 'No wonder you shorten it.'

'Hey.' He tilts his head to one side and gives me a look that almost knocks me off balance. 'Isn't Fred short for Winifred? And you're teasing me about Leopold?'

I sigh. 'Touché. What were our parents thinking?'

'Leopold was my mum's father's name,' he tells me.

'I wish I could say that Winifred was a family name, but the truth is ... my mum's just insane.'

He chuckles as if I'm joking.

Although I'm almost ready to give up on our mission and head back to the resort for breakfast, Leo – or should I say *Leopold* – convinces me to keep going. 'We're almost three-quarters of the way through the graves; we can't quit now.'

We continue a little faster until Leo stops suddenly. 'Look!' He thrusts a finger towards a small stone, half hidden by an overgrown creeper plant. 'It's Winifred.'

I can't help chuckling at his excitement, as if he's stumbled on gold, not merely someone with the misfortune of having the same name as mine.

'I wonder if Leopold and Winifred were friends,' he says.

I read the birth and death dates on poor old Winifred's headstone. 'Considering she died not long after he was born, I doubt it.' But at his mention of friends, something shifts inside me. I'm almost sad at the inevitable end of our parents' relationship because I like him, yet once my mum and his dad part ways, there'll be no reason for us to stay in touch.

That reminds me what I wanted to ask him.

'Fred, what do you think of this wedding?' he says before I have the chance to.

I look Leo dead in his beautiful brown eyes. ''Scuse my French, but I think it's fucked.'

'Oh my God.' His shoulders sag as if he's an over-pumped tyre letting out pressure. 'No apology necessary. I agree. It's a fucking joke.'

Excited to have found an ally, I almost punch the air in victory. 'I drank half a cask of Aldi wine when I first found out.'

He raises both his eyebrows. Even when his forehead's creased, he's sexy. 'That's just tragic.'

We both laugh.

'What's tragic,' I say, 'is Mum getting married for the sixth time!'

'Your mum's been married five times?!'

'You didn't know?'

He shakes his head. 'I knew she was divorced, but Dad didn't mention how frequently.' He looks away as if needing a second to digest this new information, then suddenly he nods. 'There she is.'

I spin around expecting to see Mum striding towards us, but quickly realise he's found Colleen's grave.

'Well, that headstone's a little disappointing.' I lift my phone to take Bee's requested photo, but I might have to send a preamble warning her that it's nothing to send pictures home about.

The stone is not much bigger than a shoebox, jagged at the top and tarnished on the front, making it appear a lot older than its ten years. On a metal stake at the back stands a tiny Norfolk Island flag – the kind you buy at tacky tourist shops – and a small, solitary bouquet of cream and violet roses rests against the base of the headstone. For someone who wrote copious tomes throughout her life, it seems bizarre that aside from her name, birth and death dates, the only word etched into the stone is 'Writer'. What about daughter, sister, partner? *Friend?*

I feel an odd tightening in my stomach, thinking about what my gravestone will say. Or maybe I'm just hungry? 'Wanna go into town and find a café for breakfast?'

Leo blinks at my question. 'Aren't we supposed to be doing breakfast as a *family*?'

I silently groan at the thought of having to sit through another meal with his delightful nieces, not to mention Mum and Paul staring adoringly at each other as if they're teenagers again. Having to spend the rest of the day with that lot will be punishment enough.

'Are you always such a rule follower?' I ask. 'Is it because you're a teacher? I bet you were one of those boys who sat right up the front of the class and was the first to shoot your hand into the air whenever the teacher asked a question.'

'I was *not!*' he exclaims, clearly offended by the picture I've painted. 'I spent more time in detention than I did in the classroom.'

Really? Now that is intriguing. 'Well then, Leopold . . .' I smile. 'I read in a brochure in my room that the Olive Café is nice.'

He smiles back and gestures up the hill towards the car park. 'Lead the way, Winifred.'

6

FORMING AN ALLIANCE

The centre of town is busier than I expected, and we have to park a short walk away from the café in front of a big, cream and beige building housing 'Madisons Jewellers'. The most bizarre thing about it is not that an island this size needs a place that has 'Diamonds Galore', but the Egyptian graphics on the wall and the sign out the front that invites us to come inside and experience Tutankhamun's Tomb.

Leo and I exchange bemused looks as we climb out of the car. I immediately miss the air conditioning inside it. Although it's not even eight o'clock, it's already starting to get muggy. Leo tells me that February is the most humid time of the year here. Apparently, I'm the only one who did little to no research before coming.

'Just our luck our parents chose this month to get hitched.' But Mum is a romantic, and as well as wanting to get married ASAP, she likes the idea of having a Valentine's Day anniversary.

We walk down the rough pathway towards our destination with its red tin roof forming a sharp triangle towards the sky before giving way to a flat roof on either side. Several people are already sitting at tables out the front beneath big, black sun umbrellas.

Even before we go through the open glass doors the tantalising smell of coffee hits me.

'I hope that tastes as good as it smells,' Leo says as we enter. 'I love the smell of coffee,' I tell him, 'but I can't stand the taste.'

He gapes at me like I've just admitted I'm a conspiracist who believes Beyoncé is a leader of the Illuminati. 'Seriously? You like Aldi wine but don't drink coffee? I'm not sure we can be friends.'

'Pity you can't choose your family,' I say with a wink.

He chuckles and looks longingly at the coffee machine. 'I think jet lag is hitting me. I'll need a strong caffeine boost if I'm going to make it through the day.'

'I definitely need sustenance. What's that?' I ask the young woman behind the counter, pointing to some sort of yellow-white loaf cake that looks deliciously crumbly.

'That's the famous Norfolk Island Coconut Bread,' she says. 'And you won't taste a better one anywhere else on island.'

'Sold. I'll have a slice of that and . . .' I scan the fresh juice section of the menu. 'A watermelon, mint and apple juice, please.'

'Let me get it,' Leo says, whipping his phone out from the pocket of his boardies.

'Definitely not.' I give the young woman a look that tells her not to even think about allowing him to do so.

Rule #9 – Always pay for yourself on dates!

Not that this is a date, but his family has already paid enough for me this week.

Leo holds up his hands at my fierce opposition, then once I've paid for my order orders a large flat white with two extra shots and a big breakfast with the lot. We take our number and find a table in the far back of the café.

The best thing about the Olive Café is the wi-fi. As we find a table, I notice the password on the wall behind us and immediately punch it into my phone. Free wi-fi here is not to be wasted. As I text the less-than-satisfactory photo of Colleen's grave to Bee, knowing it's still practically the middle of the night there and she won't reply for hours, Leo walks around looking at the pictures on the walls and checking out the books available on the exchange shelf. He doesn't sit down until our drinks arrive, quickly followed by my warm coconut bread with a dollop of cream on the side, and soon after his overflowing plate of greasy breakfast fare.

'Oh my God.' Forgetting my manners I moan through my mouthful. 'This is to die for. Honestly, it's almost as good as sex.'

Leo raises an eyebrow at me as he shoves a forkful of scrambled eggs into his mouth. He's already downed half his coffee.

'Tell me then,' I say, forcing myself to push the image of Leo and sex out of my head, 'what's wrong with your dad?'

He swallows and frowns. 'Nothing. He's the best. He and Mum have supported me through heaps of—'

'Nope.' I shake my head. 'Sorry, not buying it. My mum doesn't marry fabulous men. She marries arseholes and pricks, men who cheat and gaslight her.'

'Dad's not like that at all. He was married to Mum for thirty-five years and they were really happy, but he's not thinking straight at the moment. I'm sure Tracy is a lovely person, but it's clear this sudden engagement is his reaction to grief. He was totally cut up when Mum died. She was his "One", and we didn't know how he was going to go on living without her.'

'You believe in The One?'

He cuts off a slice of bacon – 'Course I do' – then pops it into his mouth. 'Oh, that's right, you don't.'

'Course I don't,' I scoff. 'It's merely a romantic con, invented by writers, poets and jewellers who want to flog their work. Like everything, there's dollar signs behind it. Just because only fifty per cent of marriages end in divorce doesn't mean the other half are living in wedded bliss.'

'What about love? Do you believe in that?' he asks in the same way one might ask if someone believes in God or Santa Claus.

'Of course I believe in love – family love, love between friends, and I guess romantic love . . .' I think of Bee and Sully, of Xavier and Rory, Persephone and Nick, and of Janine – my old boss – and her husband, Dave, who are living it up in a caravan as grey nomads. 'But I'm not sure the latter is worth the heartache and inevitable pain that so often comes with it, especially for the woman. So often they give up their agency and independence in the name of love.'

'That's so cynical,' he says, but he's looking at me with pure pity. My hackles are raised. 'Don't feel sorry for me. I don't need *love* to be happy. A woman doesn't need a man to live a happy and fulfilled life. Or a woman. Or anyone for that matter. All she needs is a cat.'

He holds up his hands. 'Okay, okay. Sorry. What's your cat's name?'

'Aunty. Short for Agony Aunt. Want to see a photo?'

He nods. 'Sure.'

I swipe open my photos, which are ninety per cent Aunty with the rest made up of food, books or my friends, and hand him my phone.

'She's very cute,' he says, endearing himself to me again. 'Is she as snuggly as she looks?'

'She can be. When it suits her. Do you have any pets?'

'No. I'd like a dog one day – maybe a golden retriever – but my living arrangements aren't really conducive to it.'

'Do you live in an apartment?'

Leo shakes his. 'On a narrow boat. In a canal.'

My jaw drops open. 'Serious? I don't think I've ever met anyone who lives in a houseboat. Have you got photos?'

In reply, he slides his phone out of his pocket and shows me a very well taken care of home. It's blue and green with white trim and a polished deck at the front.

'How long have you lived there? Do you move around? Why?' I have all the questions.

He chuckles at my interest, then shrugs. 'I've just always fancied one. I bought it not long after I left home and worked on it on the weekends and holidays while I was studying. Mum helped me fix up the interior – she was good with stuff like that.'

'Certainly looks like it,' I say. 'So you obviously like living on it?'

'Yeah, I like that I can move around and live in different parts of London. I meet all sorts of people and never get bored.'

'Where are you now?'

'In Islington, just south of the canal tunnel. It's close to the school where I work.'

I tell him I live close to work too; it's lucky that Waylen chose to buy not too far from the library.

'You live with your brother?'

'For now,' I say. 'I'd love to have my own place one day, but the market is crazy at the moment and almost impossible with only one income. If only we had canals in Freo.'

'You and Waylen must get along well.'

'We do. Although there's five years between us, we've always looked out for each other. What about you and your sisters? They seem quite different. Scarlett is all smiles and a little effusive, where if I'm honest, Juliet is slightly terrifying.'

He laughs. 'Don't tell her I said so, but she's a softie at heart. Occasionally things get a little fraught between them – Juliet thinks Scarlett lets her kids run wild, and Scarlett wonders why

Juliet's even bothering to have any if she's going to put her baby in daycare almost immediately – but mostly we all get along pretty well.'

I turn the conversation back to the matter at hand. 'Speaking of your sisters, how do they feel about the wedding?'

He wipes a smudge of avocado off his chin and shrugs. 'I think they're both just happy that someone else is going to be looking after Dad. We were all worried about how he'd cope when . . .' I watch his Adam's apple slowly move up and down as he swallows emotion. 'When Mum died. Scarlett's so far away and so busy with her brood and whatever it is she does on Instagram that she can't help, and Juliet's a workaholic and is going to be even busier once the baby comes, so they think your mum is a godsend.'

'But you don't agree? Are *you* happy to take care of your dad?'

'He's only fifty-eight and he's fit as a fiddle due to all the outdoor work he does. He hardly needs a carer just yet.' Leo puts his cutlery together on his plate like the polite Englishman he clearly is, then leans back a little. 'And anyway, once the fog of grief lifts and he realises what he's done, he'll either feel trapped or he'll break up with Tracy. I don't want her to get hurt when that happens.'

'So you came for my mum?' I ask sceptically.

He shakes his head as he picks up a serviette and starts to tear it apart. 'No. I came for *my* mum, because even if this is the biggest mistake of his life, she'd want me to be here for him. That's what family is about.'

Wow. That's the kind of speech that Bee would bawl her eyes out over. *Me?* I'm sure you can already tell that I'm far less affected by this sentimentality.

'Why did *you* come?' he asks me.

I sigh, experiencing a rare stab of guilt for my motives. 'I wasn't going to, but I'm on a tight deadline and I thought a week in paradise might give me some time to write.'

'Ah, right, the anti-love book.' He smirks, but I suddenly realise it doesn't matter if Leo and I disagree on the fundamentals of love and life, because we agree on one very important thing.

This wedding – this marriage – is doomed.

I do a quick calculation; today is Sunday and the wedding is scheduled for Friday, which means we have four and a half days to stop it from going ahead.

'Leopold,' I begin, my heart-rate quickening, 'do you want to form . . . an alliance . . . with me?'

His lips twist slowly into a grin. 'Absolutely I do.'

And the fact he knows my reference to *The Office* only makes me like him more.

'What exactly will this alliance involve?' he asks, leaning forward.

'Did you just say yes to something without understanding it?' I ask, chuckling.

He shrugs one shoulder. 'There was only one answer to your question. Mostly I'd say British TV trumps American every time, but the exception is *The Office*. Oh, and *Schitt's Creek*.'

I smile; maybe we have more in common than I think. 'I think *Schitt's Creek* is actually Canadian, but you're right, it's the bomb.' I glance around quickly just to make sure none of our family members have also escaped the hotel. 'Anyway, we both agree that our parents getting married will be a terrible mistake, so all we have to do is convince them – or at least *one* of them – of this fact.'

He nods slowly and rubs his chin. 'And how do we do that?'

'Hmm . . . that part of the plan I haven't worked out yet.'

We stare at our empty plates as we think long and hard. After a while, Leo reaches for his phone.

'What are you doing?' I ask.

'Googling ways to break people up.'

'Clever.' I should have thought of that; maybe I really am a terrible librarian.

Google proves rather helpful and while Leo reads off suggestions, I take notes in my phone of the ones we think might have merit.

Talk lots about Leo's mother, Amelia, and encourage Paul to share lots of memories of her so that Mum starts to wonder if she'll ever live up to her predecessor, and hopefully Paul starts to realise that she can't.

Find out what fundamental values they don't share and then make sure they learn this immediately.

'What are your mother's political leanings and religious beliefs?' Leo asks. Google tells us that these big picture issues often cause major relationship rifts.

'She's a lifelong Liberal voter. Super conservative. What about your dad?'

Leo's eyes sparkle. 'Staunch Labor voter. Couldn't be more progressive.'

'And where do you fit?' I ask, finding myself oddly curious.

'I think they're all as bad as each other.'

'Me too.'

We grin at each other as if we've both just been given the winning Powerball numbers and I feel a stirring low in my belly. His smile is magic.

'What's the next thing?' I ask, ignoring my errant hormones.

Uncover deep, dark secrets about one of them that the other doesn't know.

'Does your mum have any deep dark secrets?' he asks.

'You mean aside from the fact she's been married five times? I mean, I guess that's not a secret.'

Should I tell him about what happened after Husband #5?

As much as I want this marriage not to go ahead, that feels like too much to share with someone who's practically a stranger. And too much of a risk – I don't want to hurt Mum, I just want to make her reconsider rushing into yet another marriage. Vowing to only bring up that bastard Bernie as a last resort, I shake my head. 'Can't think of anything right now. What about your dad?'

'Nope. Nothing.'

'There must be something – everyone has skeletons in their closets.' As I say this, I find myself wondering more about Leo's skeletons than our parents'. *Concentrate, girl.*

'I guess if we knew about them they wouldn't be skeletons though,' he says.

I nod – 'Good point' – and we move on.

Get someone to try and crack onto one of them and then take incriminating pictures to show the other.

'The only people we know here are related to them,' I say. 'Unless we enlist the help of an islander,' he suggests with a wicked wiggle of his eyebrows.

'Oh my God,' I exclaim. 'You *are* naughty.' I add the idea to our list. 'This is so good.' I'm so excited that my fingers aren't typing as fast as usual and I'm making heaps of typos. 'It'll be like *The Parent Trap* but in reverse.'

Leo frowns again and I might have to tell him to stop doing that because every time he does, my hormones dance a jig. I resist the urge to reach out and smooth a finger over those cute little creases as he says, 'The *what*?'

'You haven't seen *The Parent Trap*?' When he shakes his head, I add, 'Not even the terrible nineties remake with Lindsay Lohan?'

A shrug accompanies his blank look.

I give him the run-down. 'It's about identical twins who are separated at birth because their parents get divorced and take one each. The girls have no idea the other one exists until one summer they meet at camp and—'

'The parents take a child each and like, abandon the other one?'

'Yes. I agree. It's horrible, but divorce wreaks havoc on people's lives and makes people do terrible things. Why do you think I don't want my mother to go through another one?' I shake my head. 'But that's not the point. When they meet again at summer camp, they freak out but as they start to talk to each other about their lives and show photos of their parents, it all clicks, and they realise something fishy is going on.'

Leo's leaning forward again, listening intently. 'So what do they do?'

'By this time, they've become so close they can't imagine not living together, so they decide to try and get their parents to fall in love again. They hatch a plan to swap places so that when their parents realise they've got the wrong child, they'll have to meet again to do the switch. They go to all sorts of lengths to show their parents that they're supposed to be together – as a couple and a family.'

'Sounds like a hoot,' Leo says, downing the last of his coffee.

I smile. 'And we're just like Sharon and Susan, except we're not twins, and we don't want our parents to be together.'

'Absolutely not,' he agrees. 'And did the twins' plan work?'

I nod, steepling my fingers together and wriggling them in wicked delight.

7

OPERATION BREAK-UP

'Where've you two been?' Mum asks as Leo and I enter the resort foyer to find our families waiting for us, alongside a stout, grey-haired woman dressed in navy shorts, a pale blue shirt with the tour company logo on its pocket and bright green Birkenstocks.

Before either of us can answer, the woman steps forward, smiling as she offers her hand first to Leo and then to me. 'It's okay, we work on Island Time here. I'm Raquel Quintal and I'll be your tour guide for the morning.' She looks around the rest of the group, counting everyone off on her fingers. 'If we're all ready, we may as well head off.'

'I'm sitting in the front!' TJ announces, already racing outside towards the faded yellow tour bus we'd noticed when I parked the rental car.

The rest of us follow her, Miller squirming in the sling she's trapped in on River's chest. TJ doesn't get her wish because Juliet pulls the pregnancy card, informing her niece that her morning sickness will only get worse if she adds carsickness to it as well. I suspect Juliet doesn't have either ailment but just wants to sit up the front where she doesn't have to suffer Kayla pretending to be a cat. And I don't blame her. Don't get me wrong, I like cats, but a child pretending to be feline isn't something I realised I found irritating until last night.

Way and Benji sit right up the back, probably so they can fool around uninterrupted. Kayla climbs into the van on all fours, then proceeds to bicker with TJ about who gets to sit next to Mummy. I ignore the lot of them, carefully engineering it so I can sit next to Paul. 'I feel like we haven't had a chance to really get to know each other yet,' I say, giving him my best smile as we fasten our seatbelts.

'Well, where am I supposed to sit?' Mum asks, glancing around the twenty-seater mini-van like the kid on a school excursion who no one wants to sit with.

Leo waves at her from a seat a few rows back. 'Come sit next to me, Tracy.'

Good man, I think. Not only will this give us each a chance to seed doubts in our parents' minds, but keeping them apart as much as possible is also part of our plan.

Let Operation Break-up begin.

Raquel slams the door and treks around to the driver's side, putting a headset on so she can speak into the microphone and 'those of you right down the back can hear me while we're driving'. 'You're in good hands with me today, folks,' she promises as we start down the resort driveway. 'I'm going to take you right round the island and show you all the main points of interest, giving you insight into what life is like here now and how it has been in the past. I'm an eighth-generation islander – my family have strong ties with the Bounty mutineers – and I married a fifth-generation islander, so ask as many questions as you like. If I don't know it, no one probably does, but I can always make it up.' She chuckles. 'We islanders are good storytellers. Colleen McCullough might have been our most famous author, but she's not the only one, you know.'

I find myself grinning as I think of my morning with Leo hunting for her grave.

'Do you know what a fear of books is called?' TJ shouts. Raquel frowns into the rear-view mirror. 'Excuse me?'

'You can be scared of books. It's called bibliophobia.'

'Well, you learn something new every day,' Raquel replies, clearly unsure what to make of this interruption.

'How can you be scared of books?' Benji asks, smirking.

'It's not the fear of the actual paper,' TJ explains, 'but rather what the books stand for and how they can influence people. Bibliophobia has been the cause of book banning and even book burning.'

Wow. I'm impressed at her knowledge. Maybe this unschooling business isn't such a sham after all.

Raquel clears her throat as if trying to take back the conversation. 'I love doing these private tours for special groups like yours, and it's so lovely that you're all holidaying together as a family despite your children being grown-ups.'

I immediately set her straight. 'We're not *family*.'

'Nope, not family,' Leo agrees loudly from the middle. *God love him.* 'Most of us only met yesterday.'

'Oh?' Raquel says, her voice tinny through the speakers. 'Then how do you know each other?'

Paul turns to give Mum a reassuring smile and I don't need to look at her to know she's fuming at my comment. Well, *she* wanted me here.

'Tracy and I,' he tells Raquel, 'we . . . uh . . . we were friends at school but—'

'They married other people instead,' TJ calls. 'And then when Granny died, Pop met Nanna Tracy again at a school reunion and now they're getting married here on Friday.'

Not if Leo and I have anything to do with it. I resist the urge to turn around and wink at him.

'Wow. Isn't that just lovely?' Raquel exclaims. 'I love a wedding!'

'So does Mum; this will be her sixth,' I tell her gleefully.

I see the tour guide's eyes boggle in the rear-view mirror. She clearly has no idea what to say to this, but lucky for her we've just bumped over the cattle grate at the edge of town, and she has to slow the van for a cluster of cows. She clears her throat. 'As you've probably guessed, the cattle have right of way here. This grate is supposed to keep them from grazing up and down the street near the shops, but they've free run on the rest of the island.'

Scarlett leans out the open window to snap photos of the cows – no doubt for her millions of followers – and Paul asks, 'Who do they belong to?'

'They're all owned by island families. Almost all of us have some – it's cheaper to grow your own meat, so to speak, than import it – but there's a maximum of ten per person. Saying that, there's no age minimum to own cows, so if you have a baby, you can get them a couple as well.'

'Hear that Miller?' River says, tickling her chin. 'Shall we get you a couple of these cute beasties?'

I'm surprised they don't have one already.

Kayla frowns and shakes her head. 'No, Daddy, I don't like cows.'

TJ rapidly flicks through the pages of her book. 'Maybe she's got bovinophobia.'

Several cars ramp up behind us and the kids start to get restless. I wish Raquel would take a breath so I could speak to Paul and am beginning to wonder if we live here now, in this van, forevermore, when she says, 'This is the closest you get to a traffic jam on island.'

'Can't you beep the horn to clear them out of the way?' Juliet asks, waving a tour pamphlet against her face. I get the impression she doesn't like sitting idle.

Finally, the cows amble off to the side and we continue in the direction I'd gone this morning. As she drives, Raquel talks about the island's history – 'East Polynesians were the first to settle here, but they were long gone by the time the British arrived in 1788' – and delivers other random facts.

There are more chickens here than people. And while they don't have the same right of way as the cows, they think they do.

TJ informs us that a fear of chickens is called alektorophobia and I'm thinking maybe she should sign up for *Hard Quiz*.

You can't buy fresh milk – all these cows are for beef, not dairy, which seems silly to me, but what do I know about farming?

The islanders speak their own language – a blend of English, Tahitian and West Indian Creole.

This is one of the few places outside of America to celebrate Thanksgiving. It's even an official public holiday here.

'Our first stop today is the World Heritage Kingston and Arthur's Vale settlement area,' Raquel continues. 'If you're not already booked into any historic tours, I highly recommend doing so – they go into much more detail than I will today – and the museums are also must-see.'

Mum tells her that Wednesday is our history day. I'm sure there's not a tour she hasn't booked us in for.

Norfolk's capital, Kingston, is the second oldest town in Australia. The island's anthem is 'God Save the Queen'. Now 'King'.

Everyone in the van gasps as we turn a corner and the historic buildings come into view with the crisp blue ocean behind them. Even though I only saw it an hour or so ago, the postcard perfect vista takes my breath away. Yesterday's rain has vanished, although the moisture still lingers in the air, and the sun is now high in the sky that's almost as blue as the water.

If I could paint, I'd want to paint this!

'This area we are coming into, while undoubtedly one of the most beautiful spots you will ever see, has a shocking and brutal history,' Raquel explains. 'The penal colonies here were two of the worst, most gruesome of their kind and the convicts often staged uprisings and mutinies against their captors.'

'What do you mean by two?' Way asks. He loves a bit of history.

'There were two convict eras. From 1814 to 1825 the settlement was abandoned, and the island lay uninhabited,' she says as she turns down a road called Pier Street. 'The second convict era only lasted until 1846 and then the baddies were sent to Tassie.'

We're heading towards the historic buildings and ruins closest to the ocean, passing yet more cows grazing in the green fields on either side of the bumpy road.

'Oh, isn't this lovely,' Mum exclaims, smiling out the window at some ruins.

Raquel parks the van down by the water, in front of a building identifying itself as the Pier Store and Museum, encouraging us all to get out and enjoy the fresh sea air.

Despite being at the front, Paul and I are the last to leave the van. He's a gentleman who lets everyone else go first and I purposely hang back beside him. Keep your enemies close and all.

'Thanks so much for agreeing to come here, to be part of the wedding,' he says in a quiet voice. 'It means so much to Tracy. She was worried you weren't going to.'

I snort. 'Why wouldn't I? I'm an old hand at this wedding business. I've been to so many ceremonies thanks to her that I reckon I could become a celebrant myself!'

For a moment I wonder if I'm laying it on a bit too thick, but then again, we have limited time and I'm only speaking truth.

Paul nods, his expression solemn. 'I imagine all that

disruption must have been hard for you and Waylen growing up, but I know Tracy appreciates you being there for her, especially when she . . . uh, separated from Bernie.'

'She told you about that? About her depression?' I'm shocked.

It's not a period of her life she's proud of. 'Yes, of course.'

'Then you should be able to understand why I'm concerned about her entering into yet *another* marriage. She's very fragile, and I think another divorce might actually kill her.'

'I promise you that's not going to happen,' Paul says firmly. 'I'm here for the long haul. Trace and I were very good friends at school and I'm so glad Fate brought us together again and has given us this chance. I love her with all my heart.'

'That's what they all said,' I counter, because it's true. No one enters a marriage thinking it's only going to be a short-term thing. Unless they're in their twenties and marrying a rich octogenarian. Before Paul can say anything to that, I add, 'But aren't *you* worried about her track record? Granted, most of her husbands have had massive faults, but . . .' I think of Jeff. 'It's not always been all on them. The fact is Mum loves romance. She loves the thrill and excitement of a wedding, but she's not so great with the whole till-death-do-us-part thing. I don't want you to get hurt either.'

Paul smiles warmly and pats my arm. 'That's very sweet of you, but I promise you've got nothing to be worried about.'

Before *I* can say anything to that, he strides off after the others.

Dammit. I hope Leo's doing better with Mum than I am with his father.

Hurrying to catch up with everyone, I almost trip on a giant crack in the bitumen.

Leo is there to catch me, and his hand on my elbow and in

the small of my back almost makes me forget our mission. 'You okay?' he asks.

'Yes,' I whisper. 'Don't tell me these roads are also heritage-listed, so they can't renovate them?'

He chuckles. 'What were you and Dad talking about back there?'

'Leo, Winifred, over here,' Mum calls, waving from over near the wharf. 'We need a family photo by the water.'

'Kill me now,' I mutter as we trundle over to join the others. 'I'll take the pic,' Raquel says, taking Mum's phone and ordering us all to 'squish in close'.

Scarlett thrusts her mobile at Raquel as well. 'Can you take one on mine too, please?'

Leo and I are standing next to each other, and his arm wraps around me as we force smiles for the camera. I try to concentrate on Way on my other side instead, not the heat of Leo's body pressed against mine.

'Say "wedding bells",' Raquel shouts over the squall of the wind coming in off the ocean.

'Wedding bells,' we all echo.

Afterwards, Raquel leads us even closer to the edge and waves at a couple of fishermen pushing a boat into the water. River clutches Kayla's hand as we all look at the drop.

'This is one of the two loading bays on island. The other one is at Cascade – I'll take you there near the end of the tour – but it all depends on the weather as to which one is used. Supply ships arrive to deliver groceries and other necessities once a month—'

'Once a month!' Juliet exclaims.

She's not the only one horrified. No wonder the fruit and veg in the general store looked dire.

'What's that for?' TJ asks, pointing to a yellow crane perched almost at the end of the jetty.

Raquel smiles down at her. 'The ships can't get close enough to shore to unload, so all the freight is loaded into whaleboats and then the crane lifts it off the boats and onto the pier. It's a pity you won't be here to see this month's delivery because it's quite a sight.'

'Swim, swim, swim,' Kayla chants, tugging on River's hand.

Scarlett is still busy taking photos. 'I wanna go swimming.'

'You can't swim here, darling.' Raquel chuckles. 'I'll show you a spot that Mummy and Daddy can bring you back to after the tour.'

Kayla pouts and I want to remind her that cats hate water.

Would that be *catty*?

More questions are asked and info deposited as we amble away from the pier towards the prison site, such as that half of the islanders are descended from the HMS Bounty Mutineers.

Paul is hanging on Raquel's every word, fascinated by everything she says. Maybe we can convince her to meet us again and crack onto Paul, but then again, it might be better to find someone

to put the moves on Mum instead. Her track record means she's much more likely to be lured to other pastures than Paul, who stayed with one woman for *thirty-five* years.

'Where is your wedding going to be?' Raquel asks Mum as we leave the prison area and walk back to the van. 'Sometimes people set up marquees down here, although it can be very windy so close to the water.'

'We're having the ceremony and reception up at Captain Cook Lookout.'

'Ooh, that's a beautiful spot too.'

While Mum and Raquel talk ceremony, TJ runs ahead and Leo piggybacks Kayla, I take another chance to grill Paul. 'What was your wedding to Amelia like?'

He glances in Mum's direction before he speaks, clearly a

kind soul who doesn't want to upset her with talk of his dearly departed wife. 'It was huge. Amelia had a lot of friends and family.'

'I imagine not all of your friends and family are happy about you getting married again so soon after Amelia's death.'

He frowns. 'I can't imagine why you'd think that. My friends are very supportive. They know I loved Amelia, and they just want me to be happy.'

'If that was the case, I'd expect more of them to be coming to the wedding.'

'It's a long way to come at such short notice.'

'You could always postpone?' I say hopefully.

He chuckles. 'Why would we want to do that? The most important people are already here. Trace and I don't need a big fancy do; we just need the support of our loved ones.'

'And where did you and Amelia meet?' I ask, not wanting to dwell on that point.

'She used to work for the National Trust, and I was doing some gardening work for one of their houses.'

'And was it love at first sight?' I try not to choke on these words – as if I believe such nonsense.

'No. We were friends first and from that, something more grew.'

'You said she *used to* work for the National Trust. What did Amelia do before she passed?' I feel terrible pressing the poor man on his dead wife, but surely if he was that upset over her death, he wouldn't be rushing straight into holy matrimony with someone else and I really need to get to the bottom of this if I'm going to save Mum from making yet another mistake.

'When we had the children, she wanted to stay at home and take care of them, but in recent years, she did a lot of charity work. That kept her very busy.'

Charity work? Once again I wonder how they have so much

money when Paul is a mere gardener and Amelia didn't toil at all. Maybe they won Lotto? It would be rude to ask.

'We better get a move on,' Paul says, politely putting an end to this conversation. 'Everyone else is already at the van.'

As if scared of me – *Fredophobia!* – this time he takes a seat next to the Queen of Phobias herself, so I head up the back next to Way and Benji.

My brother glowers at me and at first, I think it's because he doesn't want me on their loveseat, but then he opens his mouth. 'What's your problem?' he hisses.

'What do you mean?'

'I heard the way you were talking to Paul, asking all about his wife and their wedding.'

I shrug and offer him an innocent smile. 'I was just being friendly and making conversation like you told me to.'

'And what were you thinking, telling Raquel this was Mum's sixth wedding?'

'Well, it is. Did you want me to lie to her?'

'I want you to think about how what you say might affect other people – *that's* what I want,' he whispers and then turns his back on me as if he can't bear to look at me any more.

Although annoyed at Way's reprimand, I know I'm doing the right thing. If he wasn't so lost in his own bubble of lust, he'd agree with me, but thankfully I don't need him because I have Leo.

My gaze drifts with my thoughts to where he's sitting a few rows in front with Mum. They look to be deep in conversation, and I hope he's waxing lyrical to my mum about Amelia.

As we drive away from the ocean, we turn down Quality Row with its beautiful old houses on one side of the road and lush green gardens surrounding Government House and a golf club on the other. Raquel tells us the history of these houses, which were originally built to house civil and military officers and clergy. Now some are museums and others private residences.

After telling us about the Australian Government disputes with islanders over who owned what and who was in charge, including islanders burning some of these houses to the ground in protest, we come to the cemetery where Leo and I were this morning.

TJ is particularly interested in a place called Murderer's Mound, and when the rest of us get out for 'more fresh air and a look-see', Juliet chooses to stay in the van and rest her swelling feet. I'd stay inside too, except I'm feeling a little car sick, and I also want the chance to check in with Leo.

'How's progress?' I ask as we hang back from the group. 'Not great,' he says with a sigh. 'You?'

'Same. I think we need a more concrete plan.'

Kayla runs up and grabs Leo's hand. 'I found a cat on someone's dead stone. Come see?'

'Hang on a sec, sweetheart.' He looks back to me. 'Do you want to meet up later, after dinner when everyone else has gone to bed, so we can put our heads together properly?'

I nod. 'Meet you in the games room, once the coast is clear.'

He grins – 'I can hardly wait' – then lets Kayla lead him off to the other side of the cemetery.

Me either, I think.

And, if I'm honest, it's not *just* because I want to stop this farce of a marriage before it begins. I'm also looking forward to hanging out with him again.

8

HEARTBREAK #1

By the time we arrive back at the resort, the kids aren't the only ones frazzled and in need of a nap. Juliet and Leo are fighting jetlag, and I'm looking forward to spending some one-on-one with my phone and maybe even my manuscript. The pool is looking particularly inviting in the mid-afternoon sun, so maybe I'll head out there and work on my tan while I sit and write on one of the loungers.

'See you all at dinner,' I say, practically skipping into reception. 'Have you forgotten something?' Mum asks, right behind me.

I tap my head making sure my hat is still there and that I didn't leave it in the van. Now that I'm bald I have to be vigilant with sun protection, but on the flip side, I save a lot of money on shampoo.

She shakes her head in irritation. 'We've got an appointment to go get our hair and make-up done for the wedding.'

'Today?! But I don't have any hair, and the wedding's not 'til Friday. Am I not supposed to wash my face until then?'

She laughs as if this is the funniest thing anyone has ever

said. 'This is just a trial, silly. So Petrice can play with colours and styles and see what suits us for the big day.'

Petrice. Why does that name sound familiar?

Mum reluctantly allows me ten minutes – 'and ten minutes *only*' – to wash off the sea and sand from my early morning swim, but the moment I get into my room, I reconnect to the wi-fi to see if Bee has replied to my photo of Colleen's resting place.

She has. In fact, there's a barrage of messages that have come in while I've been out.

Bridget Jones (Yes, I have her full name in my phone; yes, it annoys her): *That grave is a total let-down. If I was Colleen, I'd have had a shiny gold pyramid or something. Are you going to see her house for me? xx*

Bridget Jones: *Morning swim sounds nice though. And OMG I can't believe that Hot Guy from the airport is your mum's fiancé's son. What are the odds? Xx*

I'd sent her that important detail last night, post dinner, but she'd been out at the movies with Sully, and I'd been in a comatose sleep by the time she'd tried to call me.

Bridget Jones: *I have library goss. You'll never guess who's dating!?!?!?!*

Bridget Jones: *Go on . . . take a guess. xx*

Bridget Jones: *You're no fun. Where are you? xx*

Bridget Jones: *Fine. Since you twisted my arm. It's Edgar and Daisy!*

Bridget Jones: *Hey, just had a thought. Maybe Leo will be your 'stepbrother' book boyfriend. xx*

Bridget Jones: *Where ARE you? Have you died? I need more goss. What's the rest of the family like? What's PAUL like?*

Me: *EDGAR AND DAISY?!!*

This is a startling revelation – Edgar and Daisy are both members of the senior book club that Bee runs, but I'd never have expected romance between them. She's English and quite proper,

and he's what you'd call a little rough around the edges. Sweet though.

Bridget Jones: *Thank the Lord above you're alive!! I was about to book a plane ticket to come look for you. Why haven't you answered me? Don't tell me you've been off bonking your stepbrother. xx*

Me: *One – I think you're spending too much time with old people. No one says BONKING any more.*

Me: *Two – I should be so lucky re the stepbrother. Mum's kept us occupied ALL day and I told you there's no coverage on the island so I can't message unless I'm in my hotel room or a café.*

Bridget Jones: *Which one are you in now?*

Me: *Three – Edgar and SULLY'S grandmother?!!*

Bridget Jones: *Never mind about Edgar and Daisy. I want to know what's happening THERE!*

Me: *Actually. A lot . . .*

I flop onto the bed and lean back into the pillows but have barely begun to type my update when my phone rings. Of course it's Bee.

'Hey there.'

'Don't "hey there" me,' she shrieks. 'Tell me everything. What are Paul's family like? What's Leo like?'

'I don't have long. I'm supposed to be getting ready to go to a hair and make-up trial.'

'Ooh, how exciting.' I snort.

'Sorry, I know you hate this stuff but—'

'But you love it.' My prediction is Sully will propose any day now and then she'll lure me into helping her with her own big day. At least theirs is a marriage I'll be able to get behind. 'So . . . the family are nice enough. Scarlett, Paul's oldest daughter is a bit loopy and too-sweet-to-be-true. I'm not sure what to make of Juliet yet, and Leo . . .'

'And Leo is gorgeous!'

I laugh. 'Well, there is that, but more importantly he feels exactly the same as I do about Mum and Paul getting married. Together we're going to make sure it doesn't happen!'

'What do you mean?'

I fill her in on Operation Break-up. 'We haven't quite worked the whole plan out yet, but two heads are better than one, right?'

She takes a moment to answer, then says, 'Oh Fred, are you sure that's such a good idea?'

My heart sinks. 'It's one of the best ideas I've ever had.'

'I'm just worried someone might get hurt.'

'The whole idea is to *stop* that happening,' I say, annoyed she's putting a dampener on my plans.

'Okay. I just hope you know what you're doing.'

'Don't I always?'

She laughs. 'What's Leo short for anyway? What's his last name?'

'It's Leo – short for Leopold – Lewis,' I say as someone starts pounding on the door. 'Sorry, that'll be Mum. I have to go. Talk later.' I disconnect, open the door and glare at my mother. 'You'll wake the dead.'

She glares right back – 'Ten minutes was up five minutes ago' – then looks me up and down. 'I thought you were having a shower?'

'I meant to but—'

She reaches inside and grips my wrist, dragging me towards her. 'Well, there's no time now. We don't want to be late for Petrice.'

On our way down the main street, we pass a little bar called the Black Anchor. With its modest, brown weatherboard facade, large, clean, glass sliding doors at the front and a shiny anchor sign overlooking timber benches, it is the first place I've seen on the island that looks edgy and like maybe it belongs in this century. I'm excited until I see the sign saying it's not open until Thursday night. Right now, that feels like ages away.

'I'm so happy to get you alone,' Mum says, linking her arm through mine like an eager schoolgirl. It's so humid that my skin is sticky beneath my summer dress and I'm really regretting not having that shower. 'What do you think of Paul?'

'He seems nice.'

'I knew you'd like him as soon as you met him. And don't you just adore Scarlett and her children? Tallulah-Jane is so smart, Kayla cracks me up with her cute little cat antics, and I could just eat Miller up.'

'Um . . . they all seem nice, but I haven't really had a chance to get to know anyone yet.' Somehow, I manage not to comment that neither has she – we haven't even been here twenty-four hours.

'Really? What about Leo? You two looked quite friendly when you came in this morning. Where were you?'

The last thing I want is her getting suspicious that Leo and I are up to something, so I try to sound nonchalant. 'Oh, I went for a drive because I couldn't sleep and ran into him on a run. I gave him a lift back to the resort.'

'He seems a little quiet, reserved.'

I remember the sound of Leo's laughter this morning as we plotted together. Quiet is *not* how I'd describe him.

'Maybe it's because his mother only just *died*,' I point out, wondering how my own mother can be so blinkered. 'He's still grieving, and you marrying his father so soon is probably hard to get his head around.'

She slows her walking and for a moment I think maybe I've got through to her – that maybe she can see there are other feelings aside from hers and Paul's to consider here – but then I follow her gaze to see we're already standing in front of the beauty salon. Her grip tightens on my arm. 'We're here.'

I sigh as we head inside. This island is tiny and the town even smaller, so I'm not sure anyone could ever finish a whole conversation even if you walked the length of it.

A woman who I immediately recognise as the car hire lady puts down the book she's reading and leaps out of her seat when we enter. 'Hello! You must be Tracy!' She draws Mum into a hug. 'So glad to meet you in person. Aren't you going to make a beautiful bride!'

After their long embrace, during which I check out my surroundings – soft blue walls, more modern than the resort, less modern than the Black Anchor Bar – she turns to me. 'Hello again. I didn't catch your name when we last met.'

'Fred,' I say, before Mum can say 'Winifred'. 'I didn't expect to see you here. I thought you had a car hire business?'

Petrice half laughs. 'We all do two or three jobs around here. Some of us more. I'm a Jill of all trades – I also have tourists at my place for a progressive dinner at least twice a month. Now, can I get you ladies some tea or coffee or would you prefer champagne since it's a very special occasion?'

'Champagne,' Mum and I reply in unison. At least we're on the same page about that.

'Splendid.' Petrice grins, then calls over her shoulder, 'Tommy, grab that bottle I put in the fridge.'

'Are you enjoying that book?' I ask, pointing to the copy of *The Bee Sting* she discarded when we arrived.

She glances over at it. 'Oh, yes and no. It's the pick for my book club this month and I need to finish it by Thursday night. Have you read it?' When I nod, she adds, 'I'm enjoying the story, but the lack of punctuation is driving me batty.'

A teenager dressed like an old man, who Petrice introduces as her genius apprentice, appears with three champagne flutes and a bottle. All thoughts of books evaporate as I stare at the label. Moët?! How much is Mum paying this woman? Or rather, how much is Paul?

Mum thanks Petrice for squeezing us in at such short notice and also doing our trial on a Sunday afternoon when the salon isn't normally open.

'Oh, it's my pleasure. I've got a jam-packed week, but I *love* love and what you told me of your story is so romantic that I had to make it work. You even made me think about reaching out to my own high school crush, until I remembered I'm already married and he turned out to be a total douchebag. Anyway, I can't wait to make you and Fred sparkle for the big day.'

She clinks Mum's glass, then reaches out to do the same to mine, but it's already at my lips, half the liquid gone.

'Right, let's get started. Thank you for sending me photos of your beautiful gowns – you're both going to look stunning.'

I take another sip of Moët as Petrice and Mum put their heads together and discuss what style she wants for her hair, the colours that work best with our palettes – lucky we're both fair skinned – and then our dresses. Mum and I spent almost a whole day the weekend before she flew to London going from shop to shop all over the city trying to find the perfect dress. And by perfect, I mean one that doesn't make me look like a middle-aged spinster who spends more time knitting and baking scones than on the Peloton. You should have *seen* some of the gowns she suggested. One of them was honest-to-God the colour of baby poo with a neckline so high I feared I might strangle myself. *If* I am going to stand next to Mum and sign my name on her marriage certificate, I plan on looking amazing while doing it. Knowing Mum, she'll splash the photos all over social media and I wouldn't want a possible Tinder date to see me looking less than my fabulous self.

In the end, I got my way – *of course* – and if the wedding does go ahead on Friday, I'll be wearing a cherry-red, just-below-the-knee chiffon gown with a low neckline and an open back and sexy, hot-pink kitten heels on my feet.

'And of course Fred's make-up colours will depend on what shade of wig she decides on,' Petrice says. 'I've got a few here to choose from.'

'Wig?' I exclaim, shooting daggers at Mum as I lift my hand to caress my scalp.

She bites her lip and looks at me like I'm a wild animal. 'I just thought . . . *you* might feel more comfortable wearing one.'

Yeah, right. Everyone except her thinks I look good right now. I don't know whether it's the bubbles making me mellow or the fact that I don't plan on there being a wedding – so my hair or lack of it is a moot point – but I decide not to make a scene. The sooner we get this over and done with, the sooner I can head back to my manuscript.

'Show me the wigs,' I say as I hand my now empty glass to the apprentice, hoping he'll refill it.

The first three are 'definitely nots' and she only has five. Luckily, number four is a dark-brown chin-length, jagged bob that makes me look like Mia, Alan Rickman's mistress, in *Love Actually*. 'This is the one.'

Mum and Petrice approve, and so we move on to the make-up. I quite enjoy watching other people get their faces done up and Tommy does refill my glass, so listening to Petrice and Mum prattle on about all the special touches planned for the wedding is bearable. Until Petrice tells me I must be so excited that Mum has chosen me as her maid of honour.

I make a non-committal sound. The only time I've ever been excited about one of Mum's weddings was when she married Jeff when I was eight.

I'd loved him from the moment she first introduced him to us and, back then, I was naive enough to think marriage was for life, despite the evidence to the contrary. I blame books and TV. I loved watching Disney movies that always had a happily ever after, but I'm no longer a naive little girl who can be won over with pretty dresses and promises of a new family. As an adult it's clear why the movies never showed what happened after the wedding. Who says Belle and the Beast didn't go through a tumultuous divorce in which she took half his library and the castle? Who says Ariel and Prince Eric's marriage didn't end in a bitter custody battle? There's a reason we never saw what became of their lives – kids don't want to see reality, especially when we're living it.

Those years when Mum was married to Jeff were the happiest and most stable of my childhood, filled with visits to the zoo where he'd put me on his shoulders so I could see the meerkats, fun family dinners and trips to the beach. He came to my assemblies and school Father's Day breakfasts, which was more than my real father ever did. For the first time ever I understood why my friends raved about their daddies, but was all that worth my heartbreak when it ended?

'How long have you lived on Norfolk?' I ask Petrice, ignoring her comment about my excitement. It was more a statement than a question anyway.

'All my life,' she replies, 'except for the few years I went away to Sydney to hairdressing school and a couple of years after that. But my husband is from here, and we both wanted to raise kids on island. Most of us find our way back eventually.'

As Petrice finishes Mum's make-up and then moves on to mine, she tells us about growing up here and how it's one of the safest places in the world. 'We don't have any of the venomous animals found on the mainland, and we have next to no crime – well, except for the awful murder that happened in 2002.'

At twenty-eight, I'm too young to remember this shocking killing that apparently garnered the attention of global media, but Mum does and Petrice was friends with the victim, so we spend a lengthy time discussing it.

'We're just so thankful it was an outsider who was found guilty in the end,' she says, swivelling my head to look in the mirror. 'What do you think?'

I stare at my reflection. 'Wow!' I can't help smiling, forgetting the murder for a moment *and* why we're here, because Petrice has done what so few make-up artists ever manage to do. She's made me look like I'm stepping out for a red carpet or something, yet not in an over-the-top, will-I-ever-get-this-make-up-off-my-face kind of way. 'I love it. Thank you.'

'My pleasure.' She stands and wipes her hands on her black pants. 'I'll let you get back to your family now, but enjoy the rest of your week and I'll see you both bright and early on Friday morning.'

I'm almost disappointed that if Leo's and my machinations are successful, she won't get to do my make-up again. A selfie for Bee is definitely in order. I snap one to send later.

When Mum and I arrive back at the resort, we find Juliet, Leo, Paul, Waylen and Benji sitting on the couches in reception, playing cards. Benji wolf-whistles as they all look up and, as Paul leaps up to kiss Mum hello, Juliet smiles at me.

'Fred, you look stunning.' She elbows her brother in the side. 'Doesn't she look stunning, Leo?'

He nods – 'Yeah, stunning' – and as his gaze meets mine, heat zaps through me.

If we'd met on the apps, there's no doubt I'd have swiped right, and I get the feeling he would have too.

9

THE NEXT BIG THING

There's no time for any writing between getting back to the resort and our dinner reservation, but I'm starving anyway. Bailey's Restaurant, a very short drive from the resort, is a gorgeous restaurant at another hotel called Governor's Lodge Resort, in a beautiful, old restored cream house that Paul tells us was built by one of the early settlers. It has palm trees out the front and a verandah that wraps around two sides of the building. We step into the bar and are quickly escorted into one of the private dining rooms by a young man with curly dark hair and an Italian accent who introduces himself as Marco. Miller is dropped into a highchair and the rest of us scramble to find seats. Leo and I try to separate Mum and his dad, but when this doesn't work, we end up next to each other instead.

Oh well, there are worse places to be seated.

We all peruse the menu – there's a brief disagreement between River and Scarlett about whether they should encourage Kayla to have more than just chips – and then Marco takes our order. When the drinks arrive, Paul lifts his half-pint of beer and makes yet another gushy toast about Mum.

'Let's play a game,' I suggest, nursing my wineglass in my hand once he's done.

'What, like "I Spy"?' Kayla asks, her head barely visible above the table.

'I hate "I Spy",' TJ declares, rolling her eyes.

'So do I. But that's not what I'm thinking. This is a get-to-know-each-other game.'

'What a great idea,' Leo says, his knee nudging mine. A rather distracting thrill runs through me at the connection.

Scarlett's smile grows even wider than usual. 'I love a good game. How does it work?'

'We take turns going around the table,' I say. 'Each of us asks a question like "What's your favourite movie?" and the rest of us have to answer.'

'Sounds boring,' TJ says, but thankfully everyone else thinks it's a fabulous idea. Mum in particular looks pleased that I'm making an effort.

'Do you want to go first?' I ask her.

'Ooh okay.' She takes a sip of her wine, thinking for a moment. 'When you were a child, what did you want to be when you grew up?'

'Great question,' Leo says. 'I wanted to be an astronaut.'

I smirk at him. 'The only thing *more* clichéd would be a fireman.'

He tips his wineglass towards me. 'Well, what did *you* want to be?'

'A wizard. I was devastated when my Hogwarts letter didn't arrive on my twelfth birthday.' That was also the year Jeff and Mum got divorced – not a great time of my life.

Leo snorts. 'As if that's not cliché. At least there's a possibility of becoming an astronaut.'

I poke my tongue out at him.

Mum laughs and digs Paul in the side. 'Look, honey, they're acting like siblings already.'

More questions and answers are offered. We talk about favourite foods, languages we know, where we'd hide a body if we needed to, and then Leo asks about religious beliefs.

'Oh, I've been a Catholic all my life,' Mum says. 'I've been to so many masses, I could probably conduct one myself.'

'Really?' Leo perhaps sounds a tad *too* happy about this. 'But Dad's Church of England.'

Paul laughs. 'Well, I guess technically, but I'm lapsed.'

'Dad's a Christmas and Easter Christian,' Scarlett interjects.

'Hey! I also go to church for other things. Christenings and funerals, for example.'

'Aren't you worried about having such different beliefs?' I ask, not willing to let humour sideline us.

Paul takes Mum's hand and smiles – I don't think he ever *stops* smiling. 'No, not at all. The important thing is we respect each other's beliefs.'

I silently sigh, my fingers tightening around my glass. Religion hasn't worked, so I'm going to have to bring politics into the conversation, but first Benji wants to know everyone's star signs.'

'Don't tell me you buy into that baloney,' Mum says. 'Actually,' Paul begins, 'I'm not so sure there isn't something to be said for the stars.'

I feel a tingle at the back of my neck. I doubt opposing beliefs about astrology have ever broken anyone up, but it's a start.

'I used to be a disbeliever until I met Amelia,' he explains, 'but she taught me a lot about it. And now I do believe the time we are born influences our personalities and that strange things happen when Mercury is in retrograde.'

Way rolls his eyes; he's always been a complete sceptic. 'What kind of strange things?'

Paul shrugs. 'People misunderstand each other, flights are delayed, folks who'd normally never consider cheating are tempted to do it. And then there's technical mishaps – computers failing, emails getting lost in cyberspace, that kind of thing. These all sound like things that can happen anytime, but once you know when Mercury *is* in retrograde, it's impossible not to notice that more of them occur during this time.'

'Thank God Mercury isn't in retrograde this week! We wouldn't want it to affect the wedding.' This comment from Leo has me staring at a painting of a Mutineer on the wall as I try not to laugh.

Juliet looks towards the door of our private room into the rest of the restaurant. 'When's the food going to be here? I could eat a horse.'

'You can't eat horses,' Kayla says from under the table and Miller, previously content sucking on her dummy like Maggie from the Simpsons, also starts to grumble.

We're in the middle of discussing dream holidays when Marco and his colleague, whose name tag says 'Estelle', appear with our dinners.

'Thank fuck,' Juliet mutters as she picks up her cutlery.

Our 'game' is put on hold as we all get stuck into our dinners. I cannot fault the food. My risotto is quite possibly the best I've ever had and, judging by the exclamations of delight around the table, everyone else's meals are equally good.

'Aunty Juliet, you haven't asked a question yet,' TJ says through a mouthful of tiger prawns.

Juliet sighs. 'Okay . . . um . . . let's see . . . If you were facing bankruptcy, would you start Only Fans or join an MLM?'

Ooh, that's a good one.

'Impossible choice!' Paul shakes his head at his daughter. 'As if anyone would want a middle-aged, slightly paunchy man like me on Only Fans, but only someone stupid would be taken in by what are practically cults.'

Oh boy. I see Waylen's eyes widen across the table. Mum is the Queen of MLMs. I don't think she's in one currently, but growing up she was always signing up to what perky, pushy women assured her was going to be The Next Big Thing. Her house back in Perth is still full of Tupperware containers and old Amway catalogues. Here Leo and I thought we were going to have to talk about big issues, like sex, politics and religion, but Paul has just unknowingly burnt my mother and proved just how little they know about each other.

Of course, Way's not going to say anything, and Mum's gone a sickening shade of green. Part of me feels cruel blurting out, 'I guess that makes Mum naive then, because I've lost count of how many pyramid schemes she's tried,' but sometimes you've got to be cruel to be kind, and people really should know who they're getting into bed with.

'Oh ... Uh ... Well ... I ...' Paul seems lost for words. I bet he's wishing the island was volcanic and would erupt right beneath us.

'It was tough being a single parent.' Mum sounds close to tears. 'Of course, Toby and Simon sent me maintenance money, but it was never enough. There was always something extra we needed, and I never seemed to get enough shifts in my casual jobs and—'

Paul puts his hand on Mum's again. 'It's okay, you don't need to explain yourself. Besides, I hear some people can be quite successful in these sche— I mean businesses.'

He's doing his best to backtrack and Mum says it's fine, but she takes back her hand, the damage clearly done. If there was a mood-o-meter in the room, it would have plummeted from animated and cheerful to solemn and tense. For what feels like an hour but is probably only a few seconds, all we can hear are the scrapes of our cutlery on plates and indistinguishable chatter coming from the other parts of the restaurant.

I feel a little bad that she's upset, but then remind myself that it's better she finds out about any rifts between her and Paul now than after the wedding. The whole idea of this game is to shine light on how different they are, and it seems to be working.

'Is it my turn to ask a question?' Kayla asks, oblivious to the vibe among the adults.

'I think we've had enough questions tonight,' Paul says, shutting her down.

She bursts into tears.

Marco and Estelle choose that moment to start clearing away the empty plates. He points at Mum's half-eaten fish. 'Are you still eating that?'

She shakes her head. 'I'm no longer hungry.'

'I hope it was okay,' he says.

'It was fine,' she snaps.

He blinks. 'Great. Can I offer anyone dessert?'

'Not me,' Mum says. 'I've developed a bit of a headache. I want to go back to the hotel.'

In the end, only Juliet gets dessert to take away – 'It can be my midnight snack when this one wakes me up practising their karate chops' – which she slips into her white Marc Jacobs tote. Bee has an almost identical one from a recent trip she and Sully took to Bali, but something tells me Juliet's is the real deal. Then, pretending

we're *all* just tired, we pile into the cars and head back to the resort. Awkward goodbyes and see-you-tomorrows are exchanged before I escape to my room until enough time has elapsed that no one will catch Leo and I when we rendezvous in the games room.

My phone springs to life with texts and notifications. Bridget

Jones: *OMG why didn't you tell me he's famous?!! xx* Me: *Who's famous!?!!*

Bridget Jones: *LEO!!!!!!!!!*

My heart slams into my chest. Me: *What? How?*

My phone rings. I answer it immediately. 'What do you mean he's famous?'

'His uncle's a bloody duke.' She sounds like she's just run up ten flights of stairs. 'His mum was *Lady* Amelia. His family is distantly related to the royals!'

'What! No fucking way.'

'His dad has a really prestigious gardening company – landscapes for the mega rich and famous and has received awards at the Chelsea Flower Show.'

Oh my God. So much for gardening for 'run of the mill people'.

Why didn't Leo tell me any of this when we were plotting ways to split up our parents? Surely this is considered vital intel – not to mention it explains Paul's seemingly endless bank balance. Men can be so dense.

Then again, perhaps he thought I already knew.

More to the point – why didn't Mum bloody tell me? Maybe she didn't want me to think she was marrying Paul for the money. *Could* she be? Or maybe she did tell me during one of the times I zoned out. No, surely I'd remember something like this!

'Fred? Are you still there?'

'Sorry. Just . . . digesting this. How wealthy are we talking?'

'Well, the uncle – the Duke of Edlermoor – has billions, but his younger sister, Lady Amelia, would have had a pretty good dowry, I'd say, so I reckon Tracy's man would have inherited a not-so-small fortune when she died. Oh, and Leo's sister Juliet is married to a lord.'

'A lord? I thought he was a surgeon?'

She chuckles. 'Guess even rich people need jobs.'

I'm impressed by everything she's managed to uncover, but before I have time to absorb this information, she adds, 'And Leo is on the up in his own right.'

I blink. I don't know how much more I can take. 'What do you mean?'

'You know how he was carrying that instrument when you first saw him at the airport?'

'Yeah, it's a ukulele.'

'Uh-huh, and he's in a band that looks to be pretty popular in England. They're called The UkePros – as in professors, because they're all teachers. They're known for playing fresh and unique medley covers of classic songs.'

My phone beeps with a text and I see Bee has sent a link to one of their videos.

'His niece did mention he was in a band,' I say.

'They're really good. Listen to it, then call me back.' She disconnects.

I lie there for a few moments, frozen except for my still-thumping heart, before I finally click the link. After an annoying advert about incontinence pads that I'm forced to watch first, the screen reveals four men, all around Leo's age, on stage in a dimly lit pub. Seconds later a medley of ABBA fills the room. My eyes

skim over the band members all dressed in skin-tight, sparkly silver shirts. There's one with jet-black hair, a brunette and another blond, although lighter than Leo's hair colour. All of them have facial hair in various lengths and that slightly unruly look, giving the impression they don't care about their appearance, but I'd bet my minimal life savings that *much* effort goes into maintaining that hipster-chic look. Aside from Leo, none of them are what you'd call classically good-looking, but their music and their charisma has the crowd screaming.

My eyes zero in on Leo, who appears to be the lead singer

and, oh my goodness, is he *good*. No wonder girls are shouting from the audience that they want to have his babies. He's also a gun on the strings. I watch in awe as his beautiful fingers whip back and forth across the bar. That's probably not the technical term but, you know what I mean. My mind is too distracted, imagining what those fingers might feel like sliding across my skin – *Oh God, I might have to have a cold shower* – to care about the correct names for all the parts of a ukulele.

Maybe I'll ask Leo to give me a lesson.

Totally mesmerised, I lose myself in the band's Instagram account, scanning through more photos of them dressed in various costumes, including three-piece suits that make them look like the Beatles and leave me very hot under the collar. I almost have a heart attack when my phone buzzes again. It's Bee.

'Well, what do you think?' she asks.

'I think Leo and I have a *lot* to talk about.'

10

MORE THAN JUST BOOKS

hen it's time to debrief and celebrate a rather successful start to Operation Break-up, I find Leo in the games room perusing the shelf of ratty-looking board games. The main building of the resort is practically empty, except for the dude behind the reception and someone vacuuming in the bar. Not wanting to raise suspicion, we waited half an hour to be sure no one would see us together.

Leo dips his head as if tipping an imaginary hat. 'Evening, Winifred.'

A zing shoots through me. How come when Leo says my name I have such a different reaction to when Mum says it?

'Evening, Leopold. Or should I call you *Lord* Leopold?'

He runs a hand through his hair, which isn't tied back like it usually is but falling wildly around his face in the manner of a lion's mane. If anything, it makes him look even hotter. 'Have you been researching me?'

I almost tell him that no, my best friend has, but that would look even worse than admitting to an Insta-stalk myself, because then he'd know I'd been talking about him. 'I thought I should find out a bit about the person I've agreed to go into partnership with.'

He frowns. '*Partnership*?'

'Don't get your knickers in a knot – I'm not cracking onto you; I just meant partners in our *plan*.'

He looks relieved and I can't help being disappointed. Not that I want to get into a romantic partnership with *anyone*, but it's unsettling to know the attraction I'm feeling towards him might not be reciprocated. That isn't something that happens often, but it's probably for the best. Everyone knows that mixing business with pleasure is a recipe for disaster.

'So . . . you're practically royalty and the band you're in isn't just a little group of friends who get together in a garage occasionally to jam, but a big freaking deal.'

'I'm definitely not royalty, and if my band was a big deal, don't you think you'd have heard of us?'

'You have over one hundred thousand followers on Instagram,' I counter.

He shrugs. 'Beyoncé has over three hundred million. We're really just four guys who like jamming together – we never intended for it to become a thing. We started out doing the occasional gig in the local pub and then recorded a few medleys for charity and one of them went what I suppose you'd call viral. That's when our social media numbers shot up, and things have been a little hectic since.'

'How so?'

'A music agent recently reached out to us,' he tells me. 'He's offering us representation and reckons he can get us some bigger gigs in Europe, maybe even overseas.'

I detect a 'but' in his voice.

'And you're not excited because . . .'

Leo rubs his hand over his jaw. 'I don't know. I *like* teaching. It's important to me. And if things do kick off the way this agent is talking, then I'd probably have to quit. I like playing with the Pros too, but I'm not sure I want the lifestyle that comes with being a rockstar.'

'What do your band mates think?'

He sighs. 'That's the problem – they all want to pursue these new opportunities.' He points at a game. 'Do you want to play chess?'

Clearly, he's over talking about his band. 'Leopold dearest, you can't hold down a serious conversation while playing chess, and we have serious business to partake in.' Not to mention the whole royalty thing, which I'm definitely not done with.

'Yeah, you're right.' He sighs, glances around, then asks, 'What about pool?' as he gestures to the table, which has also seen better days.

While I happen to think facing off in pool is super sexy, we are not here for foreplay. 'Can't we just sit and talk?'

He shrugs 'We can try . . . but I'm not particularly good at that.'

'Oh?'

'I have ADHD.'

'Ah, I see.' I point to the ping-pong table; ping-pong is almost as unsexy as socks and sandals. I don't care who tries to tell me it's fashionable; I will never bed a guy with such bad taste. 'What about table tennis?'

He hits me with a disarming grin. 'That could work. As long as you don't mind losing.'

'I wouldn't know.' I shrug as I sashay towards the table and pick up one of the bats. 'I never have.'

'Is that right?' He chuckles as he picks up the other bat. 'Well, there's a first time for everything. Who's serving?'

I toss the ball towards him. 'Losers first.'

'Cocky much?' But he catches the ball in his hand and executes a near-perfect serve.

'Not cocky, just confident,' I say, smashing it right back to him.

We hit back and forth a few minutes, warming up and setting our pace.

'Why didn't you tell me any of this?' I demand.

He hits the ball back to me. 'What? That I'm a pro at ping-pong?'

'Ha-ha,' I say. 'No, that you're a bloody royal.'

'I'm not a royal.'

I snort. 'Close enough.'

'I thought you knew,' he says.

'No idea.' I hit the ball to him and this time he misses. 'Point! And this could be really useful for us.'

He retrieves the ball and serves. 'How do you mean?'

'We can make Mum out to be a gold-digger.'

'It did cross my mind that maybe that was her motivation,' he admits as the ball flies towards him. 'Not that Dad isn't a catch on his own, but this has been very quick.'

'Why didn't you say anything?'

'I didn't want to offend you.'

'Aw, how sweet.' He's so polite and English. 'But I'm not easily offended. I actually don't think that *is* her reasoning – she's more sentimental than sensible – but that doesn't mean we can't make your father think it is.'

'Maybe we won't have to stoop to that after tonight.'

I grin at him. 'I know. That was a pretty awkward end to dinner. Juliet couldn't have asked a better question if we'd primed her.

We should buy her a case of champagne to thank her once she's popped out that giant baby.'

Leo laughs. 'She's huge, isn't she? I was worried they got the dates wrong and she might have gone into labour on the flight here.'

We hit back and forth a few more times.

'Are you a fan of seventies punk rock in general or just the Ramones?' he asks, gesturing at the T-shirt I changed back into after dinner, along with my denim shorts.

'Huge fan,' I tell him. 'Give me the Ramones, the Sex Pistols and the Buzzcocks over Taylor Swift and Kanye West any day.'

'Gotta agree with you there, although don't tell my sisters – they're huge Swifties.'

'Really?' Scarlett seems too hippy for Tay-Tay and I can't imagine Juliet listening to music at all. She seems more the business podcast type.

He nods. 'I think it's the only thing they have in common – but you weren't even born when those bands were big. How'd you get into them?'

'My stepdad – well, one of them. Jeff is a huge music nerd. He took me to my first ever music concert – Good Charlotte – and after that I wanted to listen to everything he loved, most of which was punk rock. We still go to concerts together sometimes.'

'I got the impression you didn't like the men your mum was married to. Never mind keep in touch with them.'

'Most of them, I don't,' I say, whacking the ball back to Leo so fast he misses it. *Yes!* Another point to me. 'But Jeff's the exception. He's awesome. He's been more of a dad than my real father ever was. Until the last couple of years, I probably saw Jeff more than Mum.'

Scowling, Leo picks up the ball and hits it back to me just as hard. 'Why don't you see him as much any more?'

'Oh, I still see him just as much – we catch up at least once a month and message every few days – but now I also see Mum more than I used to. This is the longest she's been single, so we've spent more time together than ever before.'

'I see,' he says. 'So who *is* your real dad?'

'Ah, now that would be Simon Darling.' One of the few things I really like about him is his surname. 'He's a Woolworths area manager. They broke up when I was five, so I can't remember much of them being together, but Way says it's a miracle they lasted that long. Apparently all they did was fight and the two of us used to hide under the bed to get away from it all.'

His eyes grow wide. 'Physically fight?'

I shake my head. 'According to Way, cutting words were their weapons of choice.'

'Do you and Waylen see much of him?'

'Oh, Simon isn't Way's father – his dad lives in the UK like you.'

'Huh?' Leo's confusion loses him another point, giving me our first game.

'Way was the result of Wedding Numero Uno,' I say, serving as I begin to explain.

'Our mum met Toby in Chelmsford when she was working at a fancy hotel in her early twenties. He was a local boy, working a summer job while home from college. They weren't dating for long when they found out Mum was pregnant, and Toby did the right thing – he married her. On Way's second birthday, not long after Toby got his first proper job at a law firm, he came home and announced he was leaving her for one of the firm's

secretaries – such a cliché, but they're still together all these years later – and Mum's relationships have devolved from there.

'She threatened to bring Way back home to Australia, hoping that Toby would fight for them both to stay, but he didn't. She came home anyway, because aside from Way and Toby, she had no family in England. A few years after that she met Simon when Way was having a full-blown, screaming, kicking tantrum in the feminine hygiene aisle in Woolies.'

Leo snorts out a laugh and misses yet another hit. I'm pretty sure my track record as Table Tennis Queen is safe. 'If I were your dad, I'd have run a mile.'

'I reckon he probably wishes he did,' I say. 'Flirting with a single mum and distracting a kid with ice cream for a short time was one thing, but I don't think he was ready to settle down and have kids.'

'So . . .' Leo's brow creases as he tries to keep up with the game and the conversation. 'First husband was Waylen's dad, Toby. Second husband was your dad, Simon, and third husband was Jeff.' He smiles as if pleased he's keeping track. 'How did they meet?'

'In some online forum for single parents. He had two sons from a previous marriage. He was from WA but flew to Brissy to meet Mum, and then would come and visit every couple of months until he finally proposed. Then he asked us all to move to Perth with him, so he didn't have to move away from his other kids.'

Another stark difference between Jeff and my dad and Waylen's dad – ours didn't worry about living away from their children, whereas Jeff couldn't bear it.

'And that's where you still live?' Leo clarifies, shooting the ball back to me.

I nod. 'Way was just starting uni when Mum and Jeff split, and I was in my first year of high school, so even though Mum's parents were in Queensland, we stayed put.'

'But you said this was her sixth marriage, so who was husband number four?'

'Four was Colin Rodgers. Mum literally ran into him in the street one day.' We volley back and forth as I continue. 'It was raining, and she didn't have an umbrella, so she was hurrying round a corner trying to get undercover and slammed straight into him coming the other way. He insisted on buying her a hot chocolate to warm her up, and then dinner. Over the next year he love-bombed her something chronic and asked her to marry him on the first anniversary of their meeting.'

'Romantic.'

'Hah.' I scoff and cut to the chase. 'Until three years later when a woman arrives at our house, yelling and screaming and accusing Mum of having an affair with her husband.'

'No way?' Leo blinks, then shakes his head slightly. 'Colin was already married?'

'Yep – for thirty years. He claimed he loved both Mum and his real wife, but the wife gave him an ultimatum and they had kids together and a grandchild on the way, so in the end, he chose her over Mum.'

'Wow.'

'I know. If I was her, I'd have kicked him to the kerb.' I'm thankful I'd learned my lesson with Jeff and had given little time to getting to know Colin, so their break-up didn't have much of an effect on me. If only Mum had learned her lesson then too, we could have avoided the debacle with Bernie and we wouldn't be wasting our time here.

Not that spending the evening with Leo isn't enjoyable. When I hit the ball back to him, he catches it in his hand.

'Hang on . . . if Tracy's and Colin's marriage wasn't legal, then I guess that means, officially, Dad will be husband number five.'

I think for a moment. 'I guess it does, except that we're not going to let that happen, are we?'

Leo grins – 'Nope' – then serves. 'We most definitely are not.' I hit the ball right back.

'And who was husband number five, or four if we're discounting Colin?' he asks, returning my shot.

'For Bernie, we're going to need a drink,' I say, slamming the ball over the net, so it bounces and shoots out of his reach. 'Game. Take that, sucker!' I do a little victory dance on the spot.

Leo laughs as he puts his bat on the table. 'No offence, but you're not very librarian-like.'

'Offence taken!' I raise my eyebrows and plant my hands on my hips. 'What *do* you think a librarian should be like?'

He gives me the answer I suspect – thanks to books and movies, everyone thinks librarians are quiet, meek and mild. Sometimes a little highly strung, judgemental of anyone who knows how to have a good time, often dull, and terribly boring.

Basically, the opposite of me in every sense.

'That is such a stereotype,' I say. 'My colleagues and I are nothing like that. You should see some of the parties we have.'

I tell him about Bee being one of the bubbliest people you'll ever meet; that Persephone would put a spell on him if she heard him speaking about librarians in such a disrespectful manner; and that Xavier's Story Time sessions get louder and louder every week.

'Aren't libraries supposed to be quiet places?'

'Oh Lord, don't tell me libraries in England are still stuck in the Middle Ages, enforcing stupid rules like that?'

'I wouldn't know, to be honest. If I want a book, I just buy it.' Of course he does. He might be on a teacher's wage, but let's not forget he's rolling in family money.

'Come on, let's go to the bar and you can buy me a drink.'

This isn't a date, so I don't need to worry about Rule #9.

Unfortunately the bar is closed and even I can't manage to charm the barman, who's just turned off the lights, into letting us buy drinks to go. Disappointed, we head back into the main area. The night receptionist is asleep in his swivel chair, head tipped back and mouth wide open like Mr Whatshisname from the Faraway Tree and the whole place now feels like a ghost town.

'If I had an acorn I'd pop it in his mouth,' Leo says with a chuckle.

I snort, unable to believe just how close our thoughts are. 'What are we going to do now?'

He's quiet for a moment and I can almost see the thoughts ticking through his head, then he holds up a finger. 'Wait here and keep watch.'

'Where are you going?'

He winks – 'I'm getting us a drink' – then he slips back into the pitch-black, now-empty bar. Less than sixty seconds later he reappears carrying two bottles of beer.

I can't help laughing. 'Did you just steal those?'

'Shh.' He nods towards reception, but our friend there hasn't stirred, then whispers, 'Course I didn't steal them. What do you take me for? I left twenty-five dollars in the fridge. Come on.'

'Where are we going?'

'Outside. It's too nice an evening to be cooped up in here anyway.'

The door leading to the pool is locked, so we head around to the gate, but it's also locked. I'm about to ask Leo back to my room – purely so we can drink the beers somewhere comfier than the games room – but he has other ideas.

'Here, hold this.' He thrusts his bottle at me, and I think he's about to haul himself over the fence, but instead, he pulls a fancy pen out of his pocket, unscrews it and takes out the little metal coil at the top.

'Not as great as a bobby pin,' he says, starting to unwind it into a straight line, 'but I figured you probably didn't have one of them on you so . . .'

I watch in awe as he unpicks the padlock – I guess he's already stolen beers so a little break-and-enter is nothing – and opens the gate.

Grinning, he holds it open and gestures for me to go through. 'Ladies first.'

'Should I be worried you know how to pick a lock?'

He closes the gate quietly behind us. 'I think you should be thanking me. How gorgeous does the pool look?'

'I'm not going swimming,' I tell him, surveying the water glistening in front of us, only just visible due to the moon above and the light shining from the reception area.

'Chicken.' He sits down on the edge. 'But at least put your feet in.'

Slipping off my sandals, I sink down next to him, sucking in a breath as my feet hit the cool water. At least I tell myself that's what's responsible, not sitting so close next to Leo that I could count the hairs on his very manly legs.

He smiles and holds out his bottle to mine. 'Here's to a successful first day of Operation Break-up.'

'Cheers,' I say as the glass clinks, then, 'Was it your lock-picking skills that got you thrown in detention at school? Don't tell me you stole a teacher's car or something.'

He puts the bottle to his lips and takes a long, sexy sip. I swallow, look away and gulp my own beer. 'My detentions were for far more boring things – talking back, causing disruptions in class, skipping class and smoking behind the gym, although I did once spray cans of fart gas all over the headmistress's office. Her office was near the science labs, and they thought there was a gas leak. Whole school was evacuated.'

'Oh my God.' I almost choke on a mouthful of beer. 'Doesn't sound like you enjoyed school much?'

'Hated it.'

'Then why'd you become a teacher?' I ask, swirling my feet in the water.

'Well, I eventually saw the light and changed my wicked ways.

I want to help kids like me stay on the straight and narrow.'

'How noble of you,' I tease, although I mean it. 'But if you're such a fabulous musician, why are you teaching English rather than music?'

He laughs. 'I'm not. Don't get me wrong, I always liked music and Mum and Dad always had something on in the background, but I could never sit still long enough to practise anything. I only picked up the uke a couple of years ago as a bit of fun with some colleagues. All of us work at this underprivileged school, and one day we were letting off steam in the music room – Mitch and August are music teachers – and they joked we should start a band. Farouk, that's our fourth friend, and I couldn't play anything, so they said they'd teach us the ukes because they're one of the easiest instruments to pick up.

'It kinda grew from there and we started getting gigs at pubs. Honestly? We couldn't believe people were actually taking us seriously.'

'I've watched a couple of your songs on YouTube,' I admit. 'I can see why they do. You guys have a great presence and you're a really good singer.'

Leo smiles but doesn't meet my gaze. 'Probably from all those years singing in the shower.'

'I love singing in the shower, although the complaints I get from Way make me think maybe I'm not quite as good as you.'

'I'm sure you have lots of other talents,' he says, and although he doesn't seem to mean anything suggestive by it, warmth flows through me at his words.

I clear my throat. 'So . . . was English your favourite subject at school then?'

'I thought we'd established I didn't like any aspect of school, least of all English.'

I remember what he told me earlier that evening. 'Is that because of your ADHD?'

'That was part of it, but . . . it was when I got diagnosed with dyslexia that I finally got the help I needed, and school stopped being so awful.'

'You have dyslexia too?

He nods. 'Not sure if you know, but dyslexia is often called the hidden disability. It's not that we come across as dumb. I could understand what I was learning and talk about it, but I struggled when I had to put it into words on paper. Mum wondered if there was more to it, but I was at a good school and all the advice she got from teachers was that it was my ADHD – my inability to concentrate – holding me back. When I started high school, I was behind everyone else and I felt so stupid, so I acted out, became the class clown, to take the attention off my terrible grades.'

I listen as he recalls how his dad and teachers were furious, but his mum decided enough was enough. She took him to see a private educational psychologist, who recognised his dyslexia immediately. 'Mum and Dad had the money to get me extra help, and things started to look up for me at school. I didn't feel like such an idiot and slowly I even started to enjoy learning, but I know that's a privilege. Not all kids have the kind of mum who won't give up, or the resources to get extra help, but early intervention is crucial. If I had teachers who recognised my signs and symptoms earlier, school might have been a totally different experience for me, so now, that's my aim. To work out why kids are misbehaving, rather than just write them off as so many teachers did to me.'

A lump grows in my throat at Leo's words and the conviction in them. Here I was judging him, thinking that because his family had money he must have led a charmed life, but that's clearly not the truth.

'I chose English in particular,' he continues, 'because knowing how to communicate is the key to living a fulfilling life. Being able to read, write and express yourself, analyse text and that kind of thing, opens you up to so much more of the world. I want everyone to be able to have that experience.'

No one has ever put it to me this way before, but that's exactly why I love books too.

'Kids either do music because they're forced to by parents who regret quitting the piano themselves, or because they live and breathe it. The passionate kids are eager to learn and those there because of their parents are rarely going to be truly motivated or interested. English is not so beloved, and everyone has to do it,

so I find this is where I can really inspire kids, have big conversations and help them grow as people.' Before I can respond to this, he says, 'I'm guessing you became a librarian because you're a book nerd?'

'Hey!' I glare at him. 'I'm not a nerd!'

He holds up a hand. 'Sorry! But to me that's not an insult. Books are great.'

'They are. But I guess it was more libraries than books per se that made me decide to become a custodian of them.'

'Oh?' he says, before taking another sip.

Talking about my childhood and adolescence is something I rarely do, but Leo has been so open about his own that I find myself doing the same. 'After Mum and Jeff broke up, home was a pretty stressful place for a while. I missed him so much and I hated her for pushing him away.'

'That's why they broke up?

I nod. 'No matter what he did, it wasn't good enough for her. She was always at him that he worked too hard, and then got it in her head that he must be having an affair. He wasn't, but in the end, he couldn't handle any more of her paranoia and histrionics. So he did exactly what she was scared he'd do – he left. Jeff was my hero; I was heartbroken when they split up. I wanted to go live with him but she said he wasn't my real dad so

I couldn't. I cried for three long months and didn't talk to her for six.'

Leo's eyes widen. 'You didn't talk to your mum for six months?'

I nod. 'She tried to speak to me. And my pretending she didn't exist infuriated her. She'd yell through my bedroom door, "I'm your real parent. Blood's thicker than water," but that just made me angrier. During that time, I spent as little time as home as possible. I started hanging out at the local library after school and on weekends. It became like my second home – probably more like my proper home. I got to know the librarians and instead of being annoyed by me always being there, they took me under their wing. They'd give me afternoon tea and ask me about my day and I'd help them shelve books. Eventually they offered me a part-time job on Saturdays, and I saw that libraries are about so much more than books.'

'What do you mean?'

I smile; there's nothing I love talking about more than my job. 'Libraries are the beating hearts of communities – they're a place where locals can learn, make connections, shelter from danger or harsh weather. We hold movie nights in the winter for homeless locals, and we have a counsellor on staff so people suffering domestic violence can come and discuss options for escape. Dangerous men often watch what their partners do and where they go, but they don't seem to be suspicious of the library.'

I tell him about the other programs we run at Freo Library. In addition to kids' activities and myriad book clubs, we host workshops and seminars. Our classes on computer literacy are very popular with the seniors, and we also have a number of clubs, from Mah-jong to Lego. 'The best thing about the library, though, is that it doesn't matter about the colour of your skin, your age or financial status, everyone is welcome. When I finished school, I couldn't imagine working anywhere else and I still can't. I love it.'

'That's awesome,' Leo says, 'but where does the writing fit in?'

'Well, I've met lots of authors through work and obviously I like reading. I also love a challenge so about a year ago, I decided to write a book.'

'You must be pretty good if you've only just started and you're already getting published.'

A laugh bubbles out of me. 'The one I'm contracted to write isn't the book I started. I tried to write a novel first.'

'What kind of novel?'

I shrug. 'I thought it was genre-bending. It was about an alien and a cannibal, kind of a literary-erotic-fantasy-anti-romance, or at least that's what I was going for, but Bee read it and basically said that it's a steaming pile of dog poo that no one would want to read if it was the only book on the planet.'

'What?' He sounds horrified. 'I'm sure she didn't say exactly that!'

'She tried to be tactful – being mean isn't in Bee's nature – but in the end I got it out of her and that was definitely the gist.'

'That must have hurt.'

'Yeah, it did.' I shiver. Not because it's cold – it's a lovely, mild, summer evening – but because something about Leo has me letting down my guard, admitting to him what I couldn't even admit to Bee or Waylen. 'I thought I could take constructive criticism but apparently not. I told her I wasn't giving up, that I'd take her feedback into a new manuscript, but every time I thought of a new idea, I'd think of what she said about my original one and decide it was stupid as well. I totally lost the ability to put pen to paper.'

'That sucks,' Leo says, then downs the rest of his beer. 'You've obviously got your writing mojo back now though?'

'I wouldn't exactly say that.'

He frowns – 'Oh?' – but I shake my head. I don't want to ruin what's turning out to be a lovely night by talking about my inability to get past Chapter Three, so I point to his arms instead. Finally I'm close enough to read them. 'Tell me about your tattoos.'

Leo stretches out his arms in front of him as if he'd almost forgotten the images were there. Then he points to the quote on

his left forearm, which I recognise as a song lyric from Pearl Jam's 'I Am Mine'. 'This is to remind me that certain things in life are predestined, but we can choose how to live, and the other is from—'

'Goodbye Yellow Brick Road,' I say, grinning.

He nods. 'I like the reminder that there's more to life than fame and fortune. Both these lyrics are philosophies I try to live by.'

'Are they the only ones you have?' I ask, my tone cheeky.

In reply, he lifts his shirt so I can see his perfectly sculpted abs, but I have no idea what I'm looking at.

'They're sound waves,' he whispers. 'From the last voicemail Mum left me.'

Oh my goodness. It's one of the most beautiful things I've ever seen. Shivers cover my skin and emotion rushes to my throat. I can only imagine having the kind of relationship with either of my parents that propels me to do something like this. If I were Leo, there's no way I'd have agreed to be best man at his father's wedding when his mother hasn't even been gone a year.

I want to say something profound, but all I manage is, 'That's so precious.'

He drops his shirt again. 'What about you? Any ink?'

'Yeah.' I pull up the sleeve of my T-shirt to reveal the tiny red heart tattooed on my left arm.

Understandably, Leo frowns, then chuckles. 'But you don't

believe in romance? What right do you have to have a heart tattoo?'

'It's not about romance,' I tell him. 'It's a reminder that I'm all I need. That loving yourself is the most important thing you can do.'

'And do you?' he asks, his voice low.

I swear there's a frisson in the air between us and it makes me weirdly nervous, but also excited. 'What's not to love?'

He laughs. 'We should probably call it a night,' he says, pushing to stand.

I guess I had nothing to be nervous about.

11

AN ALMOST PERFECT SPECIMEN

First on today's agenda is a boat cruise of Emily Bay and the neighbouring Slaughter Bay, which I think is a shocking name for what I hope will be as beautiful as the bay Leo and I swam in yesterday morning. Was that really only yesterday? After last night, I feel like I've known him for so much longer.

I'm wondering if Mum might still be upset about the dinner conversation, but when she and Paul join us all in the foyer, she's giggling at him like a teenage girl, and he can't wipe the smile off his face. While Leo and I were sharing confidences by the pool, our parents were probably having old-people-make-up-sex.

Ew. I shake that thought from my head as a tour van pulls up outside.

A middle-aged man comes inside to collect us, introducing himself as 'Mike, a sixth-generation islander'. He drives us down to Emily Bay, which gets more beautiful each time I see it, and his non-identical twin Trevor is waiting for us on the sand, our boat bobbing in the water a few metres behind him. Trevor is very good-looking for someone probably twice my age – he's got a fit body, a lovely mop of curly brown hair and a smile that lights up his eyes. My heart leaps when I notice he's not wearing a wedding ring. Not because I'm looking for an island fling with an older man, but because if he's single, maybe he's the person Leo and I can enlist to crack onto Mum.

We'd failed dismally in making more concrete plans last night – distracted by conversation that kept going off track – but this was one of the suggestions we thought might have merit from our google. The question is, how can we make it happen? Perhaps we could pay Trevor?

After all, everyone has a price, and Leo can probably afford it. As we climb into the glass-bottomed boat, once again Leo and

I try to separate Mum and Paul, but they're still clasping hands like it would kill them to let go, so he finds a seat between TJ and Kayla, and I end up on the other side of Kayla, next to Way, who is of course sitting beside Benji. It takes both River and Scarlett to try to control Miller, who has decided she doesn't want to be trapped in the sling but would rather crawl around the boat, checking everything out, as we push off into the water. Despite her screaming when they won't let her climb atop the glass, they never lose their cool.

Did I mention Juliet made excuses not to come? When she'd announced this morning that she had a heavy workload and swollen feet, I'd considered telling everyone that I also had to stay back and work on my book, but I didn't think it would be fair leaving Leo to play Anti-Cupid on his own.

Kayla is the first to spot a fish. 'Look, Fred!' she shrieks, pointing through the glass at a stripy yellow and black fish, which Mike tells us is a yellow-banded wirrah.

'That's pretty cool,' I say, 'and look at that one next to it. Looks a bit grumpy.'

Mike chuckles. 'That's a Norfolk Chromis – otherwise known as a kissing fish.'

'Ew.' TJ looks horrified.

Perhaps she has a phobia of kissing, I think, amusing myself. 'Nothing wrong with kissing,' Scarlett says, turning to River and planting a big one on him that makes Kayla giggle and TJ screw her face up even more.

'Why are they called that?' Mum asks.

Trevor calls over his shoulder from where he's steering the boat, 'If you keep looking, you'll no doubt see more of them, and you'll often find pairs courting. They do this dance and often press their mouths together as if they're kissing.'

'I want to see fish kiss,' Kayla says, peering even more earnestly towards the glass.

I find myself smiling at her enthusiasm as we continue further out. In addition to the fish chat, our tour guides tell us about the historical significance of the area, most notably that it was where the *HMS Sirius* shipwrecked in 1790.

'Is that why it's called Slaughter Bay?' I ask.

Mike shakes his head. 'It was christened after an Old English word meaning slow-moving water, which makes it the perfect place for snorkelling.'

'Hey, I know a good joke about snorkelling,' Paul announces. We all look to him. 'What's a scuba diver's favourite game?' He pauses a moment, then says, 'Squid and seek.'

TJ rolls her eyes – 'That's not funny, Grandpa' – but I find myself giggling and Paul notices.

He grins at me. 'Fred thought it was. What do you think of this one? What did the ocean say to the scuba diver?'

'I don't know,' I say.

'You've got a lot of depth.' He slaps his thigh and Mum shakes her head.

'Don't quit your day job, honey.'

'You tell him,' Leo says. 'His dad jokes have always been the worst.'

Paul points at him. 'All right, son. Let's see if you can do any better.'

Leo thinks a moment. 'What do you call a fish with a degree in philosophy'

'A deep thinker,' I reply immediately.

Leo tries to scowl but his smile betrays him. 'You must have heard that one before.'

I wink. 'Or maybe I can just read your mind.'

We stay out on the bay for an hour, sharing terrible jokes and taking photos of fish and pretty coral. You might be forgiven for thinking we are a normal, happy family who have known each other our whole lives. I'm usually immune to or at least suspicious of charm, but I have to admit to laughing at a few of Paul's attempts to tease me and I'm even warming to the kids, or at least Miller and Kayla, who are both rather adorable. But it's probably our blissful surroundings and my lack of sleep warping my judgement, and I tell myself to get a grip.

Lunch is in someone's actual house on the far side of the island. As soon as we arrive, we're ushered into a large country-style kitchen with stunning views of Norfolk Pines, cliffs and the ocean in the background, and gather round to watch our hosts demonstrate how to cook some traditional dishes that have been handed down from their Tahitian ancestors. As Raquel mentioned on our tour yesterday, much of the food we eat was grown here on the island.

Over our meal, River and Scarlett talk about their own small-holding where they grow most of their food as well, and although she does take more photos than a teenager for her social media, I've got to admit they sound like they genuinely enjoy and believe in their lifestyle.

'How did you guys meet?' I ask.

'Do you want to tell the story or should I?' Scarlett asks River. 'You do it.'

He smiles at her. 'You're so much better at it.'

She gives him a quick kiss before she begins. 'We actually met while I was backpacking around Australia in my early twenties and we both got work on a mango farm in the Northern Territory.'

'I was so in awe of her,' River chimes in, pushing his dreadlocks out of his face. 'Travelling alone and working with a baby strapped to her chest in a sling.'

Scarlett raises her eyebrows at River. 'I thought I was telling this story.'

'Sorry,' he says sheepishly. 'Go on.'

I just assumed all Scarlett's kids were River's, but I learn that Scarlett became pregnant to some guy she spent one night with at the Green Man festival. Although she tracked him down, he didn't want anything to do with the baby.

'People told me having a baby would ruin my life. That'd I'd be tired and tied down and not able to live the adventures I'd always dreamed of, so I decided to prove them wrong. When Tally was a couple of months old, we set off to Australia together. Because Dad was born here and I'm half Aussie, I always wanted to spend more time here.'

'We thought she was insane, jetting off to the other side of the world all alone,' Paul says, digging into his plate of fish salad, which is to die for.

Scarlett beams. 'Best thing I ever did. If I didn't take the risk, I'd never have met River and had the rest of our beautiful family.' She glances down at the other end of the table, where TJ and Kayla are miraculously busy with pencils and paper gifted by our hosts.

'You don't miss England and your family?' I ask.

She shakes her head – 'I hate the cold' – and visibly shivers. 'I could never live in the UK full time again, but we spend our summers there, and Mum and Dad have always visited lots.'

I refrain from asking who looks after their goats and chickens and veggies when they're not there, figuring they probably just pay someone. Money is clearly not an issue for anyone in this family.

'We don't see Juliet and Leo as much as I'd like,' she adds, 'but we FaceTime a lot. Kayla's Sunday night video call with Uncle Leo is her favourite time of the week.'

'Mine too,' Leo says, before shoving a forkful of corn pilhi into his mouth.

I try my own. It tastes a lot better than it looks.

'How did Juliet and Henry meet?' Benji asks.

Leo and Scarlett exchange an amused look.

'They were both doing different degrees at different universities,' Scarlett explains. 'Him medicine at Cambridge, her a double degree in business and marketing at Oxford, but they were both in the debate clubs.'

'It was not love at first sight,' Leo adds with a chuckle.

Scarlett shakes her head. 'They faced off in a massive tournament. She thought he was a know-it-all and he thought she was stuck-up. It was only later in the pub that they got talking and they haven't stopped since.'

'Who won the debate?' Way asks. Surprise, surprise, he was also into debating.

Leo snorts. 'Have you met my sister? She'd never marry someone she couldn't win an argument with, but . . . it was close.'

'Is everyone ready for dessert?' our host asks once the main course plates are cleared up. 'We're serving local green banana fritters today.'

'What kind of question is that?' Leo replies. 'I'm always ready for dessert.'

Yet, he still has a sixpack most guys only ever dream of.

I'm not generally a big fan of bananas – far too healthy – but maybe I've been missing out, because these are delicious.

'Good, aren't they?' Leo says through a mouthful as I moan my approval.

As I nod, I notice there's some icing sugar on his face. 'You've got a bit on your chin,' I say and without thinking, reach up and wipe it off with my thumb.

'Thanks, Winifred.' His voice is husky as he looks into my eyes.

My finger tingles where it touched his skin and my stomach flips.

'Geez, you're game, Leo,' Way exclaims. 'No one calls Fred "Winifred" and gets away with it. I'd watch your back if I were you.'

'Yeah, watch your back, Leopold,' I warn, injecting a playfulness into my voice I don't feel.

Everyone laughs.

'I think it's a lovely name,' Paul says, popping a piece of fritter into his mouth as Mum looks at me with suspicion.

It's mid-afternoon by the time we arrive back at the resort and miraculously we have a few free hours before dinner at some steakhouse down the road. Scarlett, River, and the kids disappear to put Miller down for a nap, and thanks to my full stomach and late night, I want one as well, but I force myself to crack a Diet Coke and open my laptop instead. After a quick check of the apps – nothing of interest there – and more messages from Bee wanting to know whether my fancy almost-relatives all wear designer clothes and speak like they have a silver spoon in their mouths, I get to work.

Or at least I try to. I've barely typed two sentences before a whimpering sound begins next door. Is it a baby crying? But no, Benij and Way are on that side of me. The whimpering grows louder and I hear a shriek. Maybe an animal has snuck into their room – after all, this island does seem to have its fair share of them – and one of them is trying to shoo it out, but then I hear Way's voice loud and clear – 'God, Benji. Mmm, yes, baby. Yes. Yes. Yes!'

My hands rush to cover my ears. Was that a *spank*?! *Oh, dear God.* The only thing worse than listening to my brother and Benji enjoy an afternoon delight would be overhearing Mum and Paul going for it like mammals on the Discovery Channel.

What did I do to deserve this?

I never hear them at home, but then again, I'm often out at night or engaging in similar activities of my own with my latest Tinder date. No such luck here.

There's only one thing for it. I have to get out of here. Quickly changing into my bathers and throwing on a summer cover-all, I take my Diet Coke and laptop out to the pool area, delighted to find I'm the only one here. Bliss. Laptop on my knee, I settle into one of the sun loungers, determined to wipe what I just heard from my memory and lose myself in *21 Rules for Not Catching Feelings*. But every word I punch out feels like drawing blood from a stone, and the last thing I recall is a sick feeling at the thought of having to pay back my advance – long gone – if I can't finish this or, worse, the publisher doesn't like it. I'm not sure I've ever felt such fear in my life.

I jolt awake who knows how long later to the pool gate clinking. TJ and Kayla are coming towards me, both wearing bathers and carrying the resort's blue-and-white striped pool towels. It's the first time I've seen TJ without her book and Kayla without her tail. So much for peace and quiet.

'Fred,' Kayla shouts, running over and dropping onto the lounger next to mine. I'm not sure anyone has ever been so happy to see me, except maybe Bee's adorable dog.

Still, I've had my fill of kid-time on our tour this morning, and I really do need to write. I'm about to make excuses and retreat to the bar to work when Leo appears at the gate.

My mouth goes dry. He's wearing nothing but dark sunnies and a pair of simple, navy blue boardshorts. *Holy moly!* How can I not admire his broad chest, his tattoos or the curve of his butt in those slightly too-tight shorts?

'You two were supposed to wait for me,' he says, reprimanding them as he steps through and then sees me. 'Well, fancy meeting you here, Winifred.'

'Leopold,' I manage, telling myself to get a grip. It's not like I haven't seen a hot guy before. I think maybe it's his accent that gives him that extra edge and also the fact that he's off limits because he's Mum's future stepson. It could be a case of wanting-what-I-*shouldn't*-have.

Taking a hair band off his wrist, he nods towards my laptop as he scoops his hair into a bun. 'Doing a bit of writing?'

'Trying to,' I reply as TJ launches herself into the pool without a word to me.

'Are you coming swimming, Fred?' Kayla asks, pulling yellow goggles down over her eyes.

I shake my head. 'I just came here to work.'

'Oh.' Her disappointment is written all over her face and I'm about to tell her I will, when Leo chuckles and ruffles her hair. 'I thought you wanted to swim with *me*. Come on, let's leave Fred in peace to write.'

Kayla slides off the lounger and allows Leo to take her hand as well. They head to the shallow end of the pool. TJ is in the deep end doing some kind of synchronised swimming, only without the other swimmers.

'Remember Mummy said you have to stay close to me,' Leo tells Kayla as she gets in.

She nods earnestly, then says, 'Can you give me a piggyback?'

'Sure.' He drops into the water beside her, then scoops her onto his back.

I watch him charge down the pool towards TJ, ducking under the water every now and then. Kayla's head stays just above but she shrieks every time he does it as if terrified, before begging him to 'Do it again!'

Which he does. Over and over and over.

He's so sweet and patient with her and I can't help watching. I'm pretty sure I don't even want kids, but watching Leo with his nieces has my ovaries quivering. Or maybe it's just the way his arm muscles bunch and drip with water every time he emerges. When he catches me gawking, I make a concerted effort to return my attentions to my laptop, but have you ever tried to work with two kids and a hot guy larking around in water three feet away?

I'm trying to take a surreptitious photo for Bee – who, even though totally crazy about Sully, can still appreciate analmost-perfect specimen – when Kayla calls, 'Fred, puh-leese will you come in and play with us?'

'Yeah, Winifred, come in and play with us. Doesn't look like you're getting much work done anyway,' Leo says, swimming over to the side of the pool and flicking water at me, only narrowly missing my laptop.

It's impossible not to note the wicked gleam in his eyes.

I'm so confused. Last night I could swear he'd friend-zoned me, but if he's not flirting with me now, I've lost all ability to read the opposite sex. I should resist – for all the reasons I've told myself before – but instead, I close my laptop and shove it back in my bag for safekeeping. 'You're gonna regret that,' I say, ripping my sun cover up over my head as I stand.

When I look up, I see Leo's gaze trained on me. In my simple black bikini, I know I look good and it's obvious he thinks so too.

'Really?' He looks up from my chest to my eyes. 'What are you going to do?'

In reply, I jump into the pool right next to him, and the moment I emerge through the surface, I use the force of both my hands to splash him as hard as I can.

TJ laughs and Kayla's brown eyes widen as if she can't believe what I've done.

Leo wipes the water from his eyes and grins. 'This means war.' The kids squeal as he launches at me, then dives down and grabs my legs, hauling me over his shoulder like I'm a very naughty girl. He effortlessly walks me up the steps.

'Where are you taking me?' Now I'm shrieking like the kids, but it's hard not to make a fuss when his warm hands are on my bare thighs and my nose mere millimetres from his butt. If there weren't little people around, I'd be very tempted to bite it. That'd teach him.

'Stop squealing,' Leo orders, using what I can only imagine is his stern teacher voice as he strides around the pool. It's incredibly sexy.

'You'd better not drop me!'

'That's exactly what I intend to do.' He stops at the edge of the deep end.

My heart is thumping against his back, and I can't tell if it's because I'm aroused or terrified – maybe a bit of both.

But I can't let two young, impressionable girls watch me go down without a fight.

As Leo tries to get me into a position so he can hurl me into the water, I tighten my arms around his waist and kick my legs against his rock-solid chest.

'Settle petal,' he says as he loses his balance.

We plunge into the pool together, both of us letting go and sinking beneath the surface, exploding seconds later, laughing. The water feels much icier than it did moments ago, and I can only imagine that's because being so close to Leo has skyrocketed my body temperature.

'Shall we call that even?' he asks, grinning as he thrusts his hand out to me.

I pretend to contemplate this a second, before sliding my wet hand into his. 'Okay, deal.' Despite the water, his grip is firm and I'm sure I'm not imagining the spark between us.

After that, the four of us play a terrible game of Piggy in the Middle with a blow-up beach ball. Terrible because the ball is so light the wind keeps catching it and carrying it out of the pool, and also because Kayla can only stand in the shallow end. We give up and play Sharks and Minnows – Leo and I taking turns being the shark.

I can't believe I'm actually enjoying myself, and this is better exercise than the gym or kickboxing, which Bee has become obsessed with recently.

I'm catching my breath, sitting on the steps in the shallow end while Leo charges around the pool, pretending to eat his giggly nieces, when Kayla dog paddles over to me.

'Can I touch your head,' she asks, already reaching up to do so.

'Sure,' I say, thankful she's doing so now when she's disinfected with chlorine rather than earlier when her fingers were covered in lavender gelato.

'Ooh.' She grins as she rubs her hands all over my scalp. 'Feels like a cat. I wanna shave my hair too.'

I stifle a smile. As liberal in their parenting as Scarlett and River are, I'm not sure they'll go for this.

'Can I touch too?' TJ asks, arriving beside us.

Over the last half-hour in the pool, I've mellowed towards her, and nod.

Hands on my head feel tickly but innocuous, until Leo barks,

'My go' and the girls' fingers drop as they make way for him. 'May I?' he asks.

'Why not?' But I can't help sucking in a breath as he places both hands on my head and trails them slowly back and forth over my skin.

'That does feel good,' he admits.

Goosebumps spread from my neck to my arms as our eyes meet. Heat floods through me. Nothing has ever felt so sensuous. If his nieces weren't right beside us, I'd be hard pushed not to jump him.

Leo suddenly clears his throat, breaking my gaze as he glances at his wrist – even though he's not wearing a watch. 'Time to get out, girls. We need to get ready for dinner.'

Kayla starts to cry that she doesn't want to sit through another boring dinner, she wants to stay in the pool all day and all night and forever, but I leave Leo to deal with that. I need to get out of the water asap and into a cold shower.

The last thing I need is for my head to be fuzzy with lustful thoughts of Leo when we both need to be on our game, trying to drive a wedge between our parents at dinner tonight.

We only have three more days to succeed.

12

ONLY ONE THING FOR IT

After dinner at Bounty Bar & Grill, where the best thing about the evening is my burger and my coconut cocktail, a board game night back at the resort is on the agenda. Honestly, I can't think of anything worse. Taking a leaf out of Juliet's book, I make the excuse that I need to write. To be fair, it's not really an excuse.

The usual stack of messages from Bee is waiting on my phone when I escape back to my room. The first few are photos of Aunty, the next couple general chitchat and then she gets serious.

Bridget Jones: *Hey, I've been thinking . . . Maybe Leo will be your PRINCE book boyfriend. #royalty xx*

Me: *I thought you said he was going to be my stepbrother one????* Bridget Jones: *Yeah, but that was before you told me you guys were going to stop the wedding, which I still think is very bad idea btw. You really shouldn't mess in matters of other people's hearts. xx*

I barely register her disapproval; all I can think about is the fact that if Leo and I do succeed, he will no longer be off limits. Could an island fling with a spunky Englishman be on the agenda after all? My heart – or rather an organ much, much lower – zings at the thought.

And then I remember dinner – our efforts to try and paint Mum as a gold digger at dinner this evening were less than successful. Maybe Paul doesn't even care, and he just wants another woman to cook his dinners and iron his undies. *Sigh.*

Me: *That's not going so well anyway. Paul's clearly one of those men who needs a wife to feel good about themselves. Mum's hardly going to be the one to end it, so I may be donning my red dress and pink heels on Friday after all. Anyway, I need to work.*

Thinking about not having sex with Leo is too depressing.

Bridget Jones: *How's the book going? x*

Me: *Don't ask.*

We've been here almost three days and I've barely even opened the document, so instead of curling up in bed with a book or Netflix, which is what I really want to do, I fill a glass of water and sit down at the little desk in my room with my laptop.

It's time to tackle Chapter Three.

Rule Three: Chemistry Matters, Connection Must Not

You know that spark when you walk into a room, look someone in the eye and BAM! You feel it in your nether regions. Or when you're waiting in line for a drink and someone accidentally brushes past you, barely touching the naked skin on your arm and yet you feel

As I type, my mind drifts to Leo's fingers on my head mere hours ago. The heat in his eyes when his gaze roved over my bikini-clad body, and the spark I know we both felt whenever we touched – accidentally or on purpose.

No, Fred. Stop!

Fantasising about what Leo might look like naked will not

get my book finished. I try to shake him out of my head and focus.

Two more sentences are written, but I immediately need to read them back because I have no idea what I've just typed. What is wrong with me? I realise then that apart from Way and Xavier, I very rarely hang out with men who aren't potential bed buddies, and I've been spending a lot of time with Leo. It's just instinct to think of him in terms of a sexual partner.

There's only one thing for it.

I open Tinder. Maybe I can find someone local to take my mind off Leo. Do people even use dating apps on here? Might get awkward when half of them seem to be related.

Nope, it's hopeless. Literally no one available within a 1400-kilometre radius to swipe right on. I find myself scrolling The UkePros Insta page instead, and also Leo's personal one, which does nothing to ease my lustful thoughts.

I toss my phone on the bed and let out a frustrated scream. If Tinder won't work, I'll just have to try the old-fashioned way.

After fixing my make-up and hooking sparkly, dangly earrings into my lobes, I slip my shoes back on and walk the short distance to the Castaway Bar next door. Where better to find men than at a brewery?

But the place is deserted – no music, no people vaping outside, the only light coming from the moon and a couple of security lamps. What kind of bar isn't open past 7 p.m.?

'Only place you can get a drink tonight is over there.'

I almost jump out of my skin and look up to see a nearby shadow pointing back towards the road.

'At the RSL Club,' he adds cheerfully. 'But you should definitely join us for Happy Hour tomorrow.'

I traipse across the road – no traffic visible in either direction – and into the red and white fibro building with the words *RSL*

Sub Branch Memorial Club stamped across the entrance. Inside is dim – not because of mood lighting, but because the lights are sparse – the carpet looks like the sunset threw up on it, and mildew mixed with fried oil permeates the air. I screw up my nose as I take in the rest of the scene. There's an on old-fashioned radio behind the very old-fashioned bar playing talk-back, which the bartender and two blokes sitting at it appear to be listening to. An elderly couple are eating a late dinner at one of the tables.

Aside from that, the place is empty. Neither man at the bar looks like anyone I'd want to get up close and personal with, and although the bartender is quite cute, it's hard to miss the thick gold band glinting on his ring finger.

I might not be able to relieve my pent-up sexual energy, but at least I'll have the next best thing: booze.

I weave through the tables, past the couple deep in conversation. 'Evening,' the bartender says, polishing a pint glass. 'If you're wanting dinner, I'm sorry but the kitchen just closed.'

'No, I was looking for . . .' I can hardly tell him that I'm looking for someone who can take my mind off my hot future stepbrother. 'Just a drink.'

He nods. 'What's your poison?'

'Um . . .' I glance at the rows of hard liquor behind him but decide on a house white.

'Coming right up.' He's barely opened the bottle when he looks towards the entrance and acknowledges that someone else has arrived. Instinctively, I turn to look.

No freaking way.

So much for trying to escape my thoughts of Leo; he's striding towards me right now. And of course, he's looking like something I could gobble right up in jeans and a simple black shirt.

'What are you doing here?' I ask. 'I thought you were playing Scrabble or something.'

'Uno, actually, but I saw you sneak past and decided to follow. Had to wait till the game was over. Luckily there aren't too many places to disappear around here. You don't mind some company, do you?' He pauses. 'Unless you're meeting someone?'

I scoff as heat flares in my cheeks. 'Who am I going to meet here?'

Leo smiles. 'Excellent. Thought it could be a good time to discuss how our plan is progressing and whether we need to up the ante.'

I think we both know we need to up the ante.

'What can I get for you?' the bartender asks Leo as he places my wine in front of me.

'Just a pint of whatever you have on tap, thanks.'

We take our drinks over to a table so far from the bar and other patrons that we're practically in the dark.

'Shouldn't you be working on your book?' Leo asks, wiping a little beer froth off his upper lip.

I glare at him. 'What are you, my publisher?'

He holds up his hands as if I might shoot him. 'Sorry, just asking.'

I gulp down some wine. 'It's not going so well, if you must know.'

'How so?'

I take another sip and then tell him about how I fell into my book deal and now, despite my looming deadline and constant emails from my editor telling me how excited everyone at the publisher is about the book, and the major marketing and publicity campaign they're planning, I'm struggling to get past the first few chapters.

'Anything I can help with?' he asks.

I laugh as I shake my head. With his soppy belief in The One and Happy Ever Afters, he's not exactly my target audience. 'Anyway, I don't want to talk about my book right now.' I angle my glass towards him. 'Do you actually know any of the royal family?'

He sighs as if this question bores him. 'A few.'

I narrow my eyes. 'Who? *How* few?'

'I wouldn't say I *know* know them, but I've met some a couple of times; at garden parties, polo matches, you know . . . that kind of thing.'

'No, I do not know!' I shriek, almost spilling my wine. 'There aren't any garden parties, never mind polo matches in my life. Have you met Will and Kate? Did you go to their wedding?'

I'm nowhere near a royalist – I believe Australia should become a republic – but *come on!* Who doesn't want to know someone in the inner circle of the world's most famous family?

'No,' he says with a dry chuckle. 'But Juliet's husband is good friends with Pippa Middleton's husband, and Mum used to be on a charity board with Sophie.'

'Sophie who?'

'The Duchess of Edinburgh – Prince Edward's wife.'

'Oh my God. I think I need a lie-down.'

'It's no big deal,' Leo says, an edge to his voice. 'They're just people.'

'You seem a bit touchy,' I tease.

'I just think there's more important things than fame and money. More to a person than who they're related to or know.'

His words chastise me. 'You're right. There absolutely is. I'm sorry.'

'You've nothing to apologise for,' he says with a shake of his head.

But still things feel tense until Leo's scowl morphs into a smile at something over my shoulder. I turn to see the elderly couple walking towards the exit. They're holding hands and he's carrying her bag.

'Isn't that sweet?' he says. 'Still in love after so many years of marriage.'

I roll my eyes. 'Who says they're married? Maybe they both have spouses off island and came here to indulge in their illicit affair.'

'Yeah, you're right.' He shakes his head. 'That's much more likely than them having been happily married for decades and still enjoying spending time with each other.'

'If you believe in love so much, why are *you* single?' I ask.

'Who says I am?'

Stupid disappointment gushes to my heart – no, not my *heart*. My loins. Maybe I *was* imagining his flirting this arvo. Maybe it was wishful thinking.

I recover to ask, 'What's her name?'

'Zoey. It's early days. We've only been on a couple of dates. I haven't even told my family about her. I was in what I thought was a pretty serious relationship before her, and then Mum got sick and well . . .' He sighs. 'Spending time with her was more important than dating.'

Pretty serious? I definitely need to know more. 'I'm getting us another drink,' I say, standing and crossing over to the bar before Leo can object.

After a quick conversation with the bartender, who wants to know if we're newlyweds, I return with a pint of beer and another glass of cheap chardy. 'What was your ex's name? And what do you mean you *thought* you were in a serious relationship?'

As his fingers wrap round the glass, he raises his eyebrows as if asking, are we really doing this?

I look him right in the eye and nod slowly – *yes, we are. What else is there to do on a quiet Monday night on an island where most people seem to go to bed at sunset?* – then lift my glass to my lips.

He takes a *looong* sip, then sighs. 'Allegra.'

'Ooh, she sounds posh!'

'She wanted to be.'

Leo tells me that Allegra was in publicity for a local historic hotel, and they met at a party of mutual friends, the girlfriend of one of Leo's bandmates. He fell for her bubbly personality, and they had loads in common – they both loved the same kinds of music and hiking in the great outdoors. After a year together, he decided he was going to propose. On New Year's Eve in front of all their family and friends.

Oh God. My gut churns as I predict where this is going. 'Please don't tell me she said no in front of an audience?'

'I never got the chance to ask her. Turns out she was much more interested in my tenuous links to nobility than she was in me. She'd heard I was the nephew of a duke and thought that meant a lot more than it does. When she met an actual duke at a fiftieth wedding anniversary party that I took her to a few weeks before Christmas, she dumped me like a hot potato. They got married a couple of months ago.'

'Bitch!' I'm enraged on his behalf. Rich or not, surely this duke couldn't be more appealing than Leo. 'Although it sounds like she did you a favour. Who wants someone so money and status-hungry in their life?'

'Yeah, better I found out what she was like before we were engaged.' He tries to keep his voice nonchalant, but I can see the pain in his eyes and realise this is why he was so prickly when I asked him if he knew Wills and Kate.

'Surely the success of your band impressed her?'

He shrugs. 'Maybe it would have, but when Allegra and I were together, the boys and I had only just started jamming. I'm glad she showed her true colours before then, because I want a partner who is in it for the right reasons.'

I shake my head. 'How can you still believe in love after she treated you like that?'

'She obviously wasn't the right woman for me, but I have faith that the right one *is* out there and that we can have a relationship just as wonderful as Mum and Dad's.'

The optimism people have about love and relationships never ceases to surprise me. It's like an aspiring tennis player losing game after game at amateur level, yet still believing they can win Wimbledon. 'And do you think this Elly might be the one?'

'*Zoey*,' he corrects, his smirk inferring he knows I knew that. 'And yeah, I think there's potential there.'

'What's she like in bed?'

Leo almost chokes on a mouthful of beer. 'Are you always this straightforward?'

'I'm not really into small, meaningless conversation. Anyway, don't you and your mates discuss your conquests over a Scotch after polocrosse?'

'Not those kinds of conquests.' He laughs, then admits, 'We haven't actually slept together yet.'

'What? How many dates have you been on?'

He thinks a moment as if counting. 'Three. No four.'

I'm rendered speechless. My jaw literally drops. If I was this Zoey woman, I'd have been climbing Leo before we'd ordered our main course!

'Tell me this,' he says. 'How many people have you had sex with?'

His question shocks me. 'Now who's being straightforward?'

'More than ten?' Leo says, like this is a crazy amount.

I turn the question back on him instead. 'How many people have *you* slept with?'

'Three.'

'Three?! Oh my God. You're practically a monk!'

He blushes. 'No, I'm not. I just prefer to sleep with people I have strong feelings for, rather than for the sake of it. Isn't sex with someone you care about better than sex with someone who means nothing?'

Uh, *no*, because sex with feelings gives power to the other person. 'I take it you're not big on dating then. Do you just wait for Fate to throw Miss Right in your path?'

He chuckles. 'No, I date. I had a bit of a hiatus after Mum died because I wasn't feeling it. But I've seen a couple of people in the last couple of months.'

'And you haven't slept with any of them?'

'No. To me, having sex means I can see a future with someone. At least the possibility. It's special, and I don't want to do it with just anyone.'

Wow. He's like a mythical creature – I didn't know there were men like him out there. Most I meet would happily get their rocks off with just about anyone.

'Don't *you* ever yearn for anything deeper?' he asks. 'Humans aren't animals – we all need connection and friendship, emotional intimacy as well as physical.'

'Who says we have to get all that from the same person?' I counter. 'I have good friends – I'm emotionally intimate with them.'

He lifts his glass to his mouth, contemplating this, then shrugs. 'Fair enough. I guess we'll just have to agree to disagree.'

'Maybe,' I say, feeling smug. 'So . . . if Allegra was number three, tell me about one and two.'

A slow smile crosses his face before he shakes his head. 'Nope. Enough about my love life. I want to hear about yours.'

I throw back my head and laugh. 'I told you I don't have a love life!'

'Sex life, then?'

'I'm not telling you about that!' I'm normally totally confident talking about sex – mine or other people's – but there's something about Leo that makes me reticent. Maybe it's because we might soon be related, or maybe it's because thinking about sex so close to Leo has my insides burning up.

He smirks – 'Fine' – then takes another sip. 'Back to the matter at hand. You never told me about husband number five.'

His mention of Bernie is almost as good as an ice bath. I take a deep breath and then another much-needed sip of my wine. 'Bernie was a regular at the café Mum was working at back then. Their daily hello-how-are-you's when he ordered his coffee got longer over the weeks, and eventually he asked her out. Six months later he asked her to marry him, and three months after that, they tied the knot. I have to admit, he seemed like a genuine kind of person, like he cared about Mum. He was quite religious, heavily involved in his church, but I figured that wasn't necessarily a bad thing. Christian people don't like divorce, right?'

Leo chuckles.

'Well, that didn't seem to stop Bernie. A month – yes, literally a month – after the wedding, he left her. Said she didn't turn out to be the person he thought she was. He told her she had one week to get out of his house and then he went to stay with his sister.'

'Fucker,' Leo mutters.

I nod. 'Mum had given up her rental property, so she moved in with me and Way, promising it was only going to be short-term while she got back on her feet, but . . . She almost didn't get back on her feet.'

'What do you mean?'

'She fell into a deep depression – stopped bathing, barely ate anything, and spent all day in bed. I know it sounds cliched, but she became a shell of herself. You'd think she'd have coped okay because this wasn't her first rodeo, but something about Bernie's rejection broke her.'

When Jeff left and when Colin went back to his wife, she'd been upset, of course, and angry, but she never took more than a day off work before picking herself up and getting on with life. Or rather, finding the next guy. I still think I was more heartbroken about the end of her marriage to Jeff than she was.

'Why do you think that was? Did she love Bernie more than the others?'

I can't help screwing up my nose, but then I shrug. 'I don't know. She was sad when my grandma – her mum – died, but this was like nothing I've ever seen before. I tried to help her. I bought ice cream, offered to watch movies with her, reminded her to brush her teeth, sometimes I even had to help her shower. She was a freaking mess.'

Crying is such a rarity for me that I don't even realise I'm doing it until Leo reaches into his pocket and pulls out a handkerchief. Talking about that time has brought it all back.

'What's that?' I ask as he offers it to me.

He blinks. 'It's a handkerchief.'

'I know what it is, but I didn't know anyone used them any more. Well, aside from grandpas and heroines in Victorian romance novels,' I say, trying to lighten the mood I've dragged right down.

'They're better than tissues for the environment. We're so wasteful these days.'

I'm still staring at it like it's a tarantula or something equally terrifying – why anything needs eight legs is beyond me – when Leo smirks. 'It won't bite.'

Fine. I take it and dab it at my eyes. It's so soft, and intermingled with the aroma of clean washing powder is the delicious scent of him. I've never been good distinguishing different flowers and spices, so I can't pinpoint what it is he smells like, but it's good. Very good. 'Thanks.'

He smiles. 'You're welcome.'

I sniff. 'I was terrified that one day Way and I would get home from work and find out she'd hurt herself. Eventually, I convinced him that her behaviour wasn't normal, and we managed to get her to see a doctor. The doctor put her on antidepressants and referred us to a counsellor. Way paid for everything, but he was too busy with work to be much of a practical help, so taking her to appointments, making sure she took her medication, all fell to me. I had to take heaps of time off work, but it was worth it, because eventually, she came out the other side.'

Leo nods as I add, 'It took almost a year before Mum was well enough to get a job and eventually find her own place again, but I made her swear off men because I never want her to go through that again. And, until your dad, I think she's kept to that.'

'Geez. Sounds like you both went through a really traumatic time. I know it's not the same thing, but watching my mum go through chemo and then still not get better was awful. So I know how it can feel to feel helpless around someone you love. She's lucky you care so much.'

My eyes swim again at this acknowledgement. 'Thanks,' I whisper.

'But no wonder you have doubts about the wedding.'

I down the rest of my drink. 'Just a few.'

'I wonder if Dad knows all this?'

'I get the feeling he does,' I reply. 'When we were on the island tour, he said something to me that indicated he did.'

He's quiet for a moment, staring into his half-empty beer. 'Dad's a good guy . . . he'd never hurt Tracy. Not intentionally . . .'

The unsaid 'but' lingers in the air between us. *But* he's not thinking straight right now because he hasn't had enough time to grieve his first wife. And Paul's intentions won't stop her heart being broken if he changes his mind.

'That's why we have to stop them getting married,' I say.

Leo rubs the side of his jaw. 'But aren't you worried about what the wedding not going ahead might do to her as well?'

It takes a few seconds for his words to register.

'*Oh God.*' I feel sick. 'You're right.' Why hadn't I thought of that? Ever since hearing about her wedding, I've been worrying about what another divorce might do to my mother, but she's clearly besotted with Paul . . . She is going to be heartbroken whether he ends it before *or* after the wedding.

I sigh, cursing the day Mum ran into Paul at that bloody school reunion. 'She's damned if we do and damned if we don't.'

Leo's quiet for a moment, his brow furrowed, then he says, 'I guess we just have to make sure Tracy's the one who decides to call off the wedding. If she comes to the realisation herself that this isn't a good idea, then she'll get over it faster.'

'That makes sense.' I nod, letting myself breathe again. 'But aren't you worried about your dad getting hurt?'

He scoffs and shakes his head. 'He's just lost the love of his life – nothing can be worse than that.'

'Can I get you guys another drink?' the bartender asks as he collects our empty glasses. 'Last call.'

Leo and I blink at him as if we'd both forgotten we weren't alone.

'We should probably be getting back to the resort,' he says. I nod and push back my seat.

'You have a good night,' the bartender says.

We bid him the same and then walk out into the balmy evening air.

'I can't imagine living in a place that never gets truly cold,'

Leo says as we cross the street. 'I bet the islanders don't even need winter coats.'

The resort is once again dead when we enter through reception. Tonight, there's a woman behind the counter who smiles a greeting as we pass through. Leo walks me to my door, which is on the way to his.

We stand just outside my room in the manner of two people on a first date, each wondering if the other will make a move. This isn't a date, but I've shared more with Leo than I have with any guy and feel a bizarre urge to say something profound. Instead,

I take the hanky from where I'd shoved it in my pocket. 'I'll wash this and give it back to you.'

He shakes his head, his smile warm. 'Keep it. There's plenty more where it came from.' And then, he pulls me into a quick hug before turning and heading in the direction of his own room.

13

NO PDAS

It's impossible to sleep in on this island. That damn rooster is once again outside my bedroom window making sure the whole resort knows of his existence. I pull the covers over my head as I try to work out what day it is. Tuesday or Wednesday? Have we been here three or four days already? They've all kind of blurred together.

In some ways it feels like I've been here forever.

Rap. Rap. Rap.

That is not a rooster; that's someone banging on the door. 'Fred? Are you awake? It's Mum.'

Groaning, I climb out of bed and cross to the door to open it. 'Of course I'm awake. It's impossible to sleep with that bird cockadoodling. Do hens really find that attractive?'

She doesn't even crack a smile. 'Can I come in? I need to talk to you.'

'Sounds serious,' I say as I shut the door behind us and head back to bed.

Mum perches herself on the desk chair. Her expression is pinched. Could it be that the wedding's off? I bite my lip to tame the grin that threatens at this thought. Perhaps Leo's and my subtle – okay, sometimes less than subtle – jibing has worked and she or even Paul has seen the light. Maybe he *is* starting to question her motives? I'm mentally preparing myself not to show relief or delight but offer the sympathetic ear she'll need when she says, 'I saw you and Leo last night.'

Oh God. My stomach turns hard.

'When?' I ask, stalling as I think about what I'm going to say. Do I deny Operation Break-up or try and make her see that if Paul's son and I both think they are rushing into this, then maybe they are.

'It was late,' she says. 'I was grabbing a book from the exchange in the games room when I heard your voices coming through reception. Where were you?'

'Since when do you read?' I literally can't remember her ever picking up a book before.

'Since I went into menopause and stopped sleeping properly.' She shakes her head. 'But never mind about that. The issue here is you getting your claws into Leo.'

My claws? I can't believe what I'm hearing. The way she speaks about me overrides any relief I might feel that she hasn't cottoned onto us. 'Excuse me? What are you insinuating?'

'I didn't come down in the last shower. I know you.'

I snort – that's debatable – but she continues her tirade. 'You've been flirting with him since the moment you met.'

'We're just friends,' I exclaim, a tad defensive considering I do have the hots for him but also outraged that she'd dare to call me out about this. I doubt Paul is having this chat with Leo. It's never the *man's* fault. 'I thought you wanted me to bond with Paul's family.'

She raises an eyebrow. 'If that was all you were doing, that would be fine, but I've seen the way you look at each other. The way you call each other by your full names. *Winifred. Leopold.*'

Wow – she's more perceptive than I thought. I always

thought Mum was too consumed with her own life and feelings to notice anyone else's, but I can't help the buzz inside me at her mention of the way we look at *each other*. If only Leo had such lustful thoughts about me. But I'm not about to tell her she has nothing to worry about.

'What would it matter if something happens between me and Leo?' I say instead.

She crosses her arms and narrows her eyes. 'It would matter because it could cause disharmony in the family if you hurt him. Leo's going to be my son too, soon, and I care about his feelings. He's not like you, *Winifred*, he's not—'

'A slut?' I finish for her.

She looks horrified. 'No! I would never say that. What I was trying to say was that he has . . . He has different values, and I just think, considering you're going to be related, that maybe you should tread carefully. He's not just some guy you can discard when you're done with him.'

'I don't *discard* people. Everyone I date knows where they stand with me.'

'Okay.' She sighs. 'I'm sorry, maybe discard is the wrong word but I—'

'Anyway,' I ride right over the top of her, 'Leo's big enough and ugly enough' – okay, that bit isn't true – 'to look after himself.'

And then I storm into the bathroom and slam the door before she can say anything else.

Different values? She seemed quite proud of those values when I sold my book on proposal. I should have known that was too good to be true. A leopard doesn't change its spots, and it looks like my mother hasn't grown at all in the last few years. Although she attended all our school events, she was always distant with Way and I, never gushy over our achievements like our friends' parents. I'd thought she hadn't mentioned my writing at the dinner table our first night here because of the 'little ears', but now I can see the truth. She's ashamed of me. Embarrassed by me. Being married five times is fine, apparently, but having a daughter who sleeps around is not.

Well, she might act all high and mighty, but we're not so different – I just don't marry every guy I hook up with, which is far less messy in the end. If this isn't an indication that the patriarchy has screwed the world, I don't know what is.

Thankfully, she has the good sense to be gone by the time I emerge from the shower, but her presence still lingers in the air like a pungent smell. I wish my colleague Persephone was here so she could cleanse the room of Mum's bad juju for me or something, but in lieu of that, I open a window and welcome in the fresh sea breeze. I have a good mind to skive off the day's activities – a walk in the botanic gardens and mini golf – but she'd probably be happy about that.

And the last thing I want to do is make her think she can dictate how I live my life.

I expected the Norfolk Botanical Garden to be a manicured park with wide open spaces of grass, the occasional statue of local heroes and colourful beds of flowers, but I guess this is one in the purest sense. Don't get me wrong, it's got a magical quality with its lush canopy of tropical plants, but the main purpose of this garden is to showcase the native flora and fauna. As the rest of our party – including Juliet, who apparently likes a good game of mini golf so is hanging with us today – walks ahead on the wooden decking paths that weave through the bushland, I dawdle, still in a mood from Mum's enlightening chat. I'm pretending to read a sign about the Norfolk pines when Leo treks back to talk to me.

'You okay?' he asks. 'You seem a bit quiet.'

You gotta love a man who's perceptive of a woman's mood. 'I got warned off you this morning,' I tell him.

'What do you mean?'

'Mum came to visit me first thing. Apparently she saw us coming back to the resort last night and sensed we were up to no good. At first, I thought she must suspect our plan.'

He grimaces. 'Oh no.'

'But she's way off the mark. She's worried I'm trying to crack onto you instead.'

'What?' He laughs, loud enough that the others pause and all turn to look at us.

'Shhh, and keep walking or I'll be in even more trouble.' As we continue, I whisper, 'She's worried I'm going to lead you off the straight and narrow, have my wicked way with you and then spit you back out again, leaving you heartbroken.'

His expression is unreadable. 'I can look after myself.'

'That's what I told her. Anyway, I'm fine. Just annoyed. I'm not even sure why she wanted me here in the first place.'

'Well, if it makes you feel any better,' he says, nudging me playfully in the side, 'I'm glad you're here. The holiday wouldn't be half as fun without you.'

I can't help smiling at his words. 'Thanks. I feel exactly the same about you.'

We catch up to the others and I ignore Mum, grabbing hold of Kayla's hand instead. Her delight when we spot a black butterfly with royal-blue markings warms my heart. I'm quite surprised by the fondness I'm starting to feel towards her. Even her feline antics aren't annoying me as much any more. This makes me think of Dad's other daughters. Ava and Mia are about the same age as Kayla, but due to the fact I don't rate my father or go out of my way to spend time with him, I've never really given the girls the time of day either. Sure, I send them

Christmas and birthday cards, but I have no idea what they're like or what they're into.

For the first time in my life, I wonder if I'm missing out.

After our walk, we pile into the hire cars and drive the short distance to mini golf. As there's twelve of us we're divided into three groups of four, although it's not like Miller will play. Mum tries to split Leo and I up, but he tells her he wants to stick with me, and we volunteer to take Kayla and TJ as well. Mum and Paul play with Juliet, leaving the other couples – Scarlett and River with Miller strapped onto his chest, and Waylen and Benji – to play together.

The couples set off first, followed by my group, with Mum's bringing up the rear.

I usually don't mind mini golf, but I've never played with a five-year-old who thinks she's a cat and an eleven-year-old who I learn is a bit of a perfectionist. My Year Seven teacher used to say 'Patience is a virtue, possess it if you can. Seldom in a woman, never in a man' but Leo has the patience of a saint and the only reason I haven't totally lost mine yet is because each time he leans over to try and give his nieces tips, I get a mouth-watering view of his butt.

Someone really should give him an award for it.

Way and Co are already at hole eight and we're still stuck on hole three, TJ refusing to move on until she gets the ball in. I'm not sure how many attempts she's had at this one – I lost count at fifteen. At this rate we'll be here all bloody day.

When it's finally my turn to have a shot, I'm so bored that I rush it, and the ball ends up in a tiny bunker. Annoyed, I storm across the fake grass.

'Hold on a sec,' Leo says as I bend down to move my ball to just outside the bunker, uncaring that I'll use another shot.

He takes the ball from my hand, a thrill shooting through me as our fingers brush. I might know he's off limits, but my hormones don't appear to have got the memo yet.

'Here, let me help.' His voice is warm and soft as he puts the ball on the ground, then, standing right behind me, wraps his arms around me and places his hands atop mine at the top of the club. It's a classic seduction move.

'What are you doing?' I hiss. This full-body contact is torture. 'I'm not that terrible.'

'Just play along,' he whispers, his breath hot in my ear. 'I'll explain as soon as I can.'

Thankfully, Leo directs the ball into the hole in one shot because my mind is someplace else entirely. Is that what I think it is, pressing into my back? When he steps away to take his own turn, my cheeks are burning, and I resist the urge to glance at his nether regions to check.

He gets a hole-in-one – thank God someone in our group has sporting talent – and we move on to hole number four. While TJ begins her turn, which we know will take at least two or three minutes, Leo takes my hand and leads me to wait near the end of the hole.

Again, my stomach almost explodes at his touch. I can't remember the last time I held hands with a guy – probably Kyle in high school. Not holding hands isn't an official rule, but I guess it comes under *Rule #10: No PDAs*. I'll be sure to spend some time on it when I get to that chapter, because this feels almost as intimate as getting naked with someone.

'I was thinking,' he begins, still not letting go – I dare not look in my mother's direction – 'that maybe we should use Tracy's suspicions to our advantage.'

'What do you mean?'

'We pretend to be together.'

I cough out a laugh, although with his hand still holding

mine it doesn't come out quite as amused as I meant it to. 'Like a fake relationship?'

'Well, not a relationship, because everyone here knows you don't do them, but an island fling could be on the cards?'

Down, hormones. He doesn't mean a real one.

'How will us pretending to be into each other help our cause to try and tear our parents apart?'

'Pressure,' he says matter-of-factly. 'It doesn't matter where it comes from, but if Tracy's worried about you and me, then she'll be more susceptible to the other doubts we seed.'

This is an interesting theory. Whether it's got merit or not, if it pisses Mum off, I'm in. I might want the best for her long-term, but right now, I'm hurt. 'Okay. How would it work? Like, what will it involve?'

He hits me with a super-cute smile. 'Come on, Winifred, I know you're anti-relationships, but don't tell me you've never read a romance novel or watched a romcom? We'll have to make it look like we can't keep our hands off each other. Share long, lustful gazes. Laugh lots at what the other says. Be seen together at times when we don't have to be together because of the itinerary.'

I swallow. The thought of having an excuse to touch Leo is all kinds of appealing. 'Will we have to kiss in front of our families?'

He ponders this for a few seconds. 'We probably don't have to go that far, but we definitely should make them think we're doing plenty of that behind closed doors.'

Dammit, but despite the lack of kissing, I'm willing to give it a shot.

After all, we only have two and a half days until the wedding. 'Okay, Leopold, you've got yourself a deal.'

'Awesome. But just be careful, Winifred, you know what happens in the movies.'

I laugh. 'Are you worried I might fall in love with you?'

He winks. 'Well, I am pretty irresistible.'

I roll my eyes. 'Thanks for the warning, but I think I'll be fine.' It would take more than a sexy smile and an award-winning bum to reform me.

'Uncle Leo, Aunty Fred! Did you see? I just got a one-in-hole!'

We look back to see Kayla dancing atop the tee-off patch and swivel our heads in the direction of the hole. Sure enough, her neon pink ball is just visible inside it.

Scarlett, hearing the shrieking, rushes over from hole eight. She drops to her knees beside Kayla and grips her skinny arms. 'Are you okay, sweet pea?'

'Mummy!' Kayla's practically crying with glee. 'I just got a one-in-hole.'

'Oh, my goodness? Really?' Scarlett, her long plaits swishing, looks to us for confirmation.

We shrug and Leo says, 'I didn't see but certainly looks like it.'

'She did. We saw!' TJ gestures to Mum, Paul and Juliet, who are waiting at the edge of hole four for their turn. 'Good job, little sis.'

Kayla beams; I get the impression that compliments from Tallulah-Jane are few and far between.

'And you two would have seen as well if you weren't lost in conversation.' Mum glares at me as she says this.

Leo and I exchange a smile – it's already working.

The rest of the game is an absolute hoot, not because TJ or Kayla get any better – her hole-in-one appears to have been a fluke – but because faking it with Leo is pure delight. He's not a bad actor and if I didn't know any better, I'd think he truly was into me. I feel like the heroine in one of Bee's beloved romance novels as I tease and touch him at every available opportunity.

I'm so talented at flirting with hot guys that I have to keep reining myself in, reminding myself there are children present. But, if the glares Mum gives me every time I catch her looking over at us are anything to go by, Leo's plan might just work.

At the end of the game, while we're waiting for our last group to finish, Scarlett and River take the younger girls off for a snack, but Leo and I stay where Mum can see us.

He digs his phone out of his back pocket and wraps his arm around me. 'Smile,' he says as he holds it up to take a selfie. 'An Insta-worthy couple if ever I saw one.'

I laugh, then ask, 'Can you send that to me?' knowing he won't be able to do so until we're back at the resort as I still haven't got around to getting a sim card.

'Of course. What's your number?'

He's still close enough to me as I rattle it off that I can see him save my contact as 'Winifred'. A warm buzz flows through me.

The only other person who has me down as Winifred in their phone is Bee.

'I thought you said nothing was going on between you and Leo?' Mum hisses into my ear as we head to back to the car park.

I give her an innocent smile – 'Did I say that?' – and then climb into the back seat of Way's rental car with my very sexy fake fling.

Our next stop is a visit to the National Park, in particular Captain Cook's Lookout, overlooking Duncombe Bay, where Mum and Paul are planning to tie the knot on Friday. We meet Blanche, the wedding planner and celebrant, here, and she tells us a little bit of the history of the area and runs through the order of service while River tries to keep Miller from crawling off the cliff into the choppy sea below. Blanche points out the Monument, an obelisk made of what look like giant pebbles to commemorate the so-called discovery of the island, and also three large rocky outcrops out at sea: Bird Rock, Green Pool Stone and Elephant Rock. 'Are there elephants out there?' Kayla asks.

Blanche smiles down at her. 'Well, I've never made it there to check, so maybe?'

We all laugh.

I thought Emily Bay was gorgeous, but this spot has a magic I can barely describe. The air is crisp and smells fresh like the trees a short distance away in the national park. It's easy to imagine what James and his crew must have thought when they stumbled across this side of the island hundreds of years ago, although how they climbed up the steep, jagged cliffs to get to land from this point, I have no clue.

The ceremony will take place on the actual lookout deck, with Mum, Paul, Leo and I standing on it, the backdrop of endless sea behind us, and the guests will stand on the grass slope that leads to it. Today the sky is a ridiculously deep blue with only a scattering of fluffy white clouds punctuating it. Post ceremony and photos – there are so many perfect places to choose from – the reception will be held in a marquee on the grass just past the monument, where we'll eat a delicious Norfolk feast catered by a local business and dance the night away under the stars.

I look to Leo, who is standing right beside me as all this is relayed, and I can tell we're both thinking the same thing: it's almost a shame that the wedding might not end up going ahead, because this really is one of the most stunning places I've ever seen.

14

ONLY ONE BED

*L*eo is one of the easiest people to get along with that I've ever met – honestly, he's a male version of Bee – but the moment he shuts my door behind us, my insides tighten and I suddenly don't know what to say. The room seems to have shrunk since I was last in here, but I know that's only my imagination. This isn't one of my fantasy novels.

Why am I feeling this way? It's not like he's here to seduce or be seduced. Continuing the ruse, we made sure our families thought we were heading off to my room to get it on. But now that we're out of their sight, we don't have to pretend to be into each other.

And that's probably the problem. Having a man in my room I'm not planning on devouring is such an alien concept that I don't know what to *do* with him. But as it's my room, it's me who should take charge and set the tone for the evening – or rather, night – ahead. Try to make him feel welcome and at ease.

'Can I get you a drink?' I finally ask, kicking off my sandals as I cross over to the kitchenette. 'I've got half a bottle of wine, Diet Coke, tea or instant coffee.'

'I'll have a coffee, thanks. If I drink any more tonight, I'm definitely going to have a hangover tomorrow.'

Probably a good idea not to add more alcohol to this awkward situation. I lost count of how many glasses of wine I downed over dinner, not to mention afterwards. Thank God Waylen drank sensibly and Juliet not at all, or the whole lot of us would have had to stumble back to the resort in the dark, risking who knows how many encounters with cows.

As I start to fill the kettle, Leo perches himself on the edge of the desk chair as if he's not sure whether he should be sitting down at all. 'Well, that was quite a day.'

I nod at his attempt at small talk. 'Tell me about it. I swear Mum added things to the itinerary just so we couldn't sneak off alone.'

After the wedding venue reconnaissance, she'd insisted we all do a walk through the Hundred Acre Reserve, followed by ice cream at *Sweeties* just off the main street, leaving barely time for a shower before we had to head out again to the Fish Fry.

'She definitely did,' Leo says, 'but that's a good thing. It means she's worried and our plan is working. I bet right now she's stressing about it to my dad.'

I much prefer the idea of them doing this over the horizontal mambo. 'Let's hope so, because I'm exhausted. Milk and sugar?'

'Yes. One, please.'

'I'm surprised I didn't fall asleep on the table after gorging myself at dinner. Let's hope we do manage to cancel the wedding, cos there's no way I'll fit into my bridesmaid dress after tonight.'

'I'm not sure I'll fit into my suit either. That coconut pie was to die for,' he says. 'I had three slices.'

'And they weren't small slices. I don't think I've ever seen so much food in my entire life.' I hand him the coffee.

Leo thanks me, then takes a sip. 'I now understand why they call it the Famous Island Fish Fry. The whole thing was quite the experience, but I had fun though.'

I smile. 'How could you not?'

Dinner was at Puppy's Point, yet another gorgeous spot overlooking the ocean. When I first saw the Fish Fry on Mum's itinerary, I thought it sounded twee – fatty, deep-battered fish with a bunch of strangers while we watched some islanders dance – and definitely not my scene, but it was actually great. The fried fish was nothing like the stuff you find in cheap takeaway joints, and I discovered it's impossible not to enjoy yourself when you're eating delicious, lovingly prepared food and watching unique entertainment while overlooking the kinds of sunsets one usually only sees on filtered Insta shots. Not to mention the dancing with Leo that happened later.

It turns out he's a really good dancer and as we pressed our bodies together under the stars, I had to keep reminding myself that our seductive moves were all for show.

I grab a Diet Coke and crack it open as I climb onto my bed. Normally, I wouldn't have caffeine this late but with only one bed between us, I'm not sure I'm going to get much sleep anyway. I've never shared a bed with a man I'm not going to have sex with, but I guess there's a first time for everything.

'Do you want to watch a movie?' I ask. 'I've got a few streaming services on my laptop.'

'I thought you were tired.'

'Doesn't mean I can sleep yet. It's been such a big day; I need to wind down.'

He nods. 'I know what you mean. What about *The Parent Trap*?'

It takes me a moment to realise he's referring to what movie we should watch. 'You want to watch a kids' movie?'

'Yeah. I've been curious to see it since you mentioned it.'

It's probably safer than a lot of other movies – it could be awkward watching anything with a sex scene together. 'Okay.' I grab my laptop and open it to find a string of messages from Bee. My phone is still tucked away in my bag – I haven't checked it since we got back to the hotel and in fact, miracle-of-miracles, I'd almost forgotten about its existence. The guys I've been talking to on the apps will wonder if I've fallen off the face of the earth.

Bridget Jones: *A selfie? A SELFIE. Please EFFING explain.*

I laugh.

'What's so funny?' Leo asks.

'Just before dinner, I sent the photo you took at mini golf to my best friend and she's freaking out.'

His mug halts halfway to his mouth and he frowns. 'Why? Do I have a huge zit on my face or something?'

Even if he did, he'd still look hotter than most men. 'No. But one of my rules is "No Selfies" and I haven't had the chance to tell her what we're up to, so she thinks this picture means something. Just give me five seconds to explain it to her.'

Leo sips his coffee and waits patiently while I type. 'Does your mum know about this selfie rule?'

I shrug. 'She might. She definitely read the article when it went viral. Why?'

'You should post it to your Instagram. If she does know about the rule, it'll confuse the hell out of her.'

I'm already getting up to grab my phone from my bag. 'You're way too conniving for such a nice guy.'

He laughs. 'Well, you're way too hot for someone who's bald.'

My heart squeezes. 'You think I'm hot?'

He scoffs. 'Don't pretend you don't know it. I couldn't keep my eyes off you on the plane, even when you were sleeping with your mouth wide open like Mr Whatshisname.'

Thankfully, my back is turned to him so he can't see the

huge grin that spreads across my face. Leopold thinks I'm hot. I *knew* I wasn't imagining it. I think about his equipment pressed against my back earlier that day. You definitely don't imagine something *that* big.

'So what are the other rules?' he asks.

What? Surely, he doesn't expect me to leave such a comment hanging.

'Um . . .' Right now, I can't remember even one of them. Bamboozled, I turn around and flop back onto the bed and open Instagram.

'I promise I won't mock them,' he says, misreading my hesitation. 'I'm genuinely curious.'

Hitting 'post' on our selfie, I turn back to him. 'Do you want me to read you the list?'

He nods, then toes off his shoes, leans back in his seat and rests his sock-clad feet at the end of my bed. They don't smell at all, and they are massive. I know it's a myth that the size of a man's feet reflects the size of his you-know-what, but in Leo's case I think it must be the truth. 'Sorry.' Noticing me staring, he snaps his feet back to the floor. 'I should have asked before putting them there.' Heat flares in my cheeks. What is *wrong* with me tonight? I'm acting like I've never been alone with a man before.

'Don't be silly,' I gush. 'I was just admiring your socks.'

Thankfully, said socks – black with colourful books and bookworms all over them – are admiration-worthy. You have to have a certain personality to get away with his quirky fashion choices – bright shirts and crazy socks – and he totally rocks them.

He grins. 'They were a gift from one of my students.'

I force a smile and open my document. 'Right. I think I already mentioned rule number one and two the other night.'

'Refresh my memory, please.'

'Okay.' I clear my throat. 'Number one: Be honest. Number two: Set boundaries before you meet.'

'Does that mean you never meet anyone organically?' he interrupts.

'Sometimes I do. I went out with a guy I met in my writing group a while ago; in cases like that, I just make sure I let them know where I stand the moment we've established an attraction. If they don't feel the same, it ends there.'

Leo nods and I continue. 'Number three: Chemistry matters, connection does not. Number four: Always meet first in a public place. Number five: Never go back to their place, and Number six: Under no circumstances allow them to stay the night.'

He chuckles. 'Does that ever get awkward? I mean, once you've, you know – do you have a specific line you use to ask them to leave? I'd feel terrible.'

'No. That's part of the boundaries you establish before you get that far. And I don't feel bad about telling someone to leave my house when I want them to. It's my house.'

'Fair enough.'

'Number seven: Expect nothing. Give nothing. Number eight: No jealous or possessive thoughts.'

'Have you ever been jealous of another woman because of a man?'

'*Please*. That rule's for the men, and women weaker than me.'

Leo smirks and drinks some more coffee.

'Number nine: Always pay for yourself. Number ten: No PDAs.'

'What's a PDA?'

'Public display of affection.'

'You mean like what we were doing all night?'

I nod, trying to push away the image of Leo's hand on my knee, on the small of my back, the fake sweet nothings he whispered in my ear whenever Mum was nearby, and his body pressed against mine on the dance floor. 'Exactly. You already know Number eleven: No selfies, and Number twelve is Keep seeing other people.'

He goggles at this. 'You date more than one person at a time?'

'Are you going to keep interrupting?' I say, feigning outrage.

He gives me a sheepish smile. 'Sorry.'

'I'll expand on all this in the book, but I can be chatting to and seeing four or five people at once. Doesn't mean I sleep with all of them,' I say before he can ask. 'Number thirteen: Limit your time together. Number fourteen: No text and in-depth conversation. Under no circumstances should you chat daily. Number fifteen: No labels. If anyone so much as infers that I'm their girlfriend, I cut them loose. Number sixteen: Always put yourself first. Number seventeen: Never see the same person more than once a week.'

I must admit I've broken this rule myself a couple of times when I've been seeing a guy who is ridiculously good in bed, but some rules are okay to bend a little; not that I plan on writing that in my book!

'Number eighteen: Friends with benefits are not a thing,' I continue.

'What do you mean?' Leo asks.

'Just like fake relationships never work out in novels, friends with benefits doesn't work in real life, because friendship equals feelings and those feelings can grow.'

'Do you speak from experience?'

I shake my head. 'No, but I've seen it happen too many times to my friends. There's a reason friends-to-lovers is another popular trope. Do you really want me to keep going?'

'Yes. This is fascinating.'

'Where was I? That's right, Number nineteen: No gifts, no favours. Number twenty: Fit your dates around your life, not theirs, and Number twenty-one: If anyone shows signs of attachment, end it immediately.'

I look up again and try to read the expression on his face. I know he doesn't subscribe to any of this, but he seems genuinely interested in what I'm saying.

'That's quite the list. Has there ever been anyone in your life who made you question them? Anyone you've broken the rules with?'

'No.' And that's the truth; long before I came up with the official list, I was already living it.

He shoots me a sceptical look. 'Surely there's been someone who's snuck under your skin, bypassed those defences . . . made you weak at the knees. Someone you couldn't stop thinking about no matter how hard you tried.'

I shake my head.

'What about in high school? Everyone has a crush on someone in high school.'

The back of my neck prickles and my stomach feels heavy at the thought of Kyle, the boy I was obsessed with to the point that I lost sleep and missed homework deadlines because I was thinking about him. Kyle, who I dreamed about marrying one day, possibly even having babies with. Kyle, the second and final guy to break my heart.

'Winifred? You okay?' Leo says, and I realise my cheeks are warm and I haven't answered his question.

'Of course I had the hots for boys, but that was purely on a physical level,' I lie. There's no way I'm going to tell Leo about Kyle. I haven't even told Bee about him.

Just thinking about what he did after we slept together is mortifying. In hindsight, I doubt the feelings I had for him were love, but at sixteen, they sure felt like it. And his betrayal – the public humiliation that came with it – was something I never wanted to expose myself to again.

'Are we gonna watch this movie or not?' I ask before he can ask me any more uncomfortable questions.

He nods – 'Sure' – and I close my list of rules and find *The Parent Trap*. It's not on any streaming services, but luckily it's on YouTube.

Leo rinses his now-empty mug in the bathroom and then sits next to me on the bed, the laptop between us. I press play and try to ignore his close proximity and how long his legs are stretched out in front of him as the cheesy music and *BLESS OUR BROKEN HOME* appears on the screen.

'Is it an animated movie?' he asks as two little plasticine cupids appear and lift up the sign to reveal the opening animation: two people on either side of a tree, tapping their feet, scowling and refusing to look at each other.

It's been years since I watched this movie and I'd totally forgotten it begins like this. 'No, and I hope you're not going to be one of those people who asks questions the whole way through.'

'Maybe I will if I know it's going to annoy you.'

I elbow him in the side as the catchy tune continues, laughing as Leo starts to bop along to it. 'You're such a dag.'

He grins. 'I love old movies – they put so much effort into their opening sequences. That was like a whole film in itself. Pity we don't have popcorn.'

I climb off the bed and grab a packet of Twisties I bought at the airport and haven't eaten yet. 'Will these do?'

'Oh God. I love Twisties. They're even better than popcorn.'

He opens the bag as I settle back beside him, offering it to me first like a true gentleman.

The movie begins proper with the twin sisters living on opposite sides of America – one with their mother, one with their father – but by some lucky coincidence being sent to the same summer camp. I discover that Leo is one of those people who talks through movies, but strangely it doesn't annoy me as much as it should. I delight in his observations of what was one of my favourite movies growing up and manage to ignore the spark I feel when our hands dive for the Twisties at the same time.

'These girls are pure evil,' Leo exclaims, his eyes glued to the screen as Sharon cuts Susie's dress completely away at the back while she's talking to a cute boy from the all-boys camp that comes to visit. Even viewing it for the umpteenth time, it's mortifying watching her head back into the dance.

'Did Scarlett and Juliet fight much growing up?'

'Yeah, but nothing like this. Then again, this is a pretty insane situation. I can only imagine what it would be like not knowing you're a twin and then meeting your actual doppelganger. I reckon you could have some fun once you found out though.'

'Oh, they do. Just watch.' Again, I think of my dad's girls, Mia and Ava – I wonder if they've ever seen this? Probably, I mean if you were a parent of twins, you'd be remiss not to educate them. 'I have identical twin sisters.'

Leo turns his head from the screen to me. 'Simon had other kids?'

I nod. 'He got married again when I was twenty. The twins are about Kayla's age. He dotes on them. Only when they were born did he start showing any interest in being a dad to me.'

'That must be tough.'

My eyes prickle and I swallow, not wanting to cry for a second night in a row in front of him. Honestly, I'm not usually the water-works type. I can count on one hand the number of times I've cried in the last decade. When Guinevere, my cat before Aunty, died; when Mum announced she was getting married for the fifth time; and when Bee told me my manuscript sucked.

Maybe there's something in the island air that's irritating my eyes.

'Do you get along well with them?' he asks.

'I barely know them.'

And I rarely talk about them. I'm not even sure my friends from work – aside from Bee – know about the girls. Does this mean Leo is becoming a true friend? I've never had a friend who is a guy before, but I find myself not opposed to the idea. Perhaps even if we do manage to stop the wedding, we could stay in touch. Be penpals, or rather *email* pals. Okay, probably WhatsApp pals. Does anyone email outside of work any more? The only emails I ever get are from shops I've stupidly handed over my details to. Lost in my thoughts, I suddenly realise Leo has said something.

I blink. 'I'm sorry, what did you say?'

'Do you not know your sisters because you haven't had the chance, or because you don't want to?'

This is a good question – one I've never really allowed myself to contemplate.

'Perhaps the latter,' I admit. 'I can't help feeling bitter that he is to them what he could never be bothered to be for me. He's always posting on Facebook about what they're up to and how proud he is.'

This confession makes me feel stupid – I mean, what kind of person is jealous of two little girls? – but Leo doesn't.

'That's understandable, considering the circumstances,' he says, 'but how your father treated you is not their fault. I bet they'd worship you, just like Kayla does. And don't tell Scarlett or Juliet I said this but . . . sisters can be pretty cool.'

'I do rather like yours,' I say, smiling. On screen, Sharon and Susie are being marched off by the terrifying camp matron to isolation. 'This bit always scared me as a kid. It seemed to be so far away from everyone else, and I kept thinking how they could get eaten by a bear or preyed on by a random woodcutter or something.'

'A woodcutter?' he snorts. 'I can't imagine you being scared of anything.'

'I'm not any more. I wonder if there is actually a phobia of woodcutters.'

'We'll have to ask Tally to look in her book.'

I chuckle. 'She's an interesting kid and has a better memory than anyone I've ever met. The way she can recall all those phobias is impressive.'

'I'm pretty sure she's autistic, but Scarlett and River aren't into labels.'

'You disapprove?'

He shrugs. 'I don't know. Being diagnosed with ADHD and dyslexia really helped me understand and accept things about myself, and I wonder if it might do the same for Tally. Anyway, this conversation is getting a bit too heavy for this time of night, and I don't want to miss any important parts of the movie.'

We continue to watch, Leo offering running commentary and asking *all* the questions, until the end credits finally appear.

'Well, what did you think?' I ask, watching him.

'I loved it,' he says, 'but if you tell anyone, I'll deny it.'

I laugh – 'Always good to have bribery material' – and snap my laptop shut. 'Guess we'd better go to sleep now. Another big day tomorrow.'

'Yeah, probably a good idea.'

'Do you want to use the bathroom before me?'

'Thanks.' He stands. 'Do you mind if I borrow some toothpaste?'

'Not at all. And I haven't used the toothbrush the resort left, so feel free to use that as well.'

As Leo disappears into the bathroom, I quickly reply to a

text from Bee, asking if I've come to my senses regarding Operation Break-up and demanding I call her with an update.

Me: *Sorry. Can't talk right now as Leo will be out of the bathroom any moment.*

Bridget Jones: *What's he doing in your room at this time of the night?*

I quickly fill her in on the latest part of our plan. Despite her loving *books* about fake flings, she isn't impressed that Leo and I are embarking on one in real life.

Bridget Jones: *This is a terrible idea. It's going to end in tears. Are you going to sleep with him?*

Me: *Of course not. We're just friends.*

Even if he does think I'm hot. Even if he does have the biggest feet I've ever seen.

Bridget Jones: *You don't HAVE male friends.*

Me: *Yes, I do. What do you call Xavier and Rory?*

Bridget Jones: *They're GAY! Nothing is going to happen with them!*

Me: *Well, nothing is going to happen with Leo either. He's practically family – he will be if we don't manage to stop this wedding.*

I look up to see Leo coming out of the bathroom, turn my phone over on the bedside table, then grab my PJs from my suitcase and head in there myself, second-guessing everything I do. Should I take all my make-up off like I usually would – do I want him to see me without my mask on? Should I wear the leggings I wore on the plane rather than the singlet and shorts I was planning to? In the end, I remind myself what I've just told Bee and do whatever I'd normally do if Leo wasn't present. When I emerge ten minutes later – fresh from a shower and lathered in coconut body butter – I find him on the floor, trying to get comfortable with a pillow and the extra blanket from the cupboard.

'What are you doing?' I ask, even though it's fairly self-explanatory.

'I'm not making *you* sleep on the floor.'

I laugh. 'How chivalrous but . . . why would either of us sleep on the floor? It's a king-sized bed, for crying out loud.'

He doesn't look convinced. Clearly, he's worried I'm a nymphomaniac who can't control myself.

'I promise I won't jump your bones,' I say. 'Okay. If . . . if you're sure?'

I don't know if he's asking whether I'm sure I don't mind sharing or I'm sure I won't jump him, but I tell him, 'Absolutely,' nonetheless. No matter what some people think of me – not mentioning any names, *mother* – I have good self-control.

Two seconds later when he drops the blanket to the floor, I almost swallow my tongue. He's standing before me in nothing but a pair of black boxer briefs, and I don't need to tell you how good he looks. How did I not notice the jeans and his shirt folded carefully on the back of the chair? When I promised not to jump his bones, I didn't know he'd be practically naked beside me.

Oh dear.

I remind myself what I just told Bee and chant to myself, *Leo is my friend, not my fuck buddy*, in the manner of the sharks from *Finding Nemo*.

'What side of the bed do you sleep on?' he asks, seemingly not self-conscious at all.

I can't even remember the words for left or right, never mind which one I prefer. 'That one,' I say, pointing to the side closest to the door so I can escape outside for fresh air in the night if his near-nakedness gets too much.

Leo is my friend, not my fuck buddy.

I switch off the main light and we climb into bed like two nervous virgins on their wedding night, the gap between us enough for at least two more people. And maybe a cat or dog. If I do manage to go to sleep, hopefully he's far enough away that I won't throw my leg over him – or worse – without realising.

Leo is my friend, not my fuck buddy.

'Well, goodnight,' he says. 'Sleep well. Don't let the bed bugs bite.'

I force a chuckle – 'You too' – and roll away from him onto my side because this seems safest, but this is not usually how I sleep.

I'm normally a back sleeper and, after a while, I give up trying to go against nature. For the next ten minutes – or maybe it's two hours – I stare at the ceiling, trying to think about everything except the man I could touch if I just stretched out my arm.

Leo is my friend, not my fuck buddy.

Is he asleep? I listen carefully to his breathing. Bee says Sully's breathing is totally different when he's asleep, but I can barely hear a sound coming from Leo.

'Can't you sleep either?'

His words jolt me from my thoughts. 'Oh my God, are you trying to give me a heart attack?'

'Sorry. I thought you were awake.'

'I was. I just didn't know you were.'

We roll over to face each other. It's not pitch black, so I can see the bristles on his jaw and the thickness of lashes that are much darker than his hair.

'Why can't you sleep?' I whisper.

'You're distracting me.'

'Sorry.' I blush; thankfully, he probably can't tell. 'I didn't think I was tossing and turning.'

'You weren't. But everything about you distracts me.' He pauses. 'It's very hard not to think about how much I want to kiss you when you're lying right beside me.'

Oh. My. God. Leo wants to kiss me!

And I can't think of anything I'd rather do right now.

All my good intentions go up in smoke – and they're not the only things on fire – as I move closer to him. So close I can smell the toothpaste he just used.

'Why don't you stop thinking and start doing?' I suggest, boldly licking my lips.

In reply, he draws my face to his, kissing me in a way that only turns me on more. As his tongue sneaks into my mouth, he rolls me onto my back and hovers above me, his elbows pressing into the mattress on either side of me while he smooths his hands all over my bare scalp. The sensations that were there when he touched my head in the pool are a hundred times stronger in the dark confines of my room. Never in all my wildest fantasies had I imagined how erogenous my scalp could be.

I should have shaved my head years ago.

Then again, I've had sex since I got rid of my hair – other men have touched my scalp in the heat of passion – but it's never turned me on like this.

I moan into Leo's magic mouth as I press my body even closer to his. I don't want even a millimetre of anything else between us. Everything about him is perfect. His chest is firm against mine and, as our legs entwine, I can feel his hair rubbing against my smooth skin. I roam my hands all over his shoulders and arms, wanting to touch every inch of him immediately but also for this bliss to last as long as possible. We break for air and this time he puts his lips to my neck, pressing tantalising tiny kisses against my bare skin as he treks lower.

'Oh God,' I groan, thrusting my breasts towards him, my nipples already tight in anticipation of his mouth.

His nose tickles my cleavage as his hands find the bare skin at my waist, pushing up my singlet top. When his large palms sneak beneath the cotton to cup my breasts, I gasp. He puts his mouth to my bare skin and swirls his tongue over my right nipple. Pure ecstasy shoots through me, heat pooling in that tender spot between my thighs.

To hell with slow.

I reach for the bulge in Leo's boxers – if I don't have him in the next few seconds, I might actually combust. We can slow things down for Round Two.

'Do you have a condom?' If not, it doesn't matter because I always travel with supplies, but his jeans are closer than the bathroom and I don't want to waste a second unnecessarily.

'Shit.' He jerks back at my words, horror flashing across his face.

'It's okay.' I chuckle. 'I've got some.'

I'm already scrambling off the bed when he grabs my wrist and turns me to look at him. 'That's not what I meant.'

'Huh?'

He drops my hand. 'We shouldn't do this.'

It takes a second for what he's saying to register and a few more for me to work out why. Then I remember he's seeing someone. Disappointment sweeps through my body like a plague.

'Right. Sorry.' I straighten my singlet, covering my bare chest. 'I forgot about Chloe.'

'Zoey,' he clarifies, then shakes his head. 'But no. This has nothing to do with her. I told you; we've only just started seeing each other. We're definitely not exclusive or anything.'

'Then what?' I blink, unable to take my eyes off his erection. It's still very evident, which tells me he's got some conflicting feelings going on.

He tears a hand through his hair but doesn't say anything.

'Is it because of our parents? Because it might make things awkward in the future if we're step-siblings?' I smile and reach

out to touch his bare chest, trailing my finger lower. 'You know . .
. if we manage to pull off Operation Break-up, none of that will
be a problem.'

'I'm sorry, Fred, but . . .' He quickly stands and grabs his
jeans off the chair. 'Even if we do manage to pull off Operation
Break-up, I don't sleep around.'

The fizz I'd been feeling turns from desire to rage in zero-
point-zero seconds. His insinuation is clear – he is *not* like me.
'Excuse me? Are you slut-shaming me?'

'No, of course not,' he scoffs but won't meet my gaze as he
yanks his jeans up his legs, cursing when his fly catches on his
still rock-solid dick. 'What you do is your business, but I told
you, I value sex as part of a relationship and don't want to just
have it willy-nilly.'

I nod towards his groin where he's still trying to wrangle
himself back into his pants. 'Looks like your *willy* might disagree
with you.'

Red fills his cheeks. 'That might be the case, but I don't want
to regret anything in the morning.'

He yanks his T-shirt over his head, and I don't bother to tell
him it's inside out. *Regret anything?* As if any guy has ever
regretted sleeping with me!

'What about our fake fling?' I ask as he picks his shoes up off
the floor and heads for the door. He wants to get out of here so
badly, he can't even spare the time to put them on.

He pauses, looks to me and shrugs. 'Isn't someone staying
the night against your rules? So . . . it probably looks more
realistic if I leave after you've had your wicked way with me
anyway. See you tomorrow, Fred.'

Before I can even say goodbye, he's yanked open the door
and stepped outside.

I startle as it shuts behind him, the sound echoing in the
otherwise silent night. He's right. I'd totally forgotten Rule #6.

Is that because I *wanted* Leo to stay the night?

I shake my head – that thought is too outrageous to even contemplate – and try to push him out of my mind and go to sleep.

But it's hard. I don't think I've ever felt this sexually frustrated in my life.

15

NOT LIKE OTHER GUYS

Miraculously, I must have managed to sleep after Leo left, because my phone wakes me before the rooster does. It's still dark outside, but there's a tiny glimmer of light about to burst into the sky. Who on earth would be ringing at this time? Thinking it's probably a spammer, I grab my phone off the bedside table to silence it, only to discover it's my publisher calling.

Immediately, I'm wide awake and sitting up, wondering what the hell this could be about. We spoke on the phone when she offered me a contract, but all our correspondence since has been via email.

'Hello, Emily,' I manage, trying not to sound asleep, although what else can she expect with a 5 a.m. phone call?

'What the hell are you thinking?' she blasts.

I blink, still half-asleep as I try to work out what she's talking about. 'Excuse me?'

'The selfie on your grid. How am I supposed to tell marketing and sales to go out and get pre-orders for your book when you're posting photos on social media blatantly ignoring your own rules?'

Shit. Last night when I shared that pic of me and Leo, I was only thinking about Mum, not who else might see it.

'Who is he?'

I glance at the empty spot beside me where Leo almost spent the night after we almost crossed his line. That kiss will be burnt into my memory for all eternity – from now on, it'll be the one by which I compare all future kisses. Damn him!

'Fred? Are you still there?!'

'Sorry.' I swallow. 'He's my future stepbrother. I'm with him on Norfolk Island for my mum's wedding.'

'Oh, thank fuck,' Emily says and then starts laughing. 'I was doing my 3 a.m. doom-scroll and almost fell off the bed when I saw it. But can you clarify that on the post? Just posting a love heart is giving off the wrong idea.'

'Yes, of course. I'm sorry. I'd had a few drinks and—'

'No need to apologise, just get it fixed ASAP. With any luck nobody else important saw it, but if he's going to be related to you, then I guess we can explain it away. Your new stepbrother is very hot, by the way. Feel free to give him my number.' She clears her throat. 'Anyway, while I've got you, how's the manuscript going? I'd love to see a few more chapters by the end of this week if possible?'

The end of the week?

'Um . . . that should be doable,' I lie. 'I am away for the wedding though, so I've not got much time to write at the moment.'

'Fair enough.' She chuckles. 'Must be weird for someone like you going to weddings. Maybe you could write a post about that – publicity and marketing are always looking for extra pieces they can pitch to magazines, and that could be a fun angle.'

'Yeah, I could probably do that.' Might be easier than writing the actual book.

'Well, I'll let you get back to sleep, but do send some more chapters as soon as you can. I know the manuscript isn't due for a couple of months, but everyone here is itching to read it. Women choosing to be single and child-free is in the zeitgeist now, so there couldn't be a better moment to bring out this book. We think it's going to be a really big seller for us.'

'That's great,' I manage. 'I'll do my best to get you another chapter or two really soon.'

Appeased, Emily disconnects to head off to her reformer Pilates class, and I open Instagram to try to save my fledgling career. One glance at the photo of Leo and me and it's obvious why she freaked out. We do look like a couple; his arm draped over my shoulder seems like the most natural thing in the world, and our smiles could blind you if you looked directly at them. The chemistry between us is palpable and I marvel at Leo's restraint and ability to step away from it last night.

He's definitely not like other guys and, as disappointed as my libido is that we didn't go the whole way, I can't help respecting him for staying true to his values. They might be in total juxtaposition to mine, but that doesn't mean they are less worthy.

In the end, I decide to remove the post altogether, because putting 'Hanging out with my new stepbrother' on it will defeat the purpose of posting it in the first place. Then I fall asleep for a few more hours until my alarm wakes me up to get ready for Museum Day.

Unplanned, Leo and I arrive together for breakfast. My stomach squeezes and I wonder if he'll still play my fake lover for the day. Do I want him to, or would that be awkward after what happened? My lips tingle at the thought of his smooshed against them.

'Morning, Winifred,' he says, offering me a coy smile as he gestures for me to head through the door in front of him.

My anxiety about how things might be between us after last

night lifts a little at his use of my full name. Maybe we can recover after the awkward mortification of how things ended and move on to friendship. Although it wasn't my doing, I give myself a mental pat on the back that we didn't cross the line. I'd have been breaking multiple rules. Chemistry and connection should never be mixed, so sleeping with Leo after we'd shared so much of ourselves, when I like him and respect him as a person, would have been a very bad idea.

I return his smile. 'Morning, Leopold.'

I'm aware of Mum's eyes on us as we join our family at the long table near the window. Everyone except Waylen and Benji are already here. It's clear she thinks Leo and I have spent the night together, and I offer her a sweet smile as I sit between Kayla and Juliet. I'm trying to work out whether to try the pancakes again or have an omelette when my brother and his boyfriend arrive.

Waylen marches straight over to me, not bothering to greet anyone else. He looks like he hasn't slept a wink, but I didn't hear any wild shenanigans coming from that side of the wall. Then again, I was kind of distracted.

'Can I speak to you, please?' Unnecessarily, he adds, 'In private.'

'Sure.' I push back my seat and follow him to just outside the restaurant. 'What's up, big bro?'

'What's going on?' he demands, his arms folded tightly across his chest.

'What do you mean?'

'You and Leo. Do you have feelings for him?'

'What?' I smirk. 'Do you even *know* me?'

'I saw the way you two were flirting yesterday. You were all over him at the Fish Fry, and I told myself you wouldn't be crass enough to sleep with our future stepbrother, but then you snuck him into your room last night.'

'We weren't sneaking.'

'And then you post a selfie with him. A selfie! Have you lost your fucking mind? I know what that means to you, and now I'm wondering if you're actually falling in love with him.'

I cough out a laugh. '*Love?* You know I don't do love.'

'Well, that's what you proclaim and that's what you've signed a contract to write about, yet one of your rules is "No selfies" and then you go and post one with a man you're sleeping with! What am I supposed to think?'

'How did you see the selfie? I deleted it first thing this morning.'

He shakes his head as if this is irrelevant but tells me anyway. 'Benji isn't a great sleeper because of all his shift work. He took a screen shot so he'd remember to show me this morning.'

I think of my mother prowling round the hotel a couple of nights ago and Emily with her doomscrolling. Does *anyone* sleep through the night any more?

'Why'd you delete it?' Way asks.

I tell him about the Emily phone call, and his eyebrows knit together.

'If it doesn't mean anything, then why not leave it there? What the hell are you playing at, Fred? And don't even think about lying to me. I know you're up to something.'

'Fine.' I sigh, then glance over my shoulder to make sure we're still alone. 'You might not care what happens to Mum when this marriage goes south like all the others, but I do. If you weren't blinded by lust, you'd agree that this wedding is a terrible idea, but thankfully, I'm not the only one here who thinks so.'

'Leo?'

I nod. 'Yes, Leo is the only other sane person in our two families. He thinks his father has lost the plot due to grief and that he's going to wake up married to our mother, whom he barely knows, and realise he's made an awful mistake. And what do you think is going to happen to Mum then? Who do you think is going to have to fly to England and pick up the pieces? We both know it won't be you, because you're too busy and important.'

With each word I throw at him, my body temperature rises.

Is this what a hot flush feels like?

'What are you trying to tell me?' Way asks coolly. 'Are you and Leo spending all this time together because you've been plotting to sabotage the wedding?'

'We're trying to save our parents from themselves!'

'So that's what that get-to-know-each-other game was all about – you were *trying* to cause a rift between them,' Way explodes, his lips practically vibrating with rage. 'And the other night, all that money talk? You were making it sound like Mum has champagne tastes on a prosecco budget. Was that to put Paul off as well? To make him think she's only in this for the money?'

'How do you know she isn't?' I spit, despite not really believing that.

He shakes his head at me, giving me a look he usually reserves for reality TV. 'Mum and Paul are grown-ups – they're old enough to make their own decisions, good or bad. It's not up to us to decide. You and Leo are supposed to be grown-ups too, but this ridiculous plan of yours exposes you as a couple of spoiled little brats.'

I can't believe he said that. 'How dare you call me a spoiled brat!'

He shrugs. 'The shoe fits.'

I jab my finger right into his chest. 'You act all high and mighty, but you're just like Scarlett and Juliet.'

Way takes a step back and rubs his ribs. 'What the hell is that supposed to mean?'

'The three of you don't really care about our parents' happiness or wellbeing, you're just thinking of yourselves. They welcome another woman to take care of their father, and you're too blinded by your feelings for Benji to see clearly any more. No one matters outside of your little bubble.'

He opens his mouth – presumably to tell me exactly what he thinks of that – but Mum appears and he shuts it again.

'What are you two yelling about?' She looks anxiously between us – even when we were growing up, Way and I rarely fought. 'Everyone in the restaurant can hear you shouting. You're disturbing the other guests and embarrassing me.'

We look at each other – Way's face is as red as mine feels. What are we going to tell her? He raises an eyebrow at me. Does he want me to confess or come up with a story and back the hell off?

Ah, bugger it, what have I got to lose? Way already thinks I'm a monster and I can't in good conscience stand up next to Mum and be her witness as she marries a sixth man.

'Leo and I don't think you and Paul should get married.'

The moment I say it, I regret throwing him under the bus. I should have taken the blame myself; I already have a tenuous relationship with my mother, but Leo is on solid ground with his dad.

Mum blinks. 'But . . . I don't understand.'

'The only reason Fred came here was to sabotage your wedding,' Way says. 'And she found an accomplice in Leo.'

'Is that true?' Mum asks.

I nod, feeling slightly sick. 'Yes, it is. Well, not exactly the full story. I came here for the free holiday, writing time and cocktails but when Leo and I realised we both had major doubts about your engagement . . . yes. We . . . *I* came up with the plan to try and see if we could make one or both of you reassess.' May as well try and save him a little, I think.

Her lower lip wobbles. 'Is that why you two were all over each other yesterday?'

I nod. 'We thought if you thought we were into each other, you might decide that us being related wasn't such a grand idea.'

Way snorts. 'That's the most ridiculous thing I've ever heard, and I've heard a lot of ridiculous things in my time.'

I glare at him, but Mum's focus remains on me. 'I didn't think you'd agree to come unless you were okay with this.'

'To be fair, neither of you really gave me much choice. You guilted me into coming – I made it clear that day you came into the library that I wasn't happy about this. If I didn't know you'd gone through menopause, I'd think this was a shotgun wedding.'

'I can you assure you Paul and I are not rushing into anything.'

'You say that, but you can't know him properly after only a couple of months.' Perhaps the shotgun wedding comment was a little mean, but I'm genuinely worried; this isn't just a game to me, and I need her to see this. 'You've both lived whole lives since you last met. I know he seems like a good guy . . .'—I've got to admit his whole family are sneaking under my skin—'but no one is perfect and—'

'Oh, he's not perfect, sweetheart. Paul's a bit of a slob to be honest. He doesn't shut the drawers after he gets his clothes out, he never makes the bed and whenever he gets a snack out of the pantry, he leaves the door open afterwards. But that's not the worst of it.' She pauses for effect. 'He watches videos of people whipper-snipping on YouTube. In bed!'

I snort with laughter – talk about red flags – but manage to stay focused.

'What would be the harm in waiting just a little bit longer?' I ask. 'Just to be certain that you're not going to regret this. Or Paul's not. However fond of you he is, he's only just lost his wife.

Dating in your fifties is scary. He's probably terrified at the prospect of being alone for the rest of his life.'

Mum looks hurt. 'You think no one would marry me unless they're desperate?'

'I think history shows you're very marriageable,' I snap. 'It's what comes after that's the problem.'

Paul appears as Mum bursts into tears. 'I was going to ask if everything is all right out here, but it's clearly not.' He takes her into his arms. 'What's going on, Trace?'

She's sobbing too hard to reply. I can't help rolling my eyes. Way answers for her. 'Fred's been plotting to break you two up.'

'What?' Paul looks up from the top of Mum's head to me. 'Not just Fred,' she sobs. 'Leo too. They're in it together.'

His expression turns dark – it's the first time I've ever seen it so. '*My* Leo?'

How many Leos does he think there are around here?

Mum nods. 'I told you something was going on,' she all but snarls, before turning on me. 'Paul thought you were just getting along well but I knew you were up to something!'

'It's not Leo's fault,' I begin, but Paul has already let Mum go and is charging back into Cook's Landing like a bull heading into the ring. *Oh God.*

'What the hell, Leopold!'

We all wince at his volume and aggression. Part of me wants to make a run for it, but I appear to be frozen to the spot.

Moments later, Paul appears again, this time dragging Leo much like one might a naughty toddler. The rest of our party brings up the rear, clearly wondering what is going on.

'What's wrong, Nanna Tracy?' Kayla asks, immediately going to her and touching her arm.

Mum sniffs and takes hold of the little girl's hand like she's a comfort blankie.

'As you can see, Tracy is very upset.' Paul steps close to her again. 'And Waylen tells me this is because Leo and Fred are on a mission to stop us getting married.'

Scarlett gasps and looks at Leo. 'Is this true?'

He runs his tongue around his lips and sighs before responding, 'Yes. It is.'

'It wasn't Leo's idea,' I blurt, throwing him an apologetic grimace. But he's not the kind of guy to let a lady take the fall. 'Maybe not,' he admits, 'but it only came up because we were talking about how we feel about the wedding. When we realised we were on the same page about you rushing into things, we decided to take it upon ourselves to . . . slow you down.'

Paul shakes his head sadly. 'I can't believe you didn't just tell me how you were feeling before we got here.'

'Would you have listened, Dad?'

He thinks for a moment. 'Of course not. Who I marry is none of your damn business. I don't poke my nose into your love life.'

'I'm thinking I might just . . . uh . . . go and pat some cows,' Benji announces.

Way snatches his hand. 'No, you're as good as family. Stay.' Benji looks like he'd rather not and I don't blame him.

'It's me, isn't it?' Mum says, looking at Leo. 'You don't think I'm good enough for your father.'

He attempts a smile, but it doesn't meet his eyes. 'You seem like a lovely person, Tracy, but my mother hasn't even been dead a year. This isn't a good look. Dad's usually such a rational, sensible person that I'm sure he wouldn't be rushing into marrying someone else if he wasn't—'

'So why'd you bother coming?' Paul demands.

I notice a small crowd has gathered in reception not too far away to watch us. I don't blame them – if this wasn't my family drama, I'd be in the front row with the popcorn as well.

Leo tells his dad what he told me that morning in the Olive Café – that he was here because of the family values his mother had instilled in him. 'But I guess you're right. Who you marry is none of my business – I'm just your *son*. Make whatever mistakes you want, just don't come crying to me when you realise that this *is* a mistake.'

Leo storms out, heading in the direction of the rooms.

'Well,' Juliet says, 'at least he's got that off his chest.'

'Did you know he felt this way?' Paul asks Juliet, then also looks at Scarlett.

They both shake their heads.

'And is there anything *you* need to get off your chests?'

'I'd like to get this baby off my bladder,' Juliet replies, holding her bump like a basketball, 'but aside from that, I'm all good.'

Scarlett nods. 'Me too. I think your love is beautiful.' She goes over and hugs Mum. 'Don't let Leo and Fred ruin your big day.'

She's speaking as if I'm no longer there, so I decide I may as well slip away. I hardly think I'll be welcome on the museum trip now anyway. I think I've managed to escape when Way catches up to me.

'I hope you're proud of yourself, Fred.'

'Actually, I am,' I snap, whirling around to face him. 'Maybe I could have gone about it in a kinder way, but at least I can sleep soundly at night knowing I tried my best to prevent yet another disaster. And I'm washing my hands of it. You can be Mum's maid of honour – you'll look fabulous in my little red dress – and when her heart is breaking in a few months, you can fly to England and help her put it all back together again. I'm done.'

At least now I won't have to wear that stupid, itchy wig!

I don't wait around for him to reply, but I figure maybe I should check on Leo. After all, his fallout with his dad is all my fault.

16

WHEN I SEE YOU SMILE

'm not sure exactly which room is Leo's, so I walk in the general direction, hoping his curtains are open and I'll see him. They aren't, but as I pass a door about five down from mine, I hear his voice crooning along to what I immediately recognise as a ukulele.

I pause and tentatively lift my hand but stop just short of knocking. Is this such a good idea after what happened the last time we were alone in a room together? My body quivers in recollection. Then again, the situation is quite different this morning, and in the light of day. Today, we are both worked up – and not in the way that sometimes leads to red-hot make-up sex. Besides, we're not fighting with each other. We're allies, not enemies, and my conscience won't rest until I've apologised for all this drama.

Decision made, I knock loudly and hold my breath as I wait to see if he will answer.

The singing stops, then the strumming, and seconds later the door opens. We both speak at once.

'I'm sorry to interrupt.'

'Do you want to come in?'

I nod and step inside, surprised at how tidy his room is – he obviously doesn't take after his father.

'I just wanted to apologise for Family Feud back there. Way cornered me and I wasn't thinking about you when I came clean.'

He shakes his head. 'Don't worry about it.'

'I hope your dad forgives you.'

'Of course he will,' he says, sounding surprised by my comment. 'I'll talk to him later when we've all had a chance to cool down a bit. I should have been honest with him in the first place, but while we're apologising . . . I wanted to say sorry for last night.'

I frown, unsure what he's apologising for. Kissing me or not following through?

'I didn't handle things well and . . . what I inferred was unforgiveable.'

Oh, of course – after everything that just happened, I'd almost forgotten what he'd said.

'I was flustered,' he continues, running a hand through his hair, 'and not thinking straight, but the last thing I wanted to do was offend or hurt you. I'm sorry if I did.'

He sounds truly genuine, and I realise his opinion matters to me. 'Thank you. I appreciate that. I reckon you're my only friend on this island at the moment.'

'I'm sure everyone will realise we only had good intentions.'

I raise an eyebrow – his family might be so tight that they'll forgive each other almost anything, but Way sounded pretty angry and I'm not planning on asking forgiveness anyway. 'I'm not sticking around to find out.'

'You're leaving?'

I nod. 'I'm going to change my ticket to this arvo's flight. I should never have come in the first place.'

Leo sighs. 'I probably shouldn't have either. It was hell

getting time off school in the middle of the term and I had to cancel a couple of gigs, which left my bandmates in the lurch as well.'

I look over at the bed, where a black ukulele that looks sexier than I've ever given any ukulele credit for is resting. 'I heard you playing just now. You're really good.'

'Thanks. I was trying to calm myself down.'

'And was it working?'

'I'd barely begun.'

I grin. 'Can you play me something?'

He hesitates and I think he's going to say no, but then he picks up the instrument. 'What do you want to hear?'

'Just play whatever you were playing before.'

As he sits on the end of his bed, crosses his knee and then rests the ukulele atop it, I make myself comfortable on the desk chair.

He takes a deep breath, then begins to play. I watch as his long – but not creepily long – fingers hover above the strings, before starting to pluck them. He plays the intro with such tenderness, but it isn't until he starts to sing that I recognise the song: 'When I See You Smile' by Bad English.

I smile. I might have a cold, unromantic heart but even I can admit the lyrics are beautiful. After a few lines, I can't help but sing along, which is insane because although I love music, I have a terrible voice and always refuse karaoke. But there's just something about Leo that puts me at ease. I don't care if I sound terrible; I just want to enjoy the moment.

And then I look up from his hands to his face and see tears silently streaming down his cheeks. I stop singing abruptly. He notices and stops too.

'Was it my voice?' I'm only half joking.

He attempts a chuckle, discarding the ukulele to wipe his eyes as he shakes his head. 'That was one of Mum's favourite songs. It was hers and Dad's wedding song. I just miss her so much.'

It's times like these I wish I could channel Bee – she *always* knows what to say, and I have no idea. In lieu of words, I cross to the bed, sit beside him and pull him into my arms.

This is why one true love is such bollocks. It doesn't only stuff up the people who think they're in love, but their families and everyone around them as well. Now is probably not the time to state this, but suddenly I know exactly what I want to write in my next chapter, and the one after that. It's not just the rules that are important but the reasons why following them can help – they protect you from a life of hurt and heartbreak.

'Thanks,' Leo sniffs as we cling to each other, our heads resting on each other's shoulders.

We stay like this a long time and after a while, I'm not sure who's comforting who.

He gives me a sad smile and pats my knee. 'Thanks for coming and checking up on me.'

I smile back. 'That's what friends are for.'

'I think I'm going to go for a jog and a swim, try to clear my head. You wanna come?'

'No, thanks. Jogging is not in my DNA, and I need to book a flight.'

'You're really going to leave early?'

I nod. 'I think it's for the best.'

We hug quickly goodbye; Leo tells me not to be a stranger – 'You've got my number now' – and then I go to leave, but just as I reach the door, I turn back.

'I know it's none of my business, but . . .' I nod towards the ukelele. 'You are so good at playing and singing – you've got such a stage presence. I can see why you've been discovered and why your band wouldn't want to lose you. I get that you'd feel bad giving up teaching, considering why you do it, but maybe you can help kids like you in another way.'

He frowns. 'What do you mean?'

'If you guys do become really big, you could use your platform to create awareness for dyslexia, even become an ambassador for early diagnosis and intervention.'

For a moment Leo looks like he's thinking about the idea, but then he shrugs. 'I don't know. Mum was so proud when I decided to teach; I'd hate to think I'd be disappointing her giving it up.'

I smile. 'I reckon your mum would be proud of you whatever you do.' Then I open the door and head back to my room.

The Qantas website informs me that the flight to Sydney this afternoon has been cancelled and there are no available seats on tomorrow's flight to Brisbane. Thinking there must be some kind of error, I call and wait on hold for almost an hour to speak to a live human, only to be told this is correct.

'But I need to leave,' I tell the guy on the other end of the line. 'How can the one flight today have been cancelled?'

'There's a freak storm in Sydney, making it unsafe to land.'

He can't be serious. *Bloody Mother Nature.* 'And there are really no seats on tomorrow's flight?'

'No. They all went moments after the Sydney one was cancelled. I can get you on the Friday arvo flight if you like?'

Only one day earlier than my original flight. My heart sinks. I can't believe I'm actually stuck on this stupid island. I knew I shouldn't have come. 'Yes, please.' One day earlier is better than nothing. I'll be heading to the airport about the same time as Mum is heading to Captain Cook Lookout to walk down the 'aisle'.

I hand over my credit card details, annoyed I'm going to be out of pocket for this trip after all, then decide if I'm going to be stuck here for almost two more days, I may as well make the most of it and actually do some work. After writing a list of supplies I'll need so I don't have to leave this room again until my flight, I head for the supermarket in the main street. Aside from Leo, I assume everyone else is at the museum trying to forget this morning's dramas, but go the back way out of the resort, past the pool instead of through reception, just in case.

I look longingly into Black Anchor Bar again as I pass, and arrive at the tiny, near-empty mall that houses the Foodland Supermarket, a bakery, newsagency and butcher. Inside I ignore the preposterous prices and throw everything I could possibly crave over the next forty-eight hours into my small trolley. Chocolate, crackers, cheese, chips, nuts, more Twisties and a ten-pack of Diet Coke.

'Is there a bottle shop around here?' I ask the young woman who serves me at the checkout.

She nods. 'The Liquor Bonds store is about a four-minute walk that way.' Of course she points in the direction opposite to the resort.

Dammit. I should have gone there first. 'Is it possible to leave my groceries here and come back and get them in about fifteen minutes?' I ask.

'Yeah, that should be fine.'

I pay, then she kindly puts my bags on the floor behind her and I promise to be back soon. On the way to the liquor store, I pass all the shops I've seen from the car but not had the time or inclination to go into, and a park with hundreds of green-painted hands stamped onto squares of white wood and arranged in rows, almost reminding me of a memorial for soldiers. Pausing, I read the sign – *Hands Up for Democracy* – to find out what it's all about. Each handprint has been done by an islander, their name signed beneath it, as a way for the locals to stand together and show tourists and newcomers that they're not happy with the Australian government imposing their rules on Norfolk, taking away their local legislative assembly and thus their true voice about what happens on their island. These hands are their visible protest and symbol of their request to have their democratic power returned to them. In the short time I've been here, I can see that life here is not the same as that on the mainland, and it seems preposterous to have officials who don't even live here and have none of the passion the islanders have for their home ruling it. If I could I'd paint my palm green and add it to this sea of hands, I would. I continue the short distance to the liquor store, which is next to the council buildings and tourist centre. I could go in and buy that phone card I so desperately wanted when we arrived on Saturday, but there no longer seems much point as I plan on holing up in my room until my flight.

After practically skipping up the steps into the large bottle shop, I look around, impressed to find it has the kind of variety you'd find on the mainland. *Halle-freaking-lujah.* I buy a cask of wine and a small bottle of gin, thinking about Ernest Hemingway's advice that one should write drunk and edit sober, and also just wanting something to ease my frustration. I don't necessarily plan on drinking it all, but always best to be prepared.

Sweat is once again pooling on my lower back by the time I collect my groceries, and I'm panting as I lug my heavy bags up the hill to the resort and round the back past the pool. It looks even more inviting than it did the other day, but I can't give in to the urge to take my laptop there. I don't want any chance of interruption by my pesky family again.

Once I've unpacked my shopping, I shower, then put my PJs on as they are the most comfortable clothes I have here to work in. I climb into bed, open my laptop, think of how broken Leo is because of love, and start writing.

The words fly from my fingers, the way people who don't

write probably imagine always happens to authors. Over the next few hours, I don't eat any of my snacks and only occasionally drink, not wanting to risk interrupting this magical flow. I finish Chapter Three – the one that has been languishing for weeks – and move on to Chapter Four, which also pours out of me. I'm actually enjoying myself, the way I did when I first started writing my novel. A message pops up from Bee, but when I see it's merely library gossip about Edgar and Daisy's blossoming romance, I ignore it and turn off my notifications. I don't want soppy stories of seniors who think they're in love to distract me.

Day turns into night, but I barely sleep – snatching an hour here and there before waking again and hammering my keyboard even more. Chapter Four, Chapter Five and Chapter Six are done by midday Thursday. I didn't even know I could think this many words, never mind type them. They're either gold or utter drivel, but it feels so good not to be staring at a blank page any more.

For each rule, I'm giving examples from my own dating history, making it personal, more like a memoir than an instructional manual. At this rate, I could almost be finished my first draft by the time I fly out tomorrow, and everyone knows this stage is half the battle. Once I have the basic words on the page, with the help of my editor I can shape them into something amazing. In fact, maybe I should send her these new chapters now. If she gets them before close of business, she might read them tonight.

Before I can second-guess this decision, I take another large gulp of my wine, press send and am about to start on Chapter Seven when a loud banging sound jolts me from my trance-like state.

It takes a few seconds for me to realise someone is knocking on my door.

'Fred! It's me. Mum.'

My heart drops to my stomach. I suddenly feel guilty for not having sought her out before now – of course when I told Bee what had happened, she told me I should, but then I started writing and have been so consumed with my work that I barely thought about my family.

Then again, neither she nor Way have come to check on me either.

I glance around the room, cringing at the empty Diet Coke cans and junk food wrappers scattered all over the bed behind me – pouring your heart out onto the page is hungry work – and call, 'Just a moment.'

After quickly swiping the carnage onto the floor where she won't be able to see it from the door, I go to greet her. I haven't brushed my teeth or washed my face since yesterday morning, but that doesn't seem important right now.

'Hey, Mum.' I don't quite manage a smile as I open the door.

'I'm glad you're still here,' she says, a quiver in her voice. 'Leo said you'd left.'

'I planned to,' I admit, 'but I couldn't get a flight.'

She nods, rubs her lips together, then says, 'There's something I need to tell you.'

'Oh?' My heart leaps. Has she finally seen sense and decided to cancel or postpone the wedding?

Her next words make this seem unlikely but also pique my interest. 'Something I probably should have told you a long time ago.'

'Do you want to come in?' I ask, wishing I'd taken the time to actually dispose of the cans and wrappers, but she shakes her head. 'This isn't something just you need to hear. Paul and I have called a family meeting. Can you come to the bar?'

'Um. Sure. Just give me five minutes to freshen up and I'll be there.' It's one thing facing Mum without brushing my teeth, but no way I'm facing Leo without sprucing up a little.

Speaking of Leo . . . As Mum retreats, I rush into the bathroom, turn on the shower and quickly text him before I get in.

Me: *Do you have any idea what this meeting is about?*

Lord Leopold: *None whatsoever. I take it you're still here then?*

Me: *Yep. See you soon.*

Six minutes later, which I think is quite miraculous considering the state I was in, I enter the resort bar. As it's only three o'clock in the afternoon, there's no one here except a guy scrolling his phone behind it, and Mum, Paul, Waylen, Leo, his sisters, and River sitting around a table in the corner. No one has a drink; the kids aren't here, and neither is Benji, who I assume must be on babysitting duty. May the Force be with him.

I quickly glance at Leo, who is looking down into his hands as if ashamed, before taking a seat next to Way, who – judging by the way he glowers at me – is still in a snit.

'Thank you for joining us, Fred,' Paul says, reaching out to take Mum's hand.

'Of course,' I reply, wondering what the hell this is about.

17

HIGH-SCHOOL SWEETHEARTS

'It has become apparent over the last couple of days that not all of you are happy about mine and Tracy's relationship,' Paul begins, glancing at each of us sitting around the table. 'And we've both had a bit of time today, and last night, to contemplate this ourselves.'

Oh my God. My heart pounds. They *are* going to tell us it's over! Will Mum ever forgive me?

She nods. 'We've been a little caught up in finding each other again and didn't think enough about how this must look to the rest of you. For that, we're sorry.'

'So,' Paul continues as if they've rehearsed this speech a few times already, working out who is going to say what, 'we think it's time to tell you the truth about our relationship.'

'Please don't tell us you were having an affair while Mum was alive?' Juliet says, her perfectly shaped eyebrows raised.

Ooh, now wouldn't that be a scandal, I think, before realising how much it would upset Leo and praying this isn't the case.

Leo rolls his eyes. 'How on earth are they supposed to have conducted an illicit affair between London and Perth?'

She glowers at him. 'Haven't you heard of aeroplanes? Cybersex?'

He screws up his face.

'Distance or no distance, I would never have cheated on your mother,' Paul reassures them. 'Trace and I meeting again at the reunion is the truth, but we weren't just friends in high school like we led you to believe.'

'I knew it.' Scarlett grins and twists her long braid around her fingers. 'You were high school sweethearts, weren't you?' She elbows River. 'Didn't I tell you?'

River nods and rubs her shoulder affectionately. 'You did, babe.'

Paul returns her smile. 'You were right. Trace and I met the first day of high school and I immediately knew she was the girl of my dreams. After a little bit of chasing, I managed to convince her as well. We started going out at just thirteen and became inseparable. We were each other's first love, first kiss, first everything. We thought we'd be together forever and so did everyone else in our class. We had our lives all planned out. I'd go to university to study horticulture, Trace would go to art school, and when we were both finished, we'd get married.'

Art school? Until she mentioned taking up pottery a few weeks ago, I've never seen Mum doing anything remotely creative. She didn't even jump on the nail art bandwagon when all my friends' mums did.

'Growing up in Brisbane,' Mum takes over, 'we'd heard quite a bit about Norfolk Island, and we fantasised about going on our honeymoon here.'

'That's why we brought you all here,' Paul says. 'We thought, why not share the magic with you all, so you had a chance to get to know each other before the wedding?'

'But it hasn't quite worked out like we'd hoped,' Mum adds.

All eyes snap to me and then to Leo. He blushes but I refuse to feel guilty. So what if they were high school sweethearts? Does it really change anything? How many high school couples go the distance?

'Why did you break up?' Juliet asks, shifting in her seat. I can only imagine how uncomfortable she must be carrying around that massive bump.

Mum and Paul exchange another quick look before turning back to face us. 'Tracy got pregnant at fifteen,' he says softly.

We all gasp. I've never once suspected that Way wasn't Mum's first child. I glance sideways at him to find he's gone pale.

'Obviously, we didn't keep the baby,' Paul explains.

Scarlett's eyes widen in what looks like excitement. 'Are you about to tell us I'm not your oldest child? Do we have an older brother or sister somewhere you adopted out?'

'No.' Paul looks to Mum as if to check she's sure about this conversation, and she nods. 'We were so young,' he continues. 'It wasn't an easy decision to make. We didn't think either of us were ready for the responsibility of parenthood, but we couldn't imagine giving up our child either. And we thought our parents would kill us if they found out, and that Trace would be kicked out of school, so . . . we chose to terminate the pregnancy.'

We're all silent for a while digesting the news. I notice Juliet's hand protectively caressing her bump, but all I can think is *Mum had an abortion*. At fifteen!

I'm gobsmacked. Never in my wildest imaginations would I have expected this of her. She and Way's dad got married *because* she was pregnant, which kind of made me think that she didn't believe in abortion. She is Catholic after all.

Part of me feels bad that mine and Leo's actions have forced them to tell us about their past, but I just don't understand why it had to be such a big secret in the first place. I know Waylen would never judge them for this decision and although I've only known Leo and his sisters a few days, I'm a hundred per cent certain they wouldn't either.

Echoing my thoughts, Way speaks in a tone I imagine he uses with his clients. 'I don't understand why you didn't just tell us you were together in high school.'

'If we told you that,' Paul replies, 'then you'd have wanted to know why we broke up, and neither of us wanted to discuss it.'

Although he says 'we', it's obvious it was Mum who never wanted to say anything. From the moment she first mentioned Paul, I've been trying to find fault with him, but it's clear from the way he looks at her every few moments to make sure she's okay that his feelings for her are genuine. I wonder, for the first time, if maybe I'm wrong – if maybe Leo is as well – about his reasons for wanting to marry her.

'It was a very dark time in my life,' confirms Mum. 'Not long after the . . . the procedure, I haemorrhaged badly.'

'Her parents had to rush her to hospital, and they of course then discovered what we'd done,' finishes Paul.

'Did they force you to break up? Was that what happened?' Scarlett asks, now clutching River's hand as tears slink down her cheeks. Perhaps I've misjudged her as well – I believed her over-the-top chirpiness and empathy was part of her influencer image, but she appears genuinely horrified by this revelation.

Paul digs a handkerchief out of his pocket – like father, like son – and hands it to her. 'No, they were great, actually. Disappointed, but mostly that we hadn't felt comfortable coming to them for help. They saw how close we were and how much we truly loved each other.'

'Then what *did* happen?' Juliet presses.

Mum looks at her sadly. 'I pushed your father away. He tried his best to be there for me, but I was so confused. So sad. So full of shame and guilt. Not only for getting rid of the baby, but that we'd been stupid enough to get pregnant in the first place.

Somehow everyone found out about it, and I couldn't bear to go to school any more.'

My heart squeezes as I think of my own high-school shame.

Kids can be so cruel.

'I dropped out and I got a job answering phones in my dad's office instead.'

'She answered calls all day long,' Paul says, 'but she wouldn't take *my* calls. Broke my heart.'

Mum looks pained as she squeezes his hand. 'I'm so sorry.'

He shakes his head, dismissing her apology. 'Anyway, Mum and Dad bought me a ticket to England for a gap year in the hopes that getting away from Queensland, from the memories of Tracy, would give me the circuit break I needed. Don't think they ever expected me to meet Amelia over there and never come back.'

'I tried to forget Paul too,' Mum says. 'I thought that if I could forget him, I'd forget the pain of what we went through together. I didn't date anyone else for a long time, not until I was almost twenty, and then this young man started working with Dad and wore me down. He was a bit of a joker, the life of the party and so, *so* charming, but it never felt right the way it had with Paul. I realised I'd made a terrible mistake letting him go and decided to track him down in the UK. His parents wouldn't tell me where he was as they didn't want me to hurt him again and you've got to remember we didn't have Facebook or emails, so it wasn't easy. I saved up for a plane ticket, and then I flew there and started working in hotels and pubs myself, travelling all over the country, spending all my free time playing detective and trying to find him. After about six months, I did.'

We're all hanging on this story like it's a movie or novel, not real life, as they explain that a couple of months before Mum showed up, Paul had started seeing Amelia.

'I was heartbroken. Feeling like I'd blown my one chance at

true love, I went to the nearest pub and tried to numb my pain with alcohol.' Mum looks over at Way. 'That's when I met your father. He noticed I was upset, and I ended up telling him the whole sorry story.'

Toby Morpeth had dried her tears, then told her he had ways of making her forget Paul. A month later she found out she was pregnant, and after what happened with Paul, there was no way she wasn't having this baby. I imagine she must also have feared going through another termination.

'He's such a wanker,' Way says, his fists clenched on the table in front of him. 'Imagine taking advantage of someone in such a state.'

'To be fair,' she says, 'he did the right thing. He married me. And he's always paid his maintenance payments on time.' Both Way and I snort at her defence of Toby.

'Did you and Dad ever see each other again?' Scarlett asks, twisting Paul's hanky between her fingers.

'Yes,' Paul replies. 'We did. It was me who told Tracy I was with someone else. It was one of the hardest conversations I've ever had and one of the toughest decisions I've ever made. I was shocked and unnerved seeing Trace again – it brought all the hurt back. Besides, Amelia and I were good together. She made me feel human again. We were excited about our future, and I didn't want to lose her. I said goodbye to Tracy, never expecting to see her again.'

'So you *did* love Mum?' Leo asks. He's as pale as Waylen.

Paul nods solemnly. 'I loved your mother very much. We had a wonderful relationship for almost forty years. That's one of the other reasons we didn't want to tell you about our past. I never wanted you to doubt that. I cherish every moment we had together, the family we created, and I don't regret the choice I made, but love is a complicated beast. It isn't finite. I don't think I ever stopped loving Tracy either, and I'd be lying if I said that I didn't think of her occasionally and ponder what might have been. When I got the invitation to the reunion, I immediately wondered if she might go and before I knew it, I'd booked my ticket.'

Mum sniffs and smiles. 'Whereas I ummed and ahhed about going. I'd avoided the earlier ones, terrified that Paul might be there and my heart would be broken all over again seeing him. Penny and Cara convinced me to go though, assuring me he'd never been before so I decided to risk it.'

'And I'm so glad you did,' Paul says. 'It was like no time had passed. Despite all the years, the connection we'd felt way back when we were kids was still as strong as ever. We couldn't resist each other.'

They exchange fond smiles, and I have to admit, they do look right together. That's something I don't remember thinking with any of Mum's other fiancés – well, aside from Jeff. But looking back, maybe I was more smitten than she was.

'Losing your wonderful mother . . .' As Paul speaks again, he looks first to Scarlett, then to Juliet and Leo. 'Well, it made me realise that we're all on borrowed time. I'm sorry if this feels hasty, but Trace and I don't want to waste another moment. We don't want to wait for whatever anyone else'—his gaze darts quickly to me—'considers a reasonable time. We *will* be getting married tomorrow, and we'd love you all to be there, but there'll be no hard feelings if any of you decide you need longer to get used to the idea of us together, right, Tracy?'

'None at all,' Mum promises, shooting a conciliatory smile my way.

'Of course we'll be there,' Scarlett gushes, looking at Leo with the kind of stern expression I didn't think her capable of. She stands, walks around the table to Mum and hugs her. 'I'm so sorry for what you went through when you were fifteen.'

Mum sniffs and hugs her back. 'Thank you, sweetheart. That means a lot.'

Paul squeezes Scarlett's hand. 'Thanks, love.'

'Well,' Juliet says, reaching for her water bottle, 'that was quite a lot to take in.'

'Yes. It is. Do any of you have any other questions?'

I have so many questions and so many thoughts, so many things I want to tell her, but I still feel awkward about doing so in front of Paul and his family.

Perhaps the others feel the same as me – or perhaps they need time to digest all this – because they all shake their heads.

'In that case'—Paul stands and puts his hands on the back of Mum's chair—'Trace and I are going to go out with our friends who arrived this afternoon. We're going to have a nice dinner to catch up, then an early night so we're both feeling refreshed for our big day tomorrow. Will we see you all there?'

Everyone looks to me as he says this, and I see the hope in Mum's eyes.

I'm no longer certain what I feel about this marriage or any of her others after hearing from her and Paul, but I'm here and I think of Bee's words a month ago when I told my colleagues about the wedding.

What if this ends up being forever and you not being there ruins what should be the happiest day of her life?

Would I ever be able to forgive myself for that? Would Bee? 'I'll be there,' I promise. She'd be proud of me.

Mum grins like I've just given her the secret to wrinkle-free skin, then rushes over and pulls me into a hug. 'I love you, sweetheart,' she whispers, before heading out with the man who is apparently destined to become Husband #6.

Before they reach the door, Juliet tells the rest of us she's going to her room to call Henry and fill him in on everything.

'You want to come to dinner with us afterwards?' Scarlett asks her.

She shakes her head. 'I think I'll just have a quiet night and order room service.'

Scarlett chuckles. 'Too much sisterly time at the spa today?'

Juliet grins back. 'Something like that. See you all tomorrow.'

Way says he might take the opportunity to whisk Benji off somewhere for a romantic dinner, but he gives me a hug goodbye, which tells me he's forgiven me. Scarlett and River decide they're going to buy fish and chips from the shop on the main street and take the kids up to Puppy's Point to watch the sunset.

'Do you two want to come?' they ask.

Leo turns down the invitation, and there's no way I'm going on my own, no matter how much I've bonded with Kayla.

As they leave to go rescue Benji from the kids, Leo gestures towards the bar. 'Would you like to get a drink? I feel like I need one after all that.'

I *should* head back to my room and keep writing, but I'm not sure I'll be able to focus after 'all that'. I knew Mum and I weren't close but, hearing about the abortion and art school, I'm wondering if I even know her at all. 'Yes, but not here,' I tell him.

He grimaces. 'Don't tell me you want to go back to the RSL.'

I smirk. 'It wasn't that bad, but no. I have somewhere else in mind.'

'Intriguing,' he says, and I do my best to ignore the little spark that shoots through me.

18

SUNKEN DRAILORS

'Do I need to change my outfit?' Leo asks as we leave the resort bar.

I take the opportunity to run my gaze down his body, taking in his multi-coloured tie-dyed T-shirt and khaki shorts. Dark brown leather thongs on his feet. Once again, I marvel at how big they are, but try to ignore that inappropriate thought.

'Nah,' I say. 'I think we're both suitably attired.'

I'm wearing a short denim skirt, a floaty singlet top and red sandals to match my red toe-nail polish. The island seems fairly casual and the Black Anchor – which I'm hoping is open on Thursdays as the sign on its door indicates – didn't look pretentious.

'Excellent.' His smile doesn't quite reach his eyes as he gestures to me. 'Lead the way.'

We give a half-hearted wave to Mr Whatshisname as we leave the resort and start down the driveway towards the main road, our shoes click-clacking in time on the bitumen.

Leo sighs. 'That was a pretty heavy conversation back there. I gotta say, I'm feeling a little guilty now.'

I want to tell him I'm not and that he shouldn't be either, but the churning in my stomach calls me out as a liar. 'I know what you mean, but we didn't have all the information when we came up with Operation Break-up.'

'Do you think knowing about their past . . . about the baby . . . would have made a difference? Would you have given Tracy your blessing then?'

'Hard to tell. Maybe. But to be honest, I'm struggling to wrap my head around what we've just learned, never mind wondering how knowing it might have changed a lot of things. Then again . . . maybe it doesn't.'

'What do you mean?

I shrug. 'I'm not trying to diminish what they went through, but they weren't the only teenagers who thought they were going to stay together forever. If Mum hadn't got pregnant, maybe their relationship would have ended another way. Instead, because of the trauma they went through, they've both been holding onto this their whole lives.'

'So . . . you don't think the fact they've never forgotten each other is a sign that this marriage will work?'

'I honestly don't know. I'm not psychic. All I ever had to go on was Mum's track record. Maybe if I'd had more information, I'd have felt differently.' But right now, all I feel is even more distant from my mother. 'Do you feel better about things?'

'No,' he admits. 'Maybe I should but it still feels wrong that he could be marrying someone else so soon after Mum died, and I feel like a fool thinking what my parents had was so magical. How can he truly have loved her if he never forgot about Tracy?' As we reach the end of the drive and turn left onto the road, Leo adds, 'If Dad and Tracy didn't get pregnant – or even if they decided to keep the baby – and they did stay together then my parents would never even have met.'

'Yeah, and my mum might have been a totally different

person,' I say, still trying to come to terms with the idea of her and the word 'artist' being used in the same sentence. 'If they'd stayed together, she wouldn't have married all those other deadbeat men, except for Jeff, of course.'

Leo half chuckles. 'Saint Jeff.'

'But they did break up,' I say. 'Your dad did marry your mum. And I can tell when he talks about her that he did love her. Maybe there are different kinds of love.'

He casts me a confused look. 'I thought you didn't believe in love?'

'I said it wasn't worth the hassle. That all it causes is heartbreak and pain.' And what we've learned today proves my point. Mum has – apparently – spent her life pining after Paul and what they might have had, rather than being fully present with what she did have. I shake my head. 'But what do I know?'

'What do any of us know?' he agrees. 'So you're staying for the wedding now?'

I sigh. 'Yeah. What about you?'

He nods. 'I came here to support Dad because Mum would have wanted that. I guess she'd want him to be happy, and it does seem Tracy makes him happy.'

Despite his words he still sounds so glum and I'm desperate to say something to lighten the mood. 'You know, if our parents never broke up, you and I could have been siblings.'

'Don't think that's how genetics work. More likely you and I wouldn't exist.'

'That's a sobering thought.'

'I'm sorry.' He stops walking abruptly. 'I'm not sure I'm going to be very good company tonight. Maybe I should—'

'No. We're in this together.' I grab his hand before he can turn back. I can't let him be alone with his dark thoughts about his parents. He needs a drink. ASAP. Thankfully, we're approaching the Black Anchor Bar and I spy a guy wiping tables out the front. 'I don't care if you're not good company. I just want your company.' I don't let go of his hand until we're right outside the bar, three tall palm trees swaying in the gentle breeze near us. 'Is it too early to get a drink?' I ask the guy.

He glances at the smart watch on his wrist. 'Officially we're not open for another twelve minutes. Unofficially, head on inside and I'll be there to take your order in just a moment.'

Leo slides open the glass door, his hand gently grazing the small of my back as he ushers me ahead of him. I always roll my eyes if I read something like that in a book, but he barely touches me, and tingles spread throughout my body. I don't think I've ever felt such an intense attraction to someone I know I'm not going to sleep with.

Trying to ignore that thought, I focus on our surroundings. Sea shanties drift from surround sound speakers, and like Darling, Darling, the Black Anchor is pirate-themed, though not quite to the same extent. There are a couple of barrels on the long bar, which is a beautiful, polished wood, with black stools in front of it. Above the requisite wall of fancy alcohol bottles are a few black boards with cocktail specials scrawled on them in chalk. One wall is painted black and there are only a few low-hanging ceiling lights, so it's easy to imagine how warm and cosy it is once it gets dark outside.

'This place is great,' Leo says, plonking himself down on one of the stools. 'And looks like we're spoilt for choice.'

We're leaning in to read the drinks menu when the guy out front comes in. He heads around the bar, then offers us a grin and his hand.

'I'm Joel,' he says, 'Welcome to Black Anchor.' He's got short, chestnut hair and wide-rimmed black glasses. His friendly smile is exactly what you expect of someone in his industry.

'Leo and Fred,' we tell him.

'What can I get you?' he asks.

'I'm going to have the Sunken Drailor,' I say.

He nods his approval. 'Great choice. And for you?'

Leo decides he'll have the same and we watch as Joel skilfully salts two martini glasses, before mixing tequila, lime juice and blue curacao. He garnishes both drinks with a curl of orange rind, some mint leaves, and a cherry.

'So, what brings you two lovebirds to Nor-fuk?' he asks as he places our drinks in front of us. 'Honeymoon? Special anniversary? Just a holiday?'

'Um . . .' My cheeks heat as I glance at Leo.

He looks as awkward as I feel. 'We're not, um, together.'

'Sorry. I just assumed. You look . . .' Joel shakes his head. 'Never mind.'

'It's fine. Easy mistake to make,' Leo says, and then we tell him why we are here. We don't go into detail about this arvo's family meeting but he's a barman and, sensing that we don't have the joyful aura most wedding-goers do, manages to get a lot more out of us than we mean to tell him.

'No wonder you need a drink. Sounds like quite the drama.' The sliding door squeaks open, and Joel waves a hand in recognition as four women in their forties come in. He introduces them as locals – Olivia, Amber, Jude and Yuri – and we learn they're out celebrating Amber's birthday.

'These are almost as good as the cocktails at Darling, Darling,' I say to Leo as Joel gets to serving the party girls.

'Where?' Leo asks.

I put the drink down, wanting to savour it. 'It's this totally lit, pirate-themed bar back home. They have the best cocktails and all you can eat there is the free peanuts. It's dark and dingy and feels like you're way back when. Sometimes there's a guy on the fiddle playing all these old sea shanties and everyone sings along.'

'I thought you didn't like the sound of your own voice?'

I scoff. 'It's different if I've had a few drinks and everyone is singing. My colleagues from the library are regulars. We go there whenever there's an emergency to debrief.'

'What kind of emergencies do you have at libraries?'

'There you go making assumptions again. We had quite our share of dramas last year, if you must know.'

Leo tips his glass towards me. 'You can't say that and not elaborate. Please, tell me about all the dramas . . . I need the distraction.'

'Okay.' I take a quick breath, readying myself for the story. 'Our old boss Janine had to retire suddenly last year and her replacement was an absolute nightmare. Think banning books and cancelling almost all activities we offered. If anything had a hint of fun about it, she wanted it gone.'

He listens intently as I tell him about Ursula killing the feel-good vibe of the library and also the hex Persephone put on her. 'Your friend really thinks she's a witch?' His cynical smirk sends a thrill up my spine.

Trying to ignore it, I laugh, delighted that he appears to be brightening a little. 'And who's to say she isn't? She still feels a bit guilty, because in the end Ursula was quite sick and Persephone blames herself. Then, there was the guy Bee dated.'

When I've finished describing what we now refer to as the Fabio Fiasco, although not when Bee's around because she doesn't like talking about him, Leo says, 'Maybe that's the book you should be writing. The life of a librarian is far more interesting than I ever imagined.'

I contemplate this. 'You know, I've never thought about setting a book there, but you might have just given me my next idea. We do meet lots of characters. Thank you.'

One of the four women leans in, clearly overhearing us. 'Are you an author?' she asks. I think her name might be Yuri.

I turn to nod at her and give her my very brief pitch of *21 Rules for Not Catching Feelings*.

'If only I'd had that book when I was dating,' says the blonde who I think is Jude. 'Maybe I wouldn't have met an islander and found myself stuck here.'

The birthday girl digs her in the side – 'Don't pretend you don't love it. You wouldn't have met us if you didn't marry Curtis' – then looks at Leo and me. 'Do you want to come sit with us?'

We exchange a look.

'Oh, sorry, you probably want to be alone.' She giggles, then takes a sip of her bright pink cocktail.

That has us both answering quickly, saying exactly the same thing: 'No, we just don't want to intrude on your celebration.'

'Don't be silly.' Brunette, Olivia – if I'm correct – waves her non-cocktail-holding hand at us. 'The more the merrier. Come on, let's go grab a table out the back before this place gets crowded.'

We follow the women out onto a verandah, which overlooks a grassy area with a few more tables and chairs. Very casual and rustic with a couple of overgrown trees and mismatched shrubs, it could easily be someone's back garden. We've barely sat one minute before Joel emerges carrying two more Sunken Drailors. 'On the house,' he tells us, placing them in front of Leo and me.

'Wow, thanks,' we say in unison as he retreats.

'He's just oiling you up so you stay longer and spend bigger later,' Amber says. 'Now, do you mind if I pick your brain? I've always wanted to write a book.'

If I had a dollar for every time someone has said this to me, I could pay back my advance and then some, but I summon a smile and ask Amber if she has an idea.

'Oh, no, not yet,' she says and I notice Leo trying not to smirk. 'Although I guess I'd set it here. I like reading historical fiction, so maybe something about the bounty mutineers.'

Over the next hour we exchange life stories, finish the free cocktails and Leo buys another round for everyone, saying it's his birthday gift. It comes out that he's in a ukulele band and the birthday gang go crazy when they check out the UkePros on Instagram.

'My goodness,' Olivia exclaims. 'You're practically famous.'

I manage not to tell them that he's also practically royalty – a guy needs some secrets – and when Joel's right hander, Roxy, arrives with the prawn tacos and onion rings the women have convinced us to order, they force her to watch one of his videos on YouTube. Leo's cheeks have turned the colour of my favourite red lipstick and it's quite possibly the cutest thing I've ever seen.

'You have to play something for us,' Jude demands.

Leo chuckles as he shakes his head. 'I don't have my uke.'

Jude looks to Roxy. 'Go ask Joel if he's still got that old ukelele out the back.'

I raise my eyes to Leo as Roxy disappears inside.

A few minutes later, Joel comes back, this time holding a ukulele high in the air like it's a trophy. 'Leo, my good man, what's this I hear about you being a famous musician?'

'No idea.' Leo laughs and shakes his head.

'I knew I kept this for a reason. It was part of the décor for a theme night we had a few months back.' Joel thrusts the instrument at Leo. 'Drinks are on me for you and Fred for the rest of the night if you give us a little live music.'

The women squeal and clap their hands in excitement.

After a little cajoling from our new friends, he gives in. 'Okay. Just one song.'

We head back inside to find the bar is now chocka-block – the tables are all full and there's little more than standing room. Joel drags Leo behind the bar to safety, cuts the background music and whistles loudly. 'Ladies and gents,' he calls, 'I have a surprise for you. Leo from England is going to play a few tunes.'

'I said one,' Leo objects, lifting the ukulele to his chest and then smiling at an older lady sitting at the bar. 'What's your favourite song?' She answers immediately – 'Sweet Caroline' – and he nods, takes a quick breath, then begins.

At first everyone listens, soppy smiles on their faces – apparently mesmerised by his talent – but gradually they join in, one by one, until almost everyone in the room, including me and Joel, are singing along at the top of our lungs. Of course, no one lets Leo stop at just one. He whips through 'American Pie', 'Like a Virgin', and 'We Will Rock You'. His talent and repertoire are varied and apparently endless, and I reckon I'm the proudest person here.

Finally, much to the outcries of everyone, he begs for a break. As Joel puts the other music back on, I hand Leo another cocktail. 'Here you go, superstar.'

'Thanks.' He lifts it to his sexy mouth and takes a long, slow sip.

'Dance with me,' I say, tugging on his hand.

He looks around. 'But nobody else is dancing.'

'So? You're not chicken, are ya?'

In reply, he hits me with a stomach-tumbling smile, puts his glass on the bar and lets me lead him into the throng of people. It's a truth universally acknowledged that as soon as one person starts to dance, others will join them and that's exactly what happens. Just like the fish fry night, I'm in awe of Leo's skills as we dance along with locals and tourists alike to all the classics like the Macarena, YMCA and the Nutbush. With so many bodies moving close together, it's getting hotter and stickier in here by the second, but I'm having one of the best nights of my life.

Guilt pricks me at this thought – if we hadn't caused a family feud, we wouldn't be here right now letting our hair down at the

Black Anchor Bar with the locals, yet I can't help being happy that we are.

'Feeling better?' I ask as we take a quick breather and each down some water.

He nods. 'Yeah. Thanks to you.'

We gaze at each other and I wonder if he's thinking about kissing me again. It's about the only thing I can think of. No matter how much I tell myself that nothing can happen between Leo and me, I can't help wishing it will. Damn him and his morals! If not for them, I'd drag him into the bathroom right now and have my wicked way. But I don't think I'm imagining it when he steps a little closer and he dips his head. *Oh God.* My mouth goes dry, and my lips are buzzing as they anticipate his touch.

Just as I swear he's about to do what he swore he wouldn't do again, Amber thumps us both on our backs. 'The girls and I are calling it a night,' she yells over the din, too drunk to realise she's interrupting a moment.

Her friends appear behind her. I could murder the lot of them. 'Can we get your numbers?' Olivia asks.

Leo and I drag our useless phones out of our pockets, and we all swap details, making what I'm sure in the light of day – when they're sober and nursing hangovers – will be empty promises to keep in touch. We also make empty promises that we'll come back and visit again.

'Do you want to get out of here?' Leo asks when they're finally gone, and the crowd is thinning.

Is he asking what I think he's asking?

I swallow. 'Are you asking what I think you're asking?'

He nods slowly and I feel like I might be about to have a heart attack.

'How drunk *are* you?'

'Not drunk enough to be unclear about what I'm doing.' He

slides his hands around me and draws me close. 'I want this, Fred. I want *you*. If one thing Dad said this afternoon made sense, it's that life's short and we never know how it's going to turn out. Even if we don't have a future, I don't want to regret not sleeping with you.'

Although sweeter words have never been whispered to me before, the voice of reason screams in my head that this is a very bad idea.

But don't worry – since when have I ever listened to the voice of reason?

'I want you too,' I tell him, pressing my mouth to his.

We barely manage to say goodbye as we hightail it out of the Black Anchor. At first, we're walking briskly towards the resort, but we quickly pick up our pace to a jog and are panting by the time we stumble hand in hand into the resort reception to find Way and Benji there, pacing.

'Where the hell have you two been?' my brother demands.

I'm tired of him acting like he's my father. 'We went out for a drink. What's it to you?'

'Looks like you had more than one drink,' he snaps, glancing at our adjoined hands. 'And we've been trying to find you for the last couple of hours.'

'Why?' My heart leaps to my throat. 'Has something happened to Mum?'

But then I realise he's looking at Leo. 'It's your dad,' Way tells him, his expression softening. 'He's at the hospital.'

19

WHIPLASH

*L*eo lets go of my hand. 'What? What happened?'

'He and Mum came back early from dinner because he was feeling a little short of breath and not himself,' Way explains. 'They'd just gone to bed when he started to get chest pain, and he said his heart was racing. They called an ambulance, and I drove your sisters to the hospital. Since then, we've been trying to find you.'

'Fuck.' Leo rakes his hand through his hair. 'I need to be there.'

Way nods. 'We'll drive you.'

I'm grateful for my brother because I don't think Leo should be driving anywhere right now. He looks distraught, even worse than he did hours earlier when I desperately wanted to make him feel better.

'I'm coming too,' I say. I might not have the power to fix Paul, but at least I can be there for Mum and Leo. Especially if something really bad happens.

Oh God. Chest pain and heart issues. He's not going to die, is he? My own chest tightens at the thought. *Please let him be okay.*

Leo has only just lost his mum and mine has only just found

Paul again. I think of how she was after Bernie left, and my heart fills with dread at how much worse *this* might be.

What was *I* thinking?!

If Paul is okay, I bargain with the universe, *I'll be the best maid of honour anyone has ever seen.*

The four of us rush outside to the hired hatchback and climb in. Although the drive to the hospital is less than five minutes, it feels like five hours.

'Do you think it could have been something he ate?' Leo asks, leaning towards Way in the driver's seat.

My brother shrugs. 'I don't know.'

'Did he have pain anywhere else?'

Benji takes this one, turning around from the passenger seat to look at Leo as he speaks. 'Not that Tracy mentioned, but she was pretty agitated when they left. We'll be at the hospital soon and—'

'Do you think they'll fly him to the mainland?' Leo interrupts.

'I'm really sorry, mate,' Way says. 'We've told you everything we know. We haven't heard anything since we dropped the girls off. We've been looking for you.'

Leo sighs. His knees are jittery, and his hands are fisted and also shaking. I reach across to put my hand over one of his, but he yanks it away, his gaze trained out the window into the darkness.

My breath catches in my throat at his brush-off.

He's angry at me, and I don't blame him. If I'd let him go back to the resort when he wanted to, he'd have been there when Paul was rushed off in an ambulance. He might not have been able to do anything, but at least he'd be with his father now. Instead, he was with me, about to cross the line he'd drawn so clearly the other night. Shock has a knack of sobering people up – maybe he was drunker than he realised and already regrets suggesting it. Or maybe he's pissed off that I dragged him into Operation Break-up in the first place.

If we hadn't put so much stress on them, would Paul still be out enjoying dinner with Mum and their friends right now?

My hands are clammy and my stomach heavy with guilt, but I can't worry about my own feelings or even Leo right now. The only thing that matters is Paul. I pray they have good medical facilities on the island.

My hope fades as Way turns off the main drag onto a road that feels more like the entrance to a caravan park than a hospital. When we pass a sign promoting a fundraiser for a new hospital, my heart sinks even further. Way parks just off to the side of a cluster of blue and white weatherboard buildings, which look like the chalets I stayed in on school camp one year.

This *cannot* be the hospital.

But Way and Benji have already been here once tonight and know exactly where to go, leading us up a long ramp to a door with a red emergency sign. We enter into a reception area with fake timber laminate flooring, white walls and the strong scent of disinfectant. At least it smells like a hospital.

Scarlett and Juliet rush at Leo the moment they see him. He wraps his arms around them both as if he's the older sibling. Juliet looks over Leo's shoulder at me and let's just say, I don't think he's the only one angry at me.

I swallow. Perhaps I shouldn't have come.

'Any news?' Way asks.

The siblings break apart. Juliet shakes her head. 'Not yet. The doctor is at book club.' She says 'book club' in the tone you'd expect someone to use for an illegal dog fighting ring or something. 'The nurses are monitoring him and have taken bloods for—'

'What do you mean the doctor is at book club?' Leo shouts. 'Have they called him? Is he on his way?'

'*She* is on her way,' Scarlett says, putting a calming hand on Leo's arm. 'Tracy's with Dad while they wait, and the nurses are lovely. Let's not get wound up just yet. Juliet called Henry and—'

'And he said the fact that Dad was conscious when the ambulance took him off is a good sign. Let's hope so, because . . .' Juliet glances around. 'I'm not holding my breath on the facilities here.'

At that moment a trim woman with a short dark bob, who I'd guess is in her late thirties, strides in from outside. She looks like she means business and gives us all a curt nod as she zips out of the waiting room and down a corridor.

'She must be the doctor,' Benji says.

I let go of the breath I've been holding. 'She looks like she knows what she's doing.'

All eyes snap to me.

'You'd better hope so,' Juliet says, and no one stands up for me. Not Leo, not Way, not even Scarlett, who normally sees the best in everyone.

I think maybe I should leave, but would that be even worse? *Argh*. As I'm pondering what to do, Leo and his sisters huddle close together on a couch, Scarlett and Juliet leaning their heads on his broad shoulders. Way and Benji take a seat on a wooden bench opposite, leaving me with an uncomfortable plastic chair I probably deserve. It takes everything I have to lower myself onto it, rather than run out the door.

I desperately want to speak to Bee, but my phone is useless because I never bothered to get a local sim card. Probably a good thing, I think, as I drum my fingers on my knees. Bee would be horrified that this has happened and possibly blame me as well. She wouldn't say I told you so – she's not the type – but she did. She told me that Operation Break-up was a terrible idea and yet, as usual, I thought I knew best.

There are no magazines – the pandemic put paid to that in

hospitals – so we sit in awkward silence, the only noise coming from a plastic clock on the wall. If this was a bigger hospital or even a bigger island, I'd offer to go get coffees or something for everyone, but I can't even see a vending machine.

And there's every chance they'd tell me to take a hike! Despite the ticking of the clock, time feels like it has stopped.

After what seems like hours, Juliet heaves herself off her seat and starts pacing. 'What's going on in there? Surely they know something by now.'

'I reckon no news is probably good news,' Benij says.

She raises a perfect eyebrow at him. 'Are you a doctor?'

He shakes his head sheepishly and I give him a weak smile. More time passes, and when Juliet eventually sits back down, Leo shoots up. 'This is ridiculous. I'm going to find out what's going on.' Heading for the corridor, he almost collides smack-bang with the doctor.

'I'm Doctor Ramesh,' she says, sidestepping him and addressing us all. 'You must be Paul's children?'

Leo, his sisters, and Way nod.

My heart hitches as I wait for her to continue. Her expression gives nothing away.

'I've run an ECG and we've tested your father's blood for troponin, which is a good indication of whether someone has suffered a heart attack. While I don't have the results of the blood tests just yet, I'm fairly certain Paul's symptoms are not related to cardiac arrest.'

I gasp, unable to hide my relief at this news.

Scarlett bursts into tears and I have to admit I'm struggling to withhold waterworks of my own.

'Then what happened?' Juliet asks, frowning as she rests her hands atop her bump.

Dr Ramesh almost smiles. 'I'm diagnosing a panic attack.

'What?' Leo frowns. 'But Dad's never had anything like that before.'

'I understand Paul has had a few stressful days,' she replies.

Once again everyone looks at me, and I wish I could apparate like Harry Potter.

'The symptoms of this intense anxiety,' Dr Ramesh continues, 'are often the same as those of a heart attack, so you did the right thing calling an ambulance and getting him here as soon as you could. Just to be on the safe side, since I don't have the blood results yet, I'm going to keep Paul in overnight for observation. Do you have any questions?'

Way nods. 'Will he be out in time to get married tomorrow afternoon?'

Scarlett presses a hand to her chest. 'Yes. And will that be okay for him? Not too . . . stressful?'

'I think Paul not getting to marry his beautiful bride would be worse,' Dr Ramesh says, finally allowing her smile to show. 'It's clear how much those two adore each other.'

'They were childhood sweethearts.' Scarlett sniffs and in that moment, something clicks inside me.

Even Dr Ramesh – a stranger – can see Mum and Paul are meant to be together.

And I finally agree. This time *does* feel different. I can't quite explain it, but all my fears about this marriage evaporate. I know she loves Paul in a way she never loved any of her other husbands and I thank the powers-that-be for not taking him away from her.

'Can we see him?' Leo asks.

Dr Ramesh nods. 'Yes, but just quickly – he needs rest – and only one person at a time. It's late and we have a couple of other patients we need to be mindful of. I'll go get Tracy and let her know you want to see him.'

She disappears and I hang back like a bad smell while the others hug and clap each other on the back.

I don't deserve to see Paul – although I want to tell him I'm sorry – but I *need* to see Mum. When she appears a minute or so later, I'm shocked by the sight of her. Her skin is pale and her eyes bloodshot, as if she's had a medical episode herself.

Instinctively, I rush to her. 'I'm so sorry.'

'What are you apologising for, darling?'

Where do I start? 'For not trusting you when it came to Paul, for trying to split you up. This panic attack is all my fault.'

She pulls me against her and for the first time in as long as I can remember, I don't flinch at her touch. 'That's all in the past now. Paul's going to be fine. Everything's going to be fine. I love you.'

'I . . . I love you, too.' My eyes well with tears; I can't remember the last time I told her this. It's only now I realise how much I mean it. She might not be perfect but neither am I, and I would be devastated if anything happened to her.

Way comes over and wraps his arms around the both of us. He doesn't say anything, but I hope this means he's forgiven me. Scarlett goes to see Paul first, then Juliet, then Leo. Benji offers to drive the girls back to the resort as Juliet particularly needs her rest, promising to come back for us after. Mum says she's going to stay the night and asks Way if he can fetch toothbrushes and some other items, which leaves the two of us alone in the waiting room.

'Are you okay?' Mum asks, patting my hand as we sit side by side on the bench.

I sniff and nod. 'I should be asking you that. You probably regret wanting me to be here this week.'

She squeezes my hand. 'I have a lot of regrets about you and Waylen but wanting you here with me for my wedding and to meet Paul and his family is not one of them.'

'You wish you didn't have us?' I hear the anguish in my voice and cringe. I don't like sounding needy.

'No.' Her decisive reply echoes around the otherwise empty waiting room. 'Of course not. I don't regret having either of you, but I do regret the mother I was to you.'

I frown. 'What do you mean?'

'I was in awe of you both, but I never felt like I deserved these two fabulous, smart, funny kids after choosing not to have my first one. Because of that, I guess I held back a little, kept my distance. I thought I was punishing myself, but really, I was punishing all of us. I'm so sorry.'

As tears fall down her cheeks, I shake my head, grappling to come to terms with this admission. 'That makes no sense. You didn't deserve punishment. You were fifteen years old. You did the right thing.'

'Really?' She bites her lip. 'Was it the right thing? I not only lost Paul because of what my guilt and shame did to me, but I also let down the two people who mean the most to me in the world.'

I blink. 'Me and Way?'

She nods and I don't say anything because I'm not sure what to say.

'I didn't feel I was enough for you on my own, and I wanted you to have the kind of family I had growing up – two supportive parents – so I tried to achieve that for you, but all I managed to do was collect unsuitable husbands and push you further and further away.'

I can't believe what I'm hearing. 'Are you saying you kept getting married for *us*?'

'In a way,' she admits. 'At least initially. Your dad was great with Way at first, and I thought the four of us could be a family. When that didn't work out but then Jeff came along and loved you both, I felt like I'd hit the jackpot, but after *he* left, I started to think there was something wrong with me. That I was unlovable. And I guess then I just wanted to prove that I wasn't. I know it might look like I'm repeating this pattern with Paul and there's probably nothing I can say to make you understand that this is different but—'

'Mum,' I interrupt, 'I can see that this is different. Even if I didn't know what you told us today, I can see that you and Paul are the real deal. I was just scared, because I didn't understand. I wish you'd told Way and I the truth a long time ago.'

She sighs. 'Maybe I should have said something, but it's not the kind of thing you tell little kids and, as you got older, you seemed to despise me so much . . . I was scared that telling you would make you hate me even more.'

'Why on earth would you think that?'

'Well, you could barely stand to be in the same room as me, never mind talk to me.'

I shake my head. 'That's not what I mean. Why would you think telling me about your abortion would make me hate you? As if I'd judge you.'

'Not everyone is as broad-minded as you, Fred.'

It sounds as if she's talking about someone specific, yet I remember Paul saying their parents would have been supportive, so it can't have been them who filled her with such self-loathing. 'Who are you talking about?'

'Bernie,' she whispers.

'Bernie?' I feel my face screw up instinctively as I say his name. 'What did that bastard say?'

Mum takes a deep breath. 'Not long after we got married, I told him about the termination. I hadn't told anyone in years – your father didn't know, and neither did Jeff or Colin, because talking about that time made me so sad. It was easier just to block it out. But it just came out one night, and he was horrified.

Called me all sorts of names and said he couldn't be married to a baby killer.'

My hands clench into fists. 'Is that why he left you?'

She nods. 'What he said brought back all the shame and sadness and guilt I'd been bottling for years. I felt like the lowest of low and—'

'That's why you were so depressed,' I say. 'Not because of losing Bernie but because he confirmed all the fears you always had about yourself.'

'Yes.'

I'm fuming. I didn't think I could hate that man more than I already did. 'Bernie is the one who should be ashamed!'

He's lucky we're practically in another country right now, because if I was back in Perth, I'd hunt him down and murder him with my bare hands.

'In some ways Bernie did me a favour.' She lets out a wry chuckle. 'Until him, I'd been burying all my trauma deep down inside me, but I couldn't ignore how I felt any longer. I started therapy and worked through my guilt, and I don't feel ashamed any more. When I met Paul again, I was in the best place I've been mentally my whole adult life. I don't think I'd have been open to letting him into my heart again if I was still holding on to all that.'

'Did you ever think about telling Way and I?'

She nods again. 'I asked my therapist if she thought I should, and she said that if I wanted to, I should. I knew you already thought me weak because of all my marriages and I didn't want to risk you thinking worse of me. So instead, I vowed to show you I could be strong and worked on turning my life around. I just wanted to move forward.'

And I can't deny she did that. These past few years I've been surprised and impressed by her independence and the focus she's had on friendships and family over relationships.

'I'm proud of who you've been these last few years,' I tell her.

'Really?'

'Yes, that's why I was so upset about your engagement to Paul – it seemed like such a setback.'

She sniffs and gives me a watery-eyed smile. 'That means a lot. Thank you. And I can see now that holding back wasn't the right decision. I'm sorry I never told you the truth.'

'That's okay,' I say, even though I can't help wishing she had confided in me. Can't help thinking it might have made a big difference to our relationship. Maybe I'd have felt less resentful taking care of her after Bernie if I'd known. My anger would have been directed at him rather than her. 'It was your secret to keep, your story to tell or not tell whoever you felt fit.'

'Maybe, but I am sorry for everything I put you through, all the terrible decisions I've made and the effect all my doomed relationships have had on you. I hate to think that because of me you've closed yourself off from love. I was hoping you being here on the island – spending time with me and Paul – would show you that we're the real deal. True love isn't just a fantasy, but something we all deserve.'

I think of Kyle. It would be so easy to let Mum believe that my decision to abstain from committed relationships was solely because of her, but that's not true. Until Kyle broke my heart, I think I still believed in the fairytale. Mum's bared her past – warts and all – to everyone today, so maybe it's time I do the same.

'It isn't just your failed marriages that have shaped my decision to stay single,' I admit. 'Something happened in high school.'

The colour had come back into her cheeks over the last few minutes, but now she turns pale again. Her hand rushes to cover her mouth. 'Did someone take advantage of you? Was it a teacher?'

I shake my head – 'Not a teacher' – and no one could be more surprised than me when what happened with Kyle tumbles from my lips. 'When I was in year ten, I had the biggest crush on this boy. He was really smart and funny, good-looking of course, and also sporty. I think every girl in our grade and some of the boys fantasised about him noticing them. We sat together in human bio and he used to make me laugh so much that sometimes I'd get into trouble, but he always owned up and said it was his fault too. 'He was so popular, and I was an in-betweener – not one of the cool girls, but not one of the total rejects either – so I never thought he'd actually reciprocate my feelings. I didn't even think he knew how I felt, but I guess maybe it was obvious.

'When he asked me to go out with him, I couldn't believe it. I thought I was the luckiest girl in the school. I was so in love with him . . . or at least I thought I was. Who knows? But he told me he loved me. He made me feel so special. And so I slept with him.'

Mum squeezes my hand; I hadn't even realised she was holding it.

'The next day at school, everyone was laughing at me. Apparently, it had all been a big joke. He and his mates had some bet about who could get one of the nerdy book girls to give them their virginity first.'

She gasps. 'Oh honey.'

A lump swells in my throat. 'I didn't know, but . . . he'd filmed us and was showing all his friends. I felt so stupid but couldn't bring myself to tell on him. He might have been expelled if I had. Instead, I vowed there and then *never* to allow another man to have that power over me again.'

'Oh, Winnie.' Mum's voice sounds like it's breaking. 'I'm so sorry, I had no idea.'

My eyes water at the nickname she hasn't used since I was a kid. 'I didn't tell you.'

She wraps her arms around me and pulls me close. 'Yes, but maybe you would have if I'd been more available. If I'd been a better mum.'

'I'm not sure that's true,' I say. 'Most teenage girls don't talk about sex to their mums.'

'Either way, I don't like to think that one awful boy has ruined you.'

'I'm not ruined,' I object, pulling out of her embrace.

She gives me a sad smile. 'Really, darling? Are you happy?'

Before I can tell her that yes, I am happy, I love my independent life and the freedom it offers me, Way and Benji stride back into the waiting room. I quickly pull back from Mum's embrace and wipe my eyes. No way do I want to share my shame with my brother and his boyfriend. I scrutinise their expressions, trying to work out if they overheard anything, but they appear oblivious. Thank God. One emotionally wrenching, mortifying conversation per night is more than enough.

'Hopefully I've brought everything you wanted,' Way says, dumping a bag next to Mum.

'Thank you, darling,' she replies as Leo appears from the corridor.

We all look at him.

'Sorry I took longer than five minutes,' he says. 'We . . . uh . . . had a few things to discuss.' The redness in his eyes tells me I haven't been the only one shedding tears, but despite this he looks lighter than he has all week.

'That's okay.' Mum stands and goes over to hug him. 'He's your father, you can take as long as you want.'

'Thanks.' Leo sniffs as he clings to her, our gazes meeting over her shoulder. He gives me what I can only describe as an awkward smile, but at least it's a smile.

When Mum and Leo break apart, Way says, 'You ready to head back to the resort now?' He's stifling a yawn, which of course makes me yawn. The plastic clock on the wall tells us it's almost one o'clock in the morning.

Leo shakes his head and gestures to the less than comfortable grey couch. 'I think I'm going to camp out here tonight. I don't want to be too far away from him, and I want to be here for you too, Tracy, in case you need anything.'

'Oh, that's so sweet of you,' Mum says, 'but are you sure? The doctors don't seem concerned, and I'll call you immediately if anything changes.'

'I'm sure,' Leo replies in a tone that tells us he won't be deterred. I guess this puts paid to any fantasies I may have had about picking up where we left off. Although it's probably for the best, I can't help being disappointed.

Being around Leo is like having whiplash over and over again. Just when I've convinced myself nothing is going to happen between us, something does. But then, just as quickly, everything changes again. *Argh.*

FRED CALLS A FAMILY MEETING

riday morning, I'm so tired – physically and emotionally – from the events of last night and also talking to Bee about it until well past both our bedtimes – that I sleep through the rooster and wake to the buzzing of my phone. I'd usually ignore a number I don't recognise, but with Paul in hospital, I decide I should answer.

'Good morning?'

'Fred?' pants a slightly familiar, female voice. 'Is that you?'

'Yes,' I reply warily.

A sigh of relief. 'It's Petrice. I've tried to call your mum but she's not answering her phone, and she listed your number as the back-up.'

'Probably because she's in the hospital and her phone doesn't work there.'

'Don't tell me she's got this awful gastro as well?' My heart thuds.

'What gastro?'

'That's why I'm calling.' She groans. 'I'm really sorry but I can't do your hair and make-up today.'

I sit up fast. 'What?'

'I've been vomiting all night. I'm as sick as a dog. I can give you the number of a couple of other—'

'Don't worry about it. I'll sort it out. Get better soon, okay?'

'Thanks.'

As the line goes dead, I tell myself this is not a disaster – I'm not bad with an eyeshadow palette and, judging by the elaborate braids in the kids' hair, either Scarlett or River is talented in that department. The only problem is the wig that Petrice was going to bring with her for me.

Oh well, if me being bald is the worst thing that happens on Mum's big day, I'm sure she'll survive.

I flop back into my pillows and, not quite awake, begin my morning scroll, giggling when I see the barrage of messages from the women we met last night in the Black Anchor. I am about to text Bee and tell her I am staying for the wedding after all and don't need the early pick-up from the airport that Sully promised me – when a notification from Emily, my publisher, pops up.

I spend zero-point-two seconds deliberating about opening it, not wanting bad news to put me in a funk when I need to be all smiles and sunshine today, but then my curiosity gets the better of me.

Just finished reading your pages over my morning coffee. I know it's your mum's wedding today otherwise I'd call, but just wanted to let you know they are superb. Better than the first chapter you originally submitted. Better than I could have hoped for. This book is going to be such a massive hit. You are going to be a superstar. Every morning TV show will want to speak to you. Now enjoy your day and then get writing again. Em.

Relief washes through me as I read her words, and the panic I've been feeling these last few weeks – that maybe I've bitten off more than I can chew – eases. I'm shooting off a quick message thanking her when my phone rings again.

My stomach tightens at another unknown number, but I swipe to answer. 'Good morning?'

'Hello,' says a voice I don't recognise, but somehow sounds a little off. 'Is that Tracy's daughter?'

'Guilty as charged.'

'My name is Rodger King, Blanche's husband.' *Blanche?* Why does that name sound familiar? 'You met her the other day at Captain Cook's Lookout. She's supposed to be the celebrant for your parents' wedding today.'

Supposed to be? Not liking the sound of that, I don't bother correcting him that Paul is *not* my dad. 'Is something wrong?'

'Yes, I'm afraid she's caught a bug. She's been up all night vomiting and had hoped she'd be over it by this morning, but if anything, she's worse. I'm really sorry, but I don't think she'll be able to officiate the ceremony today.'

'Blanche wasn't by chance with Petrice, the hairdresser last night, was she?'

'Yes, they were at book club. Why?'

I sigh. 'She's just called. She's got gastro too.'

'Oh. Really? Maybe it's food poisoning then. It was at Nora's place . . .' He chuckles. 'She has a bit of a reputation for occasionally overlooking use-by dates.'

I don't give two hoots about Nora or her reputation. No celebrant is much worse than the hair and make-up issue. 'Is there someone else on the island who can do the ceremony?'

'Well, we no longer have a Catholic priest full time on island, but you could try the Church of England minister at St Barnabas.'

'Do you know how I can contact them?' Mum and Paul didn't

want to get married in a church, but maybe the minister will be happy to perform off-site, and if not, well, beggars can't be choosers.

'Give me a second,' he says, and I hear the rumple of papers. 'You got a pen?'

I grab one from the desk and jot down a phone number. 'Good luck,' Rodger says.

'Thanks. I hope Blanche feels better soon, and please let me know if she makes a quick enough recovery to go ahead.'

'Will do,' he promises, and I take a deep breath as I disconnect, then immediately dial the Minister's number, letting out a blood-curdling scream when I get a voicemail telling me the minister and his family are currently on holidays on the mainland and will be back next week.

This can*not* be happening. My stomach roils as if *I* might have food poisoning too.

Think, Fred. Maybe there's a tourist on the island who is qualified to marry people, but how on earth would I find that out? My heart is starting to race. Was this how Paul felt last night when he had his panic attack?

But I don't have time for shame and guilt. I need to fix this, and I can't do it on my own.

Not bothering to shower, I throw on shorts and a T-shirt and run next door to Waylen and Benji's room, but there's no answer. Maybe he's having breakfast. Forgetting to even close my own door, I run towards the main building and find my brother in Cook's Landing, sitting with Benji, Juliet, Scarlett, River and the kids.

Kayla's eyes light up as she sees me but I ignore her. 'Bit of a problem,' I tell the adults by way of a greeting.

Waylen puts down his knife and fork on a plate full of mushrooms and eggs and raises an eyebrow at me. 'What have you done now?' Knowing I probably deserve that, I don't bite back like I normally would. Instead, with unsteady legs, I take a seat between him and Juliet and hit him with it.

'The celebrant's husband and the hairdresser just called me. They've both got food poisoning and can't work today.'

Everyone stares at me as if they're waiting for me to tell them I'm joking, but quickly realise I'm not.

'Oh no,' Scarlett gasps, her hand rushing to her mouth. 'Fuck,' Juliet says. 'Isn't Blanche the wedding planner as well?' *Oh, shit!* She's right.

'Aunty Juliet said a bad word,' Kayla pipes up, her eyes wide.

Thank God she can't hear what I'm thinking; the F-bomb has been on constant repeat inside my head since I heard the minister's voicemail.

River winks at her – 'Occasionally adults need to let off steam, sweet pea' – then looks at TJ. 'Do you want to take your sisters into the games room to play for a bit?'

'No,' she replies, clearly not wanting to miss any drama.

I've got that tight chest feeling again and reach across to grab Waylen's glass of water and take a sip. *Breathe, Fred.* 'We don't need a wedding planner at this stage – everything's already organised,' I manage, 'and we can take care of the hair and make-up between us, but the celebrant is an issue.'

Everyone nods, then Benji says, 'What about a minister or priest? Way and I checked out St Barnabas yesterday and it'd be a stunning place to get married.'

'We don't need a venue,' I say – at least Captain Cook's Landing can't get food poisoning – 'and I already called, and unfortunately the minister of St Barnabas is otherwise engaged.' Likely drinking cocktails in the Whitsundays or something. Do men of God get paid holidays? I shake my head; now is not the time to ponder such things. 'I was thinking we could try to find out—'

My suggestion of somehow looking for a qualified tourist is

cut short when my phone rings again. Another unknown number. 'I'm too scared to answer this,' I say, thrusting the phone at Way. He takes it from me, clears his throat and accepts the call.

'Hello? This is Waylen Morpeth. How may I help you?'

The formal way he answers the phone usually amuses me, but I appear to have lost my sense of humour as I listen to his side of the conversation. Spoiler – the caterers, two sisters who work together – are also book club members. That's the problem with getting married on a tiny island where all the wedding contractors know each other. This would never happen on the mainland.

'Oh my God.' I drop my head into my hands. 'This is a disaster.' No hairdresser. No celebrant. And now no food. Even though this is not my fault, I can't help thinking that somehow it is – that Leo and I being so opposed to the wedding has somehow summoned all this bad luck – and I bet that's what everyone else is thinking as well. If only he was here to take some of the heat.

And then he is.

'Uncle Leo,' Kayla shrieks. Always happy to see people, she's more like a puppy than a cat.

I look up and sure enough, Leo is striding towards us.

He's still wearing yesterday's shorts and T-shirt, there are sweat patches on his shirt, and he's breathing heavily. I can't imagine he got much sleep last night and he must have just run here from the hospital, but he still looks like something one might serve on a platter for dessert. Despite our current disaster, my blood simmers at the rise and fall of his Adam's apple as he reaches for Kayla's glass of apple juice and drinks.

Scarlett and Juliet speak at the same time. 'What are you doing here?'

'Is Dad okay?'

Yes, *this* is what I should be thinking about.

Thankfully, Leo nods, putting the glass back on the table. 'But we do have a slight problem.'

My blood stops simmering. *What now?*

'Another one?' Juliet echoes my thoughts, a pastry halfway to her mouth.

Leo frowns – 'What do you mean *another* one?' – and then sits between TJ and Miller in her highchair as we fill him in.

'Is this some kind of joke?' Leo says when they're finished.

'Afraid not,' Way says. 'What were you about to tell us?'

He sighs. 'The marquee for the reception up at the lookout is gone. It was set up yesterday afternoon and there was a freak wind gust early this morning that ripped it off the ground and into the Pacific Ocean. A couple of locals caught it on camera as it took to the skies and then bellyflopped into the water. They posted it in the local Facebook group. It's probably halfway to New Caledonia by now.'

'Holy shit,' Way says.

'Uncle Way said a bad word too,' Kayla exclaims, half-delighted, half-horrified.

Everyone ignores her.

'Do Tracy and Dad know?' Juliet asks. Her expression echoes my own fear – we all know that Paul doesn't need any extra stress right now.

Leo shakes his head. 'No, I overheard the nurses at the hospital talking about it and asked them not to say anything to Dad or Tracy. Then I told them I wanted to get in a morning run, so I was going to head back here and fetch a car to come collect them. I figured we'd call Blanche and get it sorted before she could tell them, but . . .' He trails off.

But Blanche is otherwise pre-occupied thanks to Nora's disregard for food safety. I don't know who this Nora is but right now, I could throttle her!

'How *is* Dad this morning?' Scarlett asks, grabbing Miller, who has started to grizzle, out of the highchair.

'He's good. Slept through the night, no more symptoms,' Leo says as Scarlett whips up her shirt for Miller to breastfeed. 'They're just waiting for Dr Ramesh to come in and give him the all-clear to leave, so they can come back and get ready for the wedding.'

The word lingers in the air as we all contemplate the fact there might not be a wedding.

'Looks like you two might get your wish,' Scarlett says eventually, looking from me to Leo disapprovingly. 'It's going to take a miracle to find a new celebrant, and what's everyone going to eat?' Juliet nods, clearly horrified by the thought of no food. 'Besides, isn't light rain forecast for this evening? If there's no marquee, we're all going to get wet.'

'No!' I say, so loudly and forcefully that everyone – even Miller – jumps. The thought of telling Mum that the wedding of her dreams to the man of her dreams is not going to happen makes my stomach turn. I promised myself if Paul lived, I'd be the best maid of honour there's ever been and I'm going to follow through. 'I can fix this. I've been to tonnes of weddings.' Half of them Mum's. 'I know I can pull one together in a few hours.'

The doubtful faces that look back at me don't make me feel very confident – it won't be easy doing so on an island not much bigger than a postage stamp – but I have to try. It's then I remember the women we met last night. If they're not too hungover, I'm sure they'll be willing to help.

'Leo and I met a bunch of locals last night,' I say breathlessly. 'We can ask them about someone else who might be able to cater, or better still find a new venue that will do both. I know it's short notice, but we can't let Mum and Paul down.'

The hint of a smile appears on Leo's face as he nods. 'That's a great idea. Those women seemed to know everyone. Perhaps we could even ask Joel at the Black Anchor if we can hold the reception there. He's got more than enough space inside for everyone.'

I love his thinking. 'Yes, great idea. He might even be able to cater.'

'Mum really wanted the reception to be up at the lookout,' Way says. 'And even if you can organise all that, there's still the sticking point of the celebrant.'

Dammit. Why does my brother always have to bring me down to earth?

'Maybe one of us could get ordained online,' Benji suggests, 'like Joey did in *Friends*.'

I'm not entirely sure he's joking.

River raises his hand. 'I'll do it. I reckon I'd make a great wedding celebrant.'

Is this *actually* a possibility? Hell, even I'd get ordained at this stage.

I think of the Facebook group Leo mentioned. 'I was thinking that maybe there's a tourist on the island who's qualified – either a celebrant or a minister on holiday? Maybe we can get one of our new friends to put the word out on Facebook that we're desperate for a Blanche replacement.'

'That's a great idea,' Leo says, giving me one of his melt-your-insides smiles.

Warmth blooms in my chest. 'Thank you. And while we're praying for that celebrant miracle, we can address all our other problems, so at least we're ready to go if we do find someone.'

'What do you need us to do?' River asks, leaning forward as if he means business. I might have thought him an oddball when we first met, but I'm really beginning to like him.

I bring up the Notes app on my phone. 'First things first,

we're going to need someone to keep Mum and Paul off the scent. Leo, you're probably best to take charge of your dad?'

He nods. 'I'll take him to brunch and then, depending on how he's feeling, we could play that game of golf we didn't get to yesterday. Either way, I'll keep him out of harm's way.'

'Excellent.' That leaves Mum. 'Has anyone seen Mum's friends, Penny and Cara?'

'Yeah.' Juliet speaks through a mouthful of pastry, swallows, then adds, 'They came to the spa with us yesterday and are staying in the room next to me.'

More guilt squeezes my heart – *I* was supposed to be at that spa day with them – but I need to focus. 'Can you track them down, fill them in and ask them to distract Mum this morning?'

Juliet nods and we all decide that for the time being we won't let the other guests – thank God there aren't many – who've made the trip for the wedding know that anything is wrong. If we end up having to change venues, we'll tell them as close to the original ceremony time as possible.

We're in the middle of divvying up the other jobs – Juliet will do Mum's make-up, River (turns out he's the whiz with the braids) will do her hair, and Way, Benji and I will work on the food and marquee problems – when one of the resort staff interrupts us.

'Excuse me,' she says, hovering by our table. 'I'm looking for Tracy, the bride. She's with your group, isn't she?'

The dread I feel in my gut is echoed in the faces of everyone else at the table, except maybe Miller, who continues to suckle contentedly.

'Yes,' Way says. 'I'm her son, but she's not available right now. Can I assist you?'

The woman blinks rapidly as if in a firing line. 'Um . . . I'm so sorry to tell you this but . . . we were storing the cake and the flowers, which were delivered yesterday, in our drinks cool room and there was some kind of malfunction last night. All the icing on the cake has melted and the flowers are terribly wilted.'

'Are they salvageable?' I ask, not entirely convinced now that someone isn't playing a cruel trick on me. Could the others have conspired to get back at me and Leo?

But the woman looks like she's about to cry – join the club, I think – and if this isn't real, I'm sitting at a table of *very* good actors. 'Not really,' she says. 'I called our chef to see if maybe she could whip up some kind of replacement for the cake, but she's got food poisoning. Thinks she ate something dodgy at her book club last night.'

'How many people are in this bloody book club?' Leo asks, echoing my thoughts.

'I'm sorry?' the resort lady says.

I shake my head. 'Never mind. Thanks for letting us know. We'll handle it.'

River lets out a disbelieving chuckle as the bearer of more bad news retreats. We all turn to glare at him. 'I'm sorry,' he says, trying to stifle his amusement, 'but you really couldn't make this kind of crazy up.'

I sigh as I add cake and flowers to my list.

'The girls and I will deal with this,' Scarlett says, pulling her top back down as she pops Miller's dummy into her mouth. 'I've made dozens of birthday cakes in my time and I'm sure we can find someone to let us raid their garden.'

'If not, I can make origami flowers,' TJ offers, her eyes twinkling at the prospect.

Leo nods. 'Great idea, I love your origami, Tallulah-Jane but . . .' He looks at Scarlett. 'What are you going to do about a kitchen?'

She smiles condescendingly at him. 'You worry about Dad, brother dearest, and I'll worry about that.'

'Maybe we can ask one of the women we met last night if you can borrow theirs?' I suggest.

'Perfect,' Scarlett replies. She passes Miller to River. 'You're on baby duty for now. Hopefully by the time you're needed for hair duty, I'll have the cake and flowers sorted and can take Miller.'

'What about me?' Kayla asks, looking anxiously around.

'You and TJ are coming to the supermarket with me,' Scarlett says, standing. 'You don't think I can do all this on my own, do you? Come on, we've no time to waste.'

The girls scramble after her as she strides out of the restaurant.

Leo stands as well. 'I'll grab some car keys and head back to the hospital to collect Dad and Tracy.'

Juliet goes with him – taking three extra Danishes for later – to find Penny and Cara and fill them in on our plan.

Way looks to me as they depart. 'Okay. What's our game plan?'

ROMANTIC AT HEART

'Hello? Jude speaking.'

I've tried her first because she was the one who seemed the least intoxicated last night. 'Hi Jude, it's Fred. We met yesterday at the Black Anchor.'

She chuckles. 'Do you think I have Alzheimer's or something? I know who you are. Glad to hear from you, actually. The girls and I thought we might have been a little bit OTT last night in our professions of life-long friendship and all that. Good to know we didn't scare you off.'

'Not at all,' I say, ignoring the fact that if we didn't have a wedding emergency, it's unlikely I'd have ever contacted any of them again. 'In fact . . . I know this might be pushing a new friendship, but I'm in a bit of a pickle and wondering if you might be able to help.'

'Oh yeah, what kind of pickle?'

I take a quick breath and fill her in on everything that's happened since that first fateful phone call from Petrice. Saying it all out loud only makes it sound even more unbelievable, but luckily Jude takes me seriously.

'Frigging Nora,' she says. 'You'd have thought she'd have

learnt her lesson after she almost killed the kids' netball team with her homemade sausage rolls. What were those idiots thinking eating her food?' It's clearly a rhetorical question and I don't have the time or wherewithal to ask about the netball team. 'You're lucky it's my one day off this fortnight and I'm an old romantic at heart. I'll help. Just give me twenty minutes to have a shower, inject some coffee and make a few phone calls.'

While we wait for Jude to get back to me, I go have a shower myself. I should probably try to eat something, but my stomach is queasy, whether from last night's booze or this morning's stress, I can't quite tell.

She calls back exactly twenty minutes later and sounds almost excited by our mission. 'Right, meet me at the Golden Orb café as soon as you can. I've gathered the troops.'

As I'm coming out of my room, I run into Juliet with Mum's friends, Penny and Cara. They live in Queensland, so I haven't seen much of them since we moved to Perth when Mum married Jeff, but aside from a few more smile lines around their eyes, they don't appear to have changed much in the intervening years. Penny is still tiny and still wears multi-coloured caftans and lots of loud jewellery, which I suspect is to make herself seen, in contrast to tall Cara, with her neat blonde bob and simple navy sundress.

They're nice enough women, but I always felt that true friends should stop their friends doing stupid things like getting married multiple times. As far as I know, they've always been entirely supportive of Mum's nuptials and I wonder if they know the truth about her and Paul.

'Winifred,' they exclaim in unison as they throw their arms around me.

'We've just heard about all the dramas,' Penny says, pulling back first and flicking her dark bob out of her eyes. 'What a shemozzle! But Juliet says you've got it all under control?'

I nod, hoping this to be the case.

Cara pats my arm. 'Well, don't you worry about Tracy. We'll meet her when they get back from the hospital and will keep her occupied until it's time to get ready.'

'Thank you.'

We walk together into the main building where Way and Benji are waiting for me. We're heading out of reception to the car park when Leo arrives with Mum and Paul. My stomach twists as she scrutinises us. For all her shortcomings as a mother, one thing she's always been good at is knowing when Way and I are trying to pull the wool over her eyes.

'Where are you three off to?' she asks, narrowing her gaze.

'Um . . .' Although Bee sometimes jokes that I want to be a professional liar – it's what she calls novelists – my mouth goes dry, and I can't think of one good answer.

Thankfully, Way saves the day – lawyers are excellent fabricators. 'Fred and I are planning a special surprise for you, and we've got to go make a few final arrangements.' Then he looks at our future stepfather. 'How are you feeling this morning, Paul?'

'I'm good. Really good.' The older man offers us a sheepish grin. 'I feel a bit silly causing such a fuss yesterday though.'

Benji pats him on the arm. 'Nothing silly about it, mate. You can never be too careful with your health.'

'Anyway, we really should be going,' I say, before they can ask any more questions. 'Penny and Cara are inside looking for you, Mum. Think they have a few treats planned for you while Leo and Paul play golf. Enjoy.' I turn to scurry away towards the car.

'You'll be back in time for hair and make-up, won't you?' she calls.

I wave my hand above my head – 'Of course. You enjoy your morning and I'll see you soon' – and climb into the backseat before she can say another word. Little does she know that hair and make-up are the *least* of her worries.

Despite the fact that rain is predicted for this evening, there's not a grey cloud in the sky as Way drives towards town and Benji natters on in his Pollyanna way about it being the perfect day for a wedding.

'Isn't rain on your wedding day supposed to be *good* luck? Maybe we should be praying for a downpour,' I say, folding my arms across my chest.

Way raises his eyebrows at me through the rear-view mirror. 'Since when are you superstitious?'

I'm not but right now I feel like any cosmic assistance couldn't be a bad thing. I just shrug.

We find a parking spot on the main street and even though I'm feeling uncharacteristically anxious, I can't help but admire the gorgeous canopy of trees we walk through to get to the Golden Orb café. We stop to marvel at a beautiful spider – presumably a golden orb – weaving a web in one of them. There's an almost magical vibe to the place and I feel my racing heart begin to slow. We head into the café, which is warm and rustic, with framed photos of local places and tables and chairs in a mishmash of wood and cane. Mouth-watering aromas waft from the small kitchen behind the counter and a young man works quickly at a large coffee machine. I'm disappointed not to have discovered this café before today. It would have been the perfect place to bring my laptop and write.

'Fred!' Jude shouts from one of the tables, where she's sitting alongside Yuri and Olivia. 'Over here.'

I introduce the boys – 'This is my brother, Waylen, and his partner, Benji' – before we all sit down.

'Why are the gay guys always the best-looking?' Olivia asks, shaking her head as she stretches her hand out to Way.

'Um . . .' He looks at Benji as if not sure how to respond and I stifle a chuckle. Way lost for words is a *very* rare occurrence.

'It's because we take care of our skin,' Benji explains, pointing to his near-perfect complexion.

Jude chortles. 'Don't mind Livvy, she's just split up with her rat of a husband who got a little too friendly with the girls on his fishing tours, so she's dark on straight dudes.'

'Oh, I'm sorry to hear that.' Benji offers her a sympathetic smile. 'Waylen is a top-notch family lawyer if you need one.'

'Is that right? Do you do mate's rates?'

Before he can answer, I clear my throat – while this chit-chat is all very lovely, we have a wedding to save. 'I assume Jude has told you what's going on?' I say, looking at Olivia, then Yuri.

Yuri nods. 'Sounds like quite the misfortune.'

'That's one word for it. The question is . . . can you help?'

A woman I immediately recognise as the birthday girl from last night arrives at the table with a tray of drinks.

'This is Amber's place,' Jude explains, 'which is why we decided to meet here, but also because she might be able to help with your catering issue.'

'Really?' Way and I say in unison, looking up at her like she's the Messiah.

Amber grins and nods and she places steaming coffee mugs in front of the women. 'It's my day off today – after last night – but when Jude called me, I came right in. How many guests are you feeding?'

'It's only a small wedding,' I tell her. 'Immediate family and a few close friends, twenty-five people all up.'

'Oh, I can definitely help you then, but before we chat menus and logistics, how about some drinks? Something to eat?'

With the stress of catering off my plate, my hunger comes back with a vengeance. Way and Benji order coffees and I opt for a green smoothie and a pumpkin and feta muffin. While Amber goes off to fill our order, the rest of us work through our other issues.

'Your stepsister can borrow my kitchen,' Yuri offers. 'And I can help with the cake as well, if she needs it. I love baking.'

Olivia calls her mum, who has a beautiful cottage garden and asks about raiding it for flowers.

'That leaves the celebrant and the marquee,' Way says as Amber returns with our drinks and my muffin.

The women agree that getting another marquee is impossible – apparently the one now swimming with the sharks is the only one on the island – but Amber offers the café as a venue instead.

Way concedes that even though Mum had her heart set on a reception overlooking the ocean, this makes practical sense. We don't have to worry about the weather or sourcing temporary gazebos from islanders – Olivia's suggestion – to create a make-shift marquee, and it will be much easier for Amber and her staff if they don't have to trek the food from the café over to Captain Cook's Lookout. Mum and Paul can still get married there and have all the photos they want, but then we can come back here to eat, drink and be merry.

'It might be hard to imagine right now, but this place can scrub up quite well,' Amber promises, pointing to the ceiling. 'We can string up some fairy lights, I have some white tablecloths that we used for a high tea out the back somewhere, and I'm sure the ladies at the Bounty Centre will have ideas on what we can use for table centrepieces and any other adornments you'd like.'

'The Bounty Centre?' I ask, after swallowing a mouthful of the most delicious muffin I've ever tasted. If this is any indication of the quality of food Amber can produce, the catering is in good hands.

'It's this huge shop on the main street,' Way tells me. 'Benji and I spent hours looking around in there yesterday. They've got everything from fancy dress to Lego, souvenirs and all this wedding stuff. There was a room off the main shop dedicated to celebrations.'

I gape at him. 'You spent a couple of hours in a shop?' He's always hated shopping, and orders everything he can online, even groceries.

Way shrugs and looks fondly at Benji. 'Shopping can be fun when you're doing it with the right person.'

Benji returns a soppy smile as he kisses Waylen on the cheek. If I wasn't so shocked, I'd probably want to puke at such sentiment. Honestly, it's like my brother has had a total personality transplant since finding love.

'I'm afraid we won't be able to start setting up until after the lunch service though,' Amber says. 'I'll see if any of my employees can work a double shift.'

Way – thankfully, because I've barely got a cent to my name – offers to pay not only for the food, but all her wages and then some. Jude, Olivia and Yuri volunteer to help in the kitchen and if I was a soppy kind of person, I'd want to kiss the lot of them.

Benji says he'll help with the fairy lights and handle the table settings. 'I love decorating.'

It's agreed Way, Benji and I will go to the Bounty Centre to source what we need, Yuri will go get her kitchen ready for Scarlett and the girls, Olivia will help Amber plan the menu, and Jude will do her utmost to hunt down a celebrant. After thanking them profusely for their help, we say goodbye, then cross the road and go over to the Visitors' Centre to buy a phone card. It's a miracle I've lasted this long without connection, and it seems a waste to buy one for the short time we've got left on the island, but having a working phone is a necessity for me right now.

As Way drives us the short distance back towards the Bounty

Centre, I insert the new sim card into my phone. Dozens of notifications from my various dating apps pop up on the screen, but I'm not the slightest bit curious to look. Instead, I call Leo on the off chance he's still around at the hotel, so he can pass on the message about Yuri's kitchen to Scarlett and give her the address.

He answers on the second ring. 'Hello, Leo speaking?'

Of course he doesn't recognise my new number and I smile at the questioning tone in his sexy voice. 'Hi, Leopold.'

'Winifred! How goes the mission?' He sounds happy to hear from me, which gives me hope we've moved on from last night. I know we've only known each other a short time, but his approval matters to me.

'Good. I think we might just pull this off.' I quickly give him a run-down of the emergency meeting with the girls and make sure he jots down the address for Scarlett.

He lets out an impressed whistle. 'Wow. Great work, Winifred.'

'Thanks.' I can't help beaming.

'What about a celebrant?'

'Um . . .' My joy bubble bursts. 'That's the sticking point still, but Jude is on it, and apparently if anyone can find one, it's her.'

He chuckles. 'That I believe. Thank God we went out last night.'

My stomach squeezes as I immediately think about what almost happened between us. Heat flushes through me, but I can't think about this right now. 'How's your dad? Have you seen Mum at all?'

He sighs. 'I think they're a little suspicious. Dad wasn't up for golf, so we're playing Scrabble in the games room, and Penny and Cara haven't managed to distract your mum. She's wondering why Petrice hasn't arrived yet and Blanche isn't answering her phone. I don't know what to tell her.'

'Can she hear you?'

'No. I stepped out to take the call.'

I breathe a sigh of relief. 'Okay. Well, here's what I think you should do. Tell her that Petrice has food poisoning, but that me and River are going to do her hair and make-up. I think you should also tell her about the marquee – that's probably why Blanche isn't answering, because she's running around getting a replacement, and Way, Benji and I are with her. Whatever you do, don't mention Blanche being sick.'

'O-kay . . .' He doesn't sound convinced.

'Hopefully this way, if we explain there are a few hiccups but we have them under control, she'll be less suss and maybe even relax a bit. Anyway, I've got to go,' I say as Way pulls up in front of the Bounty Centre.

Mostly cream with trims of green, it's one of the biggest buildings on the street. I haven't ventured inside because the signs out the front indicate it sells toys, games and souvenirs – three things I have no interest in – but the moment I step inside, all I can think is that they've undersold themselves. Way wasn't kidding when he said this place sells everything. I see books, stands of trinkets and cheap jewellery, calendars, stationery sets, travel goods and more.

The building seems to go back forever, and every surface is accounted for. I would hate to have to do a stocktake here!

Weaving our way through overflowing baskets and displays, we head towards the back and then veer left into a little room that's packed to the brim with wedding paraphernalia. 'Holy hell,' I say as I look around.

Granted, much of it is rather tacky – boxes of pastel confetti, plastic cake-toppers, 'just married' signs, satin and lace horseshoes, sickly peach-coloured organza bonbonniere bags, fake gold elaborate candelabras and much, much more. Some of it looks like it's been here for decades.

I point at a cellophane bag full of dried flowers. 'Is that potpourri? I haven't seen that since I was a kid at Granny's house.'

Way makes a face, but it's immediately apparent that Benji is in heaven. Reminding me a little too much of the crazy wedding planner in *Father of the Bride* – yet another movie I watched on repeat as a child – he starts picking things up, scrutinising them and then either putting them back or thrusting them at me and Way to take care of.

He holds up one of the candelabras. 'What do you think of these for the table centrepieces?'

I shrug. 'I have no idea.' The last thing I ever expected to be doing was picking out wedding favours and decorations, so I'm happy to take his lead.

He frowns. 'I know they look a little tarnished but if we found some pink spray-paint, we could tart them up a bit.'

'Will they dry in time?' Way sounds sceptical.

'Good question. If not, we can wrap some of this pink ribbon around,' Benji says, picking up a disc of said ribbon. 'And I can fold those pink serviettes into swans.'

'You can?' I ask, impressed. I couldn't think of anything more cringy, but Mum will love it.

He nods, then winks at my brother. 'I'm a man of many talents, aren't I?'

'That you are.' Way blushes and I find myself smiling at their sweet banter.

What the eff! All this love and wedding talk is getting to me. 'I think I saw some art supplies on the way in. I'm going to go look for pink spray-paint,' I say, leaving them to smooch and pore over the offerings.

Although we're on a mission and a deadline, I get distracted by a music section – this shop really does have everything, except the kitchen sink. There's a flute, a trumpet and a couple of guitars, but of course it's a bright red ukulele that makes me think of Leo and the way his fingers played across the strings of his instrument.

You *know* where my mind goes.

If we hadn't been interrupted last night, those sexy, skilful fingers would have been playing me. A delicious shiver scuttles down my spine as I wonder if Leo is as disappointed as I am that this didn't happen. If so, is there a chance of a do-over tonight? Then again, by that time – if Jude does manage to find a celebrant – we'll be officially step-siblings.

That should probably feel like more of an issue than it does. Future Christmases sitting across a table could be awkward if we've been intimate and have to pretend we haven't. Then again, how much worse could it be if we're still trying to ignore our raging chemistry? Maybe it would be better just to get it out of our systems and leave all that sexual energy behind us on the island.

'Fred! What are you doing?' Waylen's voice interrupts my carnal thoughts. 'I thought you were looking for spray-paint.'

'Um . . .' I have no excuse, so instead I say, 'On it' and hurry to where I'm supposed to have been. Arms loaded with treasures they found in the wedding room, Way and Benji follow, and we're delighted to find a quick-dry bottle in a gorgeous pink. If we start on the candelabras immediately, they should be ready for the reception. Everything is falling into place. I only hope Jude is having similar luck.

'I'm proud of you,' Way says as we pile all our purchases onto the counter. 'I know you had doubts about this wedding, but you're really stepping up now.'

My cheeks heat at his words. 'I only ever wanted the best for her.'

'I know.' He draws me into a quick side hug as an elderly man comes behind the counter, greets us warmly and begins ringing everything up. 'You come across all prickly, but deep down you have a heart of gold.'

I snort – 'I wouldn't go that far' – and as I pull away, my gaze catches on an open doorway into yet another room. This one looks to contain an abundance of fancy-dress costumes. My heart leaps.

'Back in a mo',' I say as I head in there.

I'm blown away by the number and variety of costumes on offer – my library colleagues would be in heaven here; we love a good dress-up – but it's the accessories I'm interested in.

Bingo. I smile as run my gaze over a row of wigs in pink, silver, rainbow glitter, ones like Marilyn Monroe and Elvis, and a few slightly less out-there (read, boring) ones. Although tempted to go rainbow or Marilyn, I behave, choosing a short brunette instead. It's not quite as cute or as good quality as the one Petrice had for me, but I know Mum will prefer it to the alternative.

I'm taking it back out to the counter when my phone rings.

Jude.

22
FEELS LIKE FIRE

ude tells me she's posted on Facebook, messaged all her friends, and phoned every hotel and B&B on the island asking them to check if any of their guests were qualified to officiate weddings, confident she'll find someone.

Five and a half hours later, however, with just one hour to go before the ceremony is supposed to start, no one has come forward. Our hope is spiralling, which is such a pity because everything else has gone perfectly.

Under Benji's bossy direction, we transformed the Golden Orb into a venue you'd expect in an enchanted fairytale. Despite the limited supplies he had to work with, his finished product impresses even me.

'If I ever get married,' I told him, 'you're hired as my wedding planner.'

He and Way laughed as if it was the funniest thing anyone had ever said and of course I joined in because the Pope is more likely to announce he doesn't believe in God than me bind myself to anyone in holy matrimony. While we were putting the final touches on the venue, Amber, Jude, Olivia and a couple of Amber's staff who'd offered to stay on were cooking, and then Yuri, Scarlett and the girls turned up with a miracle cake. I'm calling it that because I don't know how they managed to create their cupcake tower masterpiece in such a short time. And the flowers from Yuri's mum's garden are colourful and gorgeous.

River is currently in with Mum doing her hair, Leo is with Paul getting into their suits and the rest of us are sitting on the couches by reception holding a vigil, praying for a last-minute miracle. Despite being at work, Bee's been texting me hourly for updates and failing dismally in trying to make me not feel bad about this. Sensing the mood, even the kids are muted. I didn't know TJ was capable of not speaking for this long, and there's not been even a meow out of Kayla. They're sitting on the floor, quietly playing blocks with Miller when my phone buzzes, breaking our silence.

'It's Jude,' I say, my hand shaking.

'Do you want me to answer it?' Way asks.

I shake my head and press accept. 'Hello. Any luck?'

'I'm so sorry,' she says. 'I really thought we'd find someone.'

A lump grows in my throat as I struggle not to cry. 'That's okay. Thank you for trying.'

'I was thinking maybe your folks could still say their vows up at the lookout, go through the motions of the ceremony and still have the reception. It'll feel like the real deal, but they'll just have to make it legal later.'

That's an interesting idea, and I hate the thought of Amber being left with all the food. 'Thanks. I'll run it by them and let you know what's happening as soon as possible.'

I disconnect and don't need to tell the others the bad news – they could see it in my face and hear it in the tone of my voice.

'I'm going to call Rodger,' I announce. 'Maybe Blanche is feeling better now? All we need is twenty minutes of her time.

And if it is food poisoning, surely it is almost out of her system by now.'

Everyone agrees this is a very good idea.

'Ah, I wish we could help,' Rodger says, answering after the second ring, 'but she's real bad, I'm afraid. We had to get the doctor to come and give her an injection and she's zonked out. Don't think she'd wake up if an earthquake swallowed the island into the sea.'

'Thank you anyway,' I manage to tell Rodger, my eyes getting pricklier.

Don't cry. Crying isn't going to help anyone, but I don't think I've ever felt so defeated in my life.

Way stands, crosses over to me and pulls me into his side. 'You really tried, sis, but I think it's time to pull the pin.'

Sad sighs ripple around our group.

'Do you want me to tell Mum and Paul?' he asks. 'Guess we should also call the photographer, car people and the band?'

'Jude suggested we still go ahead with an unofficial ceremony and the reception,' I say, clutching at this idea. 'It'd be a shame for all their hard work to go to waste.'

'And ours,' Benji pipes up. 'After today, I'm thinking of a career change.' He looks at Way. 'Would it be weird if a divorce lawyer was married to a wedding planner?'

I gasp. 'Did you just say *married*?'

'Um . . .' Way bites his lower lip as Benji lets out a 'Whoops. Sorry. It just slipped out.'

'We didn't want to take the limelight off Mum and Paul, but yes, I've asked Benji to marry me, and he said yes.'

Oh my God. It feels like someone is running an ice cube down my back. Not Way too.

Noise erupts all around me as the others rush to congratulate the newly betrothed.

'I'm just going to update Mum and Paul,' I say.

No one wants to be the bearer of bad news, but at least it will get me away from all this for a few minutes. I can't believe he didn't tell me he was going to propose – and I can't help feeling like everything is changing way too fast.

I make my way out of reception towards Leo's room where Paul is getting ready. I figure I can start with him, and he can come with me for support when I tell Mum.

Paul opens the door seconds after I knock. 'Hi, Fred. Is everything okay?'

Everything couldn't be further from okay, but I'm momentarily distracted because Paul is standing in front of me and although he looks very debonair – that's a good word for his age, right? – up top with his shirt, bowtie and suit jacket all pressed to perfection, his legs are bare except for socks. I hope he's wearing jocks, but I can't tell because – thankfully – his jacket is long enough to cover his groin.

Realising I'm staring, I immediately shoot my eyes to Leo, who is standing over an ironing board. He's wearing his black suit trousers, and his white shirt, open at the collar, is pushed up to his elbows as he moves the iron back and forth over what I'm guessing are his father's pants. I don't believe in ironing myself, but I'm not sure I've ever seen anything sexier, and I completely forget what I'm doing here.

Leo frowns, abandons his domesticities, and crosses over to me. 'Winifred?' He touches his hand gently to my arm, but it feels like fire. 'What's going on?'

'Jude didn't succeed.'

His hand drops to his side as he curses, and my body mourns the loss of his touch. Who knew the elbow was so erogenous? And how can I even be thinking such a thought under the current circumstances?

'Who's Jude?' Paul asks, glancing between us.

'Jude is someone Fred and I met last night. She was trying to find a replacement celebrant for you,' Leo confesses. 'The hairdresser wasn't the only one with food poisoning. The caterers and Blanche have it too. And unfortunately, Jude hasn't managed to find anyone.'

Paul's eyes widen and he sways a little.

Shit. Stressing that he might be about to have another panic attack, I yank him over to the bed and all but force him down. 'I'm so sorry. We really tried but—'

Smoke fills the air and I shake my head, confused. Am *I* on fire? Has Leo's touch caused a spark?

'My trousers,' Paul cries as Leo and I both turn to look at flames rising from the ironing board. His pants are literally on fire!

Perhaps Leo isn't such a pro at this ironing business after all – even *I* know you don't leave a hot iron on the clothing.

The smoke alarm above our heads suddenly starts shrieking and Leo curses again as he leaps into action, rushing over to the fire. Yanking the cord out of the wall, he picks up the ironing board and dashes outside with it and the trousers. Paul and I watch in stunned horror through the open door as he drops the blazing items onto the lawn and looks around. I'm wondering if he's searching for a random firefighter until I realise he needs a hose.

I remember seeing one just around the corner. Hoping it's long enough, I run over to it, turn it on and hurry back.

'Thanks.' Leo takes the end from me and douses the flames. By the time the fire is out, a crowd has gathered around us – random guests, our friends and family, a couple of resort staff, and River and Mum, who must have heard the commotion a couple of doors down. Credit to River, Mum's hair looks amazing, pulled back in a braid that twists around into a bun. A few wisps of hair fall around her face, softening the look so it is perfectly her.

She glances from the wet ashes to Paul's bare legs. 'Was that your suit trousers?'

He nods. 'Sorry, love, but it looks like we won't be needing them today anyway.'

Mum's hands snap to her chest. 'What do you mean? Have you changed your mind?'

'No.' He rushes over and takes her hands. '*Never*, but I'm afraid it might be out of our control. It appears Blanche is unwell and unable to officiate.'

She gasps – 'I knew there was something wrong' – then sobs. 'Maybe this is an omen. A sign that we shouldn't get married.'

Paul's face falls as a tear slips down Mum's cheek.

'It's not an omen,' I scoff. 'We don't believe in omens, remember?' How the tables have turned – me trying to convince her to go ahead with the wedding after all. 'It's just a hiccup. You can still have a ceremony and the reception today. We're all here to celebrate with you and—'

'What's going on here?' asks someone in a deep English accent.

We all turn to see a tall, handsome redhead with a black duffel bag over his shoulder.

'Oh my goodness! Henry!' Juliet squeals in a girlish manner I didn't think her capable of and launches herself at the man who I'm assuming is her husband. 'What are you doing here?'

He smiles at her fondly. 'I'm here for the wedding and to check on my beautiful pregnant wife.'

Juliet is now sobbing – happy tears, of course. 'I can't believe you flew all this way for only a couple of days. And I called you yesterday! How did you answer me?'

He chuckles, angles her face to look into his and wipes away her tears with his thumbs. 'I was in transit at Singapore airport.'

The emergency is briefly forgotten as the kids join Juliet in her excitement to greet Uncle Henry and then introductions are made to the rest of us.

'Now . . .' Henry turns back to Juliet. 'Where's your room? I need to have a shower and get into my suit. How long have I got before we leave for the ceremony?'

My stomach clenches again with disappointment. Henry has come all this way for nothing.

'Unfortunately,' Paul tells his son-in-law, 'it looks like the wedding is going to be postponed. Our celebrant is ill-disposed.'

'And we've been unable to find a replacement at such short notice,' Leo adds.

Henry scratches the side of his neck and seems to be smiling. If he thinks not having a celebrant is amusing, wait until he hears about all the other dramas we've overcome. 'It just so happens,' he says in his clipped tones, 'I was sitting next to a chap on the flight here who might be able to save the day. When I told him I was coming to a wedding, he mentioned he was a celebrant. He's here with his college friends for a weekend snorkelling trip, but I'm sure I could convince him to step in for us.'

'Do you know where he's staying?' I ask, suddenly feeling light-headed with hope.

He frowns. 'Some B&B near Anson Bay.'

'I'm sure Jude will know of it,' Leo says. 'Let's call her.'

My phone is already out of my pocket and as I wait for the ringtone, I'm bouncing on my feet telling myself not to get too excited until we've got this man up at Captain Cook's Point. But maybe, just maybe, everything will be okay.

23

BOARDSHORTS AND THONGS

'Is this really happening?' Mum asks, her voice choked as she stands before me in her hotel room. She is dressed in her strapless, floor-length, blush-pink gown, her mother's string of pearls around her neck and a pink flower from Yuri's mother's garden in her hair.

Henry's new acquaintance has come good. Apparently he was already halfway through a bottle of wine when Jude tracked him down and celebrants aren't supposed to be half-cut when working, but we all said we'd turn a blind eye so long as he didn't slur during the ceremony.

I smile at her, surprised by how right this feels. 'Yes, it is. And you look beautiful.'

Now *my* voice is choking, and I wish I had better words to describe how perfect she looks. It's not just the dress, but her aura (yeah, yeah, I don't believe in auras, but it's the only word that works). She radiates happiness *and* peacefulness, and I'm glad I didn't manage to get a flight home on Wednesday and miss this. 'You too, sweetheart. It's a blessing you got your looks from me and not your father.'

We both laugh, despite the fact that I look much more like my dad's side of the family than hers.

'But . . .' she adds, lifting her hand to touch my cheap wig, 'you don't have to wear this if you really don't want to. I know I caused a fuss about you being bald, but everyone's right, it does suit you, and I'm in awe of how confident you are. I know I probably can't take much credit, but I'm so proud of the amazing person you grew into. I can't stop thinking about what you told me at the hospital. About that horrible boy. I'll never forgive myself for not being the kind of mum you could come to when that happened.'

I shake my head. 'Now is not the time to talk about that or any regrets. We're both here, we've both cleared the air and, most importantly, you're about to get married to a wonderful man.'

She blinks, and I thank the Lord I used very expensive waterproof mascara on her lashes. 'He is wonderful, isn't he? I can't believe how lucky I am to have found him again.'

Just as things are starting to get uncomfortably soppy, there's a knock on the door. I rush over to answer it, expecting it to be Way, but a woman wearing an orange floral jumpsuit holding a massive black camera is there instead.

'Hi, I'm Lesley,' she says with a wide grin. 'The photographer. Are you ready for the before shots?'

In all the chaos I'd totally forgotten she was due to arrive. 'Yes. Come in. I'm Fred, and this is my mum, Tracy, the bride.'

Lesley beams and then lifts her camera to take a candid shot. 'You both look scrumptious. I thought we could take a couple just outside in front of the frangipanis and then some with the bridal car. It looks so cute.'

After a final mirror check, we follow her outside to find Way, Benji, Scarlett, River and the kids, all dressed up and ready for a few photos. The girls look adorable in their frilly white flower-girl dresses and everyone gushes accordingly over Mum's appearance. I snap a few selfies with Mum and the girls behind me and send them to Bee, which she love-hearts immediately. When Lesley has photographed us from every angle and in every combination possible, it's time to get the show on the road.

The resort staff and other guests who are milling about smile and clap as we walk through the lobby – everyone loves a bride – and Mum waves back like she's royalty. Although I've been present at three of her weddings, I cannot recall her looking this radiant ever before.

Maybe this one really will be the last.

She practically floats outside to where four smartly dressed middle-aged men are waiting in front of four of those cute little Suzuki trucks that we've seen darting about all over the island. Each truck is shiny clean and adorned with the traditional satin wedding ribbons across the front. I immediately recognise two of the men as Mike and Trevor from the glass-bottomed boat cruise. Turns out they also play chauffeurs when anyone has a special occasion on the island. Petrice wasn't kidding when she said everyone has more than one job around here.

After a few more snaps of Mum in front of the first truck – a white one – we pile into the vehicles. Mum and Way, who is giving her away, go in the first one, and the rest of us split up into the other three, the kids on our laps in a manner that I'm sure is illegal but no one seems to worry about here.

Do they even have a cop?

Pushing that thought aside, I sit back and enjoy the ride from the resort to Captain Cook's Lookout. As we drive slowly through the town, people walking on either side of the road slow to watch and wave at our procession, and then just past the cattle grate, sure enough *we* have to slow for cows. A rather chubby black and white one comes right up to the passenger window and Kayla squeals as it tries to shove its head inside.

Our driver, Mike, chuckles – 'She's wondering why she wasn't invited to the wedding' – as I shift Kayla out of harm's way.

Eventually, after three more stops for wildlife, Mike turns into the National Park and begins up the winding, hilly road towards the lookout.

'We're here,' I whisper to Kayla a couple of minutes later as the truck comes to a stop behind Mum and Way's.

The sky couldn't be a clearer blue as we climb out and look over to where a small crowd is gathered down the hill by the lookout platform. I take Kayla's hand and walk towards where Way is helping Mum from the truck. I smooth her dress down as he reaches into the back tray for our bouquets.

'Thank you,' I say, taking mine.

The last two trucks have also arrived, and Scarlett and River deliver the remaining two flower girls to us – Tallulah-Jane is going to carry Miller down the hill/aisle – wish Mum luck, and then hurry down with Benji to join the other guests.

I wink at Mum. 'It's not too late to back out, you know.'

She almost throws her bouquet at me. 'You're such a little devil. Now, let's get this show on the road before it rains.'

'Rains?' Lost in the excitement, I'd totally forgotten about the weather forecast, so am shocked to see grey clouds rapidly approaching from over the ocean. *Oh my goodness!*

The quartet Blanche hired for the ceremony start to play, signalling it's time to begin.

The small crowd *ooh*s and *ahh*s as Kayla walks between them down the grass, dropping petals from Yuri's mum's garden in her wake. Next is Tallulah-Jane and a cute-as-a-button Miller, who waves frantically at everyone she passes. And then it's my turn. My kitten heels dig into the ground with each step I take, but with my eyes trained on Paul, Leo and the celebrant ahead, somehow, I manage to make it to the platform without stumbling.

As I take my position, Leo winks at me in my short red dress and mouths 'Hot' – at least I think that's what he says – and I can't help but grin back. Hot doesn't even come close to describing how *he* looks. After the debacle with Paul's trousers, Leo offered his dad his, but Paul is a little larger around the middle, so they're both wearing suit attire up top with boardshorts and thongs below. Someone who is only wearing one half of a suit *should* look ridiculous, yet Leo looks anything but.

'Good afternoon, ladies and gentlemen. My name is Johnathon Gold and I'm delighted to welcome you to this very special place on this very special occasion, where we will witness the joyful union of Paul and Tracy.'

Realising Mum has made it to the 'altar' while I was drooling – whoops – I snap to attention and focus on the ceremony. Johnathon invites Waylen up to read a poem, Juliet and Scarlett perform a love song a capella – turns out Leo isn't the only one with musical talent – and then it's time for the vows.

Ignoring tradition, Mum goes first, holding Paul's hands. Although the sky might be getting darker, the brightness of her smile shines on everyone.

'My darling Paul,' she begins. 'If I had my way, this would have been our first and only wedding, but life had other plans for us. I'm not the only person you have loved. You're not the only person to whom I've promised forever. We have suffered loss and heartbreak, together and separately, but Fate has given us a second chance and I promise to take it with everything I have.'

I can see Paul's eyes glistening; it's impossible not to see the love and the history when he looks at Mum. She sees it too, and her voice breaks slightly, but she continues on, beaming with love and pride.

'I promise to give you everything I have and everything I am. You are my high school sweetheart, my best friend, the love of my life and the man of my dreams. Now I make you my husband and promise to love you for the rest of my life.'

Paul is crying by the time she's finished, and I have to admit that even to me her words sound more heartfelt than cheesy.

She reaches up and wipes his tears so he can begin his vows. 'Tracy, sweetheart, there aren't enough words in the dictionary to describe how I feel about you . . .'

The last thing I expected to do was shed tears at my Mum's sixth wedding, but emotion clogs my throat as I hear the affection in his voice.

'I will thank my lucky stars every day until I take my last breath that we found each other again. I want to be your support and companion from this day forward. I promise to love you with my whole heart.' He brings her hands to his lips and kisses them tenderly. 'Your family is now my family, and your children are now my children . . .'

I can't help glancing at Leo as Paul speaks about us kids, and I find him looking at me too. He hits me with the most beautiful smile and all I can think about is last night and what we nearly got up to. How he decided to kick his good intentions to the kerb and sleep with me. Now that the wedding seems to be going smoothly, I can't think about anything else.

Is he thinking about this too? Does he still feel the same? Will tonight, my last night on Norfolk Island, be the one I finally get lucky?

'Paul, you may now kiss your bride,' Johnathon says, and I force my eyes back to the newlyweds. The wind is starting to whip around us, pushing that dark cloud closer, so Paul better not take too long about it.

He clasps Mum's face in both his hands, drags her lips to his and kisses her in a manner that is both sweet and X-rated. I laugh as I see Tallulah-Jane cover Miller's eyes.

Everyone cheers and then throws the biodegradable confetti we found at the Bounty Centre over the top of the newlyweds as they walk back through the small crowd of guests. The kids follow, Kayla on all fours meowing at everyone she passes, getting grass stains on her pretty white dress.

Smiling, Leo holds out his arm to me and I link my elbow through his so we can bring up the rear. 'Don't think I've ever felt so great about failing something in my life,' he whispers.

It takes me a moment to realise what he's talking about and then I nod. 'Me too.'

'Well done on saving the day.'

Although I glow in his praise, I say, 'It was a team effort. We couldn't have done it without Jude and Co, and even that would have been in vain if Henry didn't arrive.' I glance over to where he and Juliet are standing, him behind her with his arms around her, cradling her bump, his chin resting on her shoulder. 'He's not at all what I imagined.'

Leo half chuckles, half frowns. 'What did you think he'd be like?'

'Less jovial, less scruffy, less of a redhead. She seems like the type who'd want a man who's clean-shaven and serious.'

'And you say *I* make assumptions, Winifred,' he says in that lovely teasing tone I've come to adore. 'Besides, love isn't logical. The heart wants what the heart wants.'

I think we both know what I think of that, so instead I ask, 'You're now okay with your dad's heart wanting my mum's, then?'

He nods. 'We had a good chat at the hospital. His love for Mum might be different to the love he has for yours, but that doesn't mean he loved her any less. And I know she loved him too, which means she'd be happy that he's not going to be alone and has the companionship of a good woman again.'

Lesley comes over. 'Let me get a few shots of you two while your parents are being congratulated, then we'll do the whole bridal party and family. We need to get as much as we can done before the rain hits.'

Nodding, we follow her back down to the lookout so she can take our picture against the balustrades with the now choppy ocean behind us and the sun, just beginning to set, off to the side.

'Closer,' she barks, gesturing one hand at us. 'We don't want it to look like the best man and maid of honour can't stand each other!'

'Anything but,' Leo mutters under his breath as he steps closer, then slips his arm around my back and rests his hand upon my hipbone.

I swear I feel my knickers melting.

'That's better,' Lesley says, smiling at us as she lifts her camera to her face.

While most of the non-family guests make their way into town for pre-reception drinks at the Golden Orb, the rest of us race against the clock – or rather, the clouds – to get all the photos Mum wants taken around the area before the heavens open.

Spoiler – we don't succeed.

'Don't worry, Mum,' Way shouts over the whistling of the wind and the rain bucketing down upon us as we start running towards the waiting vehicles. 'As Fred will tell you, rain on your wedding day is good luck.'

'It's true,' I call, as my blasted heel sinks into the dirt and I tumble onto the now muddy grass. 'Shit!'

Mum shrieks. 'Winnie! Are you okay?'

'I've got her,' Leo shouts and, before I can even try to get up myself, he scoops me into his arms. '*Are* you okay?'

'Yes. Thank you.' I would have fallen on purpose if I'd known it would mean finding myself in his arms, mine locked around his neck as he carries me like I'm a baby – or a bride – and charges towards Mike's waiting Suzuki.

He has the door open for us and Leo slides us both in before the door slams shut behind us.

'I'm too big to sit on your lap,' I object, struggling in an aim to sit next to him rather than on top of him.

He clamps his arms tightly around me and hisses into my ear. 'Stop wriggling. You're turning me on.'

I swallow and go still – the feeling is entirely mutual.

Thankfully, or perhaps *un*thankfully, Mike jumps into the driver's side, preventing us from acting on our lust. 'What a lovely ceremony,' he says and then proceeds to make small talk that barely needs our involvement all the way back into town to the café.

It's still raining when we arrive, and Mike offers us his umbrella to make the dash from the road through the canopy of foliage. Leo thrusts it at me, telling me to go ahead while he helps make sure Mum and Paul are okay.

'You sure?'

He nods and I hurry off, ushering Kayla with me when I run into her halfway along the path jumping joyously in puddles. Where are her parents?

Jude throws towels at us as we explode into the café, where the guests are already enjoying drinks and canapés. I see River and Scarlett, who has Miller safely strapped into the sling, and TJ standing beside them, her nose back in her phobia book.

'Thanks,' I say to Jude as I take to Kayla with the towels first. 'I love rain,' Kayla says, grinning, and once again I have to bite my tongue on telling her cats hate it.

Instead, I squeeze her affectionately. 'I reckon rain loves you too.'

'Wow, this place looks unreal,' Leo says, running his hands through his hair as he follows Mum and Paul in a few minutes later. As maid of honour, I should probably check she's okay, but her new husband seems to be taking good care of her and somehow, she doesn't look half as wet as I am.

'It's mostly Benji's doing,' I tell Leo, offering him a towel.

When we're both as dry as we can be, we each take a glass of bubbles from Yuri, who is doing the rounds, and Leo plucks a butter knife off the table and clinks it against his glass.

Almost immediately the buzz of chatter dies down, and everyone turns to look at him.

'Welcome all,' he says, his delicious accent echoing around the room. 'I'd like to make a toast to the new Mr and Mrs Lewis. Congratulations, Dad and Tracy.'

We all lift our glasses and echo, 'To Mr and Mrs Lewis.'

I do the right thing and tear myself away from Leo to mingle with the other guests until it's time to sit down to our main meal. I thought the canapes were delicious, but Amber and the girls have excelled themselves with dinner, which is a choice between caramelised vegetable risotto or pan-seared kingfish with braised olives and kumara, alongside sautéed greens and parmesan aioli. All food sourced locally, of course. It's impossible to choose between them, so I can't resist when Leo suggests we take one each and share.

It crosses my mind that sharing food should definitely be a no-no for casual dating but as we aren't doing any such thing, I make a mental note to add it to my book somehow and simply enjoy the experience.

After mains, it's time for speeches. Paul says a few heart-rending – or at least they would be if I had a heart – words about Mum, then Leo does a cracker of a best man toast, offering Mum some practical advice about how to cohabit with the world's greatest slob.

'I'm not that bad,' Paul exclaims.

'Yes, you are!' Mum, Scarlett, River, Juliet, Henry *and* Tallulah-Jane shout in unison.

Everyone is in hysterics when Leo says he tried to buy them a robot vacuum for a wedding present, but all the robots had heard about his father and refused to come home with him. 'Finally,' he says after saying some very sweet words about Paul being his hero and the kind of husband he hopes to be one day, 'I want to thank Tracy's daughter, Fred, for making today possible. Most of you have probably heard of the drama we had with a few of the key wedding contractors, but Fred refused to admit defeat. Without her we wouldn't all be sitting here tonight celebrating.'

Heat floods to my cheeks as Leo and everyone else looks fondly at me. Thankfully he moves on to recognise Jude, Amber and the rest, and then sits down for Way to make his son-of-the bride speech. We decided – or rather, *he* decided when I was still anti-wedding – that it would be best he speak rather than me. He makes me cry, in a good way, but misses all the opportunities for jokes about her previous husbands and 'let's hope it's sixth time lucky' that I would have made, which is possibly a good thing.

Full from my dinner and most of Leo's, I'm surprised I manage to fit in a cupcake but when Tallulah-Jane and Kayla bring them round they're so proud of their handiwork, it would be cruel to say no. Then it's time for the newlyweds' first dance.

I should be cringing as Shania Twain croons 'You're Still the One' from the stereo in the corner and Paul holds Mum close and gently sways her around the make-shift dance floor, but I feel a lump rise in my throat instead. I hope her dreams of having that special person finally have come true.

Lost in the moment, I startle when I feel a hand slip into mine and look up to see Leo smiling down at me. 'It's our turn,' he says, nodding towards our parents.

I slip off my kitten heels, which, although sexy-as, are not practical for dancing, and let him tug me onto the dance floor for our best man and maid of honour dance. Linking my arms around his neck, I relish the weight of his hands on my hips. I've never danced with anyone to such a schmaltzy song before, but where normally I'd be laughing, it's all I can do to stop from stretching up on tippy-toes and kissing him.

'Have I told you how gorgeous you look tonight, Winifred?' Leo whispers. 'Even wearing that ridiculous wig.'

My insides tumble. 'You're looking pretty damn fine yourself, Leopold.'

He smiles and pulls me closer so I can feel every inch of his body pressed against every inch of mine. But it's not enough. As I lean my head against his shoulder, I inhale deeply. He smells so good and despite already eating my fill of delicious food tonight, my mouth waters. My lips crave the feel of his on them again. I want to taste *him*.

I want to do a lot more than just that.

I want to feel him moving inside of me. I *need* to. If we don't end up in bed together tonight, I think I'll die.

'Can I cut in?' Paul asks, tapping my shoulder and jolting me from my carnal thoughts.

No is what I want to say. Like a child with a new toy, I don't want to give Leo up when we have less than twenty-four hours left together, but he drops his hands and makes the decision for us.

'Sure, Dad,' he says, patting his father on the back.

I force a smile for my fourth stepfather as Leo goes to dance with Mum, who I suddenly feel irrationally jealous of. Paul starts blathering about how grateful he is to me for saving the day and how much he loves Mum and wants to make her happy. I try to concentrate on what he's saying, but my mind and body are elsewhere, my feet itching to dance with Leo again.

Before long Benji and Way, Juliet and Henry, Scarlett, River and the kids join us and I think it might be possible, but then Tallulah-Jane demands to dance with her uncle and so I sulkily take Kayla's hands and bop around with her. Eventually the other guests join us, TJ starts dancing with her dad and Leo makes his way back over to me and Kayla.

He holds out his hand and takes a silly bow. 'Young lady, may I have this dance?'

Kayla giggles as Leo lifts her into his arms and then shoots around the outskirts of everyone else like they're ballroom dancing. My heart melts – it's one of the cutest things I've ever seen. I can't help rescuing my phone from my little evening bag and snapping a few pics to commemorate the moment.

Finally she gets tired and thirsty, begging her parents for another soft drink, and Leo walks back over to me. His forehead is shiny from exertion and the top few buttons of his shirt are undone, exposing just enough of his sculpted chest to make my mouth dry. 'I think I need some fresh air,' he says, flapping his hands against his red cheeks.

This is my moment to get him alone again. 'Want some company?'

His gaze meets mine. 'Only if the company is you.'

24

NO MORE HANKY-PANKY

No one notices as we slip away – they are all still too busy on the dance floor – and the moment we escape onto the verandah, Leo takes my hand in his like it's the most natural thing in the world.

Rule Number Ten, says a pesky voice in my head, but I ignore it because I don't want to let him go. Maybe there are different rules 'on island'.

We walk between the canopy of trees away from the café, the music and laughter getting quieter the further away we get. It's a beautiful night. The rain has gone and although it's still humid, there's a gentle breeze wafting from the not-too-distant ocean and stars twinkling in the sky, but I barely notice any of it.

It's the man beside me who excites me, who makes the pulse race in my wrist as we cross the road and walk into in the small park next to the Visitor's Centre. The town is so quiet it almost feels like we're the only people on the island, the only people in the world. We wander towards a towering pine tree in the centre of the grass, where a handmade sign announces it as the Tree of Knowledge.

'Isn't that what the tree in the Garden of Eden was called?' I ask.

Leo chuckles and then reads the rest of the sign aloud. 'The Norfolk Pine has been both a blessing and a curse . . .'

His voice is so sexy, I could listen to him speak all day and all night. We learn this tree symbolises a tradition that goes right back to when the first islanders settled. It was planted in 1991 on the birthday of a local lady, but it represents others that were scattered around the island and used as official message trees. Locals and officials post notices on these trees to keep the community informed. Although there are no messages on the tree right now, apparently, they still use it.

'That's probably because their internet is so crap,' I say, reaching up to scratch my neck. 'I'm surprised they don't have a town crier.'

Leo snorts, then nodding towards me, jokes, 'Have you got nits?'

'Haha.' I scowl at him as I let go of his hand, needing both of mine to address the chronic itchiness that has suddenly taken hold of my scalp. 'Can you get nits in wigs?'

He smirks at the horrified expression on my face. 'I don't think so. But I'm impressed you've kept that thing on so long. No wonder you're itchy. Maybe it's time to take it off.'

I know he's talking about the wig, but my spine tingles at his suggestive words. Before I can do as he advises, he lifts his hands to my head and ever so gently pulls my fake hair off. It feels way more erotic than it should. Immediately, I feel blessed release.

'That better?' He gazes down at me as he tosses the wig over his shoulder.

I nod, my insides tightening at the clear heat in his eyes. 'Thank you.'

'You're welcome.' His voice is gruff. We stare at each other for a long moment, then he breaks the silence. 'Do you mind if I kiss you?'

Do I mind? My heart is banging in my chest and there's a heaviness between my thighs. My body has never wanted anything more. I open my mouth to say all this, but my breath catches in my lungs, so I simply tilt my head up towards his.

At first his lips just scrape across mine as if a question – *Are you sure? Is this okay? Are we really doing this?* – and I answer him by sliding my hands into his hair and pulling his face closer. I don't want any inch of air between us. A tantalising moan escapes his mouth as he cups my face in his hands, then shoves his tongue into my mouth like he can't get enough of me. Luckily, the feeling is mutual.

Leo's kiss is unlike any I've ever experienced. He's both tentative and in control, and he takes every cue from me. Like he's in complete tune with my longing. As the kiss heats up, he slides his hands from my face down my bare neck, my skin tingling beneath his touch. I kiss him like this is the last kiss I might ever get – I don't want this to end, yet at the same time, I want so much more. He pulls his mouth from mine and gasps, 'You drive me crazy, Winifred.'

'I'm taking that as a compliment,' I reply, sliding a hand between the buttons of his shirt.

He groans as my fingers meet his bare, *hot* skin – 'It's definitely a compliment' – and then pushes me up against the tree, pinning me between the trunk and his body before pressing his mouth back to mine, kissing me like he needs me more than oxygen. There's not a millimetre between our bodies. My breasts are crushed against his rock-solid chest and our hips are locked together as our need pulses between us.

And that's not the only thing pulsing between us. I can feel his erection trying to burst free of his shorts, teasing us both as it presses against me. I need him now and, judging by the way he pushes the skirt of my silk dress up around my thighs and dips his hand into my knickers, he feels exactly the same way.

'Oh Lord,' I cry as a finger sinks inside of me, finding me wet and needy.

'Is this okay?'

'Yes,' I pant, nodding desperately as I press myself into his hand in encouragement. If he stops now, I'll kill him.

He groans into my ear – 'You feel so damn good' – but I'm helpless to respond. For someone who hasn't had a whole lot of experience, he knows exactly where to touch me so that within moments I'm writhing and shuddering against the tree.

'I need you,' I order, still coming down from what might just be one of the sexiest orgasms of my life.

He blinks and glances around. 'Here?'

I nod. I don't think I've been this horny since I was a teenager; besides, not one car has passed since we arrived at the park. The whole place is still deserted, and I don't want to wait till we can get a room. I don't want to wait even one second longer.

'I don't have a condom,' he says, the disappointment etched across his gorgeous face.

'I'm safe and on the pill,' I tell him, positive Mr Three Sexual partners is also clean.

His hesitation barely lasts a moment. The second I slide my hand into his boardshorts and wrap my fingers around him, I know he's a lost cause. I pause only to take my knickers off and seconds after we shove his shorts down his legs, he picks me up, slams me up against the tree and thrusts into me. I squeeze my legs tight around his waist, wanting him as deep as he can possibly be inside me.

'Fuck, Leopold!'

'Yes, Winifred?' he whispers and then drives again, harder and faster.

Fairly certain nothing has ever felt this good, I clamp my teeth into his shoulder to stop from screaming as he takes us both over the edge. Considering his lack of experience, I'm blown away by his technique. I've had sex in a few places outside of a bedroom and this isn't my first public encounter, but none have come anywhere close to being as euphoric as this. In this moment I think I love him.

My heart has barely stopped racing when a light shines bright into my eyes.

'Well, well, well . . . what have we here?' a surly voice asks. Its owner lowers the torch, revealing a stocky man in his mid-to-late fifties wearing a police uniform.

Crap. I guess that answers my question about whether there are cops on the island.

'Shit,' Leo mutters, his hands still on my bare bum cheeks, our bodies still connected in the most basal way. 'Is that a cop?'

'Yep,' I whisper, my stomach threatening the reappearance of my dinner.

Leo presses his lips to mine briefly, then slides out of me, lowers me to standing and smooths down my dress before pulling his shorts back up his legs. Turning to put himself between me and our interloper, he dips his head as if offering the policeman a salute. 'Evening, officer.'

I can't help giggling at the way he speaks, like the perfect gentleman, like we haven't just been sprung in a very compromising position.

'Do you find this amusing, miss?' the cop asks, glaring at me.

I bite my lip and shake my head, not trusting myself to speak. Leo takes my hand and squeezes it as the policeman gives us a slow once-over.

'We don't take kindly to public displays of indecency on Norfolk Island.'

'Are we under arrest?' I should be worried about this

possibility – I mean, what is the penalty for public indecency? Could we go to prison? Or is there a fine? I wonder how much it is – I might have to ask Way for a loan – but all I can think about is how much Bee and my colleagues are going to love this story.

The cop clears his throat. 'Not yet. Names?'

'I'm Leopold Lewis,' Leo says, 'and this is Winifred Darling.'

'It's a pleasure to make your acquaintance,' I say, offering my hand. 'And you are?'

He glares at my hand but doesn't take it. 'Sergeant Parker.'

'Are you going to put us in handcuffs?' I know I shouldn't be riling our possible captor, but I can't resist. He seems so serious, and I wonder what it would take to make him crack a smile.

'Do I need to?' he asks. *No smile.*

I'm about to say, 'Yes please' – I don't hate the idea of being handcuffed to Leo – but the object of my wanton thoughts gives me a stern look, silently begging me not to make this worse. We shake our heads as the sergeant's phone starts to ring.

'No more hanky-panky,' he orders, pulling it out of his pocket.

I smirk at his choice of words as he steps a few feet away to take the call. 'Isn't that the most absurd phrase for sex you've ever heard?' I whisper to Leo.

The corners of his lips flick upwards. His hair is a mess and his shirt buttons mismatched in his haste to do them up. And thanks to the moonlight, I can just see the hot pink lipstick I wore to the wedding smooshed all over his gorgeous face.

'Should we make a run for it?' I suggest.

'If we weren't on a tiny island, I'd be tempted.'

I sigh. 'Good point. Do you think we're going to get mugshots? You'd look adorable in yours.'

'Stop. This isn't funny,' he says, but he's struggling not to laugh.

'Sergeant stick-up-his-arse should be thanking us for giving him some excitement. I bet they don't get much action – of *any* kind – around here.' Leo snorts.

'Surely they won't actually charge us. It's not like we've committed murder and no one, aside from him'—I nod towards the man still on the phone—'saw us.'

'Let's hope not. If this gets out, I'll have to quit my job – no way I can face high school students with this on my record. I'll probably get fired.'

Shit. Suddenly I feel terrible. 'I'm so sorry.' It's my fault we've been caught in flagrante; if I hadn't encouraged him, Leo would have waited until we got back to the resort.

'Don't apologise.' He smiles down at me and squeezes my hand again. 'It takes two to tango, and I wanted it just as much as you. This past week has been a rollercoaster, but the best part of it was meeting you.'

My heart swells ridiculously at his words and I smile back. 'I agree. Do you think we should call Way? He might not be in criminal law, but he'll terrify Parker.'

'You *really* want to do that?' Leo's tone tells me exactly what he thinks of this option. 'Let's just see if we can apologise our way out of this. Take my lead, okay?'

I nod, more turned on by his order than I should be, and offer the sergeant a conciliatory smile as he shoves his phone back into his pocket and focuses back on us. 'Everything okay?'

'Nothing for you to worry about,' he says gruffly. 'Now, where were we?'

Neither Leo nor I reply.

'That's right. You were about to explain yourselves to me. This is a public place – this tree is sacred to the island – and you desecrated it. You're not teenagers. What's your excuse? Honeymooners who are ticking sex in public off some carnal bucket list?'

'Is there such a thing?' I ask, annoyed I haven't heard of it. Parker glares at me again.

'We're very sorry,' Leo says, his tone more serious than I've ever heard him. 'We're not honeymooners. Or teenagers as you rightly point out. We should be ashamed of ourselves. We're at a wedding reception across the road and we just needed some fresh air. We didn't come out planning for this to happen. We're both mortified.'

'Can you promise this won't happen again?' the sergeant asks.

'Yes, definitely,' I say, feeling I should do my bit. 'It will *absolutely* not *ever* happen again. This was a one-time thing. I'm sure you've got drunk and done something stupid before.'

Parker raises an eyebrow and I realise maybe I've overstepped.

Rule #1 of Avoiding Arrest – don't insult the police officer.

'No, of course you haven't,' I gush. 'I'm sure you've always been an upstanding citizen, a role model to all the wonderful islanders. You probably don't even drink. Very sensible. I should stop too. I've been thinking about it for—'

Leo lets go of my hand and glares at me. *Shut up.*

'We're very sorry,' I conclude.

Parker looks relieved that I've stopped speaking. 'Okay, then. You're free to go, but I never want to see either of your faces, or any parts of your bodies, ever again.'

'You have our word,' Leo promises.

'In that case, goodnight. I hope the actual newlyweds had a good one.'

A puff of relief escapes my lungs as Parker turns and strides towards a police car at the edge of the grass. How we didn't hear him arrive I have no clue, but then I guess we were kind of pre-occupied.

I smile at Leo. 'Well, that was a close call.'

He frowns down at me. 'I'm not drunk.'

'I know.' We'd both been too busy dancing to have much to drink. 'That was just something I said to try to get the big guy off our backs. But I am desperate for some water. Such hot sex is thirsty work.'

'Was the rest of what you said true?'

'What bit?'

'The bit about that just being a one-off.'

'It doesn't have to be.' I wink and grab him by his lapels, drawing him to me. 'We've still got quite a few hours until our flight. We should probably go back to the reception, but then you can come back to my room and—'

'And you'll kick me out when you're done with me?' he interrupts, shaking free.

I recoil at his harsh tone. Why is he acting so cold? He should be happy we've escaped arrest. 'What's going on? Have I done something wrong?'

He sighs and runs a hand through his hair. Moonlight flickers between the branches of the tree across his face. 'No. I have. I'm clearly an idiot. I really like you. This meant more to me than just a quick fuck against a tree and I guess after today, I thought maybe it did to you as well.'

Oh God. My stomach tightens. I can't believe what I'm hearing. 'What changed today?'

'Our parents got married. And it happened because of you. You went to every effort to save the day and give them the wedding of their dreams. Why would you do that if you didn't believe in them? In love?'

'Because I felt guilty! Your dad almost had a heart attack because of the stress we put them under and that whole abortion story ... They deserve some happiness after that, and I wish them well, but that doesn't mean I want the same thing for myself. I thought you knew that. I would never have slept with you if I thought you didn't. Last night you said you didn't want to regret not sleeping with me – I thought that's why we did what we did.'

'So you're telling me I was just another notch to you? That you haven't developed feelings for me?'

How could he have got this so wrong? I want to be angry at him for jumping to conclusions, but he looks so glum. And this isn't entirely his fault. I might be a pro at keeping lust and other emotions in two completely separated compartments, but he's not. Deep down, didn't I know he was the kind of person who couldn't have sex without emotion? And yet, selfishly, I still let him smash me.

And now we're both paying for it.

'We're friends,' I say gently. 'At least, I hope we still can be.'

'*You* don't sleep with friends. Rule number eighteen.'

I'm impressed by Leo's recall, although he's not exactly right. 'Rule number eighteen is "Friends with benefits is not a thing". There's nothing about hooking up for one night to scratch an itch. That's all this was supposed to be. Even if we did both feel more, nothing about our lives is compatible. You live on the other side of the planet. You want marriage, kids, the whole shebang. You—'

'Who said I want kids?' he interrupts.

I blink. 'Don't you?' He's such a family guy and so amazing with his nieces, I just assumed.

He shakes his head. 'No, actually. The world doesn't need more babies. I'd rather do my bit teaching the ones it already has. Marriage isn't the be all and end all for me either. All those things you mentioned – even the distance – are surmountable if you love someone.'

Love? My breath feels like it's trapped in my lungs. 'You don't love me,' I scoff. 'You're just bamboozled by great sex.'

It's not the first time this has happened to me – people think only women confuse sex with love, but plenty of guys do too.

'Don't tell me how I feel, Winifred. Sure, I'm physically attracted to you, but it's more than that. The last thing I expected to find at my father's wedding was someone who attracted me on every other level as well. You're funny, smart and interesting, and you make me step outside my comfort zone and open up about things I normally keep close. I've never felt about anyone else the way I feel about you.'

'Stop,' I bark. My heart is racing. I don't want to hear such confessions. Why did he have to go and ruin such a great night? 'That's ridiculous. You've known me less than a week.'

'Time plays no role when it comes to matters of the heart,' he retorts.

I don't know – maybe that's true, but it doesn't make any difference because I don't *want* him to fall for me. I don't want anyone to fall for me, and I sure as hell don't want to fall for anyone myself.

I'm about to say all this when he says, 'I think the reason you're struggling to finish writing your book is because deep down, you don't believe what you're peddling. Deep down, you want love just as much as the rest of us. The need for connection and emotional intimacy is what makes us human.'

'Then maybe I'm not human,' I say, 'because I *don't* need it. And I'm no longer struggling with my book. That was just a blip. A little writer's block, but I spent all day Wednesday and Thursday madly writing – the words just flowed out of me – and I sent those new chapters off to my publisher.'

'Really?' Leo looks at me as if he's begging me to tell him this is a lie.

'Yep. She's already read them, says they're amazing.'

He shoves his hands in his pockets and his shoulders slump.

'Guess I really am a fool then. Congratulations. I hope it sells really well.'

'Thank you,' I say, feeling like pond scum. I hate that I've hurt him. 'And you're not a fool. We just got our wires crossed. I'm sorry I can't be what you want me to be, but I know there's someone amazing out there for you.'

He rolls his eyes at my sentiment. 'Whatever, Fred. Have a good night.'

My heart cracks – it's the first time since almost the day we met that he hasn't called me Winifred.

'Are you not coming back to the reception?'

He shakes his head. 'I think I'm just going to head straight to the resort.'

And before I can try and convince him to change his mind, he jogs away.

25

PHILOPHOBIA AND PSYCHOBABBLE

Saturday afternoon, Norfolk's tiny airport is crowded with people waiting to fly to Brisbane and I, of course, am surrounded by Mum's version of the Brady Bunch. I wonder if things were as peachy perfect as the producers made out, or if Greg and Marcia ever crossed a line like Leo and I have. I can't help looking over at him, currently jostling Miller up and down on his knee, refusing to make eye contact with me.

It's the first time I've seen him since last night and for once he looks like he got as little sleep as I did. Does this mean he's really fallen for me?

He's not the first guy who's told me this, but he's the first one I've cared about hurting. I really enjoyed our time together this past week. I like him and respect him and am kicking myself for blurring the lines of our friendship. However good the sex was, I can't help wishing we hadn't gone there. And that's also a first for me.

Well, almost. I also regretted sleeping with Kyle.

At one stage in the middle of the night, my sadness at ending things the way we did overwhelmed me, and I crept down to his room to check on him, but if he heard me knocking – which I'm pretty sure he did – he didn't answer. This made me feel guilty, and *that* made me feel annoyed at his childishness.

I wasn't the one who ruined things between us.

I wasn't the one who made outlandish assumptions and tried to change the rules!

So, while the others chatter about the wedding and make plans for a big family get-together at Christmas, I sit quietly, sunglasses hiding my eyes, pretending I have a hangover until we're called to board. Everyone makes a mad dash to form a line, but I head to the bathroom for a safety wee and then join the back of the queue. I never know why people are so eager to get on the plane first – it's not like it's first come first served. I for one don't want to be stuck there a second longer than necessary. Especially today.

I pass Mum and Paul, sitting up the front in the miniscule business section, then Way and Benji already lip-locked, and Juliet and Henry deep in conversation as I head down the aisle, reading the numbers above my head, counting down to 18C. Thankfully, Scarlett, River and the kids are way down the back – although I've come to quite like them, I'm in no mood right now for playing cats or listening to TJ tell us about all the different things one could be scared of on a plane – aerophobia, claustrophobia, germaphobia, the list goes on. I just want to pop my headphones over my ears and pretend this week never happened.

15C. 16C. 17C.

What the actual?! My heart punches my ribs. No freaking way. Is Fate having a laugh at our expense?

Leo, who is sitting in 18B next to some old lady already fast asleep against the window, looks as horrified as I am by this turn of events.

I glance frantically around us, looking for a spare seat, but I'm the last to board and . . .

There isn't one.

I swear the plane wasn't this crowded on the way over, but I guess the cancelled flight earlier in the week put more pressure on this one. Telling myself the sooner I sit, the sooner we can take off and the sooner this will all be over, I lower myself down beside him. He looks at Window Lady and I get the feeling if she wasn't already asleep, he'd be begging to switch places with her.

What a pity we don't always get what we want!

Oh well, I'm going to be grown-up about this and offer him a smile as I click my seatbelt into place, but he doesn't smile back, turning away and opening his book.

This shouldn't bother me – I don't usually give a damn what people think about me – but it does.

The captain announces we're almost ready for take-off, then navigates the aircraft to the beginning of the runway. Minutes later we are in the air, flying high above the Pacific Ocean. The second the seatbelt sign goes off, I retrieve my bag and pull out my laptop, but I can't bring myself to open my manuscript while sitting next to Leo. It would feel too much like rubbing things in his face.

I pluck the Qantas magazine from the pocket in front of me instead, flicking my eyes over an article about the best restaurants in South America, but I know I won't recall a word of it later. I can't concentrate on anything while I can feel his body heat emanating off him and see his thighs, so strong they took my whole weight last night while my legs were wrapped around him.

I reach up to fiddle with the vent, trying to direct cool air onto me, not thinking about the fact this action lands me very much in Leo's personal space.

'Do you mind?' he asks. 'I'm trying to read here.'

I glance at the title – *Me Before You*. An oldie but a goodie. I liked it because it doesn't have your cliched happy ending. 'You read that before?'

He shakes his head. 'Picked it up at the resort book exchange.'

'Seen the movie?'

'No.'

'They don't end up together. He does go to Switzerland.' His eyes widen, and I can't believe I just told him that. 'I'm sorry, that was cruel,' I gush.

Spoiling the ending of Jojo Moyes' break-out novel is like telling him that the child psychologist in *The Sixth Sense* is actually dead. I'm not usually this much of a terrible person, but he's set me on edge and I'm not thinking straight.

'Yeah . . . it was.' He closes the book and turns his head, so our eyes meet. 'Haven't you already hurt me enough?'

That isn't fair – he knew where I stood, and it's not my fault if he chose to ignore it – but I do feel bad and I don't want to leave things like this. Perhaps this is my chance to try to make things right between us. Now that his dad and my mum are married, it's likely we're going to have to see each other again.

'I didn't mean to, and I really am sorry,' I say. 'I'd like to think we can move past this.'

He sighs – 'Maybe' – then reopens the book and starts reading again.

Conversation over.

'Maybe' is a good start. I smile and go back to flicking through the Qantas mag, but I've barely read one sentence when Leo claps *Me Before You* shut again and shifts his body so he's facing me.

'You know how I said you were brave, that I didn't think you'd be scared of anything?'

This is obviously a rhetorical question, so I just wait for him to continue.

'Well, I was wrong. You're a philophobic.'

I wrack my mind trying to recall if this was one of the phobias TJ told us about. 'What the hell is philophobic?'

'Someone who's afraid of love. And you're terrified of it.'

'What?!' My shriek wakes the old lady, who glowers at me, but I don't give a toss. Leo is just like all those other men who think they know me better than I know myself. All those men who can't understand a woman who doesn't need a man to complete her. Just like so many men before him, he sees me as a challenge.

'And you're fooling yourself that there's not something between us,' he continues. 'You bent your own rules when it came to us. We became friends, and that means you *should* have resisted sleeping with me.'

I open my mouth to object – to restate what I'd told him last night about the one-off clause, even though I'm not sure this is true – but he rides right over the top of me.

'But you couldn't help yourself, because there's something raw and real and impossible to ignore between us. There has been from that very first morning at the cemetery, and I think you know it as much as I do.'

Usually, I'd roll my eyes and scoff loudly at such ridiculous sentiment, but I can't quite bring myself to do so. The utter conviction in his tone renders me speechless, and my stomach flutters in a way I've not felt in a very long time.

It's terrifying. As is the way he's looking into my eyes – searching and yet also all-knowing, as if he does somehow know me better than anyone else.

And then he puts his hand on my knee and every cell in my body jumps to attention. 'I heard what you told your mum,' he says. 'About Kyle and what he did to you.'

Hearing Leo say that bastard's name is like a punch to the

gut. I shove his hand off my knee. 'That was a *private* conversation.'

His voice is soft as he replies. 'I wasn't listening on purpose. I'd finished talking to Dad and was coming back out to the waiting room. Neither of you saw me, but I didn't want to interrupt, so I stepped back out of the way.'

'To eavesdrop,' I say, my heart thumping. Shame fills me that he knows this about me. I haven't even told Bee.

He ignores my outcry. 'Kyle was a stupid, horrible teenage boy who betrayed your trust and broke your heart.'

Anger churns in my gut, heating my whole body and replacing the butterflies of moments earlier. I can't stand the way he's looking at me with such pity. 'You should have told us you were there. You shouldn't have kept listening!'

'Maybe,' he concedes, 'but that doesn't change the facts. What happened with Kyle was a terrible thing to happen to you at such a formative time in your life, and you told your mum yourself that it's shaped your view on men and relationships. But not all men are like Kyle – or some of your mum's ex-husbands.'

'I know that,' I say harshly. 'There are plenty of good men in my life.' Until a few minutes ago, I thought he was one of them.

He gives me a sad smile. 'Yet you don't allow yourself to get close to any of them. You're scared of rejection, of getting hurt again. Because of Kyle and probably even the rejection you felt when Jeff left your mother, you're scared of putting your trust and faith in someone and being let down, so you never allow anything to get that far. You think you're protecting yourself, but you're actually punishing yourself. You've been lying to yourself so long that you now believe sleeping around is empowering.'

Any remnants of remorse I had about hurting him vanish along with all hope of us ever being friends. 'Oh my God, can you hear yourself? Thinking you know me better than I know myself after less than a week? Thinking you're so irresistible I couldn't help but fall in love with you? The problem with you – the problem with most men – is that you're so confident in your own opinions that you can't understand there might be a woman who doesn't want what you think they do!'

The old lady has not gone back to sleep; she's listening to us like we're an episode of *Days of Our Lives* as I poke Leo hard in the chest.

'Maybe Kyle and my mum's multiple marriages did make me a cynic, but I'm not *scared*. I like my life, I like the freedom and independence I have not being tied down to one mere male, so I suggest you mind your own business and leave the psychobabble to the experts.'

As I yank open my laptop, ready to use my furore to write the next chapter, Window Lady leans towards Leo. 'Some women wouldn't know a good thing if it bit them on the nose, but I do, and my husband recently went the way of the dinosaurs, so if you're looking for a good time, I can give you my number.'

Despite my anger, I snort but stifle a giggle when I glance at her expression to realise she's completely serious. Wow – you go, lady! Have at him! I certainly don't want him.

Neither Leo nor I say another word to each other the whole flight and the second we disembark I say goodbye to everyone else not coming to Perth, hurry as fast as I can through security and then make a beeline for the bus that will take me to the domestic airport.

'You okay?' Way wants to know when he and Benji finally catch up with me at the gate for our next flight.

'Yep. Just exhausted. And ready to go home.'

26
101 REASONS TO BE SINGLE

By the time the Uber drops me, Way and Benji at our place, I feel like I've been travelling for days. Norfolk Island *feels* like a whole other country. I want to crawl into my bed and sleep for a week, but not before I collect Aunty from Bee's place. Until today, I haven't really had time to miss her, but now I can't wait to wrap my arms around her and feel the comfort of her soft body against my chest as she purrs.

Seconds after I knock on Bee's door, it opens and a blur of white fur launches itself at me. Not Aunty, but Bee's rather large dog, JB, whose paws land on my chest.

Sully chuckles. 'Hey, Fred, welcome back.'

'No French kissing,' I order, pushing JB down and then ruffling his fur as I summon a smile for Sully, whose red hair is a little damp. Come to think of it, so are JB's paws. 'Did you miss me?'

'Of course, but not quite as much as Bee or Aunty.' He steps back and gestures down the hallway. 'Aunty's asleep on the couch. We've just come in from the beach and Bee's getting changed, but she'll be out in a moment.'

I head into the lounge room, JB still bouncing around me

like Winnie the Pooh's bestie. 'Darling!' I shriek as I spy Aunty curled up in a ball between two stripy cushions.

She looks up at my voice and immediately jumps off the couch and sashays over to me. Sully holds JB back as I scoop her up into my arms and nuzzle my face into her long, soft fur. Her purrs sound even better than I remembered. Some of the pent-up anger I've been feeling since I had it out with Leo begins to lift.

Who needs annoying men in my life when I have the best cat on the planet?

'Fred!' Bee shrieks and she throws her arms around me. 'I missed you!'

She pulls back quickly, knowing I'm not big on hugs. I laugh. 'I've only been gone a week.'

'Well, it felt much longer,' she says with a pout. 'Work isn't nearly as fun when you're not there. Come sit, I want to hear all about your week!'

'I've already told you almost everything,' I say. We might have been miles apart, but we've talked on the phone and messaged just as much as usual. And the truth is, as much as I adore Bee, right now, I just want to go home.

Still, she has looked after my cat for a week, so I let her lead me over to the couch, figuring I'll stay ten minutes or so, then make my excuses.

'Can I get you a drink, Fred?' Sully asks. 'Tea, coffee, wine?' He knows us well.

'I'll just have a glass of water, please.'

He and Bee frown at me. 'You okay?' she asks.

'Just a bit dehydrated after the flights.' If we start drinking, I could be here all night.

'One water coming right up.' Sully heads into the kitchen.

Bee beams after him as if he's just announced he's off to fetch the winning lotto tickets. She really is a lost cause when it comes to that guy. 'You'll never guess what I found this arvo,' she whispers.

'What?'

'Shh!' She presses a finger to her lips, then holds up the ring finger on her left hand, points to it with the other hand and beams like a loon.

My eyes bulge. 'A ring?' I mouth.

She nods. 'I think Sully's going to propose.'

Before I can charade my excitement – and I *am* excited for her, I'm pleased to find out – Sully returns with two glasses of icy cold water, a sliced lime in the top of each one.

'Thank you,' I say, as Aunty settles in my lap.

I take a long sip and then put my drink on the coffee table as Sully takes a seat on the armchair.

'So,' Bee begins, 'are you glad you decided to stay in the end?' That is a complicated question. Yes, I'm glad I was there for the wedding and I'm happy to have helped save the day from disaster, but if I'd left when I planned to, I wouldn't have monumentally stuffed things up with Leo.

My heart sinks at the thought of him. I can't explain why, but I haven't told Bee about Leo and I almost sleeping together the night Paul went to hospital or that we finally succumbed to our lust the next evening, and I don't feel like doing so now. It's not because Sully is here – he's certainly heard me talking about my sex life before – but because I'm so upset over the fallout with Leo. I fear if I talk about it, I'll start crying and not be able to stop.

I hate that we ended things so badly and the thought of never seeing him again or things being strained between us if we do, so I try to push him and his stupid theories out of my head and paste a smile on my face.

'Yeah, it was a great day,' I say, 'and I'm really happy for Mum and Paul in the end.'

Bee chuckles. 'How ironic that you went over there totally anti-wedding, and in the end, you were the one who saved the day.'

'Well, in the end, that honour really goes to Henry,' I say.

She blinks. 'He's Scarlett's husband, right?'

I shake my head. 'Juliet's.'

'Ah, right.' She looks over to Sully. 'He flew all the way from London for only a couple of days. I hope you're as doting when I'm pregnant.'

He grins as if besotted by the idea. 'I'll be *more* doting.'

O-*kay*. I think it's time for me to leave. The way they're looking at each other now, they might be about to start trying for a baby within moments. I make a move to stand, holding Aunty tight against me, but Bee says, 'Juliet looked pretty good for someone that pregnant. In fact, all of Paul's kids are good-looking, not to mention those adorable little girls.'

I smile at the mention of Scarlett's daughters. 'Yeah, I wasn't sure about TJ, Kayla and Miller at first,' I admit, 'but they grew on me.'

Bee raises an eyebrow. 'I thought you hated kids.'

'I don't hate them,' I scoff, then sigh. 'Well, maybe I kind of did, because the only ones in my life were Dad's daughters and . . . I guess I felt a bit jealous of them.'

'Aw, Fred.' Bee shifts even closer to me on the couch and I can feel her about to hug me, but I hold up a hand.

'You don't need to feel sorry for me. It was stupid to feel that way, and after spending time with Paul's granddaughters, I think maybe I want to try and get to know my little sisters.'

Bee's eyes light up. 'That's wonderful. I'm happy for you.'

'Thanks,' I say, feeling awkward at her excitement when I haven't even made contact yet. Ava and Mia might hate me, for all I know.

'So you got along well with Paul's family, then,' Sully says.

I nod. 'Scarlett and Juliet are very different to each other and to me but . . .' I think about laughing and dancing with them at the Fish Fry. 'I do like them.'

'And . . . it sounds like you and Leo hit it off as well.' Bee's tone is teasing, despite the fact she has no idea what really went on between us.

'Yeah, he's a good guy,' I say, trying to sound nonchalant when I feel anything but.

'How did he feel about the wedding in the end?' Bee asks.

I swallow. 'He was fine about it.' It was afterwards that things went downhill.

I recall the way he tenderly lifted the wig from my head. The feel of his hands on my scalp, the way he smiled into my eyes as he made me come. The way we talked late into the night – several nights – teasing each other and sometimes laughing until our chests ached.

There's a different kind of ache inside me now at the thought that none of those things will likely ever happen again. I try to remember the anger I felt on the flight, but all I can feel is sadness and loss.

'We've been listening to his band's music,' Bee says. 'I downloaded all the songs I could find on Spotify and I've even got Xavier and Ursula into them. We can't believe you know someone famous.'

I shake my head, trying to clear it. 'He's not even sure he's going to continue with the band.'

'What?' Bee and Sully exclaim in unison. 'That's a travesty,' she adds.

I shrug – the last thing I want to do is talk about Leo. As if he isn't camping in my brain rent free as it is – and down the rest of my water.

I'm about to make my excuses to leave when Bee says, 'Did you manage to get any writing done in between all that drama?'

'Miraculously, yes.' Happy to be talking about something besides Leo, I explain the wave of inspiration that took over, and the publisher's reaction.

Bee smiles. 'That's so great. I knew you'd be an amazing writer when you found the right topic. When's your deadline again?'

'End of next month. So just over five weeks. I should be able to do it if I spend all my evenings and weekends writing.'

The thought doesn't fill me with joy.

'You seem a bit glum.' Bee scrutinises me. 'Are you sure you're not upset that you didn't manage to stop the wedding?'

'Glum? I'm not glum.' I force a smile. 'I'm actually happy for Mum, and I really think this one might last. I'm just bloody buggered.'

I don't need to feign a yawn – just the mention of my exhaustion activates one. 'Sorry,' I say, covering my mouth.

Bee leaps to her feet, making Aunty startle. 'No, *I'm* sorry. Of course you're exhausted. We should let you get home to bed.'

'Thanks.' Cradling Aunty, I stand. Sully picks up the cat travel box and the three of us wrangle her inside. 'Just for the car ride home,' I promise as she hisses.

It always amazes me how she can go from placid and cuddly to wild beast in seconds, but that's one of the things I like best about cats – they don't let anybody walk over them.

At the front door, I air-kiss Bee and smile at Sully. 'Thanks for looking after my girl.'

'No worries,' Sully says. 'Anytime.'

'See you at work Monday,' Bee calls, waving me and Aunty into the car.

Once upon a time she'd have asked if I wanted to hang out with her tomorrow – we often spent weekends together, browsing the Freo markets, New Edition Bookshop or Elizabeth's, the second-hand bookstores – but now whenever

Sully has a weekend day off, she wants to spend it with him. I try not to feel put out, knowing she still loves me just as much.

Besides, it's probably for the best. I'm not really in the mood to socialise and don't I have a book to finish?

Way and Benji are already in bed when I get home. I let Aunty out to go reacquaint herself with her surrounds and wonder what will happen when *they* get married. Will Way want me to move out? Perhaps Benji will move in sooner rather than later now they're engaged – he practically lives here already. I decide this is a problem for Future Fred and that I'll start with something simpler, like washing all the travel grottiness off me – and the scent of Leo.

He shouldn't still be on my skin as I showered at the resort this morning, but I swear I can smell his aftershave as I pull my T-shirt over my head. It is not the kind of reminder I need right now.

The shower revives me a little and I decide I should eat something – let's face it, plane food is an offence, and the amount they give you on short flights barely classifies as a meal – so I make myself a couple of slices of Vegemite toast and pour myself a glass of Aldi wine. Dinner of champions, I think, taking my meal into my bedroom, where I light a scented candle and climb into bed.

Being able to eat whatever you want, whenever you want, wherever you want is one of the many good things about being a single adult. Aunty, satisfied that everything in the house is as she left it, jumps up onto the bed beside me and snuggles in as I take my first bite. As I eat, I remind myself of all the other things I love about being single.

I can do what I want when I want, and without having to think about how it will affect my significant other. I can binge-watch a TV series or write till midnight, not having to apologise to or accommodate anyone else. This bed is all mine; there's never anyone hogging the blanket or snoring – not that I've ever experienced these things, but the coupled people I know are constantly complaining about this stuff – and I can buy bedding *I* like and have as many extra pillows and cushions as I want. Frilly throw cushions aren't really my thing, but if they were, I could have a hundred!

And it's not only the bedroom benefits. There's no sharing a bathroom with gross men either. Way has an ensuite, so the bathroom here is all mine. Growing up, Mum could never afford a house with multiple bathrooms so we all shared, and while Way was probably tidier and cleaner than me if I'm honest, I'm fairly sure he's an anomaly. From what I hear, most straight men are constantly leaving the toilet seat up, peeing outside the bowl and leaving whiskers in the sink after shaving, assuming the bathroom fairy will clean up after them.

You'll never find me cleaning up after a man, but on the flip side, I can spread my make-up all over my vanity and leave my dirty sheets for another night if I so feel. Speaking of nights, I can go out every single one if I wish and stay out as late as I like with no one back home worrying about me or texting, wanting to know when I'll be home. I don't have to buy presents for a partner for their birthday, Christmas, Valentine's Day and anniversaries, so I can spend all my money on myself and don't have the pressure of getting said present right or disappointing someone.

I chuckle to myself as I shove my last piece of toast into my mouth and run my hand over Aunty's back, relishing the soft warmth of her beautiful fur. 'Looks like I might have found the topic of my next book, Agony Aunt. *101 Reasons to be Single.* What do you think?'

She nuzzles her head against my hand in reply and I take that to mean *hell yes.*

Aunty rarely likes any of the guys I bring home. If they try to stroke her, she either bites them or runs away and hides in my wardrobe. Just another reason to add to my list.

And the reasons keep on coming. I should be writing all this down, but I take another sip of wine, sure I'll remember everything tomorrow.

I'm nobody's plus-one, which means I don't have to go to dinners or parties or school reunions that have nothing to do with me in the name of being a supportive partner. *And* I can travel whenever and wherever I want without having to consult anyone else about my itinerary.

Aside from Norfolk Island, when was the last time you travelled anywhere, Fred?

That stops me for a second, as I realise the voice in my head is right. I make the decision there and then to change that. First thing tomorrow I'm going to call my dad – the real one – and tell him I'm coming to visit him, his wife and my little sisters. Leo might not have been right about everything, but he did make me remember that Way and Mum are not my only blood relations and that maybe I'd enjoy getting to know some of the others. I want to see my little sisters again.

By the time I've finished my glass of wine, I'm feeling much better, but as I fall asleep, I can't stop my mind drifting straight to Leo again. *Argh.*

27

FATE, THE COMEDIAN

Whether it's the Aldi wine or the jetlag, I sleep like the dead, not waking until almost midday, when Aunty gets annoyed at not being fed and starts to paw my head. I groan, but get up and head into the laundry to open a tin of Dine for her. Way is sitting at the kitchen table, his laptop open in front of him when I enter.

'Good afternoon,' he says teasingly.

I poke my tongue out at him. 'It's Sunday. I can sleep until dinner if I want. Where's Benji?'

'He just left. He's working today – flying to Brisbane, actually.' I chuckle as I open the fridge and stare into it.

'Want me to make you a green juice?' Way asks.

'You're an angel.' I sit down at the table and Way gets up and starts grabbing ingredients for the juicer.

'Have you seen the WhatsApp group?' I blink. 'What WhatsApp group?'

'Mum has set up a new family group chat with Paul and everyone. She says because we're all spread out, we each need to provide an update at least once a week, preferably more often, and she's already planning Christmas. We're all invited to go stay with her and Paul at the mansion.'

My heart drops into my stomach. How am I supposed to forget about Leo if I'm constantly bombarded with updates from him? 'I might not be able to go,' I say.

Way frowns at me as he pops the lid on the juicer. 'Why? Paul's paying for it all.'

'My book's coming out at the end of the year. I might be doing promo.'

He gives me an *are-you-serious* look. 'Even I know that no one does book events the week before or after Christmas. The publishers won't even be working. Is something wrong? I thought you were happy for Mum now. I thought you liked Paul and his family. *Our* family?'

'I do,' I snap. 'But that doesn't mean I want to spend all my holidays with them. I was thinking I might go travelling over the summer.'

The noise of the juicer makes conversation impossible for the next few seconds, then Way pours my drink into a glass. 'Perfect then, you can travel to England with Benji and me. It'll be fun.'

'That's if Mum and Paul are still married by then,' I say and take a sip of my drink.

Way raises an eyebrow. 'I think you and I both know they will be. Anyway, what's on your agenda today?'

'Maybe a little bit of writing.' I decide not to tell him about calling Dad. I don't want him to ask me why I've suddenly decided to make an effort with my sisters. 'You?'

He gestures to his computer. 'Catching up on all the emails I missed while we were away so I can start back at work tomorrow not feeling like I'm behind on everything.'

'Enjoy.' I leave him to it and go back to my bedroom and pick up my phone, where, sure enough, I find a billion WhatsApp notifications. Mum and Paul are sharing photos from Fiji, where they're honeymooning, and everyone else is sending pics of them arriving back home.

My eyes immediately zero in on Leo's message: *Finally walked in the door. Can't believe I have to work tomorrow. Feel like I could sleep for a year.*

Below is a selfie of him lying in bed. God, he's gorgeous. As I take in his simple black and white checked doona cover, I remember how good it felt lying in my hotel bed with him, chatting and watching *The Parent Trap*. Once again I feel such remorse that we ruined that easy camaraderie with sex. I can find hundreds of guys to sleep with, but true friendships are few and far between.

Wanting to show this somehow, I like his photo with a heart and then post a message and photo I took last night in my bed with Aunty. *Someone was very happy to see me again.*

Next, before I can chicken out or change my mind, I bring up my dad's number in my phone and press call. My pulse races as the ringtone sounds – I can't remember the last time I spoke to my father, we barely even text message – but I needn't worry, because the call rings and rings and then goes to voicemail.

'Hi, you've called Simon Darling. I can't take your call right now but if you leave your name and number, I'll get back to you as soon as I can.'

The beep sounds.

'Um . . . hi, Dad. It's Fred. I . . .' Not usually lost for words, I struggle to find the right ones. 'Um . . . I've been thinking, I'd like to come visit. Get to know Mia and Ava. What do you think?'

He doesn't call back.

I spend the rest of the day writing – Chapter Seven, Rule #7: Expect nothing. Give nothing – and checking to see whether Leo has liked or replied to my message.

First thing Monday morning, I check WhatsApp. There are several more messages from my new family, but nothing from Leo. I try to ignore my disappointment as I get ready for work. I pick up my green juice, which Way has left in the fridge for me, kiss Aunty goodbye and then jump into my faithful orange Mini. It's only a short drive to the library but a long walk and, even if I was the kind of person who exercised, I never get up early enough for such capers.

My phone rings as I'm navigating the morning traffic, Siri announcing that it's my father. Better late than never, I think, as I accept the call on speaker through my car's Bluetooth. 'Hi, Dad.'

'Fred? He sounds almost surprised that I've answered, as if he isn't returning my call. 'Is everything okay? Did I hear your mum got married again?'

'Everything's fine. And yes, she's currently honeymooning in Fiji. So . . . how do you feel about me coming to visit?'

'What? When?'

I sigh. 'Didn't you listen to my voicemail?'

'I was at the girls' soccer game when you called, and I'm their coach – the whole team are adorable, so tiny – so I couldn't answer, and then later we had a couple of their friends over for a playdate and it slipped my mind. Sorry, honey, I thought I'd just call you. Did you say you want to come visit?'

'Yes,' I reply, trying not to be irritated at the fact he never even went to a school assembly for me. This isn't about my relationship with my father. It's about my little sisters. 'I want to get to know Ava and Mia.'

He's silent a moment and my stomach twists – maybe he thinks I'd be a bad influence on them – but then he sounds a little teary. 'Are you serious? They'd love to meet you. When do you want to come? We've got a spare room – you can stay as long as you like.'

'Jackie won't mind?'

'She'll be thrilled. She's always saying how she wishes the girls knew their older sister. She's big on family. Comes from a giant one.' He chuckles. 'We'll pay for your flights. Just message me the dates and I'll sort it.'

I smile, unable to believe how excited he sounds. 'Okay, thanks. When do Ava and Mia have school holidays? Maybe I could come then so I can really spend time with them.'

'Great idea. First two weeks of April, I think, but I'll confirm with Jackie and let you know. I'm so sorry, honey, but I've got to head into a meeting now. Great to talk to you. I'll call you tonight. Have a great day.'

'You too, Dad.'

I'm grinning as I park my car in the staff car park. My manuscript is due the first of April, so hanging out with my little sisters can be my reward for finishing it.

I'm delighted to be back at the library – my happy place. My colleagues are all delighted to see me too, and eager to hear about the wedding. I humour them, giving them a condensed version of what I told Bee on Saturday, not only because I feel like a broken record but because it's almost time to open. The moment they mention Leo and his music – Bee wasn't kidding that they've all become rabid fans – I shut them down.

She frowns at me over the top of her takeaway latte but before she can ask why I don't want to talk about Leo, I glance at my watch. 'It's 8.59, bitches. Time to open the doors.'

I hurry out of the staffroom to do so and they file out after me, heading off to different tasks. We all have our strengths in the library. Bee is an expert at helping people choose their next read; Xavier is our kid-whisperer – even though he's the boss now, he's still heavily involved in our children's program; Persephone knows pretty much everything you need to know about non-fiction; Ursula is firm but kind when it comes to dealing with disgruntled patrons, and I take the lead on a lot of our community outreach programs, including making plans for all the special days.

March has a few big things for me to get my teeth into. We've already booked speakers and scheduled events for International Women's Day, World Sleep Day, Neurodiversity Week, the International Day of Happiness and Harmony Day, but I need to start collecting books for each of the displays. I grab one of the trolleys and start making my way around the library to look for suitable titles, things like non-fiction books about feminism, women's suffrage and the sexual revolution, novels written by local women, poetry collections and classics, such as *Little Women* and *Beloved* by Toni Morrison.

As I stockpile, I also do a tidy – people constantly pick up books from one section, read them for a little while in one of our seating areas and then put them back in the wrong place. We'd much prefer if they just handed them to us or put them on one of the returns trolleys than leave them all over the place. There's nothing more annoying than when someone asks us for a particular book and our system tells us it's not on loan, but we can't find it anywhere.

In the self-help section, I pull out a book that has been shoved in the wrong way – pages facing out – and almost drop it as I flip it over to check the cover.

Me Before You by Jojo Moyes. Fate must think she's a comedian.

My heart squeezes but I put the book back on the trolley and try to forget about it and Leo as I finish my task. It's much easier said than done, and by the time I take my lunch break, I'm completely annoyed by the real estate he's taking up inside my head.

I need to stop feeling guilty, not only for spoiling *Me Before You* for him, but also for hurting him. Perhaps I should try to apologise again. I head into the staffroom, grab the salad wrap

Way made me and open WhatsApp on my phone. It's the middle of the night in England and logically I know that if Leo hadn't liked or replied to my message this morning, it's unlikely he would have now, but I can't help looking.

And I can't help being disappointed that he hasn't.

That's it! I'm writing him a message. I'm reaching out with an olive branch. And if he doesn't respond to that, at least I'll know I've tried my best to make amends.

I put my wrap down on the table to concentrate.

Dear Leo Hi Leo

Long time no see, Leopold! How's things in sunny London?

Nothing I type feels right and after multiple more attempts, I give up. Perhaps it's best I just let things settle a while. After all, doesn't time heal all wounds?

As I put my phone on the table, it pings with a notification from Tinder: *Patrick has sent you a message.*

Patrick – a 36-year-old divorced orthodontist – is one of the guys I was talking to before Norfolk Island. I've not checked my dating apps since my third night there, which might be the longest I've ever gone, and everyone else seems to have given up on me.

I open the message: *Are you ghosting me? Was it something I said?*

I chuckle, then reply, explaining that I've been away and busy with my mum's wedding.

He must be between patients because he replies immediately:

In that case, do you fancy catching up for a drink this week?

Between work and writing, I'm not going to have a whole load of time for play over the next few weeks, but he seems really great and I don't want to brush him off. Besides, dating is practically work for me.

Yeah, that would be great, I reply.

Awesome. I've got my kids till Wednesday morning, but I can do Thursday or Friday night?

Thursday suits me. I never risk ruining a Friday night with a first date.

Patrick lives a few suburbs away in Melville but says he's happy to drive to me, so we arrange to meet at the Federal Hotel in Freo. I can hardly wait. Everyone knows that the best way to get over one guy is to get under another, and that's exactly what I intend to do.

28

GREEN FLAGS AND MANKY HANKIES

'It's date night,' I tell Aunty as I emerge from the bathroom wrapped in a towel to find her sprawled across my bed, taking up much more room than someone of her petite stature should be entitled to. 'What do you think I should wear?'

Clearly not interested in assisting me, she doesn't so much as twitch her tail as I throw open my wardrobe. It was forty degrees today and the temperature isn't predicted to go down much overnight, so I choose a little red playsuit I bought for a quarter of its retail price at the local Vinnies and pair it with black, platform sandals. I accessorise with chunky earrings made from old bottle tops, which I picked up at the markets, and go to town with my make-up. I've always loved wearing it, but ever since I shaved my head and no longer have to take time styling my hair, I've started having a lot more fun with bold eyeliner and sparkly eyeshadow.

'How do I look?' I ask Aunty when I'm done. She rolls over and curls into a ball.

I laugh and take a final check in the mirror. Satisfied that I'm just the right amount of hot for a first date, I run my hands over my head and immediately curse. It's a habit I hadn't even realised I'd developed until Leo touched my scalp in the pool, and now I can't do it without thinking of him.

The good mood I'd been in due to the anticipation of meeting Patrick and what might happen later shrivels. That's it, I'm growing my hair out again. I might even buy a wig to help me with the transition – at least that will please Mum. Although right now I'm not feeling very favourable towards her. If it wasn't for her, I'd never have met Leo and wouldn't be checking our family WhatsApp group every five minutes to see if he's liked one of my messages. Mum probably wonders what's come over me – I was never as active in our previous family chat – but I just hate the thought that he hates me. I'm ashamed to admit I've even scrolled his Instagram and that of the UkePros a few times, looking for evidence that he's okay and not wallowing in my rejection, but both accounts have been dormant this week.

My phone pings and I pounce on it, irrationally disappointed when it isn't a WhatsApp notification but a message from Patrick saying he's looking forward to meeting me. He seems like a really nice guy, and he deserves my full attention this evening, so I do something I've never done before. When I kiss Aunty goodnight and go out to my Mini, I don't take my phone with me. A little voice in my head tells me that this is dangerous and irresponsible – what if my car breaks down? What if Patrick turns out to be a rapist or a serial killer? – but I ignore it. People went on dates before mobile phones were invented and lived to tell the tale.

I park on the street not too far from the pub and arrive to find Patrick standing outside waiting for me. His light brown hair is in a crew cut, he has a closely trimmed beard and he is wearing smart black pants and a pale blue, short-sleeved shirt. He's tall, well built and undeniably attractive, but the best thing is he looks exactly like he does in his profile picture.

Green Flag #1, I think as I approach him. You wouldn't believe the number of men who use misleading photos – either pics from when they were much younger, AI-generated images or photos standing next to a really short person to make them seem taller than they are. A couple of guys I've met have even borrowed photos from their better-looking friends.

'Fred?' he asks, and when I nod, he leans forward and gives me a quick hug hello. I get a quick whiff of his minty breath mingling with some rather lovely aftershave.

Green Flag #2 – Good hygiene. I've met far too many guys with whom I don't make it past one drink because they can't even be bothered with the basics.

'It's nice to meet you, Patrick,' I say. 'Great shirt.'

'Thanks. I really like your . . .' His voice trails off as he gestures to my outfit.

I laugh. 'It's a playsuit.'

He nods. 'Well, it looks good. Shall we go inside?'

The place is pretty crowded – Thursday night is practically the weekend in Freo – but there are a few empty seats at the bar.

'Can I buy you a drink?' Patrick asks.

I shake my head. 'Thanks, but I buy my own drinks.'

He doesn't put up an argument and we each order from the barman – a dirty martini for me and a rum and Coke for him – then take our drinks to a high table that's just been vacated. He lifts his glass out to mine. 'Well, cheers.'

We clink and take a sip each, then he says, 'Is buying your own drinks one of your rules?'

We've exchanged a few messages this week and one night when he asked what I was up to, I told him I was writing, which led to me telling him about my book contract.

'Yes,' I tell him. 'It's Rule Number Nine – always pay for yourself.'

'What are the other rules?' he asks, and I do not detect a hint of scepticism from him, which is nice. I've found that even men who are on the same page as me about casual dating often sneer a little at the fact I'm writing a book about it, but I don't want to go over the rules with him. That will make this date feel like homework and also remind me of the last person I spoke with about them. *Leo.*

As if I need any reminders.

I hit Patrick with my best flirtatious smile. 'Nice try, but if I tell you all my secrets, you won't have to buy the book.'

'Touché.' He takes another sip. 'It's just I'm impressed by anyone who writes. I love reading and I can talk the arm off a chair – or so my patients tell me – but ask me to put a sentence on paper and I flounder.'

I like that he's self-deprecating and also appreciates what I do – or am trying to do. I tell him it doesn't always come easy to me either and that I tried and failed at fiction before getting my book contract, then ask, 'What do you like reading?'

'Anything and everything. I'm a huge Colson Whitehead fan and also love a good legal thriller. My ex used to say I was more into my books than I was her.'

Interesting. I twirl my glass between my fingers. 'And were you?'

He sighs. 'Possibly. Except when it comes to books, I've got a bit of a short attention span.'

'Did you cheat on her?'

'Geez, we're getting straight to the nitty-gritty,' he says with a chuckle.

'Is that a yes?'

He shakes his head. 'No, but I wanted to. And that's when I realised I couldn't stay in the marriage. My dad ran around behind my mum's back a lot, and I hated what it did to her.'

It could be a tale he's spinning to make me think he's a good guy, but I believe him, and my lie detector is generally spot on. 'How did your wife handle that?'

'She was sad but also, I think, relieved. I know relationships take work, but we'd both been trying way harder than you should have to.'

'Do you have a good relationship with her now?'

'Yeah. We're probably better friends than we were when we were together, and we're constantly messaging, sharing stuff about the girls. Our daughters are the most important people to both of us.'

'That's nice.' I expect him to dig out his phone and ask me if I want to see photos – that would be a no, because although I don't often date dads, when I do, I don't want to know anything about their kids. Such sharing makes things far too personal.

He points his glass at me instead. 'What about you? Do you have exes?'

I laugh. 'No. I don't have relationships or boyfriends, so can't have exes.'

'How does that work? You just have one-night stands?'

'I rarely have one-night stands. I only sleep with someone who I'm super attracted to, and then I want to make the most of it at least for a while.'

He nods slowly as if taking this in. 'So . . . you just hook up with people until it fizzles out between you?'

'Yeah, or until they become attached.'

A waitress comes over and pops a little dish of peanuts and a menu between us. 'Just wave me over if you want to order any food.'

'Thank you,' Patrick says with a smile.

Another green flag – he's polite to waitstaff. They're landing one after another.

He looks back to me. 'Will your book just be for women?'

'No.' I reach for a few peanuts. 'I mean, I guess young

women will be the publisher's target audience, but men can read it too. None of the rules are gender specific; it's a simple guide to assist anyone who doesn't want to conform to society's expectations that we pair up like pigeons.'

'But I guess it's women who normally struggle with that kind of thing. You're a rare case. Most women I've met since my divorce are after serious commitment. I guess they're just biologically wired that way.'

I shake my head. 'I'm not sure it's a biology thing – it's more that we've been brainwashed, practically since we could walk, into believing that our role in society is to find a good man, settle down and have babies. We're sold the happy-ever-after idea in fairytales and movies. It's pretty much everywhere we look. Bachelors are respected in society, while single women over a certain age are pitied. People think times have changed, but even if a wedding ring isn't the be all and end all now, we still need a partner to be validated in society's eyes.'

Patrick smiles at my rant, but the words that come out of his mouth are surprising. 'I'm sad that's still the case. Maddy and I certainly aren't raising our girls to think that way. I'll be sure to buy them both a copy of your book.'

'How old are they?'

He chuckles. 'Only three and five. Do you think I should wait a few years before giving it to them?'

I laugh. 'Probably a good idea, but you can definitely plant other seeds to break the cycle.'

He nods and picks up the menu. 'Do you want to order food? Or is that against the rules as well?' He winks. 'I'm happy to just head back to your place if you'd prefer?'

Although his wink indicates he's joking, if any previous date was going this well, I'd be inclined to take him up on the offer to go straight to dessert. Patrick ticks *all* my boxes – he's smart, kind, funny and on the same page about what he wants out of this date – but all I can think about is that he's not Leo.

I miss him so much. How is it possible to feel this way after knowing someone less than a week?

Before I realise it, I'm crying.

Horror fills Patrick's face as he puts down his glass and places his hand on mine. 'Fred? What's wrong? Is it what I said? I didn't mean to upset you. I thought—'

'It's not you,' I say, shaking my head as I dig into my bag for the hanky Leo gave me. I haven't been able to bring myself to throw it away and have been carrying it around all week. I'm desperate to smell him, but when I lift it to my nose all I get is the scent of my stale, dried-up tears, which only makes me sob harder.

'You're scaring me,' Patrick says. 'Even though I have two daughters, I'm not good with crying women.'

I see his gaze skip past me to the exit. He's wondering if it would be rude to leave me like this. Yes, it would, but I don't care; all I can think of is how much I want to make things right with Leo. How much I want to claw back a friendship that barely had the chance to begin, yet felt so real.

'I'm sorry,' I say, pushing back my seat so fast the chair falls sideways to the floor. 'This has nothing to do with you. I just . . .' Without another word I turn and run, unable to care what he might think about me. In this moment, I don't have the brainpower to worry about anyone but myself. I half walk, half run down William Street towards the prison, darting around evening revellers, then cut through Henderson Street past the row of historical warder's cottages. I'm puffing by the markets when I remember my car is parked back near the pub, but I'm almost halfway to Bee's place on Norfolk Street, so I just keep running. Running towards the only person who can possibly make me feel better.

If anyone will know what to do, it's Bee. She'll help me come up with a plan to win Leo's forgiveness.

It's only when I'm banging on her door, tears still pouring down my cheeks like gushing waterfalls, that I realise it's rather late and she and Sully might already be in bed. My heart sinks but before I can retreat, the door opens and JB explodes out of the house to greet me. I look over his fluffy head, his paws on my chest, to see Bee standing there in short Dr Seuss PJs.

'Fred?' Her eyebrows grow closer. 'Aren't you supposed to be on a date?'

I open my mouth to explain but tears slide into my mouth, their saltiness almost choking me.

Bee's face goes pale. 'Oh my God, did he hurt you?' She yanks JB off me and ushers me inside. Even the dog seems to sense that something is off, because he sobers far more quickly than usual and settles on his bed in the corner rather than trying to jump at me again.

Bee leads me into the lounge room and sits me on the couch. 'Fred, you're scaring me.' She thrusts a box of tissues at me.

'Take some deep breaths. Whatever happened, it's going to be okay. I'm going to take care of you.'

It's a few moments before my sobs ease, and then I ask, 'Is Sully here?'

'He's at the hospital. Do you want me to call him? Shall we go there to get someone to check you out?'

I suddenly realise she thinks Patrick has assaulted me. 'No! This has nothing to do with my date.'

'Then what's wrong? Is it Aunty?'

'No,' I whisper. 'I miss Leo. I miss him so much it hurts.'

She frowns. 'Your mum's new stepson?'

I nod. 'I stuffed things up big time with him, and I can't stop thinking about it.'

'I . . .' She blinks and shakes her head. 'What did you do?'

'I slept with him.'

Bee gasps. 'I can't believe you didn't tell me!'

'I know.' I drop my head into my hands and start to rock back and forth. 'I'm sorry.'

'No, *I'm* sorry. This isn't about me. What's the problem? Was it . . . terrible?'

This makes me laugh. 'Anything but, but it ruined everything.'

She stands. 'I think you need a drink.'

I take another deep breath as she marches out to the kitchen. I'm expecting her to open a bottle of wine, but she returns with a cup of tea – heavy on the sugar – and, even though I'm not cold, she wraps me in a crocheted blanket that Daisy, Sully's grandmother, made for her.

'Tell me everything,' she says.

The words tumble from my mouth in an almost incoherent order.

Bee puts her hand on my knee. 'Slow down, honey.'

'Okay.' Another deep breath. 'Leo and I hit it off the very first morning we were on the island. And as soon as we realised we both thought our parents were making a catastrophic mistake, we became a team.'

She nods, already knowing about Operation Break-up.

'And I guess we ended up spending a lot of time together. There were a few late nights, some heated moments, and the more I got to know him the more I liked him.'

'But . . .?'

I sigh. 'But Leo and I couldn't be more opposite when it comes to life and what we want from it. He's like you, Bee. He's good and wholesome and believes in the fairytale. He's looking for The One and, as you know, I'm only ever looking for someone to have a good time with. Even after he told me he was attracted to me, we both agreed that nothing should happen between us. That'd we'd be better as friends. And then everything went balls-up, and we went out drinking and dancing together. We had such a great time and at the end of the night, he told me he didn't want to regret not sleeping with me.'

'Well, you are pretty hot,' Bee says, clearly trying to lighten the mood. 'I don't blame him.'

I manage a smile. 'Thanks. We didn't sleep together that night though. His dad had a health scare, which put a pin in that, but the following night . . . we went outside alone during the wedding reception. One thing led to another, and we ended up finally giving in to our attraction.'

'That's when you had sex?' she clarifies.

I nod, a hot flush rushing through my body at the recollection, which I've been doing my damn best to forget these past few days.

'Where?'

'In a park, against a tree.'

Bee shrieks – 'Hot!' – causing JB to look up from his bed.

That word doesn't even come close. 'Yeah, it was,' I say, 'and because of what he'd said the night before, I thought we were still both on the same page about just having a bit of grown-up fun, but . . .'

As JB joins us on the couch, taking up most of the room and resting his big head in Bee's lap, I tell her about being sprung by the local sergeant. Although it should be a funny story, neither of us laugh as I explain how Leo somehow got it into his head that I'd changed my mind about love.

'He basically told me he wanted to pursue a relationship. We had a big, awful fight.' Tears threaten again as I think about it – I've never cried this much in my life. I don't even know myself any more. 'And then another one the next day on the plane. He called me a coward.'

Bee looks horrified. 'I've never met anyone as strong and

independent as you. Besides, it's not your fault he got his wires crossed.'

'Maybe.' I shrug. 'He thinks my independence is nothing but a mask. He believes that because of Mum's multiple marriages and what happened to me in high school, I'm scared of failure, rejection and betrayal. That I protect myself by not allowing myself to get close to anyone who I might fall in love with.'

'Hang on.' Bee frowns again. 'What happened to you in high school?'

I take a deep breath and tell her about Kyle. The more I speak about him, the less it seems such a big deal. What he did was a cruel, childish thing and I felt mortified at the time, but I bet no one else from school even remembers it now. And maybe if I'd spoken to someone about what he did years ago instead of bottling it all up inside me, I wouldn't have let it shape my life the way I have.

By the time I'm finished, Bee is the one crying. 'I'm sad you never felt you could tell me about Kyle, but I'm glad you finally spoke to someone about it.'

'I didn't actually *tell* Leo either – he overhead a conversation I had with Mum. I was so angry when he told me he'd been eaves-dropping. So ashamed.'

'You have nothing to be ashamed of.' Bee puts her arm around me and pulls me into her side. I lean my head against her shoulder, soaking up her comfort in a way I wouldn't have allowed myself to in the past. 'That's an awful thing to have gone through. I wish we could go back in time and I could give sixteen-year-old Fred a big hug.'

'As nice as that sounds,' I say, 'if we go back in time, can we do something to humiliate Kyle instead?'

Bee chuckles. 'Deal.'

Ignoring the tissues, I wipe my eyes with Leo's hanky again. 'Whose handkerchief is that?'

'Leo's.' I clutch it to my chest and her eyebrows shoot up to her hairline.

'What?' I say. 'He gave it to me one night when I told him about Mum and Bernie.'

'And you took it on your date?'

'I've been carrying it around with me all week.' She opens her mouth to reply but I don't let her. 'Never mind the hanky. I need to make things right. I don't know why I'm crying over a friendship that I barely even had, but it's all I can think about. I can't stand the thought that he hates me. He's not even liking my messages in the family WhatsApp group. I just want things to go back to how they were between us before we had sex! You're good at this kind of stuff . . . any ideas on what I can do?'

She's quiet for a moment – hopefully coming up with a wonderful plan – then says, 'Correct me if I'm wrong, but usually you tell me when you sleep with someone.'

I'm not sure where she's going with this, but I nod. 'I didn't tell you because I was trying to block it out.'

'But it hasn't worked out that way?'

I shake my head. 'I can't think about anything else. Thinking about stuffing things up makes me so sad. It's driving me crazy!'

'I've never seen you this upset about a guy before. You barely think about most men when you're not with them, yet you tell me you can't get him out of your head, so I'm wondering . . .' She looks a little nervous. 'If maybe . . . maybe you didn't tell me about Leo because he means something. Fred, darling, don't bite my head off, but it sounds like you might have caught feelings for him.'

'Don't be ridiculous,' I scoff.

Bee doesn't back down. 'You've slept with men before who've fallen in love with you and wanted more, and you've walked away from them without a second thought. What makes Leo different?'

It's a question I've been asking myself all week. 'We're connected through our parents, so we'll have to see each other again. I don't want things to be awkward, but also, I want us to be . . .'

'What?' she asks as my voice drifts off.

I was going to say 'friends' but it's suddenly clear I've been lying to myself.

I do want us to be friends. But I also want so much more. More than I've ever allowed myself to want from anyone.

Holy shit. Bee's right.

I've bloody gone and caught feelings for Leo.

He's broken me. He's spoiled me for carefree dates and casual hook-ups. From now on, every guy I ever meet I'll compare with him and none of them will ever measure up. What kind of hypocrite does this make me? I'm halfway through a book schooling other people in how to have sex without emotion, and I've gone and blown it myself.

If I'm honest, I think I crossed the line with Leo long before we slept together.

Maybe it was because we never dated that he bypassed my defences – I didn't realise what was happening until it was too late – but how it happened doesn't matter. The fact that it *has* happened is my problem. A *huge* problem.

'Fred! Are you okay?! Say something.'

It's then that I realise that Bee is shouting because I'm hyperventilating.

'You're right,' I gasp, trying to fill my lungs. 'Leo's . . . right.' More quick breaths. 'I *am* a coward. I *am* scared of love. Or rather, I'm scared of how vulnerable it makes me. I *was* trying to protect myself, but I failed dismally, because if what I'm feeling now isn't heartbreak, then I don't know what is.'

'It's love,' Bee says kindly. 'I've felt there was something different about you since you got home. You haven't been yourself. I thought it was because you were tired from your trip and stressed about your book, but what you've just told me – and the fact you've held onto a manky hanky – tells me everything I need to know. You've one hundred per cent been hit by the love bug.'

The word still gives me the heebie jeebies. 'How can it be love? I've barely known him a week.'

'Oh, honey.' She hits me with a sympathetic smile. 'Have you read *Sense and Sensibility*?'

I glare at her, wondering why she's asking me about Jane Austen at a time like this. 'No. Why?'

'Marianne Dashwood – one of the sisters in the book – famously said: "Seven years would be insufficient to make some people acquainted with each other, and seven days are more than enough for others."'

While I'm trying to digest this, she adds, 'The heart wants what the heart wants.'

'That's exactly what Leo said.'

'He sounds like a smart guy and a wonderful person.'

My heart swells at her praise of him. 'He is.'

Bee is my best friend in the world and as much as I adore her, she didn't see through me like Leo did. Even my own brother never questioned my stance. They both believed in my mask, but I can't really blame them, because I did too.

'So what are you going to do?' she asks.

'I don't know.' I groan and drop my head into my hands again. 'What should I do?'

Her reply is instant. 'I think you should fly to London and tell Leo how you feel.'

I look up as my chest tightens at the thought. 'This isn't a romcom, you know.'

She grins at me. 'Why can't it be? You told me not so long ago that I deserved a happy ever after. Well, so do you.

Everybody deserves to love and be loved. Even you, Winifred Darling. *Especially* you.'

Usually I'd roll my eyes at such sop, but instead I feel something crack inside me. 'We parted in such a bad way,' I say. 'I'm not sure he'll still feel the same way about me. For all I know he went back home, saw the light and is thanking the Lord for his lucky escape.'

Bee does something very un-Bee like – she rolls her eyes, then shrugs. 'Then at worst you clear the air, so family Christmases won't be crazy awkward in the future.'

'And at best?' I ask nervously.

She winks. 'I guess there's only one way to find out.'

Although the idea of putting my heart on the line is terrifying, it's also thrilling. Just the thought of seeing Leo again has every cell in my body on edge – in a good way – but then I remember the other complications. 'What about *21 Rules for Not Catching Feelings*? I can't be promoting a book about being satisfyingly single if I'm in a relationship.'

Her smile falters. 'Um . . . how binding is that contract?'

'Well, if I tell them I can't finish it, I've got to pay back my advance.' I guess I could sell my car or ask Way for a loan. 'And I'll also be the laughing-stock of the publishing world. I doubt I'd ever get another book deal.'

'I guess you have to ask yourself what you want more.'

I don't even have to think about it – 'I want Leo' – and it feels so damn good to say this out loud. 'Oh my God. I'm in *love!*'

Bee squeals and grabs me in a hug again. 'Can I be your bridesmaid?'

I laugh as JB tries to get in on the action. 'Don't get carried away. Even if he does feel the same way, marriage is going too far. Sorry, I know you want to get married, but I still believe it's an archaic and oppressive institution.'

'We'll just have to agree to disagree on that,' she says, wrangling JB, who is far too big to be a lapdog onto her lap.

'The book isn't the only problem. We live on opposite sides of the planet. If by chance he does want us to be together, then eventually, one of us is going to have to move. It might be me.'

I don't have to say what we're both thinking – for almost a decade we've lived in each other's pockets and the thought of not seeing Bee almost every day is awful.

She takes my hand again and squeezes it. 'I'll miss you, but trust me when I say love's worth a few sacrifices, and knowing you're happy would ease the pain. Besides, I hear your new family is pretty loaded, so you can come back and visit all the time, and Sully and I will come visit you as well.'

My stomach clenches. 'I could be getting ahead of myself.'

She smiles. 'Maybe. Maybe not.'

'Thank you,' I say, squeezing *her* hand. 'You're the best.'

'I know.'

I chuckle as I stand.

'Where are you going?' she asks.

'Home to book a plane ticket to London.'

'Do you want me to come with you?'

I frown. 'Home? Or to London?'

'Both,' she says, pushing JB off and getting up.

I know she means it – she'd do anything for me – and I think about her offer for a moment before shaking my head. 'Thank you. But this is something I need to do by myself.'

Bee nods. 'I understand.' Then she pulls me into a hug. 'Good luck.'

29

A LEO GROUPIE

It's just after 6 p.m. on Saturday night when I land in London. After eighteen hours in the air and a two-hour stopover in Dubai, I should probably find a hotel room to freshen up, get some sleep and face Leo in the morning, but I haven't come this far to wait. I jump into an iconic black cab at Heathrow, bark the general vicinity of Leo's houseboat at the driver, then pull my make-up out of my bag and get to work. London is so cute with its historic architecture and red phone boxes on every corner, but although it's a thirty-five-minute drive from the airport to Islington, it's impossible to appreciate my surroundings with my emotions swinging between excitement and terror the whole way. By the time the driver pulls up as close to the canal as he can, everything I ate on the plane is threatening to make a reappearance and I'm considering asking him to turn around and take me right back to the airport.

Be brave.

Listening to the voice inside me, I pay my fare, then climb out of the car, hitching my carry-on bag over my shoulder. As the cab edges away from the kerb, I shiver and wish I'd remembered that winter in England is a lot colder than winter in Perth.

But after booking my flight Thursday night, working Friday – where I begged a slightly annoyed, slightly bemused and excited Xavier for time off – I hadn't had a whole lot of time to think about packing before my 6 a.m. flight. I figured I could buy anything I needed in London, but it's already dark and bitterly cold here now, and the oversized jumper and leggings I travelled in are not cutting the mustard.

Oh well, I think as I start down some stairs that lead to the canal walk, hopefully Leo's place is heated and, even more hopefully, he lets me in. The cold is not the only thing I'm worrying about – as I get closer to the canal, the lights from the streets above fade and it's dark enough that I have to use the flashlight app on my phone to avoid stumbling and falling into the water. The hair on the back of my neck prickles as I pass a man who looks to be fondling himself, leaning against a wall. Thankfully, he appears to be in a world of his own and doesn't so much as blink at me. When Leo said he lived in a houseboat, it sounded unconventional but fun, yet tonight the water looks murky and who knows what could be lurking behind the shadows on my path?

I pick up my pace as I pass boat after colourful boat lined up along Regent's Canal Walk. They all appear to be sleeping, occasionally winking with low lights in the small round windows, bobbing up and down almost imperceptibly as people move within. On the other side of the embankment, trees are growing, their long, graceful branches trailing into the still dark depths. My phone light catches on dirty puddles on the grey paved walkway, and I almost feel as if I'm walking through a Dickensian novel, as if Fagan or one of his boys might jump out at any moment and pickpocket me. I thought it would be easy to pick out the narrowboat Leo showed me photos of, but there are so many more than I imagined and in the dark, they all look so similar. I haven't planned this out properly – why didn't I search for his place on Google Maps? Trying not to feel disheartened and ignoring the racing of my heart, I'm trying to recall any distinguishing features when a gruff voice scares the bejesus out of me.

'Will I help ya, luv?'

Pressing my hand against my chest, I look towards the voice to see an old man with a massive, scruffy beard standing on the front of one of the boats, smoking a cigarette.

'Excuse me?' I manage.

He hits me with a rusty old smile, and I swear I recognise him from an old movie, or maybe it's just his type. 'Yar looking a wee lost. I figure either yar looking for someone or ya casing the joint.'

I chuckle, relaxing at the warmth in his voice. 'My friend lives around here somewhere. At least I think so. He said he's moored just south of the Islington Tunnel Canal. Is that where I am?'

'Aye.' He nods. 'What's yar friend's name?'

'Leo Lewis. Don't suppose you know him?'

The man throws back his head and laughs loudly – 'Aye, he lives right there' – then gestures to the boat just in front of his, one little light shining above the door.

My heart leaps to my throat. Thank God. Maybe I won't freeze to death after all.

'But he's not home. I spoke to him earlier, and he was heading off to a gig at the Wenlock Arms.'

My heart sinks, but only for a second. Pubs are warm and cosy, they have comfort food and, maybe in this part of the world, mulled wine. 'How far away is that?'

'Ya got transport?'

'Um . . .' I point to my legs.

He laughs again. 'Well, I'd say it's about a thirty-minute walk.'

There's no way in hell I'm spending half an hour out in this biting cold air. 'I'll take an Uber. Thanks so much.'

'Welcome, luv,' he calls, as I start to run back the way I came. A car arrives thirty seconds after I order it, and it sweeps me through the streets of Islington, the city dark except for the twinkling of the tall, black lampposts. By the time we pull up outside the pub, I've thawed out a little, but now I'm not so focused on being cold, my nerves return with a vengeance.

'This is it,' my driver says, clearly wondering why I haven't got out yet.

I stare out the car window at the Wenlock Arms, a two-storey building on the corner that was probably built sometime in the early 1800s. It looks like almost every other pub in England. Its bricks are a deep burgundy red and I imagine the thick walls are mortared by warm ale and secrets. There's laughter coming from one end of the bar, which I can hear from the outside, as well as the welcome sight of golden light flushing through the grand windows. The door is right on the corner, and above it, the sign declares *Freehouse, Established 1835*, making it older than Sherlock Holmes.

I shake my head. Who cares about Sherlock Holmes! What the hell am I doing here?

Two weeks ago, if you'd told me I'd fly halfway across the world to declare my feelings for a guy, I'd have laughed until I choked. Do I really want to do this?

I emailed Emily late Thursday night – just after booking my flight – and told her I couldn't finish my book, and she'd called me at the crack of dawn Friday morning. To say she wasn't pleased is an understatement. When I told her it wasn't because

I had writer's block or imposter syndrome but because I had possibly fallen in love and didn't want to be a hypocrite, she told me I was having a mental breakdown and that she was going to delete the email and pretend she'd never received it.

So it's not too late for me to back out.

But that idea only makes me feel worse. I can't go back to Australia without at least seeing Leo. Maybe I'll take one look at him and come to my senses. Maybe I won't feel a fucking thing. 'Thanks,' I tell my Uber driver, who looks relieved as I finally climb out of his little hatchback. I've barely closed the door before he's screeching off down the road.

Cold air whips across the top of my head as I turn towards the entrance of the pub. People are huddled outside smoking and vaping. Chatter, the clink of glasses and the now very familiar sounds of the UkePros drift out when someone opens the door to head in.

My heart hitches as it recognises Leo's voice. I couldn't even tell you what he's singing, all I can hear is him as I take a deep breath and head inside. The pub is crowded and I follow the music. The bar is lined with people sitting on weathered stools and I can smell greasy pub grub and stale beer.

I could do with a glass of Dutch courage myself.

Someone apologises as they jostle against me, but I don't reply because I've seen him, holding his ukelele close to his chest as he croons into a mic at the front of his band. The second my eyes land on him, all the doubts I had about coming evaporate. He's every bit as gorgeous as I remember, with his dirty-blond hair tied back in that sexy man bun, but his facial hair is longer than it was on the island, as if he hasn't had the time or inclination for grooming.

My heart swells with feelings I never knew I was capable of, and I'm so overcome, I have to reach out and steady myself on a stranger.

'You okay?' the rosy-cheeked, middle-aged woman says as she looks at my hand on her arm. 'Maybe go a little easier on the drinks.'

But I haven't had a drop of alcohol since my martini Thursday night and I'm no longer in need of any liquid courage. 'More than okay,' I reply, beaming past her to stare at Leo.

As much as I want to push through the people between us and declare my feelings to him, I can't interrupt mid-song. I probably shouldn't even interrupt mid-gig, so I summon patience from the dark depths within me and order a pint of beer to sip on while I watch and wait. Although some of the patrons are bopping along to the music, most of them are barely paying the UkePros any attention as they chat and laugh with their friends. I can't understand why they're not as mesmerised as I am. I can't take my eyes off Leo, and as much as I love watching him up there in his element, I'm wishing time would speed up so they'll finish their set and I can announce myself.

They're halfway through an eighties medley when Leo glances across the audience. I see the moment he recognises me – he doesn't falter, but his brow furrows then his eyes widen as if he doesn't believe what's in front of him.

I smile and lift my hand to wave. That's when he stops playing.

He all but drops his ukelele to the floor and his bandmates stare at him in horror as he steps around his mic and strides towards me. People step aside like he's Moses parting the Red Sea, and I push off my stool so I'm standing when he reaches me.

'Winifred?' He sounds both surprised and delighted to see me, and my bones melt at his use of my full name.

'Hello, Leopold,' I manage.

He rakes his hand through his hair, which is hanging loose and wild around his face. 'What are you doing here?'

'I . . . I wanted to see you.'

His lips quirk at the edges. 'It's a long way to come just for that.'

'Well, maybe there's a little more to it.'

The music has stopped, and I can feel all eyes in the pub boring into me as Leo waits expectantly.

I swallow and look up into his gorgeous face. 'I came because I wanted to tell you that you were right. I am a coward. I'm terrified of love and getting hurt and being vulnerable with someone, but somehow you snuck under my defences. I loved every second we spent together on Norfolk Island, and since I've been home, I've tried damn hard to forget about you, but I can't. I've missed you so much. Did you mean it when you said you think there's something special between us?'

Leo's lips crack a full-blown smile. 'I've never meant anything more. This last week has been hell – worse than any break-up I've ever been through. I almost reached out to you so many times, but I knew I couldn't handle being just friends with you.'

'Well . . .' I suck in another deep breath. 'I'm hoping we can be a little more than friends. I'm still a coward, but now what I'm scared of has changed. Much more terrifying than trying to make a go of things with you is living the rest of my life wondering what if? What if I got brave and opened my heart to you?'

He doesn't reply – he simply stares at me. 'What are you thinking?' I whisper.

He reaches out and brushes his thumb over my cheek. 'I'm thinking a couple of things actually. I'm wondering if I'm dreaming, and now that I've touched you and you appear to truly be here in the flesh, I'm thinking that for someone who's always identified herself as unromantic, you say pretty damn romantic things.'

'And I mean every one of them,' I say, a rumble of relieved laughter escaping me. 'I don't know how this is supposed to work between you and me logistically, but I want to do everything within my power to make it happen.'

'Me too,' he replies, then cups my cheeks in the palm of his big, beautiful, warm hands and dips his head to kiss me.

Heat rushes from my lips to my toes as cheers erupt around us. 'You know, I still don't believe that a woman needs a man to be happy,' I say when we finally break apart.

'I agree with you, but that doesn't mean I'm not going to spend every second of every day trying to make you happier than any other woman on this planet.' He grabs my hand and leads me towards the exit. 'Starting right now.'

'We can't just leave! What about your band? What about everyone here to hear you play?'

He shrugs. 'What about them? I've got more important things to do right now, but . . . dammit . . .' He stops and sighs. 'My keys and phone are in my uke case.' Reluctantly he changes direction and heads back towards the stage where the rest of his band are still waiting. 'Hi, boys, I'd like to introduce you to Fred. Fred, this is Farouk, August and Mitch.

'Pleased to meet you,' I say. 'Sorry for, ah, interrupting.'

'That's okay,' Mitch says. 'So many people filmed that little show you two just put on, for sure it'll be viral by tomorrow. We couldn't pay for better publicity.'

Leo groans and I laugh.

Maybe it's because of this, but when Leo tells the others that he's cutting out early to take me home, none of them kick up much of a fuss.

'How'd you find me?' he asks as we step outside into the cold air, uke case in one hand and mine in the other.

'I went to your houseboat and your neighbour told me you were here.'

'George?' he asks.

'Big guy with a bushy beard?'

He nods. 'That's the one. Oh my God, you're freezing. Don't you have a coat or something?'

When I shake my head, he shrugs out of the big black overcoat he'd grabbed alongside his keys and phone and feeds me into it. It's not only deliciously warm but smells of him. I feel like I've died and gone to heaven. We catch an Uber and snuggle in the back seat all the way back to the canal. Snuggling is a new experience for me, something I always thought would feel claustrophobic, but now I wonder what I've been missing out on all these years.

This time Leo and I are practically fused together as we walk the short distance to his boat, and I don't feel unnerved at all by the shadows. I don't think I could ever feel unsafe with him beside me. He lets go of me to unlock his door and help me from the dock into his houseboat.

'Welcome to my home,' he says, stepping in behind me and closing the door. 'I can't believe you're here.'

I smile. 'Me either. And wow, this place is gorgeous.'

He grins. 'Thanks. I like it.'

I don't know what I was imagining, but the cosy interior with overstuffed bookshelves, warm-toned rugs and walls lined with photos was not it. It's really neat and tidy and smells good, like citrus. He gives me a quick tour from his tiny but immaculately clean bathroom to his bedroom, in which the perfectly made bed fills the space from one wall to the other. I'm impressed. Considering he had no idea I was coming back, I think, he must always live like this, but then it crosses my mind that maybe he spruced everything up because he thought he might end up bringing someone else here.

My thoughts immediately go to Zoey, the woman he was

kind of seeing before we met, and my stomach roils. Is she still in the picture? 'We're you expecting . . . uh, company tonight?'

He blinks. 'What do you mean?'

I glance around. 'This place is so tidy, like you were planning to bring someone back here.'

He laughs. 'To be honest, it's not usually this way, but I've been manically cleaning and sorting things out since I got back, trying to keep myself busy so I wouldn't think about you.'

'Did it work?' I ask.

He shakes his head, then pulls me towards him, closing the already miniscule gap between us. 'No, but at least it means you don't yet know how much of a slob I am.'

I snort. 'Take after your father, do you?'

'Let's not talk about my dad right now,' he says as he gently pushes me down onto his bed.

I'm desperate to have him, but Leo refuses to rush our love-making, promising we have all the time in the world, saying that he wants to explore my body in the way he didn't get to first time round. At first, as he slowly removes each item of my clothing like he's unwrapping a present but doesn't want to rip the paper, I think he's just trying to drive me insane, but as he trails his mouth over every inch of my skin, I begin to think there might be merit in his madness.

When he finally sinks into me, after already making me come with his fingers and his tongue, tears flow to my eyes.

'What's wrong?' he asks, tensing immediately as he pushes up onto his hands to look at me.

I shake my head. 'Absolutely nothing. This just feels so right.'

'It does.' He drops his mouth to mine and kisses me in a way that is both tender and hungry as he thrusts into me again.

Afterwards, we share a shower – which, let me tell you, is

quite a feat when the whole bathroom is barely bigger than a postage stamp – and then Leo makes us hot chocolate. He opens a packet of chocolate digestives – his favourites – and we devour almost all of them in his bed as we talk about everything under the sun. We may only have been apart a week, but I feel like so much has happened in this time.

I explain that because of him, I reached out to my dad and said I want to meet my sisters. Leo says that because of me he told his band that he'd spend the summer touring with them in Europe and if it goes well, he'll consider going full time with the band.

'Will you come with us?' he asks.

'You want me to be a UkePro groupie?'

'I want you to be a Leo groupie.'

I giggle in a most un-Fred-like way and lean my head upon his shoulder.

Before I can tell him that sounds wonderful, he adds, 'But if that doesn't work for you, then I'll pull out and come down under. I'm sure I can get a teaching job in Perth.'

'I'm sure you can, but you dropping out of the UkePros would be a travesty. You guys are so good. I'd be proud to be your groupie.'

'Really?'

'Hell yeah, as long as you get me a T-shirt, so everyone knows I'm with you.'

'I'll get you whatever you damn want,' he promises.

So . . . we agree that I'll spend the rest of the week here with Leo, then head back home and he'll fly out to stay with me in his half-term break. We'll talk every day on the phone in between. I'll quit my job or take extended leave to spend the summer with him, and after that, we don't know what we'll do or where we'll live but somehow, I know we'll make it work.

It's weird to be so sure about something I didn't think I even wanted, but I am.

'When should we tell our families?' he asks.

I groan. 'Mum is not going to be happy. She's going to worry I'll change my mind and break your heart, but I won't. I promise.'

'I believe you,' he says seriously. 'And they'll come round. It might be unusual, step-siblings being together, but we're grown-ups, so it's perfectly legal and they all just want us to be happy.'

He asks about my book, and although he has the good sense to look a little sheepish when I tell him I've probably ruined my career before it got started, he refuses to accept that it's over.

'There are other publishers. In fact, we have hundreds of them in London.'

'Maybe,' I say, 'or maybe I was writing to fill a hole inside of me, and maybe, thanks to you, I don't feel so empty any more.'

I don't remember falling asleep, but when I wake up, Leo is gone. If not for my surroundings, I might think I'd dreamt the last twenty-four hours. That's when I notice there's a little note on the pillow beside me.

Dear Winifred

    Don't go anywhere. I'll be back soon. Love, Leopold

I smile as I sit up and locate my phone, which has only 10 per cent charge left and a zillion text messages from Bee.

Bridget Jones: *Flight tracker says you landed. So . . .?*

Bridget Jones: *Did you find him? What was his response like?*

Bridget Jones: *Winifred Darling, I'm getting cranky now. Don't leave me hanging.*

That's only a handful of them but they're all along the same lines.

Me: *I think he was happy to see me.*

Immediately, my phone rings in my hand. 'Tell me everything,' Bee demands.

And I do, leaning back into Leo's pillows, the light from the little window behind the bed flowing over me as I relive the most perfect night I've ever experienced.

Bee sighs – 'Aw, it's just like a novel' – as I hear Leo's door open.

Seconds later, he appears at the end of the bed holding what looks to be a takeaway coffee, a juice and a large paper bag.

'Gotta go,' I tell Bee, disconnecting before she has the chance to object. 'Good morning, Leopold.'

He grins at me. 'Good morning, Winifred. Thought you might be hungry. I wasn't sure what you'd feel like, so I got croissants, Danish pastries and muffins. Oh, and they didn't have watermelon, so I got as close as I could to the juice you got on Norfolk Island.'

'Oh my God. You remembered what I like? You really are the perfect man.'

'No one's perfect, Winifred, but I am pretty damn close,' he says faux seriously.

Once again, we eat in bed, and it isn't long before I hear ducks quacking just outside. I peer out the window and shriek, 'They're on the boat.'

Leo chuckles. 'I've got into a bit of a bad habit of sharing my breakfast with them. They're not bad company.'

I smile and watch them waddling around on his little deck. In the light of day, the canal looks much more appealing and safer. I can see the magic and appeal of living on this stretch of water. The other boats look bright and cheerful beneath the winter skies, and people all rugged up are walking along the canal walk. It feels like we're in the hub of a community, while also being secluded in Leo's tiny space, far from the rest of the world.

'I really like it here,' I say, turning back to look at him.

He reaches out and touches his finger to my chin. 'I'm glad. And you can stay as long as you like.' Then he leans forward and kisses me again.

EPILOGUE

The *Best* Bridesmaid

My heart thumps as I wake to the buzzing of my phone at the crack of dawn on the morning of Bee's wedding. Or at least it feels like the crack of dawn – but when I snatch it up to make sure it doesn't wake Bee, who is dead to the world beside me, I see it's only a minute before my alarm is due to go off.

And it's Leo, not an emergency, *thank God*.

I still have nightmares about the morning of Mum and Paul's wedding and have been praying since Bee and Sully got engaged eleven months ago that nothing will go wrong on their special day. Sneaking out of the massive bed Bee and I shared last night in a fancy suite at the Esplanade Hotel, I take my phone into the bathroom – which is bigger than our bedroom on Leo's boat – to answer it.

'Good morning,' I whisper, grinning in the way I always do when I see his name appear on my screen.

'I miss you, Winifred.'

Warmth floods my body. 'I miss you too, Leopold.' Even though I saw him a mere twelve hours ago. 'Is that why you're calling?'

'Yes, but I also wanted to see if you needed anything. I'm popping out on a coffee run for Sully and his groomsmen, and I wondered if you wanted me to bring you a green juice or something.'

Leo is staying at our place, next door to Bee and Sully's house, where Sully and his friends are getting ready. Not long after I got back from London, the historic townhouse next door to Bee, which Sully was renting when they first met, went on the market. Leo snapped it right up as our Aussie base. Most of the time, we let it out on Airbnb, and the only complaints we ever get are about the neighbours. Apparently one of them plays the bagpipes at all hours of the day!

As much as I do want to see Leo, I don't want to be distracted from everything I need to do today to make sure Bee has the best time ever. First up, sustenance. 'Thanks, but I'm good. Can't wait to see you at the church.'

He chuckles. 'I can't wait to see you in that sexy pink dress.'

I whisper-laugh. 'There's only one person in the world I'd wear pink and frills for, and right now, I'd better go wake her up.'

But when I head back out into the suite, Bee is already sitting up in bed, a massive smile on her heart-shaped face. 'I'm getting married today,' she squeals, loud enough to wake anyone still sleeping in the hotel.

'I know,' I squeal back, landing back in the bed beside her. 'No cold feet?'

'As if! I can't wait. We should have had a morning wedding. The next seven hours are going to be agony.'

'They are not! Breakfast will be here in a moment, along

with your mum, Kara and Elsie, and then the four of us are going to pamper you silly until the hair and make-up folks arrive.'

There's a knock on the door. 'See? Right on time.'

I jump off the bed to go welcome our feast of freshly cut fruit, delicious crumbly pastries and, of course, prosecco. As the hotel worker withdraws, Bee's mum, Julie, and her sisters-in-law, Kara and Elsie, appear, dressed in the matching pink silk PJs I bought everyone to wear while we get ready. Kara's daughter, Sarah, is going to be Bee's flower girl but will join us in a few hours.

Right now, it's grown-up girl time!

Bee's mum, Julie, an older, slightly rounder version of Bee, is even more of a hopeless romantic than her daughter. As we enjoy croissants and bubbles, all sitting on the king-sized bed, she reminiscences about her own wedding day to Bee's dad, and Kara and Elsie chime in about their weddings to Bee's brothers.

'Will there be wedding bells for you and Leo soon?' Julie asks.

She met him last night and was immediately besotted.

Bee laughs as I shake my head. 'I prefer to live in sin.' Kara and Elsie splutter the bubbles they've just sipped.

'Well . . . maybe you'll change your mind after today,' Julie replies.

'Maybe.' I shrug, not believing that in the slightest.

Then again, if you'd told me a year ago that I'd be (mostly) living on the other side of the world with a man I'm absolutely head over heels in love with, I'd have laughed you out of town. Leo and I have barely spent more than a handful of days apart since I jumped on that plane and flew to London in what those in the publishing biz would call a Grand Gesture. I guess we're now living out the Happy Ever After part of our story.

These days, we are sort of nomads. After a very successful

summer tour with the UkePros, Leo quit his full-time teaching job to play with the band full-time and I quit the library. He still does some relief teaching between gigs, and I've been writing. Wherever we are, whatever city, whatever country, Leo is my constant. I could never have imagined feeling this strongly about someone and, if anything, I feel freer and more independent than I ever did. Leo is my best friend and although the sex is off the charts – yes, I have now ticked joining the Mile High Club off my bucket list – it's all the little things and moments that make our life together wonderful.

The way he learned to make my morning green juices.

The little text messages and funny memes he sends me even when we're sitting right next to each other on the couch.

His foot rubs.

The long walks we take along the canal, so deep in conversation that we don't realise how far we've walked.

His smile.

The way his eyes light up whenever he sees me. The leap in my heart whenever *I* see *him*.

Don't get me wrong – it hasn't all been perfect. Neither of us has ever lived with a partner before, and there have been some adjustments to get used to. We still disagree on which way the toilet roll should hang and whether glasses should be upright or upside down when stored in the cupboard. And don't get me started on the fact that he thinks Diet Coke and Pepsi Max are interchangeable – once we had a full-blown argument about this, but the make-up sex was almost worth it.

One of the downsides of our nomadic lifestyle is that we can't always have Aunty with us. She wouldn't approve of our home on the water anyway, but she seems content living with Way and Benji. The latter treats her like his firstborn child and now leaves me a long list of dos and don'ts if ever Aunty stays with us when we're in town.

As we top up our glasses, talk moves on to Bee and Sully's honeymoon plans – they're doing two weeks in Europe, ending in London to spend some time with Leo and me – and then how many babies they plan to have.

'Sully wants a whole basketball team, but I'm thinking two or three would be nice,' Bee says.

When all the food has been demolished, the day really begins. Bee may have been worried about waiting until she can walk down the aisle to the love of her life, but we manage to fill almost every second and I take my duties seriously. As well as making sure Bee is relaxed and enjoying the experience of being princess for a day, I snap photos for her wedding album, make sure she stays hydrated, pull a tube of superglue from my emergency wedding kit when Julie's heel breaks, let Sarah watch *Bluey* on my phone when she arrives and we can't get the TV to work and, when the time comes, I help Bee into her wedding dress and do up every single one of the forty-three tiny buttons at the back.

My fingers are cramping by the end of it, but my smile never falters.

The hair and make-up ladies leave, and the photographer arrives for the pre-wedding snaps. He tells us he's just come from Sully's place, where the men are looking dashing and an excited Sully is shooting baskets in the backyard to pass the time until they head to the church.

'He'd better not be all hot, sweaty and stinky,' Bee exclaims, but we all know she doesn't really care. She'd marry the man if he'd just been rolling in garbage.

Bee poses for photos with her bridesmaids and then her parents and then ... OMG, it's time to really get this show on the road. So far everything has gone smoothly – even the sun is shining in through the window. Although apparently rain is lucky on a wedding day, I'm fairly certain Bee and Sully don't need any luck.

'See you at the church,' Kara says as she grabs Sarah's little hand and follows Elsie out the door to where two Austin Princesses are waiting to drive us to the church.

Julie pulls Bee into a teary hug. 'You look so beautiful, my darling. I'm so happy I could burst.'

'Thanks, Mum.'

I manage to usher Julie out the door, and we give Bee a quick moment with her dad, who turned up looking very dapper in his suit not too long ago. While we wait, I send a quick selfie to Mum (you'll be pleased to know she and Paul are still going strong), and also to Dad to show my little sisters. Aside from finding true love, getting to know Mia and Ava has been the highlight of the last year. Leo and I have visited them multiple times, taking the girls on day trips to theme parks and Australia Zoo. Mia wants to marry Robert Irwin when she grows up. Ava doesn't want to marry anyone. I adore them both.

The door of the hotel room opens and Bee steps through, her dad holding the door. He's teary-eyed like Julie and although I've been here every minute of her getting ready, I feel a lump form in my throat at the sight of my beautiful best friend. I fluff her skirt up around her and hand her the bouquet of bright pink gerberas she's chosen for the occasion. Bee takes her dad's arm, and Julie and I walk behind them, other hotel guests pressing themselves against the walls, smiling and taking sneaky pics as we pass.

Everyone loves a bride and I may be biased, but Bee is a fairytale one.

The reception staff clap and cheer as we head outside, where the photographer takes a few more quick snaps before I get in the first car with the other bridesmaids and Bee gets into the second with her parents, who will both walk her down the aisle.

Fremantle Wesley Uniting Church is only a two-minute drive from the hotel, but our chauffeurs take their time as we cruise down Essex Street and then South Terrace, so all the Saturday tourists and locals can enjoy the show.

I don't plan on getting married, and even if I did it wouldn't be in a church, but no one can deny that this one is perfect. The sandstone building looks exactly as a church should with an arched door and windows and a steeple at the top. Strangers slow out the front as the two cars pull up, and I jump out first to help Bee out of hers. Sarah is in her element, dancing on the stone paving out the front and waving at passersby, annoyed when she has to stop and head inside to lead the processional.

'Good luck – not that you need it,' I say as I smooth Bee's skirt, then squeeze her hand before stepping up behind Kara and Elsie.

I can't see into the church yet, but I can hear the sweet sounds of Leo's ukelele as he begins Wagner's famous 'Bridal March' solo. Somehow, despite the vastness of the building, the music holds its own. I smile as Sarah practically skips down the aisle, followed by her mum and aunty, and then it's my turn. I'm not sure I've ever felt so happy as I do when I walk towards the altar where Sully is waiting with his groomsmen and Bee's dog, John Brown, beside him. Miraculously, JB isn't jumping around like the usual lunatic he is. The church is so full that people are standing at the back – Bee invited her favourite patrons, including all the members of her seniors book club to attend the ceremony. I spy Janine and Dave (back from their travels around Australia), Persephone and Nick (kid-and-fancy-free), Xavier and Rory (the latter already sobbing), and Ursula and Ali (smiling at each other as if remembering their own special day), and give them all a quick wave. Way and Benji are also there, no doubt taking notes for their own upcoming nuptials, only a few months away.

When everyone gasps, I know that Bee has entered the church behind me, and I immediately look to Sully again. The love he has for her is evident in a smile so wide it barely fits his face. Proudly, I take my position at the front and turn as the bride and her parents approach. They each kiss her on the cheek before retreating to the first pew next to Daisy, Sully's grandmother, who looks radiant in a gold pantsuit. If I have half her style when I'm her age, I'll be stoked.

I might call myself a writer, but it's hard to describe the magic of Bee and Sully's ceremony. They've chosen traditional vows rather than writing their own and there's something special about this – it suits them to a tee – but the absolute best part is when the minister pronounces them husband and wife and Sully jumps the gun, pulling Bee into a raunchy kiss before he is given permission.

Everyone laughs, except Bee's nephews, who make gagging noises, causing everyone to laugh even more.

Afterwards, we file out of the church into the afternoon sun and line up for all the guests to offer their congratulations. Then it's time for the photos. Fremantle has a zillion perfect places for wedding pics, but top of Bee's list is some snaps among the bookshelves at the library, so we head there first. The patrons are delighted when Bee descends the stairs in her gorgeous gown with her gorgeous groom on her arm and the rest of the bridal party following behind.

While we take formal and funny photos between the books, I can't help thinking about the fact that in just over a year, my own book will be on the shelves here. No, not *that* book. When I told Emily I wasn't going to finish *21 Rules for Not Catching Feelings*, she was furious. She said it wasn't just me who was going to look like a fool but also her and her colleagues, who'd been talking up my book to booksellers. She went into damage control and came up with a plan – I would finish the book anyway, and they'd publish it under a different name. 'Or better yet, we won't put a name to it at all! There hasn't been a book published by Anonymous for a long time, but it always creates such a storm. The media can't help speculating about who might have written it and people become obsessed.'

Emily had been very excited about this possibility, but I'd outright refused.

Well, maybe I'd considered it for a few seconds because it would mean not having to pay back my advance, but in the end, I couldn't in good conscience do it. I no longer believed that my rules for not catching feelings were empowering or even that they worked. And I didn't want to be responsible for putting anyone off opening themselves up to love.

And anyway, by the time she'd come up with this plan, I'd already written the first chapters of a new book.

I hadn't known I was writing a novel when I started – I thought maybe it was a short story at most – but I was so inspired by my surrounds and Leo's interesting neighbours that what started as something to kill the time on his boat while he was out teaching became so much more. *Love on the Canal* is about a woman who inherits a ramshackle boat in London and falls in love with a busker, who helps her renovate it and bring it back to its original glory. While renovating, they find a secret portal that takes them back in time to the very early days of canal life.

There's a twist, but explaining that would be a spoiler.

When I was writing the story, I didn't give a thought to whether anyone else would ever read it; I just had fun. No one was more surprised than me when it was snapped up at auction for seven figures, then sold into multiple foreign territories and optioned for film within the next month. Who knows if the movie thing will actually happen but . . . it turns out Bee was right: when you write from the heart, and first and foremost for yourself, magic happens.

'I need to pee,' she whispers, interrupting my thoughts. 'And that means . . .'

I'm required to come too. We head into the staff bathrooms, where I lift the many layers of her skirt so she can sit on the loo.

She grins up at me. 'I love you, Fred. Thanks for agreeing to be my bridesmaid, even though you hate love, romance, marriage and all that mushy stuff.'

I wink. 'You're welcome. Just don't ask me to do it again.' We both laugh, confident in the fact that she never will.

By the time we arrive back at the hotel for the reception, I'm exhausted but very happy with the way the day has gone so far, and I am pleased to report it continues in exactly the same way. Dinner is delicious, the speeches are hilarious and heartfelt, the cutting of the cake is perfectly romantic and then, finally, I can take a take a deep breath, kick off my heels and follow the bride and groom onto the dance floor. I dance the obligatory song with Sully's best man before beckoning to Leo to come cut in.

'I've been waiting to get you alone all day,' he says as he slips his arms around my waist. 'You know, you're the most beautiful woman here.'

I smile. 'Don't be ridiculous. Have you seen Bee?'

He shakes his head. 'I only have eyes for you.'

Glowing, I playfully punch him on the arm – 'You're such a sweet talker' – even though I can't get enough of him and his delicious words.

'You did good today, Winifred,' he says, looking seriously into my eyes. 'No one will accuse you of being a bad bridesmaid ever again.'

I laugh, then step up onto my tippy-toes and kiss him.

21 WAYS TO KNOW YOU'VE FOUND THE ONE

1. You find yourself being vulnerable and telling the person things you've never told anyone else.
2. You can't stop thinking about them.
3. You've got chemistry AND connection.
4. The first place you met becomes part of your relationship history.
5. You're happy to hang out at your house or theirs as long as you're together.
6. You can't bear to spend a night apart!
7. You want to give your best to each other.
8. You know you have no reason to be jealous but can't help wanting them all to yourself.
9. You enjoy giving and receiving with no expectations.
10. Controlling PDAs is a hard task.
11. Your phone is not only filled with pics of them, but your lock screen is now your favourite couple selfie.
12. You don't want to date other people.
13. You want to spend all your time together.
14. You text and talk daily even if you can't see each other. In-depth conversation is the norm.

15. The words 'boyfriend' and 'partner' are now part of your everyday vocabulary.
16. You treat each other equally and with respect.
17. You spend as much time together as possible, while not sabotaging relationships with friends and family.
18. They're your best friend and you constantly want to jump their bones.
19. You enjoy giving gifts and doing favours for them.
20. You consult each other when making decisions that affect you both.
21. You can't imagine either of you ever ending things.

ACKNOWLEDGMENTS

Writing a book is HARD, but writing acknowledgements is almost harder, as I'm always so scared I'm going to forget someone who is vitally important or supportive. Writing a book really is a collaborative process – there's practical support, emotional support and editorial support – and I'm truly grateful to everyone on Team Rach!

To all the wonderful Australian Penguins. Thanks to Ali Watts (truly a delight to work with – you should be careful or you'll give me a big head), who came up with the fab title of this novel; Holly Toohey, who says such lovely things about my books as well as being super important; Amanda Martin, whose attention to editorial detail means you're reading the best version of this book you possibly could; Bek Chereshsky and Anna Tidswell, who work tirelessly to make sure you ALL know about my book; and also to the fabulous Janine Brown, Jo Baker, Michael Windle, Sarah McDuling, Madi Du and Lily Crozier – I couldn't have a more enthusiastic and hard-working bunch of people in my corner. And to Nikki Townsend for creating ANOTHER amazing cover! You don't know how much time I waste just staring at your beautiful creations.

To the team at Bloodhound Books, who are taking my books to readers in the United Kingdom and America, thank you for championing Aussie romcoms!!

To my brilliant agent, Helen Breitwieser, thank you for being such a great champion of my work over the last twelve years.

To everyone at home, who puts up with my creative mood swings and cheers me on when I'm stressed: Craig, Hamish, Lachlan and Archie – love yas all! To Mum, who came with me to Norfolk Island at VERY short notice to help me research this book. Hope you enjoyed the trip as much as I did. And, of course, to my darling Adeline (aka Addie), who sits under my desk patiently waiting for me to finish my daily words so we can go for a walk and she can chase the ducks by the river. You're also a pretty great footwarmer on those colder mornings!

To Annie Bucknall, my virtual assistant, I'm so glad I finally took the plunge and hired you to help with the non-writing aspects of my career. How did I manage so many years without you? Well, just know I'm NEVER letting you go again.

The best thing about this job is the people I've met along the way – the writing friends who have become some of my best friends. There are so many that if I listed them all, we'd be here all year, but a shout-out to Rebecca Heath, Anthea Hodgson, Emily Madden, Tess Woods, Jem Gowen, Lizzy Dent (also a fabulous cousin), Brooke Testa and Sophie Green, who listen to me whine about my writing and talk me down off ledges on a regular basis. I couldn't imagine my life without you!

To every single member of the Rachael Johns' Online Book Club (you can find us on Facebook if you're not already a member), thanks for being part of the fab book community I run with Anthea Hodgson. Book people are the BEST people!

To all the residents of Norfolk Island, thanks for the hospitality in January 2024 when Mum and I spent a week exploring your gorgeous home. I hope I've done it justice!

To all the booksellers, bloggers, Instagrammers, Booktokkers and librarians who champion my books once they head out into the world, I might not be able to visit all of you in person, but I appreciate every single one of you. Thank you for spreading the love.

And last but never least, thank YOU for picking up this book, reading it and (hopefully) enjoying it.

BOOK CLUB NOTES

1. Winifred is a proud single woman with firm standards. Do you appreciate her initial viewpoint on marriage? What pleased or displeased you about her change of attitude by the end?

2. On their first date, Damon asks Fred if she is a 'man-hating feminist'. Do you understand why he might feel this way?

3. Which one of Fred's 'red flags' did you most relate to?

4. Fred claims she is very comfortable telling men exactly how she feels. In what ways is she less inclined to speak plainly when it comes to matters of her family?

5. Do you have a dream wedding? Or have you already had one? In what ways did it turn out to be different from what you had imagined?

6. What was it about Jeff (Husband #3) that made Fred so attached to him?

7. Leo believes that being there for each other no matter what is what family is all about. Do you agree?

8. Discuss the role that books played in the healing process Fred went through as an adolescent. Have you ever found books to be therapeutic?

9. Bee tells Fred: 'You really shouldn't mess in matters of other people's hearts.' Should there ever be exceptions made to this rule?

10. Tracy and Paul have a second chance at love, all these years on. Do you know of any other love stories – real or fictional – that feature happy endings decades later?

11. Leo says: 'The need for connection and emotional intimacy is what makes us human.' Do you agree?

12. Do you agree with Paul that it is possible to have more than one love in a lifetime?

A NOTE FROM THE PUBLISHER

Thank you for reading this book. If you enjoyed it please do consider leaving a review on Amazon to help others find it too.

We hate typos. All of our books have been rigorously edited and proofread, but sometimes mistakes do slip through. If you have spotted a typo, please do let us know and we can get it amended within hours.

info@bloodhoundbooks.com